Praise for *In the Quiet*

'Simply, *In the Quiet* is a beautiful and tender debut novel. Eliza Henry-Jones is a bright new talent in Australian literature with a voice that is accomplished, fresh and utterly engaging." – *Judges Report from Readings Prize for New Australian Writing 2015*

'A glorious book that will make – you cry, guaranteed. But it's also uplifting and tender. A surprise find.' – *Canberra Times*

'I often wonder what it would be like to step away from your family and to watch them from afar; to notice the details of everyday life and how they go about their day when you aren't there. Cate does that here. The only trouble is, she's dead but keeping watch over her husband and her three young children as they come to terms with their lives without her … Henry-Jones, in her debut novel, has structured a glorious book that will make you cry, guaranteed. But it's also uplifting and tender. A surprise find.' – *Sydney Morning Herald*

'Eliza Henry-Jones is a brand new Australian author to watch out for! This book just oozes raw emotion.' – *GoodReads*

'Reading Eliza Henry-Jones's debut novel requires something of a leap of faith, but it's well worth the effort. *In the Quiet* is an unusual but wonderful book, full of beautiful sentences, and I very much look forward to reading more from this prolific short-story writer, and now accomplished young novelist.' – *Good Reading*

'This heart-tugging first novel is a beautifully paced mixture of romance, family saga and mystery.' – *Adelaide Advertiser*

'This sad, gentle story explores love, grief and family; the nature of time and memory; the destructiveness of secrets; and the pain of letting go. It's an impressive debut.' – *Bookseller+Publisher*

'I happened to be reading this novel at a time of remembrance of a big love in my life. It tapped into that beautiful and very sad core of grief in me. Rather than being upset by this, I treasured how Henry Jones wrote about loss. It was a gift.' – *The Big Book Club*

'Eliza is a trained grief, loss and trauma counsellor and her skill and expertise dealing with the difficult subject of the death of a mother adds to the poignancy and authenticity of the novel.' – *Barbara Horgan, Boffins Bookshop*

'This is an absorbing, thoughtful and languorous debut told in such a compelling voice … it will linger in your thoughts long after you have turned the final page.' – *Book Muster Down Under*

Eliza Henry-Jones was born in Melbourne in 1990. She was a Young Writer-in-Residence at the Katharine Susannah Prichard Writers' Centre in 2012 and was a recipient of a Varuna residential fellowship for 2015. She has qualifications in English, psychology and grief, loss and trauma counselling. She is currently completing honours in creative writing – exploring bushfire trauma – and works in community services. She lives in the Dandenong Ranges with her husband and too many animals. *In the Quiet*, her debut novel, was shortlisted for Express Media's inaugural award for Outstanding Achievement by a Young Person in the Literary Arts and the Readings Prize for New Australian Writing in 2015. It has also been long-listed in the 2016 Next Generation Indie Book Awards.

ELIZA HENRY JONES

In the Quiet

FOURTH ESTATE
An Imprint of HarperCollins*Publishers*

Fourth Estate

An imprint of HarperCollins*Publishers*

First published in Australia in 2015
This edition published in 2016
by HarperCollins*Publishers* Australia Pty Limited
ABN 36 009 913 517
harpercollins.com.au

HarperCollins*Publishers*
Level 13, 201 Elizabeth Street, Sydney NSW 2000, Australia
Unit D1, 63 Apollo Drive, Rosedale, Auckland 0632, New Zealand
A 53, Sector 57, Noida, UP, India
1 London Bridge Street, London SE1 9GF, United Kingdom
2 Bloor Street East, 20th floor, Toronto, Ontario M4W 1A8, Canada
195 Broadway, New York, NY 10007, USA

National Library of Australia Cataloguing-in-Publication data:

Henry-Jones, Eliza, author.
  In the quiet / Eliza Henry-Jones.
  ISBN: 978 1 4607 5339 2 (paperback)
  ISBN: 978 1 4607 0476 9 (ebook)
  Australian fiction.
A823.4

Cover design by HarperCollins Design Studio
Cover photograph by Victoria Aguirre
Typeset in 11.5/14pt Bembo by Kirby Jones
Printed and bound in the United States of America by LSC Communications

To Jan and Ben – my story sharers.
I love you both to pieces.

I don't know how I died. That's strange, isn't it? To be dead and know *that* but to not know how it happened. To not know my last memory.

It's not something that I ever considered when I was alive.

I can see and I can hear. And when I remember back to other times and other places, I see and hear them as though I'm reliving them.

But when I remember, I miss things that are happening now. I miss chunks of time. I try not to remember. I try not to think. I watch and I listen and I hope to not miss any more time. Because time is all I have now. And how quickly it disappears.

* * *

The first thing I am conscious of is my little girl, Jessa. She's sitting on the verandah wearing the blue dress I bought her last summer. She has, perhaps, worn it twice since then. She is coming into her teenage years and the dress already seems too short, riding high above her

1

knees. She's fiddling with a nail from a horseshoe and keeps stamping her foot.

There's bull ants. That's why.

She stares left, where the big paddock is. She makes a clucking noise with her tongue, like she's coming in to a jump on her pony.

Purple flowers from the jacaranda start to fall and she shakes her head free of them and glares up. 'Don't,' she says.

And above her head Rafferty is hanging out a window, grinning, one hand wrenching a branch backwards and forwards.

'I said *don't*!'

She is on her feet, fist clenched around the horseshoe nail. She runs inside, straight into her father.

'Whoa,' he says, patting her. 'Easy.'

* * *

My husband, Bass – Sebastian – is a farm boy. He has always been prone to stroke me and make cooing noises whenever I was unhappy or unsettled. Has been prone to make clucking noises, like Jessa, if I walk too slowly down the street. When he is impatient or bored, he will blow his breath out in a raspberry that sounds like a relaxed Clydesdale.

Sometimes I sense he wants to give me a good kick, like he would when riding a stubborn horse.

I miss his hands. The warmth of them.

If I could still feel, I'm sure the yearning for them would be enough to make me ache.

* * *

My boys are sitting in their room. It is dark now. But it must be warm outside because they have the window open.

Rafferty is sitting on the sill, near the top of the jacaranda tree. He is smoking. His boxers have a hole in the side and the T-shirt he's wearing is stretched out and faded.

In the night sky, the stars are out. And there's a haze around the moon.

'Put it out,' Cameron says. He is in bed with the blankets pulled up, nearly to his neck. Rafferty turns to glance at him and takes another long drag. The tip lights up and he blows smoke rings out into the still night. It is strange, to see him smoking. Strange to see him so adult. Altered, but the same.

'Please?' Cameron says.

Rafferty sighs as though Cameron has just asked him to cut off a leg, but he slowly butts it out on the sill. He slaps at a mosquito and sighs.

'Thanks.'

Rafferty grunts and lies on his bed. His doona is kicked off the end, but he doesn't make a move to grab it. He puts his hands behind his head and stares up at the ceiling, where the moon has fanned shadows of the jacaranda branches. Rafferty blinks slowly, watching their stillness.

'Are you okay?' Cameron's voice is quiet. Barely a whisper.

'Of course I am.'

* * *

The twins came suddenly and violently at the end of spring. Afterwards, wet with blood and nauseous and trying not to cry, I stared down at two sets of eyes. They were blue when they were born, but as they grew their eyes turned an extraordinary shade of hazel. They made me think of stones in a river, lit up by the sun through water.

Bass's eyes.

They spent their first few months in nappies and singlets. When they were older I let them crawl around the verandah naked, and when I took them inside at dusk, Bass hosed the wood clean.

Those evenings smelt of earth and milk.

* * *

It is just before dawn. The same night, I think. Cameron has thrown off his blankets and is sprawled so that one foot is nearly touching the ground. I had been looking at double beds for them, before. But Bass seems to have forgotten in the after. On the other side of the room Rafferty has curled up in a ball, his head underneath his pillow, his arms curled around his stomach.

He says it so quietly, I barely catch it.

'Mum,' Rafferty whispers, his eyes pressed shut.

* * *

Sometimes I try to remember back to what happened. I often do this at night, when they're asleep. My family.

But it's rare for all four of them to sleep through the night. Cameron twitches himself awake at about midnight and does the breathing exercises the school counsellor taught him in year seven. Rafferty will often wake up at the same time and sit at the window and smoke.

Jessa wakes biting back a cry. The noise comes out as a hiss. She will lie in bed with her lips pursed, when this happens. I don't know for how long. Then she will sigh, as though she is disappointed in herself, and tramp down the hall and into our bedroom.

Bass's bedroom, now.

As often as not he will be in the kitchen when she comes looking for him. Sometimes drinking Scotch and other times drinking warm milk with a little cinnamon. It's what I make, what I made, for the boys and Jessa when they had nightmares or couldn't sleep.

Jessa and Bass will curl up in bed. Bass on my side. Jessa on his. They fall asleep back to back and always wake up holding hands. They sleep with the blankets kicked off and the portable fan in the corner of the room on high.

Nearly every night these things play out.

And nobody ever speaks.

* * *

In so many ways, the house has moved on without me. Beyond me. But some things remain unchanged. As if they are stalled. As if time has stalled without me.

There is fresh, mismatched bedding on Bass's bed. Flannelette and cotton, blue-grey and orange. He has left my pillowcase on. The blue and white patterns of it. He sleeps on it every night. It must smell more like him now than it ever did of me.

Jessa chips the nail polish off all her fingers but leaves it on her toes. It's nearly grown out, just little flecks left on her big toes. Blue nail polish. I'd put it on for her, to cheer her up over a miserable day at school.

The jar of nail polish is still on the coffee table. I want Jessa to unscrew the lid. I want her to paint her nails. I want the boys or maybe my sister, Bea, to paint the nails on her right hand, her dominant hand.

A few of the same towels are still hung in the bathroom. They have been in there for weeks, maybe months. I don't think anyone is using them, but nobody is washing them clean, either.

The radio is tuned to the golden oldies station I liked to listen to. The sound of it. It makes the world soften. It reminds me of my eyes blurring with tears.

The roses I picked from the garden and set on the sideboard in the living room have lost their colour, are rotting in water that is now mostly green. Their petals are papery and brown, under lounge chairs and puffed down the hallway and into other rooms. There are other flowers, set into corners and on tables. Flowers I haven't seen before. Dying flowers, some with cards still attached. On shelves and in dirty vases on the verandah.

There is dog hair, dust. Collecting in nests under the couches and chairs and tables. I wonder if it smells dusty, inside. Smells as stale as it looks.

Outside, the property is yellowed and browned from summer. The only green is in the beds immediately around the house. Even the leaves on the eucalypts, the silver stringybarks and lemon scented, are dulled from the heat and the dust.

A pang, like something metallic pressed against the tongue. I want them to move, one way or another. I want them to throw out the roses. I want them to vacuum. I want them to wash every piece of bedding, every piece of tearstained clothing. Blue nail polish. A tended garden. I want them to move. Be moving.

Secateurs left near the rose beds. There are clothes turning damp in the dryer.

* * *

My sister has freckles and long brown hair she always keeps plaited. She wears a baggy shirt and a tart, icy perfume that makes Bass's nose pucker when he leans in to hug her.

She sits at the kitchen table. Bass, tugging at his collar and shuffling from foot to foot, has made her a cup of hot milk and cinnamon instead of a cup of coffee.

Beatrice drinks it. They're both sweating.

'I thought Jessa could come and stay with me now and then,' she says. 'Give you a bit of time to get back on your feet and Jessa a bit of girl time.'

Bass clenches his right hand. The one that Jessa holds when she wakes from her nightmares and seeks him out, in silence. He would miss his little girl. Who, even as he and Beatrice speak, is outside cleaning the chicken run. There is sweat running down her legs and her hair is plastered to her head. Her mouth is pursed and she keeps glancing behind her at the gate of the run.

Bass opens his mouth slightly. He smiles too broadly and bobs his head. 'That's a lovely offer, Bea. Thank you.'

Beatrice smiles, but it's only a pretend smile. Her eyes don't move from his face. Don't change or widen or narrow.

'I can't imagine how much you must miss her, Bass.' Her voice cracks.

Bass looks up at her, then out the window. 'She was my wife.'

Bea's face catches in a tiny frown. For a moment, she looks young. She looks like she's bending over difficult homework, or reading something complicated in a book.

Bass cranes his neck at something over Beatrice's shoulder. He stands up in a flurry like a bird flung loose and sticks his head out the window above the sink. 'Oi! Raff! Let her out!'

Outside, Rafferty is running towards the bush tracks and does not stop.

Jessa is standing in the run with her arms crossed. 'Dad!' she yells.

'I'm coming, Jess. I'm coming.'

* * *

'She's our angry little goose,' I had said and Bass had kissed my forehead. The day she first made that frustrated hissing noise in place of a hungry cry. Jessa, born in winter.

She was six months old before I let her lie naked on a blanket stretched out on the wood of the verandah.

My summer boys have a year-long tan, as much as I plied them with sunscreen. Like their father, who is tall and tanned with brown hair, hazel eyes. Jessa is pale and freckled like Beatrice. Like me. She burns in the sun and gets headaches in the heat. She once passed out at a horse competition after insisting on riding in thirty-five degree heat.

Jessa and Rafferty both have a hardness in them. Something Bass calls guts and I call the quiet.

Bass, too, has the quiet. He spends great chunks of time sitting at my end of the kitchen table, staring straight ahead. Not moving. So still. Often it is at night, with his mug of milk or his glass of Scotch. Some nights he sits so rigidly it is almost like he is made of stone, or something dead. And I watch as he pours two glasses of milk, or else brews some of my favourite peppermint tea. He will set it next to him, in front of one of the other chairs. And he will stare at it while he drinks his milk. And his breathing will come easier.

Sometimes he swallows hard. I see his throat jump up and down. His grief, in these moments, is almost something solid.

I want to speak to him, but all I have is seeing and hearing so I watch and I listen and I am quiet.

'Cate,' he says. It comes out like a cough.

The absence of aching is a sort of ache in itself. I'm terrified of the day when they stop saying my name. Calling to me.

Because maybe I'm only here, anchored, in order to hear them.

* * *

Cameron and Jessa are sitting in a corridor with plain chairs and curling, bland posters on the walls. Sunlight, coming in through a white-edged window. It's not a room I recognise. A hospital, maybe. Or a community centre.

Jessa runs her fingers along the edge of the poster like she wants to pick it into pieces. She kicks her thongs off and knocks them hard under her seat.

I can hear a kookaburra chuckling away from somewhere outside. Cameron startles at it, sits further back in his chair.

Bass is standing next to them, running his hand around the back of his neck. He is in his usual clothes, his shirt and jeans. The clothes he wears regardless of whether he's working at the furniture restorer, cash in hand at someone else's farm or tinkering away on our farm. His farm, now. His work brings some money in. A fair amount. But not enough.

The horses I trained and sold helped. I'd mostly get the horses off the track and train them for a few months, get them out on the trails and to competitions. My friend Laura prefers to breed hers, to breed her horses and train them from weanlings.

We talked, a lot. Laura and me. We talked about combining what we did, but we never got around to doing it properly. Officially.

Jessa lets her hand drop and glares up at Bass, still running his hand backwards and forwards across the back of his neck.

'It smells funny in here,' she says.

'Oh, it does not,' says Bass, turning to face Cameron. 'Does it?'

Cameron sniffs. 'Smells the same as school, I reckon. And a bit of lavender.'

'It does not smell like lavender. It stinks.'

'Jess, drop it,' says Bass.

'I could be riding.'

'This lady's the best.'

'I don't need to see anyone.'

'Jessa …'

'I *don't.*'

He squats down next to her chair. She knocks him in the shin as she crosses her legs away from him. 'It stinks. I feel sick,' she says.

'To see your mother like that …' His voice is low. It cracks on *that*. He looks hard at the poster and Jessa glares at the bare wall and Cameron is quiet, watching them.

'I don't want to talk about it.'

'This lady …'

'With anyone.'

Bass stands up. 'Well, you need to.'

'I don't.'

'It's not a choice. It's happening.'

'I have a headache,' she says. 'I'll vomit.'

'Have some water from your bottle.'

'On *you.*'

'Don't vomit on Dad,' says Cameron.

'Jessa, enough,' says Bass.

'I won't talk.'

'Well, sit in there for an hour and twiddle your thumbs. I don't care.'

But he does. It's there, in the lines of his shoulders and the way his mouth is caught at the sides.

Jessa sees it. Watching him out of the corner of her eye.

'Maybe I'll just stop talking altogether.'

Bass cracks his neck. 'Maybe you will.'

'Maybe I will if you make me come here every week.'

'Jessa?' Cameron is slumped in his chair.

'What?'

'Shut the hell up.'

* * *

Sometimes when Beatrice pulls away from our house on the farm, she will stop the car in a shoulder not far down the road, pull the handbrake up and cry.

She cries like I haven't seen her cry in years. Not since we were teenagers and Beatrice had bad skin and too many textbooks and seemed to cry all the time.

She will sit quietly afterwards. Her head sometimes resting on the steering wheel. I wonder if other drivers coming down the road ever see her. Ever see her collapsed over the wheel, all long dark hair and clenched fingers. Ever feel a quickening of their pulse, the start of panic, and press the accelerator down that little bit harder.

I wonder if people driving past ever think that my sister is dead.

She will sit until her breathing slows back down to normal. She will tilt her head back, blow her nose on a crushed napkin, run her fingers across the puffy skin beneath her eyes. Then she will clear her throat, pull out her notebook.

Groceries?

Take boys?
Talk to Jessa (has Cate had The Talk)
Horses???

Poor Beatrice. She will set the notebook aside, recap her pen, turn and indicate back onto the road.

She has no idea what to do with my family.

* * *

I do not see Cameron in the small office with the couch and the abstract paintings and the square box of tissues. By the time I have focused on them again I see Jessa, who sits with her legs stuck out in front of her and her arms crossed tightly over her chest.

'… or your own safety. That make sense?'

Jessa stares at her.

'This is your space, okay? If you don't want to talk that's all right. It's yours.'

Jessa raises her eyebrows.

The counsellor settles back on the couch and stares out the window.

About ten minutes in, Jessa mumbles something.

'Pardon, Jessa?'

'I said, I'm not talking.'

'Okay.' The counsellor continues to gaze out the window.

'After this, I mean. Just so you know. It doesn't matter how many sessions you sit through in here with me and it doesn't matter if it's my space or Humphrey Bear's. I don't want to talk.'

The counsellor shrugs. 'Okay.'

Jessa struggles with herself for a moment. The clenching of her fingers. 'Okay?'

'What? You think I'm going to force you? I'm not here as a punishment.'

Jessa raises her eyebrows again.

The counsellor grins. 'Would you like to hear about me?'

Jessa startles. 'What?'

'Well, seeing as you don't want to talk. Do you want to hear about me?'

Jessa shakes her head, but the counsellor has closed her eyes. 'I hate spinach when it's cooked. I love baby spinach in salads …'

Jessa glares at the counsellor, but the counsellor keeps her eyes closed. 'I was allergic to dog hair when I was little, but not any more. But I still prefer cats and –'

'That's stupid stuff, though,' Jessa says.

The counsellor cracks her eyes open. 'You think?'

'Yes.'

'Why's it stupid?'

'Because it doesn't matter.'

'What makes you say that?'

Jessa is silent.

The counsellor settles back in the couch. 'Because it seems small? Because we're not likely to have spinach or cats in here?'

Jessa stares out the window.

'Because I think the small stuff matters. And I think it makes you who you are. I don't want you coming here thinking you need to launch into the big stuff. We may never get to the big stuff. And that's okay.'

I see it then. A tiny shift in Jessa's shoulders, as though the muscles there have loosened. She does not talk again for the rest of the session, but on the car ride home she stares at her reflection in the side mirror.

'My freckles kinda look like a cat,' she says.

Bass glances over at her. 'The patch on your left cheek?'

She nods.

Bass shakes his head. 'I always had that pegged as a horse.'

Jessa doesn't smile, but her face softens. And when she gets home she does not run straight inside to start dinner, or outside to do the horses. She sits on the verandah for a while, running her fingers over her cheek and making clucking sounds with her tongue.

* * *

When I was much younger, Beatrice and I would spend long afternoons stencilling leaves into exercise books. We would find them around the seaside suburb we lived in outside Melbourne. We would be running around in old sneakers with flowers tucked behind our ears. Back at home, lying tummy-down on the concrete porch or the narrow band of lawn out the back, I would label each leaf and describe its colours and where I had found it, my page a running mess of writing and smudged lead.

Beatrice is older than me. But, most of the time when we were younger, I felt older. I made the decisions. I pressed her into games she didn't want to play. Once, I made her run down to the beach with me in the middle of a thunderstorm to watch the lightning. Afterwards Mum smacked her hard enough on the arm to leave a red welt that lasted until dinner.

Beatrice, if I left her alone on those days we sketched leaves, would colour hers in and sketch fairies or trees. She came up with pretty names and drew pretty dresses.

Nothing really changed as we got older.

* * *

Bass has been careless with the horses. This is clear when Laura comes over in her old ute and sets about catching them and filing down their hooves.

Jessa is with her. Bringing in the horses from the paddock next to the house. She holds them, making cooing noises. She knows when to push them and when to back off.

The angry little goose gets that from her dad.

Henry, Laura's nephew, is sweeping up the hoof offcuts, throwing the larger bits to Mac, who is lying across the doorway. Henry always has the hollow-eyed look of a child who spends too much time watching the movements of adults.

Laura rubs her mouth and forehead with the backs of her hands. Her brown hair is coming free from its bailing twine tie. In the sunlight I can see flecks of grey, at her temples and at the nape of her neck. She is tall and fit but wears baggy clothes that hide everything but her weathered forearms and neck. 'Where's the black filly?'

'What?' Jessa says, glancing up, startled, from brushing out her pony's tail.

'The black filly your mum was breaking in.'

Jessa reddens. Her pony, Pebbles, raises his head. An almost imperceptible leaning in towards her.

'I don't know,' Jessa mutters. I watch her fingers clench hard around the brush.

'What do you mean?' Laura's voice comes out too sharply. Henry stops sweeping.

'I mean, she must still be out there.'

'Where?'

Jessa glances at Henry, who rests the broom against the wall and comes over as if he wants to pat her better.

Jessa looks at Laura, and then down. Her cheeks redden even further. The colour Jessa goes when she's trying not to cry. There's a hiss in her words. 'The bush tracks.'

* * *

My black filly. Opal. The warmblood mare with the white hind sock. The flare of her nostrils and her hooves unsettled on the ground.

I don't try to remember, you see. I try just to see and listen. When I do chance to remember I try to remember my family. My time is too precious for anything else.

It is easy to become lost in memories, to surrender to the swirling, endless flickerings of impressions and moments and feelings and thoughts. Jessa making Cameron lie underneath a pole she was jumping on Pebbles. The unfamiliar sound of Bass yelling at them.

Rustling paper and candle wax. Pressed flowers left too long, turned brown. Turned sour. Jessa pulling them out of the telephone book in her room one by one. Putting plaits of horse hair in there instead.

Cameron trying to pick things up with his toes that time Rafferty tied his hands together with Gladwrap and bailing twine.

Rafferty, tiny but made bulky by his parka, staring down at a dead calf Bass had not had time to move from the paddock. He had sat next to it, running his fingers along the planes of its face. When I'd come out to get him, I'd found him crying.

Bass letting the boys paint his face and his arms. Brown and grey and orange. The colour of our farm in summer when the sunset sky turns bruised. Jessa watching and rolling her eyes.

So many memories. The endless, flickering motion of them. I dread them sometimes. Their deepness and their colour. The way they twist and shift.

More than that, though.

More than that, I dread losing them.

* * *

Laura purses her lips and shoves her old workman's cap on. She saddles Pebbles for Jessa while Jessa runs into the shed to mix a feed and fetch a spare halter.

'Do you want to ride Gus?' Jessa asks breathlessly, vaulting up onto Pebbles, who immediately tries to walk off.

'No. Henry, bring the rest of them in, hey?'

'Sure,' he says.

Jessa leans closer to Laura. 'It's pretty hot to be walking.'

'If he can manage, so can I,' Laura says, nodding at Pebbles. 'Besides, if we find her I think I'll need to focus on leading her back. Without the bother of another horse.'

'Have you got a drink to take?'

'Yes, Mum. In the car.'

Jessa's expression flickers. Laura sighs and claps Jessa on the leg. Pebbles shies away.

'We'll find her,' Laura says.

* * *

I had bought Pebbles for the boys. A little fat, fluffy pony for the two of them to share. Sometimes in spring I had to lock him in the house garden to stop him gorging himself on the grass and foundering.

So quickly, though, he became Jessa's.

Cameron and Rafferty both preferred Gus to Pebbles. Gus, my old horse, who I had saved for when I was a teenager working in a music store.

Gus, who trotted like a train, without changing. He chugged along, head in the air. Snorting and straight.

At four Jessa was already riding Pebbles by herself, making him jump things when she thought I wasn't watching.

* * *

Here's the thing about Jessa. She wants to be grown-up so badly that her nails mark little crescents into the palms of her hands.

19

She's old enough to know that being grown-up is about planning and prioritising, but young enough to believe that it means never making a mistake.

I see it, more and more.

Bass's alarm goes off at six o'clock. He will use the hand that has been holding hers to turn it off. And when he rolls back over, perhaps intent on seeing how his little girl is, she will be heading down the hallway for her gumboots.

She makes herself a sandwich before school. If Rafferty has refrained from locking her in the chicken run, putting things in her bed or hiding her saddle, she will sometimes make him and Cameron a sandwich too.

On grey mornings she will hunt out their school jumpers from the growing pile of laundry that Bass has left in the middle of the kitchen floor. She will lift the jumpers to her nose and wince at the musty smell of them. Once she tried to spray them down with Windex.

'Thanks, Jess,' Cameron will say. On his way home from school on these days he will sometimes pick her flowers. Jessa will say 'Oh,' like she's disappointed and will leave them on the kitchen table. When nobody is looking she will secret them away into her room and sometimes the sight of them, when she wakes hissing in the middle of the night, will be enough to soothe her back to sleep.

* * *

By the light, it is afternoon. Lanky shadows stretching from the silver stringybarks by the edge of the paddock, almost to the house. Rafferty is the first home. He dumps his bag on the kitchen table, drinks milk straight from the carton and wipes his mouth on the back of his hand. We have a chalkboard on the fridge and he scrubs at it. There are curling cards from their sixteenth birthday stuck there and he pulls them down and stuffs them into the overflowing mail pile.

He writes *Jessa is a fuck head*.

He drums his hands on his legs and sits up on the sink. He considers the chalkboard.

He gets up again, scrubs out his message to Jessa and writes *Jessa is a fuck head Cameron is a …*

He pauses, chalk poised.

Jessa comes in. She puts her bag by the kitchen door, sees the message and scowls.

'You're the arsehole,' she says.

'Fuckhead.'

'You're such a pain.'

'I can't think of what to write for Cameron.'

I see Jessa's mouth tighten. She busies herself moving dishes around at the sink, refusing to look up.

'Fuck head, what d'you reckon?'

'Go away.'

Cameron comes in, shoulders rounded, cheeks blotchy. His hands shake as he dumps his backpack by the table and sits down, resting his head in his arms.

'Cam?' Rafferty sits down next to him, helps himself to the non-rotting part of an old Granny Smith apple. 'Cameron Carlton?'

Cameron almost imperceptibly shakes his head. I want Rafferty to touch his shoulder. Give his arm a squeeze.

'My twin-tuition's pinging. Think he might be upset about something,' Rafferty says.

'You're a genius.'

'Are you actually doing the dishes or just making a noise?'

'I'm cleaning bowls to have yoghurt in.'

'We have yoghurt?' Rafferty sits up straighter and spits out the apple he was chewing on. 'Hear that, Cam? There's yoghurt!'

Cameron groans.

They are quiet for a while, scraping the yoghurt out of the tub and rummaging for spoons in the back of the cutlery drawer.

'Find the black filly?' Rafferty says.

'No.' Jessa frowns down at her bowl of yoghurt and then gets up to make a cordial.

Rafferty, bowl already empty, is tossing his half-eaten apple into the air. 'Tough break.'

'Piss off.'

He studies the back of her head and half raises the apple.

'Don't you dare,' she says, not turning around.

He grins and sits backwards on one of the mismatched kitchen chairs. He takes a bite of apple.

'You going out again?'

'Yes.' She is stirring her cordial with a dessert spoon.

Rafferty chews and swallows. 'Well, do you need a hand?'

Jessa turns and stares at him, cordial in hand. 'What, so you can jump out and spook her just as I'm catching her? Or tie me to a tree like last time?'

'*Last* time? That was ages ago!'

Jessa takes a few gulps from her glass and then throws the last quarter at Rafferty's face. 'That's for the chicken run!' she yells as she sprints out towards the shed.

Rafferty mops up his face. He watches Jessa disappearing, riding Pebbles bareback towards the bush tracks. He's grinning.

'Cam. Want some cordial?' He shakes his head at Cameron, who just groans and sinks deeper into his chair.

* * *

Jessa sometimes sits in the stable, when nobody else is nearby. She will sit cross-legged in the corner where I have always stored my feed tins, the barrels and tubs of supplements. She will stick her head deep into a partly filled bag of chaff and I can hear her breathing soften, can hear it quieten.

She's stuck her head into feedbags since she was a little girl. Gradually the ritual changed from a hide-out to something comforting, something safe.

Sometimes, Rafferty has seen her, with her head deeply in a bag. He never disturbs her, never mentions it.

When she lifts her head, there is chaff in her hair.

* * *

Rafferty is trying to bleach the cordial out of his school shirt with dry powder and Cameron is sitting in the counsellor's office. I made sure my boys knew how to wash clothes. How to peg them up, make a bed. But bleaching was always a chore I kept for myself. I found it calming, the way the fabric came out of the bucket, wet and changed. The way the clothes dried, almost new, on the line. I liked white things, although I was never much good at keeping them clean. White horse boots and saddle blankets and thick white cotton rugs.

White doesn't age the way colours do. White can be brought back to life, if you bleach it enough.

I watch Rafferty trying to bleach his school shirt without water and am sorry for him. Sad. I wish I'd shown him, just once. Him and Cameron and Jessa. I wish he'd ask his father. But Bass is sitting in the hallway with the plain chairs and posters, flicking through a car magazine and glancing towards the closed door nearby.

Bass is waiting for Cameron.

In the room with the coffee table and the paintings. There are flowers in there now. I wonder if they're real. 'Did Jessa talk much?' Cameron asks.

The counsellor shifts in her seat a little. 'Sorry, buddy. Can't talk about Jessa's sessions, you know that. That's her space and this is yours.'

Cameron nods. He is slumped back into the couch, running his finger along the binding.

'How's this week been?'

'Okay.'

'Any more anxiety attacks?'

He shakes his head. Anxiety attack. It sounds boxlike. It happens, then it finishes. But the truth is that the helplessness comes in waves. I saw it that first time with Cameron. He was ten years old and hyperventilating in the sports shed during lunch break and nothing they'd tried had calmed him down.

I pressed him against me, made him match his breathing to mine. I imagined his heart beating, the slowing of it. It felt good to hold him like that, hold him close and soothe him as I had when he was smaller. I loved him so much in that moment.

I caught Rafferty's eye. His unhappy face, his arms tight around himself as the boys behind him knocked him and muttered things. We stared at each other over the sound of Cameron's ragged breathing. We continued to stare as the teacher got the rest of the students away from the shed and Cameron finally pushed away from me. 'I'm okay,' he said. The words barely there. 'I'm all right.' His breath catching, looking at Rafferty, looking at me. His eyes filling. 'I'm sorry.'

Holding him tighter. 'There's nothing to be sorry about.'

After speaking to the teacher on duty and the principal, I had put the keys in the ignition of the ute and stared straight ahead. The number for a child psychologist scribbled on a yellow note in my pocket. I'd said I'd take Cameron to our family's GP later in the week. The sudden flooded feeling of it made me press my hand to my forehead and cry.

We watched Cameron after that. All of us, but mostly Rafferty and I. We were careful with bad news, we timed our teasing. We watched for the clammy skin, the tremble in his hands. Always with our breath half caught.

Cameron's anxiety became ours.

'No more this week,' Cameron adds, still running his fingers along the couch. He isn't really watching the counsellor. He's slouched low. His shoulders are pulled in, pulled tight. He looks embarrassed. He looks too tall.

The counsellor smiles. 'That's great, Cameron. Now, was that because you were able to head them off with the mindfulness technique we …'

Outside the office, Bass is popping his knuckles. He is staring down at his boots. They are cracking, but he will not oil them himself. I always oiled them for him. We shared chores. He would do the dishes and grocery shop. He would fold up the laundry and put it away. He would vacuum. He would mop.

But I always oiled his boots. I hated seeing them all caked with mud and hardening from the weather, from the earth. The cracking, where the boot bends with his toes.

I watch him staring down at his boots. He wiggles his toes. Scuffs his heels. He might never oil a pair of boots for as long as he lives.

When I go back to Cameron, he is nodding at the counsellor as she opens the door for him.

'See you next week,' she says.

* * *

For as long as he lives. For as long as she lives. For as long as we live. The rest of my life had seemed like forever.

A little pang of anxiety, sometimes. Of how they would cope without me. On windy days watching the three of them disappear down the driveway for the school bus. Fighting the urge to run after them and give them a lift, although the bus stop is only a few metres from the end of our driveway.

Pangs when I stayed in the city, when I was away from them. Pangs when they went away from me. The bucks night in Sydney, Bass returning dark under the eyes, wincing at light and noises and movement. I kissed him all over his face until he pulled me into a hug and said I had to stop or he'd be sick.

School camps in the bush and once in Canberra.

Enjoying the quiet of the house. But reading the same sentence over and over, then getting up from the couch to check my phone, just in case.

'Just relax,' Bass would say. But I couldn't.

Mostly though, the rest of my life had seemed like forever. This certainty that it would continue. That I would *be*.

But my life has ended and I am still here.

Sometimes, I am not sure what to hope for.

* * *

Beatrice comes by after work. I can tell because she is wearing her tight knee-length skirt and shiny, expensive high heels. She works in the council offices in Garras. Her hair is plastered to her head, her plait heavy, and she drops her bag on the verandah.

'Bass?'

There is no answer. Just the buzz of flies and the sound of a tired magpie in the verandah rafters.

Beatrice picks her bag up and goes inside. There is a basket of laundry in the hallway. Mac is sleeping on the floor.

'Bass?'

Mac looks up for a moment and quickly drops back onto his side. A dragonfly skirts into the hallway and back out into the sunlight. Mac watches it without lifting up his head.

'Not much of a guard dog, are you?' Beatrice says.

In the kitchen she stalls again, setting her bag down on the counter. The table is a mess of newspapers and a half-unbuckled bridle. There are wizened apples in the fruit bowl, no dishwashing liquid by the sink.

'Christ,' Beatrice mutters.

Cameron, leaning against the hallway door, rubbing his fingers over the scratched back of his hand. 'I should've done the dishes last night,' he says. 'Would you like a drink?'

It is in this way that Beatrice finds herself sitting next to four weeks of newspapers with a lukewarm tea in her hand.

'I came here to help out,' she says.

Cameron shakes his head. 'I've got it,' he says, scrubbing tomato sauce off a plate with a bar of soap.

* * *

A few months after the incident in the school sports shed, I noticed Cameron's hands were raw and swollen. He was reaching for a jug of water. The scratches looked like they'd been made by nails. I noticed it, then. I noticed his scratching. When he was nervous or fretting or unhappy. He would scratch the back of his hands.

I had already shown Bass the number the school had given me and asked him what he thought about counselling. He had glanced at it, said nothing, and gone back outside.

When I'd mentioned it again, he'd shaken his head. 'He'll be right, Cate.'

'He's not, though.'

'What? You think sending him to a counsellor's going to fix it? He overanalyses everything as it is. Worse than you, even.'

I suppose I always thought Bass's reluctance was somehow about him. About his discomfit at fathering an unsettled, weepy boy.

But he walks slowly out of the counsellor's office. And when they reach the car, he claps Cameron on the shoulder.

Like his own father had done when he was proud of him.

* * *

Jessa trots Pebbles along the bush tracks. Tracks that Bass and I ambled along at dusk in the days before the children. Hand in hand, wearing hiking books and sometimes gummies. Once, sticky with sweat and wine, we stumbled along the muddy tracks barefoot, laughing and giddy with everything.

The tracks are hilly. Narrow, scraggly lemon-scented gum trees crowd the path where it touches our fence line, then give way to blackberries and rugged iron barks with rough skins and sticky dark sap.

The tracks smell of the bitter twist of eucalypt, of stones, and sun, and air rushed through leaves. Jessa knows them as well as the tracks of veins winding up the insides of her own pale arms. Better, even. She has spent her entire life living and breathing these tracks. First, in a pusher or strapped to my back. Then, toddling on little feet. Later, being led on her first pony.

The tangled tracks, all crossing over each other and disappearing again. It would be easy to get lost in them. To stumble out hours later, scratched and blinking in sunlight that feels too bright.

I kept a shovel near the door when the children were younger, but never used it. The snakes stayed on the tracks, or shifted so quickly when they heard me coming that I never noticed them around the house or the horse paddocks.

Once, after we'd slashed a paddock up the front of the property, we found a snake's head ripped clean from its body. Rafferty picked up the head with my snake shovel and put it on a metal drum in the shed, out of Mac's reach. He was twelve, maybe thirteen. He stared closely at the misted eyes, at the place where the head had been removed from the body. At the fangs, just visible.

Cameron said we should never slash again. He cried for the snake and Jessa told him not to be stupid.

Rafferty spent ages in the shed, just staring at the snake's head, nudging it this way and that with a stick, counting its scales and marvelling at its nostrils.

Bass and I peered in without him noticing. We watched him watching.

'Funny little bloke,' Bass said.

We waited until he'd gone inside, then Bass wrapped the head up in a chaff bag and threw it out and nothing else was ever said.

It is cooler, on the bush tracks. The air smells different, feels heavier. The branches are high overhead. Sometimes, in the wind, they rustle and stretch and creak while the world below is quiet and still.

We had gotten the land so cheap off a neighbour. An extra fifty thousand on the mortgage. The land was worth more than that but old Martin next door couldn't be bothered putting a road in, couldn't stand the idea of a house being built there, so close to his own. So we signed away, stating that we would not build anything for ten years. Martin, who was eighty, figured he would be dead by then.

Jessa inhales the heavy smell of stones, and air rushed through leaves, her hands full of Pebbles's dark and dusty mane. He snorts and she snorts a quiet echo on his back. Not even realising it.

She rides along the bush tracks each evening. Tracking Opal, whom nobody had noticed was missing.

Each night, Jessa riding along with a halter slung over her arm or across the saddle in front of her.

I don't know how many nights it is before she finally catches sight of Opal. A dusty and skinny black rump, disappearing into the swell of underbrush. A breath inhaled. And then she is gone.

* * *

Bass is reading the classifieds. He has always had this idea that he will find a prize bull listed. A great hulking creature that someone has inherited from a rich dairy-farming relative with no idea of its worth.

This, Bass has always hoped, is how he will move into the stud business.

As it is, we have a few black and red Herefords that graze in sloping paddocks behind the house and the yards. We normally have a dozen Friesian ladies in there too. We put them to good bulls and sell their calves to dairy farms. Sometimes, sadly, to the knackery. Not profitable, but Bass loves it. If we'd had the money for the initial set-up, I would have long been married to a dairy farmer.

Across the table from him, Laura is slowly sipping a coffee.

'Bass?'

'Hmm?'

'Did you put cinnamon in this?'

Bass makes a sad clucking noise and Laura snorts. 'Bloody farmers.' She puts her coffee down, cocks her head under the table. 'What the hell is that?'

'What?'

'On your feet.'

Bass stares down at his leather boots. The cracks, running through the toe joint. The mud packed tightly into every crevice. He glances back up at Laura. 'What?' he says.

Laura holds out a hand. 'Right. Give 'em here.'

'What? No.'

'Give 'em here. Go get me some oil.'

He stares at her and she raises her eyebrows. '*Quick.* I haven't got all day.'

Bass shakes his head. 'Loz, thanks, but it's fine. I'll do 'em later.'

'*Raff!*' Laura yells.

Rafferty leans back over the couch in the living room so he can see them in the kitchen. 'Yeah?'

'Go get some oil? Your father's boots are a disgrace.'

Bass glances up at Rafferty, back at Laura. 'Loz …'

Rafferty grins and jumps up. Laura holds her hand out, her eyebrows raised, until Bass, muttering things I can't quite catch, reaches down under the table and passes them across.

Laura sets them down on the local paper and Rafferty hands her the tub of oil.

'Thanks,' she says. 'Cripes alive. Get me a damp rag, will you, Raff?'

Bass watches her working the leather. She cleans off the mud and then starts working the oil into the cracks.

'Some of these cracks are set in. Might be able to get some of them out, though,' she says without looking up. Her fingers greased and stained with brown. Bass is wearing odd socks. He's jiggling his leg and he keeps lifting his empty cup up to his lips and pretending to drink. 'Thanks for … the horses … their feet, you know,' he says.

Laura grimaces at where the leather is starting to lift from the sole. 'It's the least I can do.'

'I mean it. I know how busy you are. And I don't know the first thing about horse feet.'

'Don't mention it.'

Bass sits back in his chair for a while and Laura rubs her greasy hands over and over the leather, working in the oil.

Bass watches her fingers. 'I can't believe I … I mean, how did I miss her?'

Laura looks up. 'Opal?'

'Yeah. How did I not realise she was missing?'

Laura shrugs. 'Grief does strange things to people.'

'She was Cate's pride and joy.'

'You don't need to tell me. She called me just about every night to tell me how her training was coming on. Even if I was *there*, watching her bloody training, Cate'd still call for a debrief.'

'She's worth a fortune.'

'I know.'

'I ... with the funeral and ...'

'I get it. You need to find her. You need to sell her.'

'Right.'

'How'll Jessa go with that?'

'Fine. Opal was always Cate's horse.'

'That's why I asked.'

'Oh. Right.' Bass fiddles with the newspaper on the table.

'Jessa's not the kind of kid to get waily about her mum's dresses or jewellery or Christmas cards, but Opal ...'

'She's been out nearly every arvo. Reckoned she saw her the other day.'

'Probably did. The tracks are big, but not that big.'

They sit in silence for a while. Laura nods towards a dress hung over the back of one of the chairs.

'What's that?'

'Beatrice. Trying to take Jess under her wing.'

Laura whistles. 'Good luck to her.'

'Actually, was gunna run something past you. Bea's been at me about Jessa. Wants her to come and stay on weekends and stuff. I haven't told Jessa yet — she's so pissed off about the counselling, I figure hearing she's going over to Bea's might tip her over the edge.'

'Bea's really in her own little world, isn't she?'

'What do you reckon I should do?'

'You? Let them work it out. Tell Bea if she wants Jessa to come over, she needs to discuss it with her. Bea needs to understand you can't just pack a thirteen year old off for the weekend.'

'Jessa's happiest here, I think.'

'She is. And it's up to her.'

Bass nods.

I try not to think about Laura oiling Bass's boots; try not to think about Bea buying my daughter dresses. Try not to notice the great hole that opens up in me as people step into the absence I've left behind.

* * *

When Laura and Bass were young together, they collected stones for a project at school. They waded into creeks and dams and traced each other's footsteps down the sides of the main roads of Garras.

Bass says Laura was short when she was young. And prone to being strapped for hitting classmates who annoyed her.

Laura says Bass played so much sport that by the time he was sixteen he was as broad as he was tall. Laura says he used to sketch unicorns in the sides of his workbooks. Bass says they were cows and Laura showed them to everyone.

'She was a pain in the arse at school,' Bass says.

Sometimes it is strange to think of them growing up together, being a part of the same place, the same stories, all those years I was growing up with Bea on the outskirts of the city.

That this place existed. The roads and properties, the familiar shapes of the trees and the wind of the creeks. The smell of too much jasmine curling up the trunks of gum trees in spring. The smell of smoke and wet earth in winter. That this place existed, with all these people, with the animals and the heat and winds and rain.

That it existed without me.

* * *

We all have stories that we like to tell. That those around us have heard so often that it's their story too.

Jessa always loved to tell the story of how she was left alone when she was three years old.

She'd tell Cameron and Rafferty. She'd tell Bea and the kids at school. She'd tell Laura and my mother. She'd tell Henry.

'Mum thought I was with Dad, and Dad was out with the boys and thought I was with Mum,' she'd say.

'And when they realised, they were so scared. They thought I'd disappeared into the dam.' She'd pause, in her telling. Raise her eyebrows. 'D'you know what I did? Guess!'

'I can't.' Laura, hiding a smile. Rafferty with his chin resting in both hands, pretending to be enthralled. Cameron wanting to get away but not sure how to without causing a fight.

'I caught Pebbles and gave him a brush! How funny is that? They thought I was dead or gone or scared and I was as happy as anything, in the paddock. I'd even shut the gate after him! Can you believe it?'

The story would always make Jessa glow.

'Good story, Jess,' Raff'd say. 'It's almost like I've heard it before.'

* * *

Rafferty kicks a rock with the toe of his boot. It's on dusk, dry and still. He's knocking the side of one of the water tanks, listening for a dulling of the sound that will tell him where the water level is. He frowns when he finds it. Steps back and stares up at the grey mass of it.

He wanders over to the barn and fiddles with the generator until it roars loudly to life and Jessa, grooming Pebbles outside after another ride along the tracks, swears at him.

He checks the lengths of hosing. He finds a ladder, goes up and checks the guttering on the house. Guttering we had usually checked already at the start of the season.

'What are you *doing*?' Jessa asks, shielding her eyes against the last of the sunlight.

'Just checking.'

'Checking what?'

'Piss off, Jess.' He doesn't say anything else and when Jessa asks Cameron about it, crowded over the bathroom sink, he spits and raises an eyebrow. 'He was checking all the stuff in case there's a fire.'

* * *

Cameron wakes up screaming. Normally I would come running down from our bedroom. Since I died it has been Bass. But Bass sleeps on, his hand pressed into Jessa's. It is Rafferty who gets out of bed and kneels next to Cameron's bed.

'You're okay,' he says.

Cameron is gasping, scrabbling. Sweating. Rafferty does what he saw me do, when Cameron was much smaller. What he has seen his father awkwardly attempt, then baulk at, at the last minute.

Rafferty brings Cameron into his arms. 'You're okay,' he says into Cameron's hair. 'You're okay. Just breathe.'

* * *

When he was younger, Rafferty started bringing home injured and sick animals. He never stopped moving, when he was small. If he had to stand or sit in the same place for too long, he'd bounce.

The first animal was a possum he'd found walking strangely on the footpath outside Bea's. He'd thrown a tantrum until she'd brought out a cardboard box and helped him get the possum inside it.

'He would *not* move,' Bea said, holding up her hands. 'I tried everything. Thought he was going to pick it up with his bare hands.' She shuddered. 'Good luck.'

We put the possum in an old bird cage Bass found in the shed that his father's cockatoo had once lived in. We stared at it and Rafferty said it was thirsty.

'It stinks,' Cameron said, poking his head in.

'Stinks!' Jessa agreed, only three and still unsteady on her legs when she got tired or distracted.

Rafferty fed it through the bars with an eyedropper while Bass tried to get onto some wildlife carers. 'No luck,' he said. 'Left messages.'

The next day, Rafferty insisted Bass take him to the library to find out what possums eat. Bass stared at me, wounded, as Rafferty pushed him out the door.

'Have fun!' I called and Bass gave me a look as he climbed into the car.

Rafferty called the possum Pokey. He cried when the wildlife carer picked it up. He was morose for weeks, only perking up when the carer sent him a photo of the possum happy and up a tree.

'Is it the same possum?' Bass asked me through the corner of his mouth while Rafferty showed Jessa the photo, telling her off when she tried to touch it with her sticky toddler fingers.

'Buggered if I know,' I'd muttered back.

Rafferty was quiet, around the animals. He was calm and still and gentle. Sometimes, crouched over a cage or shoebox or hanging over a makeshift enclosure in the shed, I'd mistake him – for a moment – for Cameron.

After the possum came the echidna and the blackbird. The stray kittens he'd found covered in flea dirt and crying near the church. The goat he found with a swollen leg and a raw patch where its collar had sat. The blue tongued lizard who bled out in my ute on the way to the vet. Rafferty had been twelve by then, maybe thirteen. He had pressed his face against the side window and tried hard not to cry, the lizard still in his hands. Its skin and blood still warm against his fingers.

* * *

I remember rushing, I think. Rushing, but I couldn't feel any wind. I remember words, but they're letters and scattered and when I try to arrange them they dart away like frightened fish.

I think back to Bass. Think back hard to those first moments I saw him after I died. But all I see is him standing in the rain and the dark, staring up at the house. Standing. Unmoving.

He never says a thing.

* * *

It's hard to think of my stories the way I can think of the stories of my family. Maybe because I'm watching them, their stories are still there and real and whole.

My stories seem to be slipping away. Slipping backwards.

Sometimes, I try to remember them. I think of the day I first touched a horse. A girl at school with wealthier parents than mine. We'd gone to the stables where she kept her horses in the suburbs outside the city, where the blocks and houses were huge and the paddocks picketed with white wood and blue stone.

She had a horse with spots called Casper. The first time I touched a horse, I was twelve. Margo fussed around with bandages and saddle blankets and brushed flies off her face. I stood next to Casper's neck, transfixed. I pressed each of the spots beneath his mane and when he turned his head to breathe me in, I startled backwards.

'Kiss his nose,' Margot said.

'What?'

'Just above his nostril.' She kissed his other side. 'It's like velvet and it smells like grass.'

I kissed Casper's nose. It smelt like more than grass. It was sweet, earthy. Later, I would learn it was the smell of molasses and lucerne chaff. It was warm and velvety. I could feel his heartbeat through my lips. Gentle and slow.

I dreamt about horses, after that. I lent Margot all my favourite pens so she'd let me ride Casper sometimes after school.

'You stink,' Bea would say, when Margot's mum dropped me home.

But I didn't stink. I smelt sweaty, but underneath I smelt like molasses and lucerne. Sweet and earthy and whole.

* * *

Beatrice, unmoving in the children's clothing aisle at Target. She has two T-shirts in her hands. One is blue with sequins, the other pink with a bow.

Her hair is falling out of its clasp and she blows it out of her face.

She pulls out her mobile phone and brings up a contact.

'It's me,' she says. 'Does Jessa like blue or pink better?' She pauses, listens. She clenches her eyes closed and, although there is nobody in sight, she nods. 'Okay. Thanks.' She puts the phone back in her pocket and waves down someone wearing a Target shirt.

'Excuse me! Do you have any dark green T-shirts in this size?'

* * *

Cameron is leaning against the side of the corrugated-iron demountable where he has English every Wednesday and Thursday afternoon. Cameron's never liked PE. And now, halfway through a class, he's trying to slow his breathing. Every part of him is trying, so desperately, for nonchalance.

Some of the others in the class are putting basketballs back into a big net bag. Sweaty, red faces and swatting at flies. Turning towards the PE teacher, waiting for the next instructions.

They're all sweating. The grass on the oval is gravelly and grey.

Rafferty and his best friend, Guy, are hanging upside down from the monkey bars, watching. They're sixteen, too big for them, their outstretched hands nearly touching the ground. Rafferty catcalls something and Cameron's ears go red.

His little finger is flicking and unflicking the corner of his T-shirt, beneath the crossing of his arms. And he keeps pressing his lips together. Running them between his teeth.

'Cam, you okay?' A blonde girl in a T-shirt, which is a size too small. She tilts her head. Maggie March.

Her mother died when she was young. She is staring at Cameron. Searching, almost.

Grief, I suppose, is something you think you understand once you have seen its colours, its shapes. But the thing about grief is that it is forever changing. A swell, subsiding. The waves, their curl and height and depth, each different.

She leans against the demountable and wipes her forehead. She smiles at him. 'Sweaty,' she says. 'Wish we didn't have class after this.'

Cameron smiles at her. 'Yeah,' he says. His finger stops flicking his shirt.

'You're good at running. Really good.' She tucks a strand of blonde hair behind her ear. Along the inside of her wrist, *Naomi*. Her mother's name in cursive script. Her father took her to get it done when she was thirteen years old. I remember telling the other mothers in the year level to shut their mouths and mind their own goddamn business. Because grief paints itself differently for every person.

'Not really. But thanks. For saying that. You know.' He runs a hand around the back of his neck, reminding me of Bass.

She frowns. 'You right?'

Cameron swings one of his arms. 'Just tired.'

'Yeah.' She nods at Rafferty, who is hanging upside down and chanting Cameron's name. 'Can't imagine you'd get much sleep sharing a house with the banshee. What the hell is he doing, anyway?'

'Free period.'

'Rafferty Carlton! Knock it off!' the PE teacher yells. Rafferty's arms drop and Guy hangs down next to him.

'Umm ...' Cameron looks at Maggie. 'You ... I ... I like your shirt.'

Maggie grins.

'Carlton, you're up.'

Cameron swings his arms like he has seen swimmers do before a race.

He stands awkwardly at the starting line, staring across at the other three boys lined up next to him.

'Ready, steady ...' The teacher presses the starter gun, it makes a funny *ping* and the boys start running.

But it does not look like they're running. It looks like Cameron's running and the others are jogging, except they're not. I've never seen Cameron move so fast, and when he pulls up, flustered and embarrassed, his teacher punches his arm and grins.

'Where the heck did that come from? Welcome to the athletics team, Carlton.'

And Cameron stares at her, as though uncertain whether winning the race is a happy or upsetting thing. He keeps glancing down at his legs. At the other boys. He wipes his forehead and leans down, bracing himself above his knees.

'Go, Cam!' Rafferty yells.

* * *

Sebastian Carlton. I laughed when he first told me his name.

'Sorry,' I said, trying to breathe. Noticing the numbness of my cheeks and knowing, dimly, that I was drunk.

Cate Carlton, a voice in my head chimed. How pretty it sounded.

'Cate Knot is nothing to crow about either, you know,' he said, sipping his beer. But he'd glanced at me and grinned that surprisingly cheeky grin that always somehow startled me.

'You've got the most beautiful eyes,' he said. 'They're Knot bad at all.'

* * *

Bass and Jessa, moving the cows into the next paddock. They have been at it long enough to be sweating and streaked with dirt. It's windy and sticky, with fat droplets of rain, and the cows are unsettled.

'I hate cows,' Jessa says, pulling Pebbles up. He pigroots and squirms sideways. 'And so does Pebbles. When I grow up, I'm never going to have cows. *Ever*.'

'Good for you,' says Bass. 'Quick!'

Bass is on his four-wheeler, so he lets Jessa and Pebbles do the quick work. Jessa gets the last two in and Bass slams the gate behind them. The cows trot off towards the far side of the paddock closest to the house, where their hay is thrown when the grass gets low.

Jessa glares at Bass, her face red and sticky with sweat. She swings off Pebbles and loosens his girth.

'Done and dusted,' Bass says, closing the gate behind them.

Jessa stares at him for a while longer.

'What?' he says.

'Nothing.'

'We didn't need the bike. You could've handled it all on Pebbles. Who'd have thought he'd be such a little cow pony?'

'He's not. He *hates* it.'

'He's good at it.'

She snorts and sits down, brings her knees up to her chin. I think it strange for a moment, before I remember the view into the valley from that rise outside the paddock. It's all bruised pink and purple, shadowed by the sun, just set. The wind makes Jessa's hair fly madly around her face. She bats it away and sighs.

'Jessa ...'

Jessa rests her head on her knees. 'What?'

'Beatrice says you can stay there whenever you want.'

'I *know*. I hate it there.'

'Why?'

'She hovers.'

'Well ...'

Jessa lifts her head. 'I wanna be home.'

'Okay.'

'Are you ...?' She rocks backwards on her seat bones and shakes her head.

'What?'

'Nothing.'

'Am I what, Jess?'

Jessa puts her head back down on her knees. 'Nothing, I said.'

'Seen any more of Opal?'

'No.'

'She'll turn up, Jess.'

'I know. Then you'll sell her. And buy something stupid like a tractor.'

Bass cracks his neck. 'We'll cross that bridge when we come to it.'

'Or an excavator. Even though you don't need it.'

'Jessa, you need to understand that we don't own this place, okay? The bank does. And if I can't give them enough money each week ... Well, I'm not in a position to buy any machinery. Selling Opal or not selling Opal. Things are tight.'

'I know what a mortgage is. I'm not stupid. And things have been tight for ages.'

'Do you know how much a funeral costs?' Bass winces at his own bluntness but Jessa's eyes narrow.

'Mum didn't even want any of that. She thought flowers at funerals were stupid.'

'No, she didn't.'

'Yes, she did! And she would've hated that coffin. You let Beatrice and Nana Jo pick it out.'

'They didn't want her in the ... Look, that's all over and done with. Except for the bills. The bills I'm still paying.'

'Nana Jo could've paid them.'

'Is that what she said?'

'No. But she's rich.'

'You might not understand this, but I *wanted* to pay them.'

'Even if it means things are tight?'

'Yes, Jessa. Even then.'

'Even if you don't get to buy another tractor in your whole life?'

'Even then.'

'Even if we have to sell Opal?'

'We haven't even found her yet.'

'*You* haven't even been looking. You just want me to find her so you can sell her.'

'Jess … if we do sell her, it'd be to a good home. Anyway, she'd be better just about anywhere than out there.'

'Liar.'

Bass tugs at a blade of grass and sniffs. 'What's up with you, Jess?'

'Nothing.'

'Is it going to Bea's?'

Jessa is silent.

'It's not a punishment. Going to Bea's.'

'Oh.'

'Did you think it was?'

Jessa's nose always wrinkles in a lie. Now, though, on the ridge above the house, her nose is hidden in the crook between her knees. 'No.'

* * *

An overcast day with the clouds low and sluggish over the main street. Jessa is standing in front of the pharmacy with her fists clenched and her shoulders tight and held up too high. She is pretending to inspect the display in the real estate office window.

A sudden gust of wind. It must be warm. Jessa closes her eyes as it passes her and exhales. She glances at the pharmacy again, takes a step towards it and then shakes her head, just a little. A horse unsettled by a fallen tree in its paddock, perhaps. Unsettled by a gust of wind that has set its world in motion.

Jessa sighs. The sound is like a hiss. Then she turns on her heel and heads for the bus stop.

* * *

Rafferty, Guy and Jake are in Guy's room. His mother had her boys young. Maybe eighteen when she had her eldest, Jake. She has a picture of herself in front of a birthday cake, set on the sideboard when you walk in the door. She is pregnant, in the photo. Wearing a dress that's too tight across her belly.

Yvonne. She works long hours. Guy often came over for dinner during primary school. Bass would drive him home, all the way across town, after *The Simpsons*.

'Do you mind?' I asked him once.

'No, course not,' Bass said. 'We have good talks, you know? Think he kind of likes having some man time.'

'Man time.' I rolled my eyes but I was smiling.

Guy has found a stash of porn falling out of someone's recycling bin. Rafferty and Guy are staring at the covers. Jake is poking through the pile of plates and papers on Guy's desk. There are about thirty magazines.

'Looks like someone's just discovered the internet,' says Rafferty, flopping down onto Guy's unmade bed. 'Where'd you nab 'em?'

'I dunno who lives there. One of the crappy places along Elm Street.'

Rafferty lights up a cigarette and rolls onto his back. Jake snorts. 'You're such a creepy fuck, Guy.'

'Whatcha wanna do with 'em?' Guy asks Raff, ignoring Jake. He's sitting on his wheeled office chair and spinning around. The desk is piled high with dirty clothes and plates.

They agree it's creepy to look at them together. They decide to split them. Guy gets two-thirds and the other third goes to Rafferty. They put them into plastic bags and Guy stashes his under the crap on his desk. Rafferty tucks his into his history folder.

Jake shakes his head when Guy tries to hand him a pile.

'Don't forget it's there,' says Jake, nodding at the folder. 'You'll give Mrs Codding a heart attack.'

Rafferty grins.

'Hey. Did you know that dipshit brother of yours could run so fast?' says Guy, flipping through a magazine.

'Nah. Crazy, right? Who the fuck knew?' says Rafferty.

'Cameron? Being athletic?' Jake raises his eyebrows. 'Good on him.'

Guy snorts. 'Jason was pissed. He won zone last year, don't think he was expecting Cam Carlton to beat him by that much.'

'We should have a party,' Raff says. 'A *big* one. Like how we used to, you know?'

'Sure thing, grandma. Back in the glory days, right?' Guy says.

'Ha ha.' Rafferty pauses. 'We haven't … Shit … Don't think I've been to a party since before Mum …'

Guy is watching Rafferty closely. He's shorter than Rafferty, with light blond hair and big brown eyes. Jake is similar, but much taller and broader. Guy lights up his own cigarette.

Rafferty points at a pair of muddy shoes under Guy's desk.

'Are they the ones you wore to Mum's funeral?'

'Yeah.'

'Did you buy them? For the funeral?'

'Yeah.'

Rafferty doesn't say anything, but he nods.

Guy stands up and clears his throat. 'C'mon. Let's organise this party. Raff's comeback. Here? Friday when my mum stays at Davo's?'

'Yeah.'

'Bonfire?'

'Is the pope fucking Catholic?'

* * *

I have memories that I am sure are from the last few weeks of my life. Dipping Turkish bread into an avocado salsa that Cameron has made, shyly, as a before-dinner treat.

Trimming Rafferty's hair before a date. He did not tell me it was a date, but I suspected because he was so coy and cranky. Then I overheard him asking Cameron where he picked the flowers he sometimes brought home for Jessa.

Jessa, walking through the kitchen. 'You're such an arsehole, Raff.' The clatter of the door as she went outside.

Blowing flies out of my face as I rode Opal around in the dusty arena. The ache in my stomach muscles from posting, posting, posting. The feel of her black mane against my fingers. The pinch of skin between the reins and my wedding ring.

Bass's hands. His beautiful, sun-darkened, work-worn hands. And the flickering colour of them in candlelight.

* * *

Bass masturbates once or twice a week in the shower. He stands very still afterwards and leans his head above the faucets. His shoulders shudder and his nose runs and it's the only time I see him cry. He towels himself off more slowly on these mornings.

And his expression, when he looks at himself in the mirror, is the saddest I have ever seen.

* * *

Jessa is sitting on Beatrice's toilet. From here she can rummage through the cabinet under the sink.

She pulls loose three pads, stares at them. I see her breathe out a sigh of relief.

She stuffs them into the pocket of her school jacket. The third she stares down at before stuffing her underpants with toilet paper instead. She flushes the toilet and exhales. She fixes her hair in the mirror.

'How's school?' Beatrice asks when Jessa comes back out into the kitchen.

'Good.'

'You're enjoying it?'

'Yep.'

'Your dad says you're looking for your mum's horse?'

Jessa crosses her arms. 'Yep.'

'Be careful, Jessa.'

'I am.' She glances at her schoolbag, her hand pressed into her pocket. She wants to stuff the pads into the very bottom of the bag. Wants to press them away into the dark where nobody will accidentally see them.

When she sits back down at the table, she flicks her skirt slightly, so her undies sit on the wooden chair. Not her light-coloured school dress. Beatrice doesn't notice.

'Jess, have you talked to anyone? About what happened? Because I know you're seeing a counsellor, but ...'

'I love my counsellor,' says Jessa. 'We really click.'

Beatrice nods and has a sip of tea. Her forehead creases just above her nose, the way it used to when we were younger and I snapped at her. Was impatient with her.

Jessa presses her hand still deeper into her pocket.

'Your dad seemed to think you weren't that keen to be going.'

'I'm really keen. *So* keen.'

'Uh huh.' Beatrice hesitates and then sits forward. 'You know, Jessa, if you ever need someone to talk to about anything, I'm around.'

'I know. Thanks.'

'And if you need some space, a break from all the testosterone, you can always stay here too, okay?'

'Okay.'

Beatrice's forehead stays creased. Just a little. She stares at Jessa whenever Jessa isn't looking. She puts her hand in her pocket, where she has a list torn from a notebook of things she can do to help.

They are quiet, finishing their drinks. Back at home, Jessa shuts herself in her room and puts the bloody tissues she's been using in the bin. She sets about slowly unwrapping the pad and inserts it carefully in her underpants.

She flexes her thighs experimentally. After a moment, she empties her bin and then hangs over the fence of the yard with Laura, watching Rafferty riding Gus.

* * *

When the boys were small, I always had Cameron pegged as the rider. He had a softness about him, a watchfulness. I think now that he was in many ways like a frightened horse himself. Ready to shy, ready to scramble away and stand, trembling, staring back at something that had startled him.

It was a dull pain sometimes, watching Cameron. Sometimes he tensed at a flock of birds landing in the garden. A few times, watching him startle made me cry.

But it was Rafferty who worked with the horses as though they were two halves of a broken shape coming together.

I wondered at this. Whether confidence really did mean more than gentleness. Or whether, somehow, when I looked at Cameron I confused timidity for gentleness. Confused his tendency to shy and startle for insight rather than the likeness that it was.

Rafferty, fearless. Galloping and jumping. It made my chest ache.

Equal parts pride and terror. It was exhausting.

* * *

These quiet mornings, in the stretching summer light of dawn, Laura feeds out an hour earlier than normal so that she has time to take the quad bike into the bush tracks. She goes slowly, looking more at the ground, looking for prints and poo and signs of Opal's patterns. The way she lives each day out here where there is not even really any grass.

It's autumn, I think. The claret ash's leaves are red and alive and grass greening up again after a long summer. The silver birches near the shed are dropping leaves all over the driveway. Bass glares at them but doesn't clear them.

Afterwards, Laura will stop in for breakfast with Bass and the children and they will eat in silence and Cameron will clean up and Jessa will stamp on Rafferty's foot and then start running for the bus.

Sometimes, over breakfast, Laura will point at Bass's feet with her eyebrows raised and stare up him until he hands over his boots. She will leave them oiled on the table and Bass will stare at them while everyone eats around them.

'No sign?' Bass, putting his hat on, the door held open for Laura as she puts her sunglasses on and heads back towards her bike.

'No sign.'

* * *

It is raining. Dark. Bass is down at the pub where there's a rotary raffle and an all-night happy hour. Bass is with Steve and some other guys he's known his whole life.

He's grinning, has just won a huge bag of cat food. Across town, Rafferty is seeing how close he can inch his shoes to the bonfire at Guy's before they start to melt. The rain here seems lighter, it hisses when it lands on the fire. They have put up a tarp, but it's singed and darkening from the heat.

At home, Cameron and Jessa are playing Uno on the floor in front of the fireplace.

'Let's get a fire going,' says Cameron.

'Why? It's not even that cold.'

'It's *nice*, though. A fire.'

'Not if it makes you boiling hot. It's only April.' She gets up, though. And they bring in wood and Jessa scrunches the paper for him. They light it, watch the flare of the paper going up. The settling of the flame as it starts on the kindling.

'Raff's gone out,' Cameron says.

'Well, yeah.'

'I don't want to go out.'

'Great story, grandma.' Jessa lies on her stomach and starts shuffling the cards. The oven is ticking. A lasagne, the offcuts of the veggies still all over the chopping board in the kitchen. 'And you've *never* liked going out. You're a nana.'

'It's good … Raff, going out.'

'It's good,' agrees Jessa. 'Your go.'

I try to think of the last time I have seen these two sprawled on the floor, playing a game with each other. When Jessa was five, I think. When she had the chickenpox and Cameron kept her company when she got grumpy and sick of watching Disney videos.

Cameron sits down cross-legged and puts down a two. 'Bea came over the other day.'

'Christ. More groceries?'

'She said we could stay there, if we wanted. Invited us all over for tea.'

'She wants me to stay over too. She's worried there's too many boys here.'

'Are you going to?'

'No. Draw four, arse face.'

'I feel kinda sorry for her, you know.'

'Bea?'

'Yeah. Like, she's trying so hard. With us, I mean. Trying to help but it's just ...'

'Fucking annoying? Uno.'

Here's the strange thing. Jessa loves to win. Games, competitions, arguments. I suppose she must get it from me, because she certainly doesn't get it from Bass.

Yet, I watch as she picks up instead of putting down her Draw Four card. I watch as Cameron wins and she presses her card pile quickly to the bottom of the deck.

Cameron's grinning. He pumps his fist into the air and laughs.

'Yeah, yeah.' Jessa passes him the deck. 'Your deal.'

* * *

When Rafferty was four, he pressed a book against his face and inhaled so sharply I stopped dicing vegetables at the kitchen bench.

'What are you doing?'

'Books smell like dreams.'

I remember thinking I had to write that down in the diary I kept of the things the boys said. The strange and wonderful things. 'They do, do they?'

'I'm collecting them. For when I sleep.'

We didn't really speak any more about the books or the smell of dreams. Rafferty sat cross-legged on the kitchen floor most nights and would breathe in the smell of the pages. He favoured older books. My childhood ones or the farming manuals that Bass's father had left Bass when he passed away.

As I cooked dinner. Casseroles and soups, mostly. Boiled vegetables. Things that were quick, simple.

Sometimes Cameron would come into the kitchen. I could cook at the counter and glance up to check that his small, tousled head was still visible over the back of the couch.

He would sit down next to Rafferty and Rafferty would pass him books and Cameron would stare at them, stare at the endless, marching print on the pages and at Rafferty, who was so happily absorbed.

'Can I help?' he'd ask me after a while. Putting the book carefully down on the floor. Sometimes he would do it carelessly, and Rafferty would pounce and drag him, squealing, to the ground.

Most nights, though, it was quiet.

Rafferty, endlessly turning the pages. Cameron trying to cut broccoli and carrots with a plastic picnic knife.

The quiet sound of their breathing and old pages being turned.

* * *

Rafferty is walking unsteadily home in the rain. He has his hoodie pulled up over his face and keeps stumbling on the gravel shoulder. He has a ball of easter egg foil in his hand.

'Careful, careful,' he mutters to himself and giggles.

When he reaches the farm he goes into the paddock and pats all the horses. Then he sits on the bonnet of Bass's car for a few minutes, staring up at the dark, cloudy sky.

Inside, he struggles out of all his clothes and pulls on a pair of boxers and a dry jumper. He goes upstairs and sits on the windowsill. He throws a balled-up sock at Cameron, who grunts and pulls his covers in more tightly around himself.

'You missed a ripper party.'

'I wasn't invited.' Cameron blinks at him. 'Weren't you meant to be sleeping there?'

'Yvonne came home.' Rafferty pauses, giggles. 'Had a fight with big man Davo. Wasn't too happy, dun reckon. Had to leave. So I walked.'

'You walked? From Guy's?'

'Yup.'

Cameron sighs, gets up. 'Wait here.'

Rafferty flops onto his bed and giggles some more. He starts singing a Spice Girls song and then drops his hand on the floor and starts running his fingers across the wooden planks.

'Here.' Cameron hands him a big glass of water.

'What's this?' Rafferty raises an eyebrow.

'Doesn't it stop your hangover?'

Rafferty hoots. 'I don't get hungover.'

'Right. Whatever. I'm going to sleep. Don't chuck.'

Rafferty claws his way under the covers and sighs. 'Do you reckon she remembers?'

'What?' Cameron turns to blink at Rafferty, who has stuck an unlit cigarette in his mouth.

'Opal,' says Rafferty. 'Do you reckon she remembers?'

'I don't know.' Cameron rolls over and snatches his blankets so crossly that he pulls them up off his feet.

'Mum used to reckon they remember a lot more than we give them credit for.' Rafferty lights the cigarette and waves his fingers around in front of his face. 'Can't see *nuthin.*'

'Well, I hope she was wrong. I hope Opal doesn't remember anything.'

'Why?' That provocative voice. Rafferty presses his cigarette against the sill, watching as it smoulders against the wood. The sill is dark with singe marks. I wonder if Bass has come into their room often enough to notice.

Cameron's voice is muffled. 'Because then she'll never let us catch her.'

* * *

Maybe a few days later. Jessa still has pads pressed into her schoolbag. She is still sitting down with her skirt flicked up.

'Dad,' she says, finding Bass sitting in the hay shed trying to untangle a length of electric fencing.

'Hmm?'

'Cameron made the athletics team.'

'Good. Great! That's wonderful!' He keeps untangling. 'Give us a hand, hey? Asked the boys to do this weeks ago. Got those new heifers coming. Last thing I need is for them to get next door like the last lot did. Or the road.' He shakes his head.

Jessa sits down in front of him and starts working at the other end of the tangled pile. 'Dad …'

'What?'

'We should … I dunno. Do something. Go for dinner or … I dunno.'

'What do you want, Jessa?'

'I think we need to mark it, somehow. I think we need to mark it like Mum would've.'

Bass stares at her for a moment. His hands go still in his lap. She glances up and he smiles too broadly. He tousles her hair. 'Yup! Good! Great. Let's do that. Tonight. We'll, ah, go somewhere. Somewhere nice.'

It takes them a good while to sort out the electric fencing tape. Bass texts the boys and calls up Bea. Invites her too. They end up in Rosella, at a cheap Chinese restaurant where I am sure I once got food poisoning.

Cameron is shy, happy. It's the first time in years a dinner has been just for him. Birthdays he shares with Rafferty.

They are quiet. Bea offers to plait Jessa's hair and Jessa stares at her. 'I *like* my bun.'

Rafferty makes everyone use chopsticks and Bass keeps dropping his fried rice and his ears turn red. Jessa eats a whole tub of black bean vegetables and complains about her stomach. Outside, after they've eaten, Bass squeezes her shoulder.

'I'm glad we did that,' he says. 'Really glad. Think he enjoyed it?'

'He did. Course he did.'

'Athletics. Who'd have thunk it?'

* * *

Cameron taps Laura on the shoulder. They are standing in the shed, Laura running her hand over Thai's swollen hock.

The silver birches are bare, but it is sunny. Warm. The weather, it changes. There are warm days in winter and cold days in summer. Cameron is tanned, but he runs now. He's a runner. I imagine that he may now be tanned all year round.

'Well, of course you'd do it now, just coming back into work. You bloody bugger,' Laura mutters, running her hand further down to press experimentally around Thai's pastern.

'Loz?'

'Hmm?' She straightens.

'Would bailing twine work to lead a horse?'

'What?'

'If you had to, I mean. If you had nothing else. Could you put some bailing twine over their neck and lead them?'

'If that's all you had. I suppose so.' She bends back down to Thai's leg.

'Okay. Thanks.'

Cameron is in his running shoes. His baggy shorts, his faded T-shirt. He stuffs a length of bailing twine into his pocket on his way out the door, and then he starts jogging towards the bush tracks.

* * *

Rafferty is in the kitchen. It's early. I can tell by the shivery way he holds himself, the way a body stands when it is still pining for bed. Still close enough to touch it. He was always up before Cameron, when they were younger. Always up before his body had had a chance to wake up properly. He was chatty, in the mornings. Even as he yawned and shivered.

He opens the high cupboards in the kitchen. The cupboards nobody goes into except for me. Serving dishes and fairy lights. Our wedding china, still in boxes, and ghastly little figurines given to us by Bass's Aunt Marge.

I wait to see what he will take, but he just stares up at everything for a while and then closes the door.

He goes into the lounge room and does the same thing, hands on knees, staring into the musty area at the bottom of the sideboard.

In the spare room, he runs a finger along all the folded sheets, which are in need of airing.

'Raff?' It's Jessa, watching him from the hallway.

He sits back on his heels and looks over at her. 'Have you ever noticed how little of this house we use?' he says. 'It's a big house. And all the cupboards and everything. But between the four of us, we don't use much. You know?'

'Yeah,' Jessa says.

'It's like everything, the whole fucking lot of it, still belongs to Mum.'

* * *

On our one-year anniversary, Bass and I had a picnic in the national park that bordered Garras. We had dip and crackers and smelly, delicate cheeses that seemed to melt as they touched my tongue.

'Here,' Bass said.

A box, wrapped with a bow. Inside was a scattering of sweet-smelling seeds.

'Basil,' he said.

I laughed. 'You got me basil seeds?'

He propped himself further up. 'And coriander and sunflower seeds.'

'You're a dag.'

'I know you're all about self-sufficiency.'

I smacked him and lay back, closing my eyes. 'I should've given you …'

Before I could finish he had pressed a kiss against my lips. 'So you don't have to wait,' he said.

In his hands were two sunflowers and a handful of basil leaves.

* * *

Jessa rides more slowly, these days. Pebbles wanders with his head lower, his ears flicking.

Slow blinking.

She has taken to leaving food out in a big plastic feeder on the edge of the tracks. It's always gone when she checks. She runs her fingers along the dirt around it. Sometimes it will look like a faint hoof print shape, but Opal does not have metal shoes on so her feet leave fainter marks. Jessa has no way of knowing if Opal is eating it or possums, kangaroos or wallabies.

Before tacking Pebbles up today, Jessa had gone into the room she still shares, most nights, with Bass. She opens the wardrobe that still has my clothes in it. That still has my boots and sandals and ballet flats. She hesitates, stares into it.

She brushes her hand across a brown box that is nestled down with my shoes.

Watching her, I wonder what she's smelling. Do my clothes smell like me, my perfume, when I was still alive? Or have the clothes grown stale, damp, locked away in the stillness and the dark?

She pulls my boots on. My tall, laced boots that Bass gave me as a birthday present a few years back. She kicks off her ugg boots, the scruffy, stained and smelly ones she wears inside in winter. She pulls on the tall, laced riding boots. I would have thought they would be too tall for her, would catch the back of her knees, but they're not. She has grown. The boots sit perfectly, as they're meant to. A little wide, perhaps. But my thirteen-year-old daughter is nearly the same size boot as me.

The wonder of it makes the world blur. All I can see is Jessa. Her legs, her feet. The way she turns to stare stonily at the reflection of the boots, her legs, in the mirror.

I expect her to tighten the laces, flex her feet and head out the door, with the wardrobe still spilled open. But she doesn't. She stares down at her feet, at the dull gleam of still-new leather. She runs a tentative finger down the side and then kicks them both off and puts them back in the wardrobe. Latches it. She trips on her ugg boots as she jams them back onto her feet, then charges back out to her room.

Later, riding Pebbles, they meander. Jessa, who only weeks ago rode these trails with a sort of frightened urgency, staring off into the bushes as though each thick trunk might be hiding my lost mare.

She did see the disappearing rump, though. Did see how easily Opal has slipped away.

Now Jessa stares down at Pebbles's neck and plaits his mane, the dusty strands of it.

She is wearing her old elastic-sided boots.

She's not even really looking any more.

* * *

Cameron and the other students in the athletics team are grouped and stamping in an undercover area somewhere I have never been. It is overcast, a bit windy. The others are eating sausages and bread and laughing. The ones who have already competed have a looseness to them. They're not holding their breaths; fighting nausea. Maggie March is warming up for her long jump a little distance away. She keeps glancing back at Cameron.

They all start to move off and Cameron stands up very straight. I can see him trying to do the breathing exercises, but they don't seem to be helping. His hands grip together so tightly I can almost see them shaking with the effort of it.

'You right?' the coach asks. Murray, I think is his name. He's older than most of the other staff at the school. He has been a cattle farmer, a little bit out of town, for most of his life.

'Yeah,' Cameron says, but his voice trembles. He leans down and braces himself above the knees, his breath heavy and fast. He drags a hand across his sweating forehead.

'Shit,' he mutters.

'Take a deep breath, eh?' The coach hands him a handkerchief from his pocket. 'Here. Thought this might help.'

Cameron takes it with trembling fingers. The other students are starting to stare back at him now. Curious.

'It's …'

'Eucalypt. Bit of lavender oil. Always helps me when I get nervous.' Murray claps him on the shoulder. 'Take it out with you onto the track. It'll just look like you're blowing your nose. You'll be right, Carlton. This is your thing.'

Cameron buries his nose into the cotton. He closes his eyes and I watch as his breathing slows, as his hands stop trembling. My relief, my gratitude, makes the world waver like a heat mirage.

'You'll be right,' says Murray again. It's a relay race. Cameron walks towards his starting position. He glances at Murray and Murray nods and smiles.

He tucks the handkerchief into his pocket at the last minute.

The starter gun goes off.

And then Cameron starts to run.

* * *

When Rafferty started high school he clashed with his English teacher so spectacularly that we were advised to have him tested for dyslexia.

The little boy who clawed his way through *The Lord of the Rings* trilogy when he was eight years old.

Rafferty can read. He's a reader. But with the teacher telling him to stop talking, listen more, pay attention and pouncing on every mistake he made, he was not reading. He had stopped.

What followed was long evenings trying to coax him into doing his homework. Coaxing, threatening and then losing my temper and yelling at him until Bass came in and pressed me gently out of the room.

'Why won't he just read the bloody books?' I snapped, slumped against the wall in the hallway when Bass came out ten minutes later. 'He can read them standing on his head! He's so bloody stubborn.'

'If you'd had someone telling you that you were hopeless at something every day, would you want to do it?'

I snorted, feeling like a small child.

Bass hunkered down in front of me. 'Think of him like a horse,' he said, so earnestly that I burst out laughing.

'I'm serious,' he said. 'Imagine he's a horse learning to jump, a young one. And every time he gives it a go he gets whipped on the arse and jagged in the mouth. What's that horse gunna do?'

'Start refusing,' I said grudgingly.

Bass just sat there, with his hand cupped over my knee, until I blew a big breath out. 'I need to be more patient,' I said.

He kissed my head. 'You're human, Cate.'

'You should patent that, you know.'

'What?'

'Parenting for horsefolk.' I stood up. 'Be a big seller.'

In the teacher's office, later that week, I nearly told her indignantly that Rafferty had smelt books since he was four years old. Instead I held Bass's hand. His cool fingers stayed relaxed against my own, hot and clenched.

'He's not dyslexic,' Bass said. 'He's been smelling books since he was four years old.'

My love flooded me like a sunset through a window. Overwhelming. Blinding.

* * *

Sometimes Jessa will take her dinner on a plate out to the horse paddock. She will sit with her back against the gate.

Mostly dinner comprises the old faithfuls that I made sure each of them knew how to cook by the time they were twelve. Pasta with fresh tomato sauce, salad with garlic and lemon dressing, curries and stews and vegetable lasagne. Sometimes their dinners are strange things concocted out of all the leftovers in the fridge. Salads with broccoli and strawberries. Quiches with olives and basil. They seem to eat the meals happily enough, each calmly absorbed in their own thoughts.

Jessa, cross-legged by the gate. Often the horses come up and breathe grass and sweetness into the side of her face so that she grins and swats them away. The paddocks are coming back to life. Coming back to greenness. The horses always come back and her hand will always creep up to play with the mess of their forelocks.

In the house Bass will glance up from doing the dishes, his hands slick and wrinkled. His daughter looks so small, with six big horses pressed up behind her.

Sometimes the sight of her out there will be enough to send his heart tripping forwards. Will be enough for his forehead and underarms to grow damp with sweat. But he will catch his breath.

And close his eyes.

'Raff!' he calls. 'Go outside and sit with Jessa, will you?'

* * *

'Let's go,' says Jason. Cameron blinks at him, but follows. Acquiesces. They are walking back from the shops, their arms heavy with bags full of chips and chocolate and soft drinks and cheap chocolate eggs, on sale after Easter.

'The others are coming at six,' says Jason. 'Still can't believe we won! We've never won relay at zones before. You nailed it, Carlton.'

'It was everyone.'

'Horse shit. We were losing. Here.' Jason hands Cameron a bottle of lemonade.

'Thanks,' says Cameron, unscrewing the lid and taking a swig.

'You ever even been pissed before, Carlton?'

'No.'

Jason laughs, claps his shoulder. 'Oh, man. Have I got a lot to teach *you*.'

Cameron lugs his bags a bit higher. I can see the corner of the coach's handkerchief poking out of his jacket pocket.

* * *

Parent–teacher interviews were always my thing. Bass had hated going to the local schools, so much that when he picked the children up he always sat in the ute with the engine running rather than wait for them inside the gates.

Now he sits with his hands pressed in his lap and his back very straight. He doesn't touch his neck like he normally does when he's uncomfortable or tense or feeling things he doesn't have the words for.

In this school, where he'd struggled to read and write, he was too afraid to be uncomfortable.

I was curious about words. Stories. I was curious about the names of flowers, the history of where I was living. Endlessly wondering about the places people came from, the stories they told and the words they left silent, without breath.

Bass's curiosity was for the way a flower unfurled in the morning. Was for the way cows moved across the paddock. Was for ways to bring out the beautiful texture of a piece of wood he'd just discovered on someone's front lawn in town.

Curiosity is something in itself that can be shared.

Mrs Crowther. I remember her. She once told me that Rafferty had a talent with words but that his spelling was atrocious.

'But aren't words all about the spelling in grade four?' I asked.

'Not with me, they're not.'

She smiles at Bass and he grimaces back, his hands still pressed in his lap. He looks so like a small boy. I expect him to start swinging his legs.

'So,' she says.

'So,' he says.

'How are you doing?'

'Good.'

'And the boys?'

'Good. Fine. Yeah.'

'It's been a … tumultuous time for your family. And I have to say that I think how well Jessa has been coping is a credit to you. To you both.'

Bass clears his throat. 'Thanks. Thanks.'

She smiles at him. That smile everyone seems to give my family now. As though they're damaged. Their brains. Their hearts. As though, without me, they are suddenly pitiable.

Everyone except Laura, blowing hair out of her face as she helps Jessa with the horses and sends Henry over to help look for Opal.

'I'll cut to the chase,' Mrs Crowther says. 'I have no doubt Jessa is a very intelligent girl. I have no doubt she has strong language skills. And I *know* what a dreadful time it is for her. But she won't read the bloody books.'

'Did you just say bloody?'

'I did. I'm not sure how to reach her. She's incredibly angry. The assistant principal mentioned she's doing counselling.'

'Well, she sits in the room for an hour.'

'I see.' She crosses her arms on the table and waits.

'I …' He blinks. He tucks his hands between his knees. 'I don't really read,' he says. 'Books, I mean. I can read. I can read fine. But what I mean is, I don't read so I don't know how to get her to read when I don't read myself.'

'May I suggest something?'

'What?'

'Talk to Rafferty.'

* * *

A quiet afternoon where the doors are closed and the windows are open. Bass's arm is goosebumped. He starts writing down all the horses' names. He struggles to remember some of them. And this struggle is a sort of twinging guilt that makes him squirm in his seat.

He didn't listen to me. All those hours, those conversations, the deliberations of who to sell on, who to buy. Who had ripped their rug and who had a swollen hock. Who didn't like grass hay and who spat out their supplement powder.

And he can't even remember their names.

* * *

Rafferty wanders in, trying to tune the guitar an ex-boyfriend of Yvonne's gave him when Jake and Guy both rejected it.

Cameron is on the couch, resting his head in his hands.

'Cam?' Rafferty sits down next to him, nudges his side. 'You good?'

'Yeah. I'm good.' Cameron glances up. 'I'm a bit *drunk*,' he whispers. 'I think. Maybe.'

'Oh. All right. And how's that working out for you?'

Cameron considers this, frowning. He stares earnestly at Rafferty and leans closer in. 'I'm really *tired*.'

'Go have a nap.'

'Jason made me drink heaps of UDLs. I don't *like* UDLs.'

'Do you … remember how many?'

'Two.'

Rafferty bites the corner of his lip to stop himself laughing. 'You wild party animal.'

Cameron glances down at his hands.

'Do you want a drink?'

'No. I might have a nap.'

'Okay. Good. You nap, then.'

Rafferty goes into the kitchen.

'How you doing?' Bass asks, glancing up from his list.

Rafferty glances at him, puts the guitar down against one of the cupboards. 'Fine. You confusing me with Cam?'

Bass shakes his head and takes a swig of beer. Rafferty settles back into the chair. 'What about you?'

'I'm fine. Good.'

Rafferty grins. 'Great talk.'

'Look. There is something. It's Jessa. Her reading. She won't do it and I don't read books. Not really. Not enough to really push her and …'

'You want me to get her in a headlock while you yell Shakespeare at her?'

Bass lifts an eyebrow and Rafferty exhales in a rush. 'Okay. I'll talk to her.'

'Thank you.'

'Watcha doing?' Rafferty says, opening up the fridge.

'Horses ...'

'There's no food in here.'

'I know, I know. I meant to shop today, but ...'

'What about the horses?'

'I'm doing a list.'

Rafferty glances at his father's wonky writing, the misspelled names, the question marks. For a moment his expression softens and he looks so much more like Cameron.

'To work out who to sell?'

'Yeah. And a rough estimate of prices. Laura said she'd work them a bit if we need her to.'

Rafferty sits down at the table. 'Why don't you go get some food and I'll do this.'

Bass half rises from his chair. 'You sure?'

'Yeah. Get Twisties.'

'All right. Thanks, mate.'

Rafferty grunts and starts scribbling things down on his father's list.

* * *

I didn't like the boys or Jessa being late or eating bad food. Bass didn't like them within a hundred metres of the dam.

Neither of us liked them getting cold.

Some days I didn't care what they ate, as long as I had five minutes to sit on my own. To stare out the window. To count the planks of wood on the verandah. There were days when they would climb all over Bass, knocking him hard on the way up, and all he could do was wave a hand. 'C'mon, kids ...'

Sometimes we ran out of energy at the same time. Days when the children could be naked in the rain for all we were able to coral them. But then Laura was there, for half an hour. Or Steve came around or my mother dropped in for the weekend. Bea would take them to the park, or to Rosella.

It was hard for her to squash all the car seats into her hatchback.

'Imagine being a single parent,' I said to Bass one day after my mother had taken the three of them off for a walk. Jessa, just crawling; the boys into everything, and none of them sleeping more than a handful of hours at a time. All different times. All spread. 'Imagine being a single parent with three little kids, two of them twins.'

'I can't,' he said. 'I honestly can't.'

'People are incredible,' I said. 'Aren't they?' Then I fell asleep on the couch with a tea towel in my hand. I'd woken up covered in dribble, dry-mouthed. We'd slept for two hours.

It was never just the two of us. It was never just Bass and me. Laura was always down the road. There was always the phone. There was always the car.

There were always other people.

I had never appreciated that. I had never seen it clearly. But I see it now.

My children are so lucky.

* * *

Jessa is spreading old hay in the chicken run. The chickens wander around her, hopefully. They chatter and whinge, wanting food, but are quickly distracted by the hay Jessa's dragged up from the stables.

Rafferty stops outside the run gate.

'Jess?'

Jessa whirls around. '*Don't* you lock me in.'

He holds up his hands. 'Wouldn't dream of it.'

Jessa glares at him and turns back to the hay. 'What?'

'You need to start studying.'

She laughs. 'Piss off.'

'Dad's serious, Jess. You need to study.'

'Or what? What'll he do?'

Rafferty frowns. 'Jess … do you want a shit job for the rest of your life?'

'I'm gunna be a professional rider. Like Laura. Don't need good marks for that.'

'Laura inherited a lot of money to get her started. The way our dear dad's going, all we're getting is a giant debt.'

'Piss off, Raff.'

'You need to read the bloody books, Jess.'

Jessa shakes her head, goes out of the run and marches past Raff. 'There's no point.'

* * *

My mother belonged to me. When her alarm went off in the morning, I would hear it. It would wake me, and the two of us would get up and share the quiet. Of the house, belonging to us, alone.

She was an artist, an art teacher. Our kitchen smelt of turps. There were brushes in jars like bouquets of flowers.

We would listen to the radio, dance around the kitchen to songs that Beatrice hated. Giggle, smother the sounds. On mornings when my mother painted I'd perch behind her and watch.

When I was younger, I dreamt that I was my mother's favourite. Sometimes I would test her. I would pit myself against Beatrice. Hang over the back of her while she tried to study, and then run to Mum when she finally swore and turned round to hit me.

When Beatrice really wanted us to go to the beach, I would keep my eyes open until they stung with tears. 'But I hate the beach! I get burnt and the sand gets everywhere!' and we would end up at the nature reserve or shopping centre.

On those nights I would dream of the ocean and go into Beatrice's room and climb into her bed. Sometimes she'd kick me violently until I climbed back out, but mostly she would let me sleep.

It was only after I was sure she was asleep that I would find her hand. Squeeze it.

After I became a mother myself, I often wondered why I was closer to my mother than Beatrice was. It was never an overt thing. Our closeness. But rather, of things unsaid. Of things shared. I was chattier, maybe. I called for her in the night until I was much older. When my mother hugged us, I hugged back harder. I hugged back longer. Beatrice was happiest on her own, I think. Near the water and dreaming.

Beatrice was artistic like our mother. She filled notebook after notebook with sketches. But she never watched my mother paint. She never begged to be taken to the art shop like I did.

Sometimes, when I think of the endless small and unkind things I did to Beatrice when I was younger, the regret is as sharp as a hard blow to the ribs.

Our father, Mark, belonged to nobody. He treated us well, I suppose. But we were secondary. His passion was his research. His solitude, in his study.

It had seemed enough for me. For all of us. Had seemed enough until I met Bass and, later, when we had children and he watched them as closely as I did. Breathed in the smell of their soft baby heads. Pressed his fingers against the squirming grip of their tiny, feathery palms. It was only then that I looked back at my own father and realised how lacking he was, in so many different ways.

Back then it sometimes made me watch Beatrice a little more closely. There were two of us, there were two parents. But neither spent time with Beatrice in the way my mother spent time with me. Neither watched her with a creasing eye, with a half-smile. It made my chest shudder with an odd feeling I did not, until years later, recognise as empathy. As tasting another's grief.

* * *

Cameron is drawing something. He is not a drawer. Does not draw and I find myself focusing on the paper. All red and dark and twisted.

I shy backwards from it. The world starts to shimmer towards darkness.

I focus on what he is wearing. His jeans, his T-shirt, his hoodie. It must be colder outside than it has been. There must be a chill in the air.

The counsellor is sitting across from him on the floor. She's fiddling with what looks like origami. 'There,' she mutters, pulling the paper open into the shape of a flower.

'What's it like? Drawing your nightmares?' she asks without looking up.

'It's …' Cameron sits back, stares down at the picture. 'I dunno. It's good, I guess. There's nothing really that scary, when I draw it. It … I guess I'm scared of other things.'

'Other things. Not things in the nightmares?'

'No.'

'What sort of other things?' She sets her flower down and picks up another piece of paper.

Cameron picks his pencil back up. Keeps drawing. 'Losing people, I guess. Getting things wrong. Every time I say goodbye to someone, I worry it's the last time I'll ever see them. I imagine, all the time, what I'll do when I'm told they're dead.'

'And what do you imagine that you'd do?'

Cameron frowns. Stops drawing. 'Cry, like I did with Mum. But also I scream and yell and I didn't do that when Mum died. I slam my fists into walls. I scratch my hands until I can see the bones. But it means I keep breathing, you know? It means I can keep bloody breathing.'

* * *

A wind has the horses rattled, so that they pace the fences and nip at each other. They're in their rugs now. Jessa is sitting watching them with her knees drawn up to her chest, her parka drawn close around her face.

Bass isn't home. He's at the pub. A man with black hair and a faded blue shirt is sitting next to him. Steve. Who helped out at the rotary club with Bass. Who learnt to knit when the twins were born.

After the twins were born, when I would hear the gravel of the driveway crunching and knew it wasn't Bass, I would cry. Visitors – always. The house packed with their balloons and tiny clothes wrapped up in tissue paper.

'Just tell them to stop,' Bass said one day, rubbing my back while I wept on the couch. I had just gotten the twins to sleep when Maureen Lacker, whom I had never seen outside of mothers' group, had come over with a carrot cake. It was the first time the boys had been asleep at the same time in four days. I was so exhausted I felt like I was going to vomit every time I stood up, but I had managed to make Maureen a cup of tea and say 'Oh, really?' in all the right places while she launched a half-hour attack on the shortcomings of formula feeding.

After she'd left, just as I'd come back in from the verandah, I'd heard Rafferty start to cry in the other room. I'd sat down and started to weep myself.

'How?' I snapped at Bass. 'How the *fuck* do I tell them to stop? They think they're being nice! They think it's a *surprise*! I don't know half these people and,' my lip trembled, 'now they've seen all my bad undies hanging on the clothes horse!' I started to sob again.

Steve was the only visitor, other than my mother and Beatrice, who didn't make me want to knock myself out with a brick. He didn't come in very much. He hung around outside, helping Bass do the chores around the farm that, for the last few months, I'd been unable to manage. I sat on the verandah with the boys, watching as Steve weeded the garden beds, turned the compost, tightened loose fencing, graded the arena and got a ladder to fix the blown arena floodlight.

I always asked him in afterwards and he'd sit quietly and hold the babies, or do the dishes. Once, when I went to have a shower, I came back out to find he'd mopped the floors. I burst into tears.

'Oh god. You *mopped the floors*? Now you've done it. She'll be crying for hours,' Bass said when he came inside, giving Steve a thump on the back.

Now, at the pub, Steve claps Bass's shoulder a couple of times, but they don't speak. Not for a very long time. I have seen photos of them together when they were young, both dark-haired boys, riding around on their bikes, counting down the days till they could take their clapped-out farm cars onto the road. They look like that, sitting at the bar. Young, uncertain.

Steve has smile lines, but he's not smiling. He sips his lager while next to him Bass drains his.

'Want another?' he asks.

Bass shakes his head.

And Steve claps his shoulder again and orders him another beer. They sit like that, shoulder to shoulder, for hours.

* * *

Jessa with her legs stuck out in front of her and her arms crossed. The counsellor gazing out the window at the grey day. There is incense burning on her desk, a tissue box with flowers on it next to Jessa's chair. Jessa's hair is pulled into a messy bun. Her face is pale, a couple of small pimples on her chin.

'No,' says Jessa. 'I haven't. Not yet.'

'Nothing wrong with sleeping in your parents' bed,' says the counsellor. 'Nothing wrong with that at all.'

'Yeah. Yeah, I know.'

'Can I ask you something about how you sleep?'

'I suppose. Yeah.'

'When you wake up, what makes you get up?'

'And go into Dad?' Jessa frowns. 'I don't know.'

I expect the counsellor to probe, like I would. To ask if she is scared or unsettled or angry or sad. To coax the words out. But she just sits there. In the quiet. And I don't know how she does it, I don't know how she lets that space grow, lets it fill up everything between them.

Jessa sits for a while, chewing her bottom lip, frowning. She glances at the counsellor. 'Sad. Maybe. I just ... I just don't like being by myself.'

'What don't you like about it?'

'It's too dark. Too still. I don't know. I don't want to talk about that any more.'

'Okay.' The counsellor smiles.

'What's testosterone?' Jessa asks, flushing deeply around her freckles.

'It's a male hormone. Girls have oestrogen.'

Jessa nods, twiddles her fingers against the arms of the chairs.

And then they're silent.

* * *

Rafferty, his feet on the kitchen table. He's wearing odd socks. It's late afternoon, I think. That strange still light outside as though the whole world is holding its breath, waiting for the last shadow to stretch away and out of sight. 'Reggie should get a couple of grand, same as Thai. Gus ... I'm guessing we're keeping Gus.' Rafferty keeps his eyes down. The horse he learnt to ride on when he was five. He had to clamber up onto the stable door to get on him. 'Noddy should get five, if we get him back in work, and Opal ...'

Bass leans forward. 'How much?'

'Laura reckons thirty. More if we spend a year getting her fit and back out competing. Loz reckons we could have her doing medium in eighteen months. Reckons Mum already had her starting piaffe and half-pass.'

'Shit,' Cameron says, sitting across the table. 'I thought Mum was just breaking her in.'

'Quick learner, apparently.' He set the paper down. 'That's all of them. I've drafted ads for Reg and Thai. Bam and Molly are already up on Gumtree.'

'Thanks, mate. For all that. Know it must've taken you ages. I just ...' Bass presses his shoulders back. Something makes a cracking noise.

'And all for a very reasonable price.'

Bass stares at him, confused and unimpressed.

'My Twisties! Jeez. Lighten up.'

Bass grunts.

'Anyway. We need to find Opal,' Rafferty says, tapping his pen on the surface of the list. 'She's worth more than all the others put together.'

Bass nods, glancing at Jessa who has her chin in her hands.

'What's up, Jess?' he asks.

Jessa doesn't look at him. She's staring out the dark window. 'Opal's Mum's,' she says.

* * *

We weren't expecting children, not yet. I was on the pill and we used condoms and we were so careful. I took the test because Laura made me. I wasn't late. My periods had been a bit irregular, but they were still coming. A prickle of relief, each time.

Laura and I, mixing feeds for her horses one still, mild afternoon. 'Go take a fucking pregnancy test.'

I dumped a scoop of pellets into the buckets. 'I'm not pregnant. There's no *way*.'

'If I have to hear you complain once more about how tired you are, or how dizzy you feel, or how you hate Bass's stupid cooking, I'm gunna deck you one.'

I'd laughed. 'All right, all right! Jeez!'

I bought one test and when the two lines came up in the bathroom at home I vomited in the sink and then drove back to the pharmacy where I bought four more.

I went to the café across the road, with the misted windows and the piles and piles of old, worn books.

Every test was positive.

I called my mother first. I called her from the payphone near the café, too shaken to drive home and use the phone there.

'You're *what*?'

I sobbed. I'm not sure whether it was more shock or terror, in those early moments. But I cried and cried. 'Pregnant. I think. I don't know *how*, but I am. Fuck.'

My mother started to cry. Her tears were tears of happiness. 'Oh my.' Over and over. 'I'm going to be a grandmamma!'

I told Laura, on my way home. I pulled into her place and ran into the stables, startling the horse she had in the crossties.

'What the hell's up with you?' She stared at me, her eyebrows raised. 'Holy fuck. You *are*?'

I nodded, started crying again.

'I honestly don't know what to say. You gunna keep it?'

I nodded, wiping my eyes. 'Yes. Yup. I am.'

Laura hugged me tightly and we had pineapple juice from a can, because that was all she had. I drove the rest of the way home feeling calm, feeling almost happy.

I waited on the steps of the verandah for Bass to come home from work at the antique restorers in town. We needed extra money, to set things up properly on the farm. And Bass's father had taught him how to carve beautifully. How to French polish and join and sand. He didn't love it, not in the quiet and complete way he loved farming, but he didn't mind it, and there's a lot to be said for that in a town as small as Garras.

I waited like a little kid, with my knees all wrapped up under my jumper and my fingers running over the decking, catching on every nail and stray splinter on the planks around me.

Bass whistled when he got out of the car. He had his tools with him. He liked to bring them home at night to sharpen on his father's old whetstone.

'We're pregnant!' I yelled at him as soon as he was close enough to hear.

He stopped. He stared at me, blinking, slow smiling. Then he dropped his tools and ran over, his hat coming off in the wind.

* * *

Rafferty will sometimes sit, barefoot, out the back of the house. Even if it's cold. Even if it's windy. He will sometimes take a cushion from one of the kitchen chairs, but often he will sit straight down on the grass.

Under the low branches of the stringybark. The grass, sometimes green and long, sometimes short and bleached from summer. The dirt showing through like a scalp.

He takes his guitar out there. The old one with the scratch marks that Guy and Jake didn't want.

He strums, tunes it. Flicks the pick through his fingers. He doesn't play any full songs, just pieces of melody. He hums, taps his foot.

'He's good,' says Steve one day.

Bass nods, eats some pizza. 'He is. Never plays any full songs, though. Think it just relaxes him. Kinda like Cam's running, I guess. Or Jessa with the horses.'

'What do you do?' Steve asks.

'Hmm?'

'What's your thing? Now?'

Bass opens his mouth. He frowns, glances at Steve. That helpless look on his face. School interviews, public speaking. Those few times he couldn't stop me crying.

'I don't know.'

* * *

Cameron stirs a pot on the stove. The bench is strewn with onions and celery heads and scattered grains of rice. Something near the burner catches alight.

It's not something I have taught him, not specifically. But I have taught him soups, stews, curries and stirfries.

Outside, Jessa, Rafferty and Guy are plucking slugs off the cabbages in the vegetable garden. Rafferty is holding a torch, but keeps moving it, making shadow puppets.

'Raff, *stop it*,' Jessa snaps.

'If you move that torch one more time, you can drown your own damned slugs,' says Guy.

'Guy's picking on me!' Rafferty calls out. '*Dad?* Guy says he won't help me drown the *slugs!*'

'You're an idiot,' says Guy, knocking him in the arm. 'Hold the freaking thing still! This one's *huge!*'

'Ew,' says Jessa, leaning closer to it.

Back in the kitchen, Cameron tilts his head forward.

'Maggie March,' he murmurs.

He lazily dusts out the flame, so much my son, so distinct from Bass who goes mad at any flicker of a flame larger than a struck match.

He glances out the window at the skimming torchlight.

Jessa's voice. '*Stop it*, Raff. Guy, take it off him! Arse face.'

'Do you guys do this thing? With the cabbages? Like, regularly?' Guy asks.

'When they're seedlings, yeah,' says Jessa.

'And after it's rained,' Rafferty says.

Guy shakes his head. 'Why wouldn't you just fucking go to Coles?'

'Because it's *organic*.' Raff waves the torch across the biggest cabbage. 'Because it's *wholesome.*'

'Because it's what Mum always does. Did.' Jessa gets up off her knees. 'How many?' she asks Guy, peering into the slug bucket.

'Fuck. Sixty?'

'C'mon.' Jessa presses the lid down on the bucket. 'We'll go put them in the chicken run.'

'Why?' Guy asks.

Rafferty switches off the torch. 'For the chickens, idiot. They *love* slugs. It's like chicken crack.'

Back inside, Cameron stirs his soup. He bends his head down to smell the pot. 'Maggie Carlton.' So quiet, I barely catch the sound of his voice.

* * *

I was riding Opal fast. The drumming of her hooves. Sharp against the heavy summer earth.

And it was sometime near the end. I'm sure.

I think hard. I miss whole days of my family.

But all I can feel is Opal, galloping, her mane in my face. My own weight, pressed into the stirrup irons.

I want to know how I died. I want the boys to murmur about it in their bedroom. I want Bass to sit Jessa down and try to pry free how she's feeling. What she saw. What story is choking up inside her.

But they're all so silent.

* * *

Some afternoons, Jessa tramps through the bush tracks by foot. I watch her, the rise and fall of her chest as she starts to pant after half an hour's climb. The occasional slipping of her flat-soled runners on the sloping gravel and slick dirt. The old leaves and sharp gumnuts. The brassy sound of the halter, flung over her shoulder. The bulge of her pockets, full of oats soaked in molasses.

On weekends, she rides out at dawn. After waking up with her hand linked with her father's. After getting up to hunt out her elastic-sided boots or gumboots. After sometimes leaving the boys a breakfast of soggy toast and fresh squeezed juice.

Some days Henry will be waiting for her near the yards. They saddle up Pebbles and Gus. Breathing steam in the cold of the early morning. Sometimes Jessa will press mints into his hand and they will suck on them quietly, staring out into the trees.

Jessa, invariably, scowls when she sees him.

They say little.

'You're so slow,' Jessa mutters. She will sometimes trot Pebbles on. Other times she canters and stones go flying.

Jessa and Henry. Quiet and sweating from exertion under the shade of the eucalypts.

* * *

Beatrice pulls up outside the house, just as Jessa and Henry are disappearing into the shadows of the bush tracks.

She has groceries in the back seat. A box of them. And when she bends to get them out, I notice that her hair is unplaited.

'Bea?' Cameron, sitting on the steps, unlacing his running shoes.

'Hey, Cam. You come give me a hand?'

Cameron ties his shoes back up and Rafferty comes out the kitchen door. He walks barefoot across the gravel to the car. 'That's a lot of food. You moving in?'

Bea laughs. 'No. I just know your mum used to do the shopping. That's all.'

'Well, thanks,' says Cameron.

'It's nothing.' She locks her car when they go inside.

'Dad'll flip,' Rafferty murmurs to Cameron as they follow her in with the box.

'Dad doesn't flip,' Cameron says.

'As much as Dad does. He'll flip.'

In the kitchen, Bass is writing down phone messages. He holds up a finger and scribbles down the last message before setting the phone aside. 'Bea ...' he says.

'It's nothing.' She starts pulling cans and fruit and vegetables out of the boxes.

'Mum used to do the shopping,' Cameron says and Bass rubs the back of his neck.

'Boys, can you go see if Jessa needs a hand? She's in the shed.'

'She's out riding,' Cameron says.

'Well, can you check the shed?'

'Umm ...' Cameron blinks a few times. 'Okay.'

'I'm barefoot,' Rafferty says, holding a foot up for inspection. 'They'll get chilly.'

Cameron jogs outside. I see him disappearing around the side of the house, towards the shed.

'Well, can you see if the laundry's dry?'

'What laundry?' Rafferty asks.

Bass sighs and turns back to Beatrice. 'This has got to stop, Bea.'

'What does?' She is pulling mouldy cheese out of the chiller in the fridge.

'*This.*' Bass waves at the cheese, at the shopping, at the big bottle of detergent now on the kitchen sink. 'I want you to come over and have dinner. Maybe give us a hand when we have a working bee. Not shop and cook for us. We're not invalids.'

'I *know* that,' she says.

'He feels emasculated,' Rafferty says, leaning happily over the back of the chair.

Outside there is the sound of something heavy falling and Cameron yelling out, 'Fuck! Ow!'

Rafferty presses his fingers to his temples. 'Twin-tuition. I feel a disturbance. Cameron's hurt himself.'

'Oh, get out of it,' Bass snaps, reddening. 'Go on. Go check on him.'

'Do I get more Twisties?'

'Raff. Go.'

Rafferty grins and wanders into the living room.

'Bea,' Bass says. 'I know what this is about.'

Her shoulders tense as she catches her breath. She pushes a piece of hair behind her ear and leans forward, just a little. Her voice, when she speaks, is almost breathless. 'You do?'

'Of course I do.' He sighs and rubs the bridge of his nose. 'But you can't chase her like this. You've told her that she can come over. You just have to sit and let her come to you. You know?'

Beatrice exhales and it's like that held breath was holding her upright. Holding her strong. 'Yeah, okay,' she says, turning to snap the cupboard door shut.

* * *

Cameron does not speak to Maggie at school. He never, not once, seems to be the one to talk first. He tries to, sometimes. The working of his jaw. His fingers, flicking and unflicking his shirt. I wonder if she notices. Whenever she speaks to him, his grin reaches all the way up to his eyes.

Cameron sits next to her in maths and I see him scribbling notes in his margins. *Roses? Musk? Those white flowers Mum likes????*

I am confused. Then see him breathe in deeply. Glancing, so slightly, at the gentle curve of Maggie's milky neck.

'I hate maths,' Maggie mutters, leaning closer to him to inspect his pencil case. She has, I have noticed, taken to letting Cameron copy her maths homework, look at her work in tests. Cameron, who has never understood numbers as easily as he has understood English or history or science.

She sits back, stretches, giving Cameron a clear look at the problem she has just solved.

And Cameron leans forward and writes down *Green Tea*.

* * *

Beatrice and Rafferty in the front seat of her orange hatchback. I laughed the first time I saw it. She'd wanted a grey car, maybe a steel blue.

'Shut up,' she said when she got out that first time and saw my face.

'Smells like Dad's Ford,' I said, sitting in the passenger seat.

'It's new-car smell. They all start off like this.'

I whistled. 'Jeez. Ours went terribly, terribly wrong somewhere along the way, then.'

'It's called having toddlers,' she said. 'So? Where do you want to go?'

It had airconditioning that was actually cold. And now I am watching it blowing Rafferty's hair back as Beatrice pulls off the freeway at Rosella. Guy is in the back seat, jammed in with Rafferty's guitar.

'Turn it down, Raff. It's nearly winter,' Bea says.

'I know. Sorry.' Rafferty switches it down and scratches his nose. Doesn't look at Beatrice. 'Thanks, again. For doing this.'

'I'm happy to,' she says, changes gear.

'I ... Dad ...'

'Your dad's got a lot on his plate.'

'I was gunna say he's too busy getting shitfaced tonight with Steve. Left here.'

'It's only been a few months.'

'I'm aware.' Rafferty's words come out sharper than he means them to, I think. He sighs. 'Sorry. I know. He's just doing his thing. But until I turn eighteen, that severely inhibits my ability to do *my* thing.'

'You've got a good aunty. Stop whinging, ya pussy.'

Rafferty reaches back to horsebite Guy's thigh. 'Piss off!' Guy laughs.

A car comes the other way, the headlights illuminating Beatrice's face. She is grinning, her hands are tight on the wheel.

They end up at a bar in a part of Rosella I never really stopped in. Beatrice orders both boys a beer and gets herself a lemon, lime and bitters. It's some sort of open mic night, I think.

Raff gets up with his guitar and the world falters. His holey jeans and unbrushed hair and the sagging, rolled-up shirt that once belonged to Bass. He is so tall, so broad. But, up there, he looks so small.

Then he starts playing, singing softly. A Jeff Buckley song. I can't remember ever hearing him play like that before. His guitar strumming was always obnoxious, loud. Mucking around with his friends on the wide verandah or strumming happy birthday over someone's birthday cake.

Beatrice cries and Guy gives her a scrunched-up napkin and thanks her again for the beer.

'He's good, eh?' he says. 'He's been practising a bit. At mine. I got one too. Shithouse compared to him, but.'

Beatrice dabs at her eyes. 'I wonder if Cate ever heard him play like this.'

Guy catcalls and stamps as Rafferty finishes, but Bea looks thoughtful and sad.

* * *

Cameron is sitting out behind the house with Jason and some other boys from the athletics team. There's five of them. They're eating chips and Skittles straight from the bag and have their shoes off. There is talk about getting a bonfire going, but nobody gets up. Cameron has a beer. It looks warm, barely drunk. It's dark, the rest of the house empty except for Jessa who is lying in bed, muttering to herself about the 'stupid loud dickheads'.

Mac is curled at the end of the bed, dozing. She rubs his belly with her toes. I used to try to keep Mac off the beds, off the couch. Once Jessa was old enough to call his name, that ended. He slept on our beds, rotating between the rooms, and dozed on the couch, leaving hair everywhere. Bass would always kick him out the back door whenever his serious farmer friends dropped in.

An explosion of laughter and loud voices from outside. A rude joke, I think, although I don't catch it properly. Jessa punches her pillow and stalks out onto the verandah. 'Keep it down!'

More laughter.

'I'm serious. It's nearly one. I'm going with Laura to a comp tomorrow. Dad said you could only hang here if you're quiet.'

'Get some earplugs,' says Jason.

'Don't screw with me.' Jessa crosses her arms, squares her feet. 'I've been trying to get to sleep since ten. I'm over it.'

'Want some vodka?' Jason holds out a UDL. Some of the boys titter.

Jessa walks across the lawn towards him.

She reaches out a hand.

Cameron frowns. 'Jessa …'

She hits Jason hard over the head. He grunts and ducks in surprise, slopping some of his drink down his front. 'Fucking keep it down!' she says. 'And don't offer me drink, you fucking creep!'

She stalks back inside, slamming the door behind her.

There is silence. Quiet.

Then the other boys begin to clap.

The tail-lights of Bea's car disappearing down the driveway. Guy and Rafferty coming around the back of the house. Rafferty has his guitar.

'You have *friends*, Cam!' Rafferty says. He stops walking and stares at them.

'Why are they clapping?' Guy whispers. 'It's scary that they're clapping.'

'Jessa just whacked Jason over the head and called him a fucking creep,' says Tony Waters, elbowing Jason hard in the side.

'She's very astute,' says Rafferty. He grabs a handful of Skittles. 'Your top's all wet.'

'Fuck off,' says Jason.

Rafferty nudges Guy. 'C'mon. I'm wired. Let's go play video games till I'm sleepy.'

Guy yawns. 'Yeah, all right.'

Inside, Rafferty puts his guitar in his room and pauses in Jessa's doorway. 'Good job, kid.'

'Thanks. Now go away. I'm trying to *sleep*.'

* * *

Bass is with a dark-haired woman, against the side of Steve's ute. Everyone is on the verandah of the pub, illuminated in the distance. The gas heaters they drag out in the cooler months are out and switched on. Bass has pushed his sleeves up to his elbows.

The woman has followed him out and, now, against the side of the car, she reaches out and touches his shirt sleeve. I hear Bass's breath catch. It must smell so strongly of Scotch and beer. He staggers, moves heavily. As though he is in rushing water, slowly trying to get out.

Up against the side of the car, they are kissing. Bass is unsteady, clumsy. I see the woman wince a little, but she doesn't pull away from him.

'Bass?' Steve's voice. 'C'mon, mate. You've had a lot. I'll drive you home.'

The woman smiles at Steve. A sad smile, maybe. She disappears back towards the pub and Steve helps Bass into the cab.

'Who's that?' Bass asks, staring after the woman. Tight jeans, curly hair; I've never seen her before.

Steve turns the engine on and it roars into life. 'No idea.'

Bass's breath suddenly catches and I see him press his hands together into a tight, trembling knot. A part of me hurts watching Bass. His catching breath and shaking head. But part of me wishes I had hands so I could hit him, scratch him.

I'm still here.

'Bass?' Steve starts to reverse the ute out of the parking spot, but stops. The gravel crunches under the tyres. 'You okay?'

Shaking breath after shaking breath. Bass presses his fingers tightly against his eyes. He nods his head. Steve doesn't say anything else and by the time they've reached home, Bass's breathing has almost stopped catching. His cheeks are dry but his hands are still knotted when Steve opens the cab door and puts an arm around his shoulders.

'C'mon, mate,' he says. And Bass stumbles out of the cab.

* * *

After the boys were born, I waited for things to fall apart with Bass. Not to the ground. Not to pieces. But to begin to unravel, the way I suspected all marriages did when a baby arrived, never mind two. When the sheen was rubbed away and all you were left looking at was each other. Your raw, stretched faces.

Things changed. How we slept, how we had sex. How we ate and talked and the sorts of things we did when we had a few hours to ourselves.

I once threw a plastic mug at him when he said he hadn't taken the horses' rugs off yet. I cried afterwards. Shocked at myself. At how easy it had been. The boys were so young then. I hadn't slept properly in weeks.

'Least it wasn't a mallet,' he said, kissing my head on his way back in from the horses. Covered in hair from their unrugging.

Sex was dozy, when we started having it again. In the half-light before their early morning feeding. Sex was quiet and gentle, in those first couple of years after the boys were born.

We no longer sat down for dinner. We ate on the run. Between work and the animals and feeding the boys and their napping and our sleeping. We ate standing up or, later, sitting down next to the boys mismatched highchairs, Cameron always just a little bit higher.

I lived on bananas, herbal tea and bread, which Bass picked up from the bakery for me every couple of days. We ate in passing, one of us doing the dishes when the pile became too high. Sometimes it was Steve who did them, coming inside from helping Bass with the outside jobs.

Other times it was Laura, coming in from riding the horses. The smell of her – dirt and sweat and sunshine. Sometimes the smell of Laura on those days, smelling so strongly of everything happening outside without me, was enough to make me sob.

Laura would pat my head, get me some tea. Do the dishes.

When my mother visited, we would sit outside, her and Bass and me and the boys.

'You look happy,' she'd say, bouncing one of the boys on her lap. Glancing from Bass to me. 'Knackered, but happy.'

Our relationship shifted. Irretrievably. So quickly.

But I still missed him when he went out of a room. That's what never changed.

* * *

Often in the evenings Cameron is in the kitchen cooking with Laura. Henry must be staying with her, as he's often there too.

When Henry first started living with Laura for lengthy periods of time, weeks at first, then months, I watched them closely. I always expected Henry to act out at a school he came and went from, but he never did. I worried about the stress on Laura, who already ran herself into exhaustion.

Henry was bright. I didn't think very much got past him. He noticed things that other people didn't and I wondered if it was to do with his upbringing. The upheaval of it. He was gentle, thoughtful. He was similar to Cameron in this way, I suppose. But without Cameron's timidity. Without his terror.

Bass called him an old soul, which surprised me. Bass, who had nothing to say about anyone, other than they'd done him a good turn or that they were a goose.

I asked Laura about his mother, sometimes.

'She's not well,' was all she ever said when I asked how Sylvia was going. I could have called her myself, I suppose. But I didn't. Not ever.

In the kitchen, Henry watches Cameron closely. Sometimes he'll help cut things up at the bench. When Cameron coughs, he will often cough too. Cameron doesn't seem to notice. Mostly Henry sits at the table, though. Munching on crackers and asking Cameron about everything from school to science to rock stars, while Laura shows Cameron how to dice or boil or fry something up in a way that is more complicated than I taught him when he was younger.

Cameron sometimes stares at Henry. It's as though he doesn't quite know what to do with this chatty, watchful boy who trails after Jessa and whose mother is not well.

Laura is a wonderful cook. Strange, that she is domestic in this one way. I always called her my wild lady. She showered outside until last year, because she said there were better things to spend money on than installing one indoors. She borrowed my vacuum cleaner once a year, in early September, and otherwise went no further than kicking off her muddy boots before she came inside.

'This is good, Cam,' Rafferty says one night, when he and Cameron and Henry and Laura and Jessa and Beatrice and Bass are all sitting around the kitchen table on mismatched chairs.

'It's really good,' Jessa says.

'He did it mostly himself too. All Laura did was put the onion on the stove first,' Henry tells everyone. He's already halfway through seconds.

'Thanks,' Cameron says.

I look at Bass, watch his lips as he eats. He looks no different at this table than he did when I was sitting next to him. Sadder, maybe. But it's hard to tell.

It's hard to tell how much time has passed. They are wearing spring or autumn wear, I suppose. Loose fitting, long sleeves. Henry and Jessa in shorts. But maybe a warm winter day or a very cool summer one.

It's so hard to tell.

* * *

Laura is dozing on the couch with *Horse Deals* magazine and a highlighter on her chest. Her hands are thrown up above her head. She looks young, in sleep. Younger.

It is early afternoon, sun just starting to creep along the verandah through the trees. Her yard is heavy with mud and there is roughly chopped wood on her verandah.

There is a knock at the door and she stands up so quickly the magazine and highlighter go flying.

'Crap,' she mutters, rubbing her eyes, blinking widely and patting herself down to make sure she's wearing a bra.

'Oh,' she says when she sees Steve standing there. 'What's happened?'

'Nothing, everything's cool. Just wondering if we could have a chat? I'm just stumped. About Bass.'

Laura relaxes. 'Sure. Want a cuppa? I've got some beer in the fridge.'

'Nah. A water would be good, thanks.'

Laura gets them both a drink, zips up her jacket and they sit outside on the verandah. A cockatoo begins to screech in the garden and Laura throws a pine cone. The bird caws once more, loudly, and then takes off towards the barn.

'Bloody birds,' she mumbles. Setting her drink down. 'Now. What's up?'

'Just … Bass. I don't know how to help him. It's been, what? Six months?'

'Something like that.'

'He won't talk about it.'

'No. Well, he's never been a big talker.' I can hear the impatience in Laura's voice. Something she and Bass have always had in common.

'He's been hitting the drinks pretty hard. I've been thinking about what I could bring over to cheer him up, you know? Is beer a bad idea?'

'You came all the way over here to ask me about dropping in the occasional sixpack?'

'Well, when you put it like that I sound like a bit of a moron, but yeah.'

'Look. I can't fathom what he's going through. I know what *I've* gone through, and that's been bloody agonising and she wasn't my wife. If a bit of a booze-up helps him, what's the harm? If he gets rolling drunk every second night, then we've got a problem. How often is he drinking? A night or two a week?'

'Yeah … but he hooked up –'

'What do you mean, hooked up?'

'Made out with this chick at the bar. I stopped it, you know. Before anything else happened but …'

'You stopped it? It's good for him. *Good*. If he wants to go to the pub and throw back a few every few days and he meets a lady he can be close to, let him go. It's helping him. It's a process.' She looks hard at him. 'You've known him as long as I have. You really think it's an issue?'

'No. But. I've never known anyone go through what he has. Not at our age, anyway.'

'Me neither, when I come to think of it. But I think he's doing good.' She nods at his cup. 'Now. Want a top-up?'

* * *

Cameron has begun to run everywhere. So often, when I watch him now, he is running. He runs to the bus stop, with Rafferty and Jessa yelling out rude things and bundled up in jumpers behind him. He runs from the kitchen to the bathroom and back again.

He runs after school, loops around the oval, which is beginning to turn muddy. He runs with Murray grinning at him and the other students acknowledging him with an occasional smile or joke. Sometimes he runs with Jason or one of the other boys from the athletics team. Mostly, though, he runs alone.

He runs out to the chicken run, slopping their breakfast down his front.

And, I suspect, that when he runs he is thinking always of the same thing.

The smell of green tea. The feel of it against his cheek the next time he wins a race.

* * *

They find her on a cold and windy day. Cloudless but strangely dull, as though the very light of the sun has been blown away.

Henry has been given Gus to ride and he pats the chunky old horse's neck as they meander along the trails. He has the halter over his shoulder, because Jessa doesn't like carrying it.

He still looks into the bush around him as he rides, while Jessa rides ahead, plaiting Pebbles's mane.

He pulls Gus up quite suddenly. Jessa doesn't notice.

'Jessa!' he hisses.

She slowly turns around in the saddle. 'What?'

'In here,' he says. 'I think.'

They are near a copse of lemon-scented gum. 'Come hold Gus,' he says.

'I should ...'

But Henry is on the ground, holding Gus's reins out for her, his pockets full of grains, the halter in his hand.

'Be quiet,' he says.

Jessa glares at him. She once whacked Rafferty in the head with a salad bowl when he told her to chew with her mouth shut.

Henry disappears into the trees. Everything is quiet. Still.

Jessa fidgets in the saddle and Pebbles nips at Gus's face. 'Henry?' she calls finally.

There is no reply and her fidgeting grows worse.

He comes out slowly, walking the filly who is mangy and skinny and wanders with her head low to the ground, like she doesn't really care any more.

'You got her,' Jessa says flatly. She is sitting straight in her saddle, sitting still.

Henry grins up at her, pats Opal's neck. 'She just let me catch her.'

'Why'd it take so long then?'

'Because I didn't want to scare her off. I went up really quietly.'

They begin walking back towards home. Jessa on Pebbles, leading Gus. Henry on his feet, leading Opal.

'She's big,' Henry says.

'Not that big.'

'She's bigger than Trinity. And Trin's seventeen hands.'

'That's not so big.'

'Oh, Jessa,' he says. And he sounds so old. Like they've been married and bickering for fifty years and this argument, this petulance, is an echo of all the years they have known each other.

* * *

Laura is with Bass and they are drinking wine on the verandah. Laura has her mittens and her beanie on, but she's always preferred being outside, even in the cold. They are talking about a bull Bass has found in the *Trading Post* but Laura is shaking her head.

'If you're serious about it, I mean, *really* serious, get a loan out and buy a decent bull.'

'Cate ...' He stops himself, but it is enough to make Laura stare at him for a moment with something close to pity. Bass clears his throat and leans forward, his arms on the tops of his legs. 'She hated loans.'

'Do you hate loans?'

'Not carefully planned ones.'

'Well there you go.'

Henry and Jessa come into the yard, Henry leading Opal like an old grandmother wedged up against a walking frame. Laura grins and sets her wine aside.

'You got her!' she says.

Bass stumbles forward, full of urgency. Full of purpose. But then he stops, just shy of the horse. Opal raises her head, flicks her ears. Bass glances at Henry, then at Jessa.

'You got her,' he says.

'Henry did,' says Jessa. Grudging. She dismounts and pats Pebbles on the neck.

And Bass stands and stares at the two of them, with Gus and Pebbles and Opal. Jessa busies herself picking knots out of Opal's mane. The mare tilts away but does not move. I can see the whites of her eyes in the falling darkness. It's Henry who frowns and says, 'Bass, are you okay?'

Bass nods and Laura nudges past him. 'Let's go get this girl a feed and a look-over, shall we?'

She takes Opal off Henry and he takes Gus off Jessa. They lead the three horses quietly to the stables. Only Henry looks back and it's to see Bass, still standing in front of the house. His arms by his sides. He is not watching them. He is staring up at the jacaranda.

* * *

When Henry and Jessa first met, they were two years old and Laura was crying on the verandah.

Her sister had disappeared again.

I squeezed Laura an orange juice and she shredded the jacaranda flowers that had blown all along the front side of the verandah with her fingers.

'What the hell am I meant to do with a two year old?' Laura asked, draining her glass like it was a vodka shot.

Henry was learning to blow spit bubbles. He was walking, not steadily, and Jessa was sitting in a little toy trolley the boys liked to put her in. They eyed each other with the equal mix of wonder and disgust that seems to be the domain of the under-threes.

'Jessa,' I warned as Henry got closer. Jessa, the angry little goose, already had a penchant for clawing at faces she did not take a liking to.

But Henry did not go near her face. He did not get close enough to be clawed by her fierce little hands. Instead we watched as he staggered to the trolley's handles, arms thrown every which way to keep his balance, and began pushing Jessa, backwards and forwards.

She glared at him the whole time.

'I don't know, Loz. Did she say? Anything?'

'Not since I picked him up. It was just meant to be the weekend, but she's not answering her phone, nobody's seen her. I'm thinking of calling the cops.'

'Really?'

Laura blew out a breath. 'No. Not *really*. I know she's just nicked off. If I got the police involved … well, I think she'd disappear for good. Just to spite me.'

We stared at Jessa and Henry. Henry leant down and kissed Jessa's head.

And she hissed and clawed the side of his face.

* * *

The shed is still and dusty. The cobwebs need to be brushed off the rafters. Jessa is wearing a white skivvy that makes her freckles stand out against the milkiness of her skin. Rafferty is leaning against the door of the nearest stall. Behind him the tack room is dusty. Unused. The floor is dirty with mud tracked in from the winter yard.

'Jessa,' he says.

'Hmm?' She doesn't stop what she is doing.

'Jessa Carlton!'

She ignores him.

He grabs a broom and snaps the end of it down against the cement floor. 'Jessa, will you bloody stop for a second?'

Jessa stops brushing out Opal's mesh rug. 'I'm busy.'

'You're cleaning summer rugs in June.'

She gets up off her knees and dusts herself down. 'What?'

'About study …'

She drags the rug up into her arms. 'Oh, here we go.'

'He's worried.'

Jessa starts to awkwardly fold the rug. The dusty creases of it stick out at strange angles and she drops it in a sudden temper. 'I fucking hate school.'

'Well, tough tits. You need to do your best.'

'Why? There's nothing useful I'm going to learn. And teachers go blah blah, you need this, even running a farm, but so what? You don't need it to be a rider like Laura. And if I need it to run a farm, I'll learn it myself.'

'Bullshit.'

'Why are you lecturing me? You hate it even worse than me.'

'Just read the books, Jess.'

'No.'

Rafferty leans in closer, as though it's a secret he's sharing. 'He'll sell her, you know.'

Jessa tenses. 'What?'

'Dad. He'll sell her. He's tossing up whether to sell her now anyway. She's worth heaps and he's pretty skint.'

'He wouldn't tell you that.'

'Well, he did. When we were sorting out the horses prices and all that.'

Jessa stares at him and narrows her eyes. 'Bull.'

'Well, you're welcome to take a gamble.'

Jessa looks out the door and scowls. 'Okay.'

'Okay what?'

Jessa tries to kick him. 'Piss off! I said okay.'

* * *

Steve starts coming around every Friday night with a couple of sixpacks of beer. He and Bass have steak and chips and sit and drink beer on the verandah. It's cold, this time of year. But they seem to like it.

Cameron cooks up a vegetarian lasagne and they eat that one night, sitting out on the verandah while the kids sit inside around the fire.

'This is *good*,' says Steve. '*Really* good. Like, I love meat. But …' He pauses to chew. 'It's … it's almost *better* than meat ones. Fuck me.'

'He's a good cook,' says Bass.

'What's this?' Steve holds up his fork.

'Eggplant,' says Bass, trying not to smile.

'Eggplant? Don't think I've ever had that before. Eggplant. Is that what makes it taste sort of meaty?'

'I have no idea. You'll have to ask Cam.'

'Wow,' says Steve, closing his eyes and chewing. 'Wow.'

In the nights that follow, Bass will stand in front of the fridge and stare in. The milk and the beers on the same shelf. He always considers both. Stares down, at one to the other. Some nights he has a beer. Some nights he has three or four. One night, stumbling, he has seven. Most nights he grabs the milk. Has a coffee or a Milo or hot milk with cinnamon.

* * *

Rafferty has a box of old flowers under his bed. When he first brought them out, I thought they were buds of marijuana. But when I focused, I recognised them.

Roses, from my garden. Dried and pressed inexpertly between pieces of thin wood. Some just thrown in. They crunch when Rafferty touches them and he winces like he's breaking something precious.

It seems strange, out of character. Rafferty has never particularly liked gardening. He's never shown any interest in my roses. But he'll bring them out, sometimes. And run his fingers over them and breathe deeply and I wonder if it makes him think of me.

I wonder if the roses make him sad or happy.

I wonder if they make him calm.

* * *

Cameron and Rafferty, pulling shoes out from under their beds. It's gloomy outside, the window pulled shut against the bruised colour of the sky

'Will these do?' Cameron asks, waving a pair of nearly new Volleys.

'She said *nice clothes*,' Rafferty says, putting on a voice. 'Do you reckon Beatrice classifies Volleys as *nice clothes*?'

'No.' Cameron jams them back into the dark.

Rafferty dislodges an old tennis racket from under his bed and throws his hands up in the air. 'Fuck. Forget it. I'm wearing my thongs.' He leans against the windowsill and stretches his back.

'Where's Jessa? She needs to get ready too. Bea'll flip if we're late.'

'Bea flips,' Rafferty says.

'Jessa?'

'Is writing a practice essay. Shakespeare.'

Cameron sits back on his heels. 'Bull.'

'Nup.' Rafferty lights up a cigarette and unlatches the window.

'I'm wearing my Volleys,' Cameron says, propping himself up on his bed. 'Where's the restaurant?'

'Rosella. Dad said we're leaving at six. You signed the card?'

'There's a card?'

Rafferty sticks his head into the hallway. '*Jessa!* You got the card?'

'Shut up!' she yells back down the hallway. 'I'm *concentrating*!'

'She's concentrating,' Rafferty says.

'Shit,' Cameron says.

'What?'

'It's … it's just weird. You know? Going out to dinner in Rosella without Mum.'

'We've been before,' says Rafferty. 'We went when you got onto the team.'

'I *know*,' says Cameron. 'I know that. But it's still weird.'

Rafferty sighs and rummages under his bed. He holds out a brown, flaking rose from his box. 'Here.'

Cameron tenses. 'Ew.'

'It's from Mum's garden.'

Cameron blinks. 'You know you're meant to throw them out before they get that manky.'

Rafferty rolls his eyes and stands up, still holding out the rose. 'They're the last ones she cut.'

Cameron's body relaxes. 'Oh.'

'Thought you might … I dunno. You always carry round that stupid handkerchief. Thought maybe you

114

could put it in there. Or something.' Rafferty pushes the rose into Cameron's hand and turns around, nudging the box gently back under the bed with his toe.

Cameron brushes his finger along the shrivelled petals. 'Right. Thanks. That's really nice.'

Rafferty grunts and stalks out of the room. Cameron sits still for a minute and then kneels down and gently presses the flower back into Rafferty's shoebox. He dusts the flakes of brown petals off himself.

Rafferty's voice echoes from downstairs. 'No, Dad. We gotta wait. She hasn't finished the essay, yet.'

* * *

Bass and I were married at a pretty little artist's retreat near where my mother lived. It was all wooden eaves and handmade glass and naked brick.

I pulled Bass aside before the place was booked. 'Do you mind? Not getting married in Garras?'

'Look, I think if my folks were still alive, we'd be discussing it more, but they're not. The place means lots to your mum.' Bass shrugged. 'I don't care, I just want to marry you.'

Bass's parents were already in their mid forties by the time he was born. His mother had died of liver cancer and his father of a heart attack when he was in his late twenties. He had never really talked about how they'd died. What it had been like for them, for him. He never really talked about them much, either. My sense of them came from the photo albums that Bass kept in boxes in the shed, from asking around town and listening to the stories.

Bea and Laura were my bridesmaids. I'd only known Laura for a couple of years, but I'd lived with her. We'd stayed up until three in the morning talking horses, which always ended with Laura noticing the time, muttering, 'For Christssake!' and stumbling to bed without brushing her teeth. We had gone to competitions together, cleaned our gear, got drunk and discussed Sylvia in great and serious length. Laura had let Bass move in with us, once he and I had got together. I loved her.

I asked my mother to walk me down the aisle. My father stood in the front row with his hands clasped and cried when he saw me.

I was so young.

My mother made me drink champagne at home before the ceremony and talked like it was the only wedding we would ever have in the family. Bea's lips became tighter and tighter and finally she went outside and stood on the porch while Mum finished my hair.

'Stop talking like Bea's not going to get married,' Laura said to Mum. 'Unless you want her to *actually* start crying.'

'Oh.' Mum's hand went to her mouth. Those wide eyes. 'I didn't realise I was.'

Laura blinked at her. She and my mother confused each other.

'I am *so* looking forward to your wedding, Bea!' Mum said when Bea came back in. Bea rolled her eyes and Mum gave a little wink over her head at Laura and Laura rolled her eyes too.

'You scrub up all right,' Laura said, staring at my reflection from over my shoulder.

My cream dress. I'd never liked white. Simple, floor length. I walked down the aisle with flowers picked from the garden.

I'd told Laura and Bea to get their own dresses. Something colourful, something they felt beautiful in. Laura had fretted about it for a few weeks, as much as Laura fretted about anything, and then had gone out and bought a beautiful green dress the first time she went looking.

Bea went to twelve stores. She made me go with her. It took longer to find her dress than it did to find my wedding dress. Mum came once, but got tipsy halfway through when we stopped at a bar for tapas.

'*Drink,*' she'd said. 'I need *drink.*'

We were quiet, on the drive to the retreat. We were quiet and my mother held my hand and Bea stared out the window. She looked happy, for most of the drive. But when we pulled into the driveway it looked as though she was trying her hardest not to cry.

* * *

The restaurant in Rosella is orange and loud and not a place I would have thought Beatrice would pick for her birthday dinner. But she is smiling and Rafferty keeps sending a coin spinning across the table to Jessa.

Bass and Rafferty. Cameron and Jessa and our mother. There is an empty seat at the end, slung heavy with bags and light jackets.

'Oh,' she'd said when Bass had raised his eyebrows at the empty chair as she started ordering. 'He's sick.'

'He? A boyfriend "he"?' Rafferty asks, wiggling his eyebrows.

'Man flu,' my mother mutters and Beatrice shoots her a look. My mother. It makes me giddy to see her with the rest of my family. I wonder how many times she has seen them, since I died. She is wearing a dark top and a plain grey skirt. She has a dark orange scarf, the same colour as the walls of the restaurant, hanging on the back of her seat.

'He's just a friend. And he's sick,' Beatrice says again.

'What is this man flu?' Rafferty asks.

'Who wants cake?' Bass says, shoving a plate across at Rafferty so forcefully it sends his coin spinning onto the floor.

Beatrice had ordered herself a cake with *forty* written on it in white icing. The wait staff bring it out with candles and everyone at the table sings happy birthday.

It's a narrow table. And when everyone stops singing, when she bends to blow the candles out, I realise how small they look. What a tiny group they are.

* * *

I remember being young. I remember infatuation as the tripping of my stomach, the feeling of it full of something warm.

I remember Brent Hardwick from pony club. I didn't have a horse, not then. But I went every month with Margot and hung over the arena fence as the other children rode. After, if Margot was tired or distracted, she would ask me to untack Casper, to brush him down, while she went into the club house and had a lemonade. I loved those days. I would brush him slowly in the shade of the horse float. Casper would doze and I would wonder if anyone seeing us would mistake him for mine. Would think how lucky I was to have such a lovely horse.

My stomach first tripped when I was twelve, watching Brent jumping a brick wall that was higher than my elbows. Then there were boys at school. Shirt sleeves rolled up to elbow joints. Cheap cologne, and letters pressed into lockers. My first kiss was with pursed lips against a tall picket fence not far from the house I grew up in. I was fourteen, I think. Maybe fifteen.

Bass. That trip when I first saw him. That smile. How quickly he consumed me. Every part of me wanting him. So soon after meeting him, it was unnerving. I told myself it was a crush, an infatuation, that I hadn't had enough dates so I got silly about them.

But the feeling never went away. It changed, as all experiences of such intensity must do, but I was always consumed by him. That tripping, fluttering part of me never tripped for anyone else. Just Bass.

* * *

Sometimes I wonder if Beatrice is happy. Or, rather, I wonder if she is unhappy. With her small cottage and her quiet rooms. She has few friends, a handful, and those she sees only sporadically. She dresses beautifully. Her cottage could be in a magazine.

But there is something cold about Beatrice. Something bracing, that means we were sisters rather than friends.

And it has leaked around her, filled her up. Saturated her.

I wonder if she feels it. Or if it is like swimming in the ocean on a cold day. Only those on the edge can feel the coldness.

The sharpness of it.

* * *

Jessa and Cameron hang over the stable door, staring in at Opal, who stares right back with her mouth full of hay and chaff. It's morning, the light stretching in through the barn door.

'Give her some space,' says Rafferty, coming in from setting up a grid of jumps in the arena. He's wearing jeans and riding boots and a thick jumper that had once belonged to Bass. 'Just let her settle. She's never been in the stables much.'

'I *know*,' Jessa says, rolling her eyes.

She turns around and watches as he gives Thai a quick brush and starts saddling her with my favourite old jumping saddle. The one that was so old it was soft and gentle enough to fit any horse.

'When's the last time you rode?' Jessa asks.

'Yesterday.'

'Before now, I mean.'

'Ages,' he says, fiddling with the buckles on the plain leather breastplate.

'Why now?'

'Because you don't ride them,' he says. 'And Laura doesn't have time. And they need to be ridden. They need to be sold.' He tightens the girth and gives Thai a pat on the neck.

'I do ride them,' says Jessa.

'Bullshit. You mope around on Pebbles and now we've got Opal you're going to be mooning over her. And nobody has the energy to fight you about it, Jessa. No one has the energy to make you.'

'I'll ride Moon! I'll ride her right now!'

'Whatever.' Rafferty does his helmet up and leads Thai out into the arena.

'I do ride them!' Jessa tells Cameron.

Cameron is staring after Rafferty with a strange look on his face.

'What?' Jessa snaps. 'You agree with him, don't you? You always gang up on me. You're both such –'

'Shush, Jessa.'

'What?'

'The saddle … it's the one Mum was riding in.'

Jessa is quiet, staring out at the arena where Rafferty is walking Thai around on a loose rein.

'Does he know?'

Cameron shrugs, turns back to Opal. 'I dunno.'

Cameron, who only likes riding Gus and only at a walk, trot or very slow canter. Cameron, who has always been a bit too nervous to compete, to school the younger ones, to ride out in the wind.

'He's a good rider, isn't he?' Jessa says, still watching Rafferty out in the arena. The gentle, sharp directions he gives. The stillness of his hands. I'd hoped, when he was in his early teens, that he would take up competitive riding. He had the knack for it. The quick reflexes, the soft and independent seat and hands. The utter lack of fear, but without tripping into recklessness. He respected horses, trusted them. But he didn't love them, didn't breathe them the way you need to if you want to make the big time. So after a while I gave up encouraging him and watched, quite sadly, as he pottered around on Gus, refusing to go to any competitions.

'You're being silly,' Bass said when I lamented over Rafferty.

And it makes me feel full, feel a strange sense of satisfaction, watching him riding Thai so beautifully in the arena.

Cameron sighs. 'Mum always thought so.'

* * *

I remember the day. Hot, sticky. The boys just about to turn three. Bass with them and Jessa on the verandah. He and Steve were watching them while I rode in the arena.

Laura, riding her warmblood.

Rafferty started toddling over. Quick little legs. Steve followed a few steps behind, ready to catch him. Raff toddled all the way across the yard. He toddled up to the arena fence and held up his arms to me. I got off, thinking he wanted me. A cuddle. Too old, now, for a feed.

His arms, still outstretched.

I held him over Gus's saddle, his little bottom in the seat of it. He reached for a tuft of mane. He beamed and squealed and wrapped it up in his tiny fingers.

I turned to Steve. Grinned.

'Would you look at that!' Bass called from the verandah, where Jessa was asleep in his lap. I could just see them around the bulk of the grevillea.

Raff, mesmerised by the twist of mane. The top of Gus's shining shoulder.

He wanted to ride Gus.

He wanted to ride.

* * *

My mother is here to visit. Scarves and kisses. She puts her bags in the spare room and kisses Jessa all over her face. Winter. Jessa's birthday.

Nobody else notices the way my mother stares at the roses by the verandah, the photos of me curling on the fridge. She brushes her fingers along an old horse ribbon slung over a drawer handle and I hear her sigh.

'Let's cut your hair, Jess,' she says, picking up a pair of scissors from the kitchen drawer.

'I *like* it long.'

'This will make it grow even *longer*.' My mum kisses Jessa's head. 'Don't wiggle. Or you'll end up with hair shorter than your brothers'.'

Henry and Laura come over. Laura hands Jessa a present. 'I know it's early, but birthday eve and all that.' She kisses Jessa's cheek, points at Henry. 'This one made you a card.'

Henry reddens, holds it out. Jessa slips it out of the envelope. A beautiful pen drawing of a black horse and a blonde girl. 'Wow,' she says. 'That's amazing. I didn't know you could draw like that.'

Rafferty stares at it over her shoulder. 'Shit, Hen,' he says.

'It took him *ages*,' says Laura.

'Not that long,' he says. He smiles at Jessa, looks away. 'I'm glad you like it.'

'It's amazing,' she says. 'I've never seen a drawing this nice in my whole life.'

'Are we doing presents?' Bea stands up. 'I brought mine over too.'

'You want presents now, Jess?' Bass asks, stretching his arms high above his head.

Jessa half shrugs and Bea goes into the other room.

'Fourteen,' my mother murmurs, sitting sideways on the armchair.

'You're just really, really old, I suppose, Nan.' Rafferty sits down on the floor and pulls Mac into his lap.

'Hmph,' my mother says, closing her eyes.

'I'm broke, Jess,' Rafferty says. 'So I cleaned all your tack. Happy birthday.'

'Hey, thanks!'

Cameron gives her a little brown package that has a hand-carved horse figurine inside from a pretty little shop in Rosella.

She smiles and tucks it into her pocket.

Bea comes back inside, car keys jingling. She puts the big bag of presents on the table. 'Happy birthday!' she says, pushing them towards Jessa.

Dresses and jewellery and horse stationery. I don't think Jessa has ever had so much to unwrap from one person before. Everyone just stares as she unwraps present after present.

Bea goes to put the paper in the recycling bin and Rafferty lets out a low whistle.

'Don't start,' says Bass.

'Didn't say anything,' says Rafferty, picking up *Spirit: Stallion of the Cimarron* and putting it into the DVD player.

'Thanks, Bea. Thanks heaps,' says Jessa when Bea comes back.

Bea kisses her. 'Go put one of the dresses on. I want to see!'

Rafferty opens his mouth and Bass makes a cutthroat sign from the other side of the room.

'Yeah, okay. Cool.' Jessa gets up, glares at Rafferty and takes one of the floral dresses into the bathroom.

'Disney movies? We're watching them now?' Cameron asks.

'Well, I *like* them,' my mother says. 'And that's entirely your fault. Hadn't even *heard* of Bambi before you were born.'

Laura snorted. 'I know what you mean, Jo. They've got a sort of strange appeal, don't they? I still have *The Little Mermaid* songs stuck in my head.' She nudged Henry. 'It was this one's favourite.'

Henry had reddened. 'Was not.'

'I remember!' Jessa says, coming back in. 'I remember! You got Mum to sew a pair of her old stockings together and pretend it was a tail!' Jessa bursts out laughing.

Rafferty rolls over on the couch. '*That's* right. I'd forgotten that.'

'I was *three*!'

'More like six,' says Laura.

'Girls are going to love you to death when you get older, Hen,' Mum says, tousling his hair as she gets up to take plates into the kitchen. He follows with the rest of them and puts them on the sink.

'You reckon?' he asks quietly, his ears reddening.

'Absolutely!' she says, giving him a kiss on the head. 'You'll be fighting them off with a stick!'

Henry smiles. 'I still kind of like *The Little Mermaid*,' he says.

My mother bursts out laughing. 'Oh, atta boy!'

* * *

Laura inherited her home, her property, from her parents. The bluestone cottage, the barn and stretch of paddocks. I asked her about it, once. A few months after I moved in. It already felt like I had known Laura forever.

'They wrote Sylvia out of the will,' she said, drinking a cup of tea and staring hard out the window. 'She didn't have Henry, when they died. So they wrote her out. Were so ashamed of her, all the shit she was doing. They never really got that she was mentally ill, you know? They had kids late. They were too old for all the lying and the chaos. And after Mum broke her hip and Dad got diagnosed with cancer, she didn't visit them. She didn't visit them *once*.'

I shook my head. Bent my knees up tighter to my chest.

'I sold off half the place. That place next door? With the new house? Well, not that new now, I suppose. But that all used to be ours.'

'Why?'

'So I have money. When Sylvia needs it. Sometimes *my* money gets too tied up in horses. I'm always investing and reinvesting. Selling. I don't have much money just sitting around. So I sold the place. Means when she gets into binds, I have something to give her.'

'Why don't you just give her all of it?'

'And what would she do with half a million dollars?'

'Yeah, okay. Dumb question.'

'She'd spend it. And then what happens to Henry if things go to shit down there? It's for him. He'll get all of this one day, anyway. But for now. For when she doesn't pay her dealer. For when she gets behind in rent or when Henry needs to go grocery shopping because she's eating out with men and forgetting about him. To keep him safe when he's not here. That money's for him.'

* * *

Jessa is lying on her back in bed, staring out at the moon. A full moon. A clear sky. There are some birthday cards on her dresser. I can hear my mother humming down the hallway as she washes her face and puts on her face cream.

'Please,' says Jessa. 'Please. Please. *Please.*'

Her nails are dug into her palm.

She has a picture of me riding Opal, poking out from under her pillow. She stands up, sudden and fluid. She stands by the window, where she can make out Opal dozing in the empty paddock.

'*Please* give me Opal. *Please. Please. Please.*'

* * *

One day Bass came outside to find me crying in the arena, sitting on Gus who flicked his ears back at me. Spring, I think. The twins a few months old.

'I'm like a giant piece of jelly! I'm riding like *shit*!' I yelled at him.

'You just had two babies.'

I continued to cry.

He came closer, put a hand on my leg. 'Cate? C'mon. I'll make you some tea. It's natural – isn't it? Isn't that what the nurse said? It'll take a while to get your core muscles back? But – '

I threw my whip at him.

Laura, hanging over the other side of the fence, raised an eyebrow.

'She's sleep deprived,' Bass told her.

'I'm riding like *shit*!' I wailed. 'I didn't think I'd be riding *this* bad *this* long afterwards.' The balance, it was gone. How effortlessly I had kept my hands still, my ankles flexed, my legs strong. How easy it had been to move one part of my body without everything else following.

'What even *is* this?' I'd asked Laura, pointing at my still swollen belly.

Laura jumped down off the fence and patted Bass's shoulder. 'I'd watch your man bits if I were you.'

* * *

Jessa, sitting at the kitchen table reading a dressage magazine. Her ankles are crossed and she is wearing a dress with thermal pants underneath. Something Beatrice must have bought her. It's the same green as her eyes.

'The vet's coming out tomorrow,' she tells Cameron.

'For Opal?'

'Yeah. Laura reckons she just needs her vaccinations and a check over. Reckons she's much better since we wormed her and did her feet.'

'Wow,' says Cameron.

'You told him already!' Rafferty calls through the kitchen window. He, Guy and Jake are out on the lawn. They've just been trying to explode Coke bottles and have now settled into running barefoot in grass that is green and muddy.

Cameron is cutting broccoli. The wok is steaming on the stove and outside Rafferty goes back to singing loudly while he waters the potted herbs. The same pots that the seeds Bass gave me all those years ago were planted in.

Rafferty is in a pair of Bass's old jodhpurs, from the early days when I was still hopeful that I could coax him into being my riding companion.

'I'm vegetarian,' Jessa says. She is staring out the window, watching Jake trying to climb the sycamore at the end of the yard.

Cameron looks up at her. 'This is broccoli.'

She nods and keeps reading, her eyes flicking up now and then, watching as Jake hoists himself up into the thick dark branches.

In the living room Bass is drinking milk frothed with cinnamon. He is thinking deeply, staring at the wall, even though the television is on. Something occurs to him and he smiles. A quiet smile, just to himself.

I wonder if he's thinking of me.

* * *

Beatrice sitting opposite a school friend I vaguely remember. Her name is Chloe or Kendra. It's a nice restaurant, with high ceilings and gentle lighting. Some place in the city. Beatrice must be spending the weekend at our mother's.

'It must just be so difficult,' the woman is saying. She has tightly curled hair and a watch so big and loose that it keeps clunking onto the side of her wineglass. I watch, transfixed. Wondering if it will break. Thinking of the spill of red wine across the pastel tablecloth, onto her light denim lap.

'It is,' Beatrice says. 'I miss her like crazy. But not as much as they do, of course. I do my best. It's kind of nice that they rely on me to pick up the slack. It won't be forever, of course. But it's wonderful to be able to help them, you know?'

'You're a good woman.'

'Anyone would do the same. And they're so grateful for the help.' Beatrice has a long sip from her wine. 'Well. You step up. Sometimes you just need to step up.'

I notice it then, the tremble of her fingers.

'Yeah,' says the woman. 'You're family.'

The tremble. Whether she is thrilling at the lie, or tremulous with the misery of it.

* * *

Sometimes Bass rummages in my dresser. He will push aside my makeup and my hairpins. He will push aside the spare buttons from my hacking jacket and the white gloves I saved for competitions. He will push aside the scribbled shopping lists and receipts that I threw in there when I was in a hurry. That I wish he would sort and throw out. He will rummage in my dresser for a small perfume bottle that I kept for many years. I only ever wore it occasionally. Always sparingly.

The first bottle was a sampler a friend gave me for my twenty-first. It was a rich smell. Bass always liked it. Said it made me smell like Riesling. Smell like summer and grass and the fires that made the air thick in spring.

'It makes me think of the first time I snuck out to a party,' I told him once. 'And I put Mum's perfume on. Just one dab. I was so scared she'd realise some was missing.'

The second bottle was larger, only slightly. Bass gave it to me after the twins were born.

He opens the bottle and inhales it and the whole shape of him softens.

* * *

Laura and Rafferty ride the horses in the short afternoons after school. Rafferty mostly works Thai, who is developing nicely along the top of her neck and through her back. Laura rides Bam or Molly and sometimes Jessa will tag along on Reg.

They mostly do flatwork, getting the horse to soften and become more elastic and rhythmic in the arena. They set up showjumping courses and grids and get Bass or Henry or Cameron to take photos and videos for the ads.

'God, he's strong,' Laura says, pulling Bam up after going through a low grid. He throws his head and rounds his back and Laura has to turn him in a tight circle to settle him.

'Brave,' Rafferty corrects.

'What?'

'In the ad. Instead of strong, you just put brave.'

'And instead of spooky, you put sensitive,' Jessa says, wandering around on Reg without her stirrups.

'Put your feet back in your irons,' Laura snaps. 'He's four and he just tried to buck you off.'

Jessa shoves her boots back into the stirrups and gathers him up. 'In his ad you'd put scopey and full of character.'

'If they're maniacs who never want to stop galloping, you say they're nice and forward moving.'

'And if they rear, you put good elevation and potential for piaffe.'

Cameron starts to laugh. 'Remember Pebbles? Rolling you off on the water? You'd say loves cross-country.'

'And Thai jumping out of the paddock.'

'Bold jumper!' says Rafferty.

They're all laughing now. And the horses' ears are twitching at the sound of it. How Rafferty and Cameron laugh so differently. Cameron's laugh, guttural and coming from right down deep in his belly. A surprising laugh, right from when he was small. Rafferty's laugh is almost a cackle, when something funny takes him by surprise. It's high and charming and difficult not to join in with.

I see Bass, standing to stare out the window at them from the small office next to the living room. He has a bemused look on his face, somewhere between a grin and a headshake.

* * *

Jessa's breath comes out in puffs of haze. She is wearing a woollen beanie my grandmother knitted for me years ago. My grandmother, who died when Jessa was three months old. I have wondered where she is, here in the after, but I never sense her close.

'Jessa, hold up!' Michaela Cross, from down the road. She and Jessa went to playgroup together. They were close until Jessa discovered ponies and Michaela discovered her allergy to them.

'Hold up?' Jessa raises an eyebrow.

The boys are further up the road. Their arguing voices carry back on the morning breeze.

Michaela catches up to Jessa and they start walking again. Michaela is wearing mascara. Lip gloss. A slight powdering of foundation on her cheeks and forehead. She has pimples but you can barely see them. She grins at Jessa.

'What are you wearing?'

Jessa's hands fly up to the beanie. The squashed grey shape of it. 'It's my mum's,' she says.

'No,' Michaela says, reaching towards Jessa's jacket. 'This!'

Jessa looks down. The whole front of her uniform is covered in hay and chaff. She groans. 'Ah, crap. I was feeding Opal. Didn't even notice.'

'Mrs Dunkins sure will. Here.' Michaela pulls her to a stop and deftly yanks the jacket off her. She flaps it wildly over her head and dusts the strays off with her hands. 'There.'

'Thank you.'

As they walk Jessa glances sideways at Michaela. 'Your hair looks nice.'

Michaela flicks it over her shoulder. 'Thanks.'

On the bus they sit in their usual places, but smile as they take their seats.

* * *

Jessa is impatient to ride Opal by herself. She is impatient to have the big black mare to herself, to not have to worry about Laura or Bass or the boys watching her with their breaths held.

She starts to creep out of bed before Bass has woken. She drinks cold Milo in the kitchen, shivering in her socks. She closes the door quietly, so Mac doesn't start to bark, and goes outside to the stables.

Most mornings, when she does this, it is to find Laura already in the stables with Moon or Reg or Noddy half saddled.

'Great,' she'll say. 'You can ride Molly.'

But Jessa yearns for Opal. For the shiver of her dark skin, for the way she raises her neck when she hears something unusual or unexpected. I wonder if this yearning has anything to do with me. I find myself hoping it does.

* * *

It is the strangest thing, watching people I don't know coming to trial my horses. Laura meets the prospective buyers on our property and chats away, tacking them up and pointing out, quietly, all their good points. Bam has the most wonderful hooves, never needs to be shod. Thai is by a world cup showjumper – just brimming with scope and would you look at her? Just not caring one bit about that tractor roaring along next to the barn?

Thai is bought by a young girl whose mother does all the talking. Beautiful Thai, who used to jump out of her paddock and make me cry. She'd been such a rangy young thing, all legs and flickering ears, but she's grown into herself, now. Bam is bought by an older woman who wants to get back into adult riding club. Bam, who falls asleep when he's stabled and startles himself awake with his own snoring. I want to tell her that Bam prefers carrots to apples, that he gets upset if you get angry at him. Laura doesn't say anything like that. She knows the horses, she knows them better than anyone, now. But she doesn't know them the way I do.

The paddock slowly empties and I see the purse of Bass's mouth slowly ease as the money transfers come through.

A cold, still day.

Laura and Rafferty help load Bam onto a pretty new float and then walk quietly into the stables as it trundles away. 'Jessa's probably better at doing this,' Raff says.

'It'll upset her. She's funny about your mum's horse stuff, you know that.'

Raff grunts, sits down in the messy, dusty tack room. 'So? What does Dad want to do with all this?'

'Sort it. He was going to help, but he's such a hoarder. Runs in the family. You and Cameron are probably bloody hoarders too.' She hunkers down and starts pulling out boxes of old leather, saddle blankets, rugs.

'Sort it,' Raff repeats.

'Bare minimum, your dad said. For two, maybe three horses.'

'Maybe three? He's still selling Opal?'

'I dunno, Raff. That's his call. We'll make sure there's enough stuff for her, but I don't know what his plans are. He's not a big talker, your dad.' Laura starts throwing reins, girths and martingales into a pile just outside the door.

'Now,' she says. 'That's the to-be-oiled-and-then-sold pile. Get Cam and Jessa to give you a hand with that later. This is the keeping pile. This is the tossing pile. Sound good?'

Rafferty sighs, runs a pair of my old gloves through his fingers. 'Yep,' he says. His fingers tightening around them.

* * *

Bass drives Cameron to race meets on the weekends, where he watches with his eyebrows raised and his mouth slightly open as Cameron wins every single race he's in. The shelf in the room he shares with Rafferty is starting to become crowded with ribbons and medals.

He runs into town where he treats himself to a sweating glass of lemonade at the café where Maggie works. The place with the books, across the road from the pharmacy. If she's working she brings it out to him with a muffin and a wink.

Cameron smiles into his lemonade.

And I wonder if this is enough for him. Because Maggie's expression is indulgent, softened. There is no sign of the longing that made the edges of her face sharpen. There is nothing but warmth.

Softness.

I hope it is enough. I hope he thinks of it, running home along the sides of heavily treed roads.

I hope it is enough.

* * *

Rafferty follows Jessa out into the chicken coop. It's early, chilly. Their breath is a ghost. That's what they used to call misty breath. 'Mum, I'm breathing ghosts!'

'If you lock me in, I swear to God I'll glue your dick to your leg.'

'That's not very ladylike.'

'Piss off.'

'Was just going to see if you wanted a lift, grump. Guy and Jake are coming by to pick up the chainsaw and then Jake's dropping us off at school.'

'Oh.'

'Well?'

'Yeah. Okay. What time?' Tyres crunch on the gravel driveway. 'Shit. Okay. Just let me finish getting the eggs and changing my shoes.'

'No rush.'

Jessa turns as Rafferty steps up onto the verandah. 'What about Henry?' she calls from the door of the chicken coop.

'Too early for bellowing,' says Rafferty, looking pained. 'Cam had early training. There's room for Henry.'

'Good.'

'Hey ... what's that on your face?'

'What's what?'

'On your face. That black stuff.'

'Mascara.'

'Isn't that meant to go ... like ... on your eyelashes?'

'Shut up!' Jessa snaps and goes back to the nesting boxes and Rafferty goes inside and starts buttering toast.

Behind them, behind the house, the paddocks are starting to firm up again. The marks the cattle leave in the mud don't fill with water. Spring, then. Early spring.

Bass is sitting at the kitchen table with some cinnamon milk, his chin propped in his hands.

'I really want a bull,' he says.

* * *

Bass and Rafferty are restacking hay into the shed. They had to empty it after the roof began to leak. Months ago.

'I'm getting a job,' says Raff.

'Are you, now?' Bass heaves the last bale up onto the stack and then sits, wipes his face on his jumper.

Rafferty flops down next to him. 'Feed store. Reg Fainter said he could use me, loading up and that.'

'Hmm.'

'It's just … I know you've always said we only work
on the property and that's it, but … I want to …'

'Do something else?'

'I can start paying board. I know how tight things are.'

Bass grins. 'Lot less tight with those horses gone.'

'Yeah, but. You know what I mean. It's just down the
road, ten minutes. And I know I don't have my licence,
yet. But the feed store's not far. And Jake might be able
to help run me down. And I can ride. Ride the bike.
Waddaya reckon?'

Bass thumps Raff on the back, tousles his hair. 'I think
you're a good kid. C'mon. Let's go have a milk.'

* * *

Every rug in the house is rolled up, dragged out into the
shed. The thick one in the living room, the long narrow
runner in the hallway. Steve comes over one afternoon
with a sixpack of beer and raises his eyebrows at the
exposed wooden floors.

He stares at Rafferty. 'Why?' he asks.

'Spring cleaning! None of us are much chop at staying
on top of the housework,' says Raff, sitting on the table
and opening a bag of Twisties. 'We figured it'll stink less
this way. Particularly with Peggy Sue inside all the time.
And Mac moulting like nobody's business.'

'Peggy Sue?'

'Our stolen chicken.'

'You stole a chicken?'

Jessa comes in, sits down at the table. Her front is
covered in dust and dog hair. '*Cam* stole a chicken,'

she says. 'He found her on the road. She belongs to the Thompsons, but they don't even have a *coop* for her, so when he saw her on the road, he stole her.'

'She's retarded, though,' says Rafferty sadly.

'Very happy, but she nests behind the wood heater. And in Mac's food bowl.'

'Slow but happy.'

'She loves a cuddle,' Jessa says.

'Umm … right. Okay. I'm just gunna …' He squeezes past them and puts the beer in the fridge. 'Where's your dad?'

'Trying to work out how to empty the vacuum.'

'We haven't used it in months. We just didn't know how dirty everything was until the rugs got moved,' says Rafferty. He points at the floor in the hallway. '*Filthy*, right?'

'Right. Umm. Well, I might go see if your dad needs a hand.'

They wave at him.

'We scared him,' says Jessa.

'I think the retarded chicken story pushed him over the edge.' Rafferty opens the fridge. 'Wanna drink?'

* * *

A cloudy, windy day. The sort where you don't particularly want to be outside or inside. Unsettled. I think it is the midmorning, but it's difficult to tell. They're all wearing T-shirts. Laura's arm is goose-bumped and she rubs a hand across her forearm. 'Jessa …'

'No. I'll be fine.'

Laura looks over at Bass, who holds up his hands. It's still a bit muddy in the round yard. Jessa is holding Opal. Both she and Laura have their helmets on.

'Jessa. If she puts you off, it'll be a bad fall. She's not balanced. She's not settled. I think it'd be better if I rode her first.'

'No.'

Again, Laura glances at Bass, this time mouthing, 'You!'

Bass leans on the round yard fence. 'Let her go, Loz.'

'What?'

'She can sit anything.'

'I can sit anything,' Jessa agrees.

Laura nods, giving Bass a sharp look before turning back to Jessa. 'I'm staying in here with you.'

I wonder if Laura, somewhere between now and when I was alive, has become more motherly. Softer, maybe.

'Okay.' Jessa bunks herself up onto Opal's back as easily as she bunks up onto Pebbles.

Laura and Bass hold their breath, but Opal turns her head and stares up at Jessa and snorts and shakes her head.

'I'm going to walk her,' Jessa says.

Laura nods once and stays close as Jessa touches Opal's sides. The mare moves forward like she's done it a million times. Like she isn't young and half wild, just brought in from the bush tracks.

'How does she feel?' Laura asks.

'She feels fine. I'm going to trot.'

'Jessa.' It's Bass this time, leaning over the fence like he's ready to catch her. Jessa ignores him and suddenly

Opal is calmly trotting and Laura and Bass both let out a sigh.

Without warning Jessa sits and asks for a canter and the mare shifts pace and does a small pigroot, ears pricked. Jessa grins and brings her back to a trot.

'See? Fine. I told you she's fine.'

Bass is nodding but Laura narrows her eyes. 'You've already ridden her by yourself.'

'No. Henry helped me.'

* * *

Cameron and Rafferty, staring out the kitchen window. Cameron has an apple in his hand, Rafferty a mug of coffee. It is the same day, the same time. Bass, hanging over the round yard wall. Laura standing rigidly in the centre as Jessa rides around and around, the track of the round yard growing thick and heavy.

'Well, she hasn't been bucked off yet,' Cameron says. He tosses the apple up and catches it. He hasn't taken the first bite yet.

'Only a matter of time,' Rafferty mutters. He doesn't move from the window, though. 'Dad's crazy to let her ride it.'

'Her. Let Jessa ride *her*.'

Raff grunts, sits down at the table. 'I talked to Dad about getting a job.'

'And?'

'He's all for it. I just ... I'd feel better if I could pay my own way a bit more, you know? He's so fucking stressed.'

'It's a good thing,' says Cameron, biting into the apple. 'Maybe I should get one too.'

* * *

Bass has always hated my roses. I watch him, waiting for him to dig them out. I wait for him to pull on his old leather gloves and kneel out there until his neck goes red. I wait for him to drag them up from the garden bed and into garbage bags, or onto the burning-off pile. I wait for him to harrow the beds. To plant something practical.

My mother grew roses when we were young. They were white and tiny and she kept them in pots on the cement steps of the back porch. I would wait for the flowers, I would count the buds. I loved the smell of them, the velvet feel of the petals which later reminded me of a horse's nose. Bea and I tried to squash and bruise the petals into perfume, but the water only ever went brown and smelt like something rotting.

The first time I saw the overgrown beds along that side of the house, I had it pegged as a place to plant roses.

Sometimes Bass goes out there with a spade and the secateurs that were left in the rain after I died and are rusted and stiff.

He will look at the roses, stare down at them. Eventually he will set aside his spade. Set aside his gloves. And he will put his face to the leaves and breathe in. That same shuddering, uncertain drawing-in of breath that makes me think of him after an orgasm.

He will bring a cutting of roses inside if they're flowering. They're in bud now. Spring coming. I yearn to brush my fingers against them, feel the dew. Their tightness.

All three of our children look at them on the kitchen table. Only Cameron ever comments.

'They're really nice, Dad.'

Bass will nod, just once. I wonder about the day when he does pull up my roses. I wonder what it will mean.

* * *

When the boys were fourteen Bass sat them down on the verandah. Autumn. The yard thick with leaves, the paddocks – already yellow from summer – slowing down for winter. Receding.

'You're going to start dating soon,' he said, all serious.

'Bass!' I remember my laughter. How it had made me gasp. Had made adrenaline course through me. The panic of helpless laughter. 'Bass, don't!'

'One, girls like you to open doors for them. Some won't like it, but it's a nice thing to do. It's respectful. And if they don't like it, they can tell you. And then you stop. But don't ever just not do it. Don't assume. Okay?'

Rafferty rolled his eyes. Cameron leant in, eyes wide. 'What about giving them your jacket if it's cold?'

'He's having us on, Cameron,' Rafferty said.

'That can be annoying. If you've packed something warm and they're in something cold and dopey. But if you really like her, you offer. Because chances are she's dressed that way for you. Now. Two, asking a girl out for dinner means it's a date. Coffee can be a bit hazy, unless you pay for it. If you pay for her coffee, you're making it count as a date.'

'Bass!'

Bass holds up three fingers. 'Three. If you ever sleep with a girl ...'

'Not for a long time,' I said. 'A very, very, very, *very* long time.'

'If you ever sleep with a girl, don't go blabbing to your mates about it. It's special, you know? And it makes it less special if you blab about it. It's ... Just don't.'

'Don't kiss and tell. Right. Can we go now?'

'Bass, they're fourteen.'

Rafferty gave me a look then. A fleeting one. And my stomach shifted a little, quaked. I realised that he was not disinterested because these things did not yet concern him. He was disinterested because he had already learnt them for himself.

Being a mother is a fullness. Pregnancy gives way to exhaustion, love, anger, weeping, frustration, wonder. The emotions, they fill you up till you think you don't have room left for anything else.

On the verandah, no longer laughing. It was the first time being a mother had made me feel hollow. For the first time, that tug of emptiness, as my children started to pull away from me.

* * *

When I was fourteen, maybe older, I walked in on Beatrice having sex with a boy on the couch. I did not know what I was seeing. Not at the time. The mess of feelings, of sharp things in my belly, of matching up the uncomfortable reality with the serenading, perfect scenes in movies. It took time.

Beatrice saw me and tried to push the boy off, but by then I was running. I had practised climbing the cyclone fencing that ran along the back perimeter of our narrow garden. On the other side was a mess of dumped cars.

I heard her call me. But I didn't stop. I knew she wouldn't follow. That she was scared of spiders and snakes and rough sheets of metal.

* * *

I am proud of Rafferty. I am proud of how hard he works at the feed store and how he rides there and back on days when Jake and Bass can't drive him. I am proud of how quickly he picks up the mechanisms of the cash register, how the deliveries are logged, where all the different types of feed and bedding are kept.

He is strong, sinewy. I watch as he hurls around bails and bags and gives people advice on what feed they need.

'You're doing great,' says Reggie. 'Is that twin of yours any good? We could do with a second one of you.'

Rafferty laughs, doesn't answer. He can't imagine Cameron dealing with how high pressure the job sometimes becomes.

Rafferty's back aches. He never says anything, but halfway through his ten hour shifts on the weekend, he will roll his shoulders back, he will stretch forward until he touches the floor and wince when he stands back up.

'You get a bit stiff to start off,' says Reggie. 'But you'll be right. The muscles build.'

Rafferty's back keeps him awake at night sometimes. The dull, throbbing ache of muscles pushed too far. He supposes he has always been able to stop when he got sore. Got tired. When he was doing things on the farm. Have breaks when he felt like it.

He stares down at his schoolbooks with a more knowing and yearning expression than he ever has before. He can't imagine doing a job like this for years and years. Can't imagine how much he would ache at forty, at fifty.

Back aching, halfway through year eleven, Rafferty begins to study.

* * *

Weeks when Jessa tries to churn cream to butter with a manual set of beaters and Rafferty drinks a bottle of vodka.

'I vomited mandarin seeds,' he tells Cameron when they are sitting in their room with the window flung open.

Cameron slaps at a mosquito. 'Oh, yeah.'

'I haven't had a mandarin since we tried to add mandarin juice to a cosmo at the Ryans' place.'

Cameron stares at him.

Rafferty lights up a cigarette and exhales in the direction of the window. 'Make sure you don't swallow them. That party was three fucking years ago.'

Cameron nods again and rubs his calves.

'Your shoes stink,' Rafferty says.

'Sorry.'

'Why do you keep bringing them up here?'

'Sorry,' Cameron repeats, straightening his legs and drumming his hands on the bed.

'Hey … can you …' Rafferty scratches his nose and stares out the window.

Cameron stops drumming. 'Can I what?'

'Don't you dare tell anyone.'

'What?'

'Can you give my back a rub? Just between the shoulders? Sort of?'

'You should probably share some of your Twisties with me first.'

'Oh, fucking forget it.'

Cameron laughs. 'C'mon. I don't mind. Lie down.'

'No.' Rafferty stares down at the lit end of the cigarette. 'You going to Maggie's?'

Cameron shrugs. 'I dunno. I don't really know anyone. Except for her. Don't think Jason or any of them are going.'

'So? You get to know them. That's the point of a party.'

Cameron drums his hands on the bed and Rafferty drags on his cigarette.

'You know,' Rafferty says. 'It's always been your problem. You let people freak you out too much.'

'I suppose so.'

'You just need to chill out.'

'Yeah. While I'm at it, I need to be good at maths and stop having panic attacks.'

Rafferty stares at him, cigarette hanging limply from his fingers. 'Are you as tight-laced as I think you are?'

Cameron seems to consider this for a moment. 'Probably.'

'I can help you out. But if you tell Dad, if you tell *anyone*, I'll fucking throw all your shit out the window and put a deadlock on the door. And *then* I'll glue your dick to your leg.'

'Right.'

Rafferty stares at him a moment longer then stubs out his cigarette. 'Close your eyes,' he says.

'When has that ever ended well for me?'

'I've matured.'

'You threw a cow pat at my face.'

'Are you still sore about that? Jesus. Shut your damned eyes.'

Cameron closes his eyes and purses his lips tight. Across the room Rafferty slips his hand behind a poster on the wall and comes out with a handful of condoms and a baggie of what looks like weed.

Not taking his eyes off Cameron, he rolls two joints and then puts everything back behind the poster.

'Right,' he says, twiddling the joint in his fingers.

Cameron opens his eyes and struggles off his bed to his feet.

'Is that cannabis?'

'Cannabis? You serious? Fuck. Sometimes I wonder whether you've grown up under a rock, but if that's true then so have I. Yes. It's weed. It'll chill you out.'

'No way.'

'Suit yourself. I'm sure you'll have fun standing awkwardly in the corner with your arms crossed, asking people when they walk past whether they know if it's zucchini or cucumber in the dip.'

'Hey,' says Cameron. Wounded.

'You want some or not?'

'No.'

Rafferty rolls his eyes, taking one joint and setting the other aside.

Cameron watches him. 'Are you cross?'

'Why would I be *cross*?' Rafferty demands, lighting the joint with his head sticking out the window.

'You look it.'

'I'm pissed off that you're such a pussy, if that's what you mean.'

'That's the same as cross.'

'You're actually the most annoying person I've ever met. Ever. *Including* Jessa.'

'Yeah, well.'

Rafferty stares at him, his cheeks puffed with smoke. When he exhales his whole body seems to relax. 'How's the therapy going, anyway?'

Cameron shrugs and picks at his bedspread.

'Jessa told Henry about it. She hates it.'

'Oh.'

'So. Is it any good?'

'The therapy?'

Rafferty rolls his eyes again and Cameron shrugs. 'I dunno. It's okay, I guess. The lady's pretty nice. I don't know what I'm meant to say, though. I've been going for so long and I still don't know what I'm fucking meant to be doing there.'

'Whatever the hell you want.' Rafferty jumps up off the bed and stuffs the butt of the joint into his cigarette jar. 'See ya.'

'Are you going to Maggie's?' Cameron calls after him.

His only answer is the sound of Rafferty's feet, the heavy falling of them down the stairs.

Rafferty veers by the stable yard where Jessa and Henry are brushing Opal.

'She's getting fatter,' he says, reaching out to run his hands through her mane.

Jessa stops brushing. 'Raff?'

Rafferty doesn't answer.

'Oi, arsehole!'

'What?' he snaps.

Henry grins and swaps his currycomb for a dandy brush. Opal shifts her weight from one foot to the other but otherwise doesn't move. It looks like she's dozing.

'You're standing in a pile of shit.'

Rafferty stares down at his feet. 'Well, fuck,' he says and walks slowly back out to the driveway.

Henry and Jessa both burst out laughing.

'What's up with him?' Henry asks. They pause to watch Rafferty pushing his bicycle towards the gate.

'That, young Henry, is a very stoned boy.'

* * *

A week after I'd seen Bea having sex on the couch, I'd glanced sideways at her and cleared my throat.

'What does it feel like?' I'd asked. Washing up after dinner, perhaps. The taste of green tea in my mouth.

She was silent. Playing with a drink on the table. Maybe it was daylight and we were doing gardening. All I remember is that she shrunk in on herself. Became focused on a task.

'Bea?'

'It hurts.'

'How? I mean …'

'Work it out for yourself, Cate.'

But her words, they stuck inside me. Fastened there. I began to think of it as a dentist's drill. As the quick, unquenchable pain of stubbing a toe hard against wood.

Out with my friends, I kept my distance from the boys we hung around with. Mostly, they ignored me. I would drive my nails into my palms. Tell myself I didn't care. Over and over.

A few times, sitting with Mum, reading or cooking or sorting through old clothes Mum liked to donate to the local charity shop, I would start to speak and then stop.

'What, Catie?'

'Nothing.' Beatrice, on the couch. What she had been doing.

I wanted to tell Mum. I wanted to see her face harden. I wanted, even then, to pitch myself against Beatrice. To win. But with this one thing, I didn't. I bit my tongue. And although Beatrice never said anything to me about it, I know that she had expected me to tell.

When I was sixteen I went out with Brent Hardwick and he saved the red Smarties for me when he had a pack at pony club. I made him cards I never sent and wrote him letters I ripped up and threw out as soon as I had finished writing them.

After Brent, I relaxed more around boys. Especially after I started hanging out with Sylvia when I was eighteen. Sex was awkward but not unhappy. It was never what I had expected, when I was younger. But it was always different to what I had seen Bea doing on the couch. It was better. And that, for many years, was enough.

It was not until I met Bass that I finally unwound.

And the wonder of it put me in a fog of happiness. Golden. Smelling of wood smoke and the beady taste of sunflowers.

* * *

Cameron has beer stains on the shirt he has paid Jessa to iron for him. He is standing in the Marchs' kitchen, prodding the dip with a cracker that I doubt he will eat. He clears his throat a few times. Outside there's firelight and laughter and the thrum of music that was new so long ago that it's back in fashion.

Cameron is watching Maggie.

She is outside, passing marshmallows and sticks to the people sitting around the fire. He watches as she drops a kiss on someone's head and pulls someone up for a hug. She whispers into the ear of a girl from school and laughs so hard she has to curl her arms around her middle.

Cameron eats his cracker.

When she comes back inside her cheeks are red and her eyes are watery from the smoke. She is wearing a black shirt and cut-off jeans.

'C'mon,' she says. She takes his hand.

Cameron follows. His fingers playing with his beer-stained shirt. Rafferty, sitting at the base of a tree with someone's homemade bong, glances up as they pass. I see him raise his eyebrow and then Guy elbows him and Rafferty glances away and passes the bong along.

The garage is a mess of old furniture and car parts.

'I've started getting things together for when I move out. Mum's stuff mostly,' Maggie says, sitting down on what looks like a jumble of old couch cushions.

She touches her tattoo. Often and briefly. I wonder if it still makes her think of her mother or whether it has numbed into a thoughtless habit.

She rolls over and pulls Cameron down against her. She presses his hand to her chest, her lips against his.

He trembles, breathes deeply.

Maggie pulls back a little, her forehead against his. 'You okay?' she murmurs.

Cameron nods, stares up at the ceiling. I can see him trying to catch his breath.

And then my boy begins to cry. And I can't watch any more. I can't be with him. Suddenly I am outside. I am watching Rafferty. Watching as Rafferty stares up at the thick branches of the tree. The heavy sky behind.

* * *

When Cameron and Rafferty were born, I couldn't stop crying. The nurse said it was normal. That my hormones were all over the place. That birth, for all its splendour and ordinariness, was trauma.

That I needed to regain my balance. That my body would have to catch its breath.

It took me a while to get the hang of breastfeeding. Swapping babies and nipples. Learning how to offer it to their tiny, pursed mouths.

Once I got the hang of it, I started to feel more composed. But not altogether, not on the inside. On the outside I felt okay. And I learnt to focus on the outside, learnt that if I focused on my breathing, on the room, on the smell of the two boys, I could detach from the sadness. From the blue murk of it.

But then a thought struck me, watching Cameron crying. The more unsettled baby, existing with an anxiety that Rafferty seemed to completely lack.

I never quite knew how to settle him.

And, watching him grow, this feeling never went away.

* * *

One day Beatrice tried to hug my father. Tried to ask him about his day. She was sixteen, I suppose. Her hair was cropped at her shoulders. She only ever cut it short once. It was around the time she took to wearing lavender oil dabbed on her neck, in the crevice of her elbows, in place of perfume.

'Can't you see I'm busy?'

She wandered around the house for a while. I remember that. She kept standing and staring out the windows, which were dirty and scratched and laced with spider webs. Then she sat down on her bed and scratched the back of her hands raw. Just that one time. After that one sentence.

I found Mum when she got back from work. I peered over her shoulder at the mirror while she plaited her long dark hair. 'Mum, Bea's sad.'

'Is she?' Her fingers working through her hair, staring at my eyes in the mirror. 'Why?'

'Can we take her out somewhere?'

My mother blinked. She was always exhausted after work. Was generally asleep by eight o'clock. But she nodded. 'Yeah, all right. We can go down to the wharf, get fish and chips. As long as it's not a late one.'

When I see Cameron, see his scratched hands, I think of my father with his glasses pressed up high on his nose. The smell of ink and paper from the table.

Bea picked at her fish, stared out at the water. My mother yawned and rested her head in her hands, but still insisted we stay for a dessert of salty-tasting mousse from the frosted fish and chips freezer.

We were very quiet, sitting on plastic chairs at a plastic table by the wharf. At home, our father didn't ask us where we'd been.

When I see Cameron, his hands swollen and burning, I think of the smell of lavender. Even now. So much later.

* * *

On this day of clear sunshine and distant clouds, Jessa sits in the stables mixing feed and chatting about a dressage competition Laura has coming up. I see Henry spin around to the wall to hide an erection. Jessa doesn't go into the tack room much, any more. She leaves the things she uses in boxes outside the nearest stall.

It is spring. Spring sunshine. My roses blooming and the yard thick with seed fluff from the silver birches.

Henry is damp, pink and trembling. He stays there, staring at the spidery bricks, the flaking cement.

'What are you doing?' Jessa, bridle in hand. 'C'mon!'

'Give me a minute.'

'*C'mon*! It's going to get dark soon and you still need to get Pebbles.'

'I said, give me a minute!' His voice is sharper than it has ever been, speaking to her. The voice reserved for his mother, maybe. For boys at school who stand too close and laugh if he drops something.

Jessa stares at him. 'I'll get Pebbles,' she says.

Heading out to the paddock with Pebbles's frayed halter over her shoulder, she is frowning down at the ground. When she glances back at Henry, he is still turned tight towards the wall.

* * *

Jessa, frowning into the pages of an old book that Rafferty once inhaled. Her hair keeps falling into her eyes. Her sharp, angry fingers pressing the strays back behind her ears. She is wearing mascara.

'What's wrong with your face?' Cameron asks, sitting down at the table.

'What do you *mean*, what's wrong with my face?'

Cameron frowns, peers at her. 'Have you got mascara on?'

'Piss off.'

'You *do*. Your eyes are all black.'

'Michaela gave it to me. Go away.'

Cameron grins and heads outside, glass of water in hand.

Jessa waits until Cameron has disappeared from view. She glances towards the kitchen door and slowly begins to set the book down on the table. She is rising, slow and quiet, when Rafferty's voice calls in from the lounge room, where he's highlighting a biology textbook.

'Keep reading!'

'Piss off. I've had enough.'

'Say bye bye to Opal then.' Rafferty comes into the kitchen and sits backwards on a chair, his chin resting on the back of it. 'Where you up to?'

'I don't bloody know. I can't concentrate. It's a stupid book.'

'C'mon. What just happened in it?'

'Some stupid guy said something stupid.'

'Do you think anyone at school likes reading Shakespeare?'

'Probably.'

'Bullshit. The difference between someone who gets an A in English and someone who gets an F is that the A person actually reads the books. And talks about them. And uses their brain. Doesn't mean their brain is any good, just that they use it.'

Jessa stays quiet, drumming her book on the table.

'Look. You're in year eight now. If you don't pull

your finger out, what do you reckon Dad's going to do with Opal? Seriously, Jessa. She's worth a fortune.'

Rafferty stands up and goes back to his highlighting. Jessa stares out the window, at the chicken coop and the grazing cows. Then she sighs, picks the book back up and begins to read.

* * *

Jessa still wakes up next to Bass, with her hand linked up in his. She wakes up earlier, though. While it's still dark. And she rummages for her boots and leaves the boys out some cereal.

She no longer makes them sandwiches. No longer digs through the laundry for any clothes but her own. Her time, when it is hers, she gives to Opal. Opal, who paces the paddock when Jessa is not on the farm, as though waiting for her to come back. To come home.

Outside, on her way to the paddock, Jessa always pauses just off the verandah, right near the jacaranda. And even though it's not flowering and its leaves are tight and green, she will squat down at its base and press her fingers into the dirt.

She will breathe deeply, sometimes with her head resting against the rutted base of it.

And then she will get up and dust her hands and whistle.

And out of the darkness, right up against the paddock fence, Opal will appear.

* * *

Bass is sitting outside with Steve. Steve, who wants to be a father so much it chokes him up. Who knitted the boys beanies when they were small and had no hair.

They are sitting on the verandah at dusk and they are bundled up in their boots and fleece. Inside Rafferty is playing his guitar and Cameron is watching re-runs of the early seasons of *Law and Order*. Bass yawns and stretches his hands high above his head. He is drinking ginger beer. He keeps running his fingers around the glass rim.

'Thinking of doing it myself,' says Bass. 'Money and all that.'

Steve is shaking his head. 'Nah. With how steep that part of your block is? Get someone in. Get Tim. He did the Mulders' fencing. And remember that drunk driver? Who went in through their front paddock? Well the fencing barely busted.'

'Money,' says Bass, setting the glass down and pressing the heels of his hands into the hollows of his eyes. 'Fucking *money*.'

'Well, I can give you a hand. If you decide to give it a go.'

'Thanks. Thanks, mate.'

They are quiet for a while, then. Bass pours himself some more ginger beer and Steve shakes his head when Bass waves it at him.

'Bass?'

'Hmm?'

'I'm … I'm gay.'

Bass turns and blinks at him. 'I know, mate.'

'Oh. Right.'

'Did you think I didn't?'

Steve shrugs, glances down at his drink.

Bass yawns. 'Anyway – what about the Gunns? Their son's just starting out doing contracting, yeh? Maybe he'll give me a hand for cheap. Put it down to experience.'

Steve has softened, exhaled. He reaches for his ginger beer and I can see his hand is shaking.

Jessa is sitting in the living room, scrolling through YouTube videos on mane pulling. She glances sharply towards the window.

Rafferty wanders in, guitar in hand.

'Steve's *gay*,' she whispers.

'How long has it taken you to work that out, idiot?' he whispers back, then more loudly, 'Cameron scared himself watching *Law and Order*.'

Jessa goes back to scrolling. 'Of course he did.'

Outside Steve is breathing deeply, his whole chest moving. I think Bass is the first person he has told. And the relief of it is like a flood, carrying everything else away.

* * *

When I brought Bass home to meet my parents and Beatrice, it was autumn. We kicked our way through crunchy leaves and breathed steam as we waited on the doorstep.

'My sister'll be rude,' I told him, linking my fingers with his. 'Don't take it personally.'

Inside, my mother had soft instrumental music playing. A lit candle on the coffee table. I remember the way the flames flickered when the door was closed. My father was out somewhere. Probably at the library. He didn't like being around when Mum had visitors over. Even me.

'Welcome!' my mother called. 'Bea, get them a drink. I'll be out in a minute.'

'What do you want?' Beatrice asked. She was wearing an old dress and her hair was frizzy at the front, how it always went after being washed.

'Just water please,' Bass said.

'He'll have a beer,' I called after her. Bass gave me a look and I held up my hands.

'Here you go,' Bea said, coming out with the beer. She holds it out for him. 'Bass, right?'

'Yeah.'

'Short for anything?'

'Sebastian.'

'Right. Funny name for a farmer.'

'Well, I'm not really. A farmer.'

'He's doing up his parents' old place. Getting a loan out.'

'What happened to your parents?'

'They're dead,' said Bass, shortly. He had a long draught of beer. 'A few years, now. But they'd been living off the farm for years before that. Couldn't keep up with it. The house, the whole farm, needs a lot of work to get it liveable and useable again.' He glanced at me. 'That's all.'

'Oh.' Beatrice sat down on the floor. 'Mum'll be done soon. She's just dishing up.'

My mother did not believe in appetisers or entrees. Every meal I had ever seen her cook involved about six dishes on the table. Fish, vegetables, salad, seasoned rice.

My mother and I looked at each other across the table while Beatrice asked Bass about his family, his studies, his favourite sports.

She laughed at his jokes and filled up his glass of lemonade.

Bass kept raising his eyebrows at me, and when Beatrice and my mother got up to clear the table, he grinned.

'Man-eater, hey?'

I had a sip of my drink. 'You charmed her. She's not normally this nice.'

'Huh.'

'Don't huh me.'

He grinned at me across the table.

At the end of the night Beatrice hugged him closely and my mother rolled her eyes at me over her head.

'Lovely meeting you, Bass,' my mother had said.

Bass grinned and on the way down the street to the car he threw his arm over my shoulder.

'You're very quiet,' he said as we started driving.

'I'm sleepy. Her house is always chilly and I ate too much.'

'Your sister left both testicles intact.'

'Good for you.'

'Hey, what's up?'

'You flirted. The whole night, you flirted with her.'

'That wasn't flirting. That was being polite to my girlfriend's sister.'

'What's flirting then?'

'Remember when I met you at the Savannah Hotel? That first time I saw you?'

'Yeah.'

'That, dear Cate, was flirting.'

* * *

They are sitting around the table, Bass and our three children and Laura and Henry. They are eating pasta with rocket and smoked salmon that Jessa spits out and presses down under the table to Mac.

'I'm getting a bull,' says Bass, staring around the table.

'Umm. Good. Dad,' says Cameron.

Bass is almost bouncing up and down on his chair. 'Steve's helping with the fencing. Which means we can get a *bull*.'

'Fucking brilliant, that's what it is,' says Laura, raising her glass. 'To well-planned debt!'

'An investment,' says Bass.

'He knows we've got bulls already, right?' Jessa mumbles to Henry.

'I think he's getting a *special* bull,' says Henry, grinning.

'Oh god. He's going to sell Opal and get a special bull.' Jessa puts her head down on the table and Henry reaches over her for the jug of juice.

* * *

I cannot remember how Beatrice came to be in Garras. It was three months after I brought Bass into the city to meet her and my mother. She drove into Garras in much the same way I had, with everything squashed into the back of her old car.

She pulled up outside Laura's bluestone cottage where Bass and I were living while we waited for the farmhouse to be restumped.

'What the hell are you doing?' Barefoot on the verandah, I watched as she pulled out suitcase after suitcase. 'I thought you were just staying for the weekend!'

She stayed in the cottage for three days and then moved into the flat above the book-filled café on the main street.

I cannot remember why I drove to Garras, why I chose that strange little town at the base of the ranges, but I had always planned to live somewhere rural. Somewhere I could nudge aside my kitchen curtains and see my horses.

Beatrice, so sharp-edged and shadowed. I could not see then, cannot see now, what joy this little town held for her. Beatrice, who hates bushwalking and has no interest in farming. Beatrice, who never came willingly to visit the horse I bought when I was nineteen. Beatrice, who likes shops and music and drawing fairy villages in her notebook margins.

When I asked Beatrice why she had come, why she had followed me, she said only that it was beautiful, that she missed me and that I'd always been too egocentric.

I'm not sure why I hated her for it. But I did. As sharp and clear as glass.

* * *

Jessa, sitting cross-legged in the counsellor's office. She is nursing a coffee. She has her jodhpurs on and keeps sneezing. I am not sure whether she is getting a cold or whether the counsellor has lit too much incense. I always made her drink honey and lemon drinks and stopped her getting wet outside with the horses when it rained. Even in spring the rain in Garras is cold. It chills you.

'Your dad says you're doing much better at school,' the counsellor says. 'Much, much better. He's very proud of you.'

'It's so he doesn't sell Opal.'

'Your horse?'

'Yeah. If I do well at school, he'll let me keep her.'

'If you don't do well at school, he'll sell her? Why would he do that?'

'Because she's worth a lot of money and he needs it. He wants to buy a special bull.'

'And what would happen if he did sell her?'

Jessa presses her lips together and looks out the window. A tremor runs through her. Terror, passing like a breeze. 'How much longer? I need to ride.'

* * *

Laura and I never speak of it, but I knew Henry's mother before I knew her. Her name was Sylvia and, for a while, I only felt properly alive when I was out with her. When we were dancing and drinking and squashed into places tight and loud.

It was when I still lived at home and watched Beatrice out of the corner of my eye. When my life was working at the music store and saving for a horse.

Early on, I think a part of me was trying to test my father. To work out his limits, to see if he cared enough to have any.

My father took no notice. My mother stuffed condoms into my purse.

Beatrice, slowly, spent more time at home. She would watch me leave from the couch, in her comfy pants with a book on her lap.

How I had lived for those nights. When even the dappled tree shadows, sent spiralling by the streetlights, seemed like a sort of omen.

Her hand, warm in mine on the scuffed dance floor.

Standing by Sylvia was a sort of dry shiver, too.

* * *

Rafferty walks out of school, his bag slung over his shoulder. He is chewing on a lollypop stick. It looks like a cigarette. He pauses at the gate, exhales and cracks his neck. The stiffness, that isn't going away, from working at the feed store. He pulls a muesli bar out of his pocket and starts chewing as he walks.

'Raff!'

He turns. It's Maggie, breathless. A finger pressed to her tattoo.

'Hi. Sorry. Just … Is Cameron all right? He's been really quiet, lately. Even for him.'

'Yeah.' Rafferty keeps walking. 'He's okay.'

She nods, almost to herself. Then she sighs and bites her lip, catching up to Rafferty. 'He's not very happy, is he?'

'None of us are very happy. That's what happens when your mother dies.'

'I know,' she says sharply. That sharpness. When she looks at Rafferty her face is not soft. There is nothing gentle about her.

Rafferty glances at her. 'I know you do. Sorry.'

'It's okay.'

Rafferty softens. 'It was a good party by the way. I liked the marshmallows.'

'Yeah? I didn't see you.'

'You wouldn't have. I spent most of the night under the tree, then I was down the back with Pearl Saunders.'

'Fair enough.'

'Listen, I heard about what happened with … you and Cameron.'

She stiffens. 'I …'

'It was nothing to do with you. He's … weird like that. He's always been weird. And since Mum …'

'I get it. I do.'

Rafferty glances sideways at her again. They keep walking. He nods.

* * *

Sylvia had long blonde hair and a laugh like raindrops falling onto iron. She smelt of Chanel No. 5. A scent, she said, her grandmother used to wear.

Sylvia and I met when I was working in the city, saving up for a horse.

'Don't bother with that,' she said. We were both working the counter at a big music store. It was empty, the fans humming. Outside it was forty-two degrees and the chocolate vinyls we had on display had started to melt.

'With what?'

'*That.*' She nodded at the Windex and paper towel in my hands.

'Makes the time go faster,' I said.

She rolled her eyes, rocked backwards on her heels. 'You one of the summer casuals?'

'Yeah.' I kept scrubbing. It was better than just standing there with my back starting to ache, watching the clock at the bottom of the screen. Even if just three minutes slipped past, they were three minutes that I hadn't had to watch disappear.

'You studying?'

'No. Not yet.'

'Oh.' She kept rocking. 'I'm visual art at Melbourne. Second year.'

'Good for you.' She was snapping her gum. Had been snapping it for the past hour.

'You ever go to the Green Monkey?'

'The what?'

'It's a bar.'

'No.'

'It's cool there. They have a three hour long happy hour.'

'Cool.' I unrolled some more paper towelling.

'Where do you go?'

'Jaggers,' I lied. 'Sometimes MC.' I hadn't been out in months. I was exhausted from year twelve. I was tired from forty plus hours a week on my feet all day. Mostly

I didn't go out any more than Beatrice did. Which was so depressing that sometimes I had to sit outside on the narrow cement porch rather than sit next to her on the couch, inside.

'Huh,' she said. 'What are you doing after your shift?'

'Umm … meeting some friends. Maybe. Why?' The thought of the leftover pasta I had put in the fridge and the second season of *Mad About Time* popped into my head.

'Come out with me. We'll go to the Monkey.'

'I don't –'

'*C'mon.*'

The Monkey was stuffy, full of people. The drinks were poured generously, though. And there was a joint floating around that made me feel like the world had slowed down, beautifully. Perfectly.

Sylvia and I, we danced. She got up onto a table and showed the room her sparkling purple bra. I'd never met anyone like her. It was flattering, almost. I'd never had anyone chase my friendship before. I'd never had anyone demand my company the way Sylvia did.

The next week, before heading out with some other work colleagues to Chinatown, we went to her place in Carlton and she showed me her artwork. It was paintings, mostly. Colourful with a lot of black.

'Abstract,' she said.

I didn't bother telling her that I had just finished studying two units of art at school and *knew* what abstract was. She nattered on about her classes and drank a bottle of white wine.

Her room had plaster caking off the walls and lots of scarves and big fans nailed on the walls. 'I hate this room,' she said. But she loved it. The floor was worn. It shone. And she had a dream catcher hanging above her sagging double bed.

'Hey,' I said. 'That's so nice.' I pointed at a rearing brass horse on the windowsill.

'That? My sister gave me that. She still lives at *home.*'

'In the country?'

'In the sticks. She trains horses.' She hopped up off the bed. 'C'mon. We'd better scat.'

Sylvia made me forget my aching back, my dismal bank account, the fact that I had no idea what I wanted to do. Mostly when I was away from her I couldn't really fathom why I'd stayed up until three am playing drinking games with her and some guy she liked. But then I'd see her again and I'd end up being awake until four.

She was strange, always startled. Always moving. Things were different when she was around. Terrible alcohol was suddenly drinkable.

Sometimes I try to unpick why I loved spending time with her so much. Looking back, her erratic thinking and irritability and the quick shift she could make from one thing to the next dominate every story. She would ask me questions I'd never been asked before. About what I wanted to do, about what I thought. She listened like what I said mattered. Even at her most unsettled, her most shiftless, Sylvia always listened.

She was thoughtful, when she remembered to be. When she wasn't distracted and moving.

She was different.

All those months, the years, we spent with each other. I don't think I ever really knew her.

* * *

Beatrice sits on the edge of the stable yard fence, watching Jessa lunge Opal. It's dusty, the ground hard-packed in places, boggy in others. Beatrice runs her hands through her hair.

'Jess, you nearly done?'

'She used to buck and rear when Mum lunged her. Now look!' Jessa points at Opal, who snorts and throws her head.

'Did that dress I dropped off end up fitting you?'

'*Trot on! Opal, trot on!* Look at that elevation!' Jessa calls, Opal trotting a perfect circle around her. 'She's gotten even better, even with the gummy hooves!'

'Was thinking we could still get that coffee, if we leave pretty soon.'

'If I rug her she'll go black next summer!'

'C'mon, Jessa. Time to finish up.'

'I'll be able to compete her soon! Just waiting for her topline to build up. That's why Laura said to lunge her and take her out on the trails. It'll help her top line build.'

Beatrice stares at her and Jessa grins back. And when she pulls Opal into the middle of the yard, it's to press a kiss to her nose. 'I love you, beautiful girl,' she says.

Beatrice goes inside while Jessa untacks. She sighs, flops down onto the couch and pats Mac, who wanders up with his tail wagging for a cuddle.

'What's that?' she calls, noticing a dark clucking mass tucked up next to the fireplace.

Bass comes in. 'What's what?'

'*That.*' Beatrice points.

'Oh, that's Peggy Sue.' Bass wanders over. 'Little Australorp Cam found on the road. Ages back now. She's such a character. Keeps getting inside and nesting, but she hates the other chickens.'

'She's nesting?'

'Yeah. Behind the wood heater. Not the sharpest pencil in the box. But that's not what chickens are known for, hey?' He squats down and strokes the chicken's small, dark head. She makes a whingey noise and fluffs her wings. Bass grins and sits down on the couch next to Bea.

'Jessa's untacking,' says Bea.

'Right.'

'She's … she's not that keen on me, is she?' Bea asks, staring down at her hands.

'She's Jessa,' says Bass. 'She's … she's just her own strange, grumpy little person. Always has been. I think being here, being around the horses, I think it helps. But I don't know. They're my kids and mostly it feels like I don't even know them.'

I don't think Bass has ever spoken to Bea like this before. The chicken fluffs out of her nest and he scoops her up, settles her down on his lap.

'Good girl,' he murmurs. 'My old man would roll over in his grave if he saw me with a chicken on my lap. Used to go berserk when I named them.'

'Hmm …'

'Bea? She'll come around. She will.'

* * *

Another day. Henry and Jessa, riding along the bush tracks. Cold and windy, both in jumpers. Everything shooting around them. The bush tracks in spring. Henry is on Pebbles, Jessa is riding Opal.

'She's pretty bold,' Henry says. Opal is playing with the bit, fussing from side to side on the trail. I wish I could tell Jessa to soften her hands, to loosen her legs. Let out the breath she's been holding since I died.

Jessa has wrapped Opal's legs in white bandages. She has polished Opal's bridle and washed all of her white saddle blankets, which had grown dusty and dull sitting in the shed.

Jessa glances at Henry as they approach the Hill, a green expanse leading up to the back of the apple orchards. 'You want to race?'

'Why? We know you'll win.' But Jessa is already cantering Opal on.

* * *

Beatrice didn't tell me about the time I walked in on her until she was twenty-one and I was twenty and golden from Bass.

'He forced himself on me, you know.'

She had just moved to Garras. We were sitting in the grassy memorial park by the café.

It was spring. I remember the prickle of my legs against the jeans I had put on against the morning frost but which had since grown heavy and hot, too thick for the afternoon sun.

'You mean he raped you.' Not a question. How cold it was, to correct her. Self-satisfied. In a glowy haze and removed from such troubling things.

I had, after all, found Bass.

'But I didn't say no.'

Kicking my feet up. Watching them against the sky. My jeans nearly the same colour as the gaps between the clouds. 'A no can be implied. A yes should never be.'

I can't remember what Beatrice did or said after I said that. I am overcome by regret. It clouds the rest of our conversation. I wish I'd hugged her. Told her I was sorry. Raged again how awful men were.

I had been cold. I had been cruel.

And I'd never bothered to bring it up with her. To apologise. To say the things I should have said at the time, all those years ago.

* * *

The same café in town, my favourite, with the old books falling apart in the corners. Where Beatrice lived when she first came to Garras. It is Rafferty and Maggie I am watching. The window is misted up. Maggie's scarf and beanie are on the table next to her mug of hot chocolate.

'And it's like nobody knows how to treat you any more,' Maggie says. 'And you end up feeling bad for them because they're uncomfortable. So you end up trying to make them feel better.'

'Instead of yourself.'

Maggie nods. 'You got it.'

'It's weird, though. When you think about it, everyone's lost someone. You know?'

'It's not just about losing someone, though. I don't think you'd get the same treatment if it was a great-aunt or a ninety-year-old grandma who died in her sleep. It's how you lose someone, I think. More than just losing someone.'

'Your mum ...'

'Yeah?'

Rafferty scratches the back of his neck.

'You can ask me.'

'Did it get easier?'

'Of course it did. Look, there are still days when it really hits me. My mum's dead. You know? She died in a car accident. It doesn't seem real. It *hurts*. But those days get further and further apart. And when they do come, they're less paralysing than they were at the start. And that's not to say that I don't miss her. I do. Every day. But the pain. It comes less and less.'

Rafferty nods. 'Thanks.'

Maggie smiles at him and glances at her watch. 'Shit! It's five. I've gotta run.'

She picks up her wallet but Rafferty shakes his head. 'My shout.'

* * *

Laura comes over early most mornings to help Jessa school Opal. They never talk about it. How Jessa gets up at five to tack her up. How Laura jacked Henry up on her shoulders so that he could fix the floodlighting in the arena.

Sometimes Henry will ride with her. He will ride Gus, who lumbers around like a big ship, or Pebbles, who tries to buck him off. He uses his saddle blanket, the one that Laura gave him a few birthdays ago.

'It's my favourite colour,' he told me on the day. 'This sort of blue.'

Henry, who still let me give him a proper cuddle when he came over, even though he was already thirteen years old.

A dark blue that was almost black. It made me think of the sea at night.

'Don't let your outside rein flap, Jess!' Laura calls, now. She's sitting on the arena fence with a cup of coffee in her hands. It's chilly, her breath coming out in steam. 'Drive her forward! Good! Now, half-halt. Get her off the forehand. Legs on. Half-halt. Good! Soften, Jessa! She's getting it!'

Jessa, grinning. She smells of horse sweat and mud all day at school. She notices but does not mind. She concentrates in the classes she needs to concentrate in. She puts her hand up. She asks questions.

In between, she stares out the window. Her fingers doodle Opal's shape. Again and again. Along the margins of her notebooks.

'You off in ponyland?' says Michaela when she sees Jessa daydreaming.

Jessa making quiet clucking noises with her tongue.

* * *

When I told Beatrice about the sunflowers Bass had given me one year to the day since our first date, she pursed her lips. Summer, sitting in the vacant block next to the café. She was living in her cottage. I remember her hands were icy with the paint she had used for her bathroom.

'They're my favourite,' I say.

'I know,' she snaps.

We sit in silence for a moment. 'Well,' I say. 'You know all about this stuff.'

'What stuff?'

Dumb stuff. 'Different stuff.'

Beatrice glared at me and I shrugged. 'I don't mean it badly.'

'Huh.'

'C'mon. What do sunflowers mean? I know you looked them up in a book.'

Beatrice sniffed and tugged at a tuft of grass. She told me that sunflowers meant faith and healing. Meant luck and longevity. Pleasure. Light. Life.

'Do you think Bass knows?' I asked.

She snorted. 'We look at flowers and try and work out what they mean. Men look at flowers and wonder if they'll score them a blow job.'

* * *

Laura is sitting at the kitchen table with Bass when Jessa gets home. Jessa dumps her schoolbag on an empty seat and goes straight to the fridge.

'Good day, Jess?' Bass asks.

Mouth full of juice, cheeks fat with it, Jessa shrugs and swallows. 'All right, I guess. Where's Henry?'

'Back with his mum,' Bass says, glancing at Laura.

Laura is sitting upright in her chair with her arms crossed. She's picking at something caught in her teeth. She looks untroubled, settled. As she used to look to me when I was alive, when I shared rooms with her and was not just looking in, watching, as I am now. When I look at her now, I can see that she's hurting.

It's her eyes that give her away. They're bloodshot. Watery.

Jessa's whole body slumps. But it's a subtle thing, like a breath let out. I wonder if Bass notices.

'Since when?' she asks, putting the juice down. 'He rode with me this morning! We were going to take Pebbles and Molly out tonight. Before the buyer comes to look at Molly.'

'I got a call at lunchtime. I went and picked him up from school. I just got back from driving him.'

'He had a test this afternoon. He'd been studying all week.'

'Jessa …' Bass says, nodding towards Laura.

'It's not fair, is it?' Laura says. She sighs. 'He'll be back.'

There's a grimness. A tiredness. And Jessa, on the other side of the room, nods and wants to give her a hug. Breathe in her smell of horse and soap and hay.

She almost starts forward, almost leans in towards Laura. But Jessa, whose only contact with another person's flesh and warmth and pulse is waking up in the morning with her hand linked tight with Bass's, is no longer used to hugs.

* * *

One day in the summer I invited Sylvia over to meet my mother. Beatrice was there, sprawled in the garden, reading, still wearing her work shirt. It was early evening.

'This is Sylvia,' I said. 'She's a painter. She's studying art.'

Sylvia was charming with my mother. She complimented all of the paintings my mother had done and asked her about all kinds of things, from the sorts of brushes she preferred to whether she stretched her own canvases. She talked at length about what she was learning in her course, about how she was going to open an art shop with a gallery and studio attached and how she was going to enter into all of these prizes.

My mother poured us green tea. 'Is that so?' she asked whenever Sylvia paused for breath. Bea came in halfway through, raised her eyebrows over Sylvia's head and went to her bedroom.

'Are you sure you can't stay for dinner?' my mother finally asked at eight o'clock.

'No. I've got to go. Plans, you know. But thank you for the tea and showing me your beautiful work.' Sylvia smiled at her and my mother kissed her cheek and we stood at the door and watched her walk off down the street.

'She's great, huh?'

'Is she on drugs?' Bea asked, suddenly, in the hallway.

'No!' I snapped. 'She's just vibrant! She's interesting!'

'She certainly thinks a lot of herself,' my mother said, shutting the flyscreen door and going back into the kitchen.

'You love confident people,' I said.

'Hmm.'

I stared at my mother. I wanted them to like her. Be impressed by her. Be impressed by *me* for making such a charismatic friend. For making friends with someone so beautiful and clever.

Someone with dreams.

I sat down and twirled Sylvia's cup around on the table in front of me. It was a deep disappointment. The sort that leaves a bitter taste in the mouth.

* * *

I watch Bass a lot. At nights, in particular.

Sometimes he will get drunk at the pub and there will be women there I do not recognise. He does not kiss them. Steve is with him mostly, on these nights. Steve orders him a bowl of chips when he's had too much to drink, and drives him home.

When I was alive, I kissed with everything I had. My body, pressed in. My hand dragging him closer. The other tracing his jaw or laced in his hair.

I still think of that woman Bass kissed beside Steve's ute. How they kissed awkwardly, quickly.

It's one of the saddest things I have ever seen.

* * *

Michaela sometimes comes over in the afternoons. She doses up on antihistamines and always sits a little way off from where Opal is tied. She and Jessa talk in yells across the shed, about school and classmates and music.

On this day, the silver birch has a curling of fresh leaves and the grass is shooting up, green and living. There is a sudden loud bang from outside the shed. Opal startles and Michaela pokes her head out into the watery sunlight.

'What is it?' Jessa asks.

'Cameron just backed the quad bike into the compost bins.'

'Oh.' Jessa stops brushing. 'You can tell them apart?'

'Who?'

'My brothers.'

'Of course I can.'

Jessa raises her eyebrows. 'Lots of people can't.'

'Really? It's so easy.'

'How do you tell?' Jessa puts down her brush.

'Rafferty walks around like a grown-up, you know? He sort of strides and holds himself really tall. Even when he's pissed. Cameron hunches and looks down heaps. Like he's a little kid skipping school.'

'Cameron's a wuss.'

Michaela ignores her. 'And their eyes are different. Rafferty always looks sadder.'

'You mean Cameron?'

'No. I mean Raff.'

* * *

There is a man that Beatrice has over every month or so. She sets the table in the same way. She irons the napkins and picks ferns from the garden.

She dusts everything, from the keys on her computer keyboard to the sunlit faces of her wooden venetian blinds.

This man is all sharp angles and quickness. Not fast like a horse galloping up a hill. Quick, like a rainbow lorikeet is quick. Lighting on something and then taking off again. The motion there, but without the power.

He notices things. How she sometimes has a stray dish or a messy coffee table on the days when he happens to come on Jessa's heels.

'Your niece?' It becomes their joke. The first flicker of warmth between them that I have seen.

A bird poos on the window as they do the dishes. 'Your niece?'

An earthquake or a flood or some political upheaval on the news they sometimes watch over dip and biscuits before sitting up at the table. 'Oh. Your niece?'

She will take his jacket, peck his cheek and they eat quietly. He eats quickly. Afterwards she will always wash and he will dry and she will ask if he would like a cup of coffee.

They end up on the couch. They have sex in silence and afterwards he will leave.

One night, on the couch, there is a loud farting noise and Beatrice's embarrassed intake of breath, sharp and damp with tears close by.

'Oh,' he says. There is a pause. 'Your niece?'

And Beatrice bursts out laughing, surprising both of them and causing another farting noise.

These two things I have noticed.

He never gets his coffee.

She has never shown him to her bedroom.

* * *

Steve and Bass are in Steve's truck. They are quiet, not speaking. Between them the radio is muffled and wavering, and the road outside is slick with spring rain. Bass exhales and drums his hands on the dash. He hates being a passenger.

'Thanks for doing this,' Steve says.

'Not a problem. The number of times you've bailed me out.' Bass shakes his head. 'Well, I owe you more than an afternoon.'

Steve frowns. 'You always do that.'

'What?'

'Talk about owing this or owing that. Like doing good stuff comes down to balance sheets.'

Bass is silent, drumming his hands. 'It's more than that. I know. I didn't mean it like that.'

'The other day, when I was picking up that lucerne. I heard you talking to Jessa.'

Bass stops drumming.

'And she was thanking you for letting her sleep in your bed after she woke up from a nightmare.'

'She does that a lot.'

'I know. You've told me. C'mon, mate. When she thanked you, you told her it was okay because she took care of the horses so well, like you owed her. Like letting her come in was doing her a favour. Making you square.'

Bass clears his throat and stares out the window. When he did that whilst I was talking to him, I always imagined he was wishing himself away into one of the paddocks stretching from the crumbling edge of the road.

Steve drops down into a lower gear as the road becomes steeper. 'It's like you're holding back.'

'I told you, I –'

'Not from me,' Steve snaps. 'I'm not talking about me. You'll lose her. You're her parent and you'll lose her.'

* * *

Later that night, Bass takes his hat off and flexes his shoulders, the front windows stained red by Steve's tail-lights as he disappears down the driveway.

Bass's boots are getting cracked again. He leans into Jessa's bedroom. She is asleep, curled into a tight ball. As he watches, a quiver passes through her and she grimaces.

I think, for a moment, that he will say that he loves her. That he is proud of her. That he needs her close at night as much as she needs him.

'You don't owe me anything,' he tells her, pulling the door gently closed.

* * *

It's raining. And I'm watching Rafferty take off his jacket and wrap it around Maggie March, with the long blonde hair and beautiful face. She's smiling at him. That half-smile when a girl has shivered with intent and a boy has, miraculously, taken the hint.

I see her turn her face, so slightly, in order to breathe in the scent of his jacket. Of horse and aftershave and coffee. He is holding her hand.

My boy.

He opens the café door for her.

'Thanks,' she says. Murmurs. Again, with that half-smile.

And Rafferty pauses. He bends, as though to inspect something. I'm the only one who sees the big breath he takes and the way he closes his eyes as he lets it back out.

* * *

When Bass and I met, our love was infused with dirt and roses and laughter. I don't remember sleeping much, or eating. My world was thrilling and filled with light.

We ate peanut butter with spoons. The first thing we did on the farm was set up a little herb garden. I'd wanted to plant my roses, but Bass had been adamant. The grit of the soil. It had been in Bass's family, the farm. For more years than he knew. But nobody had lived there for a very long time. The house was falling apart, slowly disintegrating back into pasture. We had had to mortgage the place to get enough money to repair it.

Bass nudged me. 'Horse poo.'

'What?'

Bass pointed at the raised garden bed. 'Horse poo! It's great for gardens. And we'll have an endless supply once we get the fencing sorted and move Gus over.'

Coriander and basil. Thyme, oregano, rosemary and mint. Sage and chives and parsley. I tended to them, I kept their seeds and when spring came I planted them all over again.

The smell of that little garden bed, when I went out there after dusk or at dawn to water them with water from a bath or a bucket kept in the shower. Jessa and the boys liked to crush the leaves in their hands. They liked to blindfold each other and guess what was being held under their nose.

Bass and I, running out barefoot in the time before the boys came. Basil for a pizza or coriander for a stirfry. Mint for a cocktail or a fruit juice. Chives chopped with cream cheese for a dip. Parsley for a chicken noodle soup that we made each other when colds came. When flus and tonsillitis and ear infections struck.

It lived, that garden. It was alive.

And as I think of this, the dreaming way of it, all I can really think of is Cameron. Of him bending over the steaming stove and murmuring Maggie Carlton's name.

* * *

Jessa helps Bass lug hay lucerne bales into the shed from the delivery truck. I always made her wear long pants when she moved hay. My winter baby, her skin more delicate than the rest of ours. Pale and beautiful.

How she hates it.

The fronts of her thighs are red and raw after moving the half-dozen bales into the shed and stacking them.

Lucerne for summer. It must be getting closer. Close. The pastures are browning off. That's what everyone calls it. Browning. Except it's a bleaching. A whitening. The countryside pales in summer. Becomes a ghost.

'I miss Henry,' she says. Bass glances at her, eyebrows raised, and then he quickly looks away.

'I know, Jess. It's … It sucks.'

Jessa smiles a bit. 'Yeah, it sucks. It just seems so unfair. Like, he has to work so hard to catch up on projects and people are mean –'

'Mean? Who's mean?'

'Oh, just kids at school. They don't bully him. Exactly. But he misses so much and they don't help him catch up, you know?'

'Does the teacher?'

'I mean, he misses the stuff that happens. Who's ... who's with who and who's not talking to who and jokes and stuff. He has to work so bloody hard to fit back in.'

'If I could help Laura keep him here, I would. He wants to go back with his mum, though. He's between a rock and a hard place.'

'I *know*,' she snaps, drums her heels on the hay bale. 'I just miss him. That's all.'

Bass tousles her hair and reaches up to straighten one of the bales.

'Dad,' she says. 'I'm doing better at school.'

He glances up at her. 'I know you are, Jess. It's great.'

Jessa fiddles with a piece of binder twine. 'I don't want to see the counsellor any more. I hate going. I hate having to talk, talk, talk.'

'Jessa ...'

'Please, Dad. I'll work really hard, I promise. I'll do all my homework. Raff's been helping me. And I'll ask the teacher when I don't understand stuff.'

'I think you need to see the counsellor, though. After what you saw ...'

Jessa stamps her foot. 'It's not even me who needs it! It's Raff!'

* * *

Laura is watching television with Cameron and Bass when her mobile rings and she goes out onto the verandah for more coverage.

'Where are you?' Laura asks and Cameron mutes the television.

'Right,' she says, pressing the end call button.

She comes back inside. 'Sylvia's having a meltdown. Need to go get Henry.'

'It's late. I could come? You shouldn't be driving that far.'

'You've got work tomorrow. I'll be fine. It's not the first time,' says Laura.

Bass reddens.

'Drive safe,' says Cameron.

Laura grunts. Her keys clatter when she picks them up. She leaves clumps of dried mud in the hallway as she pulls on her shoes.

As Laura slams her car door shut and Cameron turns the television off mute, Jessa hisses and opens her eyes.

* * *

Steve and Bass are sitting on the verandah, drinking herbal tea. Bass is sitting with his back to the verandah post, looking towards the house. Steve is sitting on the bench, elbows on knees, looking out at the paddock where the cows are starting to mill for their dinner.

'It *is* good,' says Steve. 'Never really drunk tea before. Apart from the milky crap Mum gives me when I go over.'

Jessa tramps out onto the verandah, the door nearly whacking Mac on the nose behind her.

'I'm just going to go. To Laura's,' Jessa says, pulling her boots on.

'She's gone to pick up Hen.'

'I know. But for when they get back.'

'Jess, just stay here, hey?'

'Why?' She throws her boot onto the verandah and turns her whole body to face him. I wonder when she became so combative. She has always had it in her, that fierceness. That stubbornness. But it has morphed into something heavier. The world, for her, is one long battle. Each little thing something over which to wage war.

'He'll be tired. He'll have had a rough time, I reckon,' says Steve. 'Why don't you shoot Loz a text and ask them for dinner or something? So if they're not tired they know they can come over.'

Jessa softens a little at that. 'Okay,' she says. She gives her father a deeply unimpressed look and goes back inside.

'She's a handful,' Bass murmurs under the sound of her feet stomping up the stairs.

Steve smiles. 'She sure is.'

'Actually, she said something weird the other day.'

'Hmm?'

'She said it wasn't her who needed therapy. She said it was Raff.'

'What do you reckon about that?'

'I think she's lying. She doesn't want to see the counsellor any more. And you know Raff, he's doing great. He's doing better than any of us.'

'Have you talked to him about it?'

'Not yet.'

'Well, you need to.'

Bass swills a mouthful of tea. Sighs. 'I know.'

* * *

Something occurs to me as I watch Bass. He is watching Rafferty closely. Rising from the table when Rafferty rises, seeking out the sofa when Rafferty is watching television. Rafferty glances sideways at him a few times, but otherwise he doesn't respond. Doesn't comment on Bass's sudden attentiveness.

It occurs to me that Bass is scared of Rafferty. This one child he thought was doing okay.

When Rafferty catches him over dinner, Bass looks away and Rafferty glances at Jessa, who glares back. And Cameron watches them all with that worried expression he gets and they eat quietly.

'Henry and Laura didn't come,' Jessa says. When nobody says anything she scowls and stuffs too much spinach into her mouth.

Fucking speak! I try to yell. *Fucking talk to each other! Just now! Just once! Just fucking SPEAK.*

Nobody looks around, nobody stops chewing. Except Rafferty who, for a moment, shivers and closes his eyes.

* * *

Jessa is hunched at the kitchen table. The following morning, with last night's dishes still piled next to the sink. She is writing on lined paper, her copy of Hamlet by her elbow. It is dog-eared, marked with her messy handwriting. She mutters swearwords under her breath, but when she finishes each paragraph her mouth quirks up into something like a smile.

When Henry comes into the kitchen she startles and her pen skids onto the floor.

'Sorry,' he says. 'Watcha doing?'

She stretches down for the pen. 'Homework. You're back!'

'Loz picked me up last night. Only just woke up.'

'Oh.' Jessa fiddles with the cover of *Hamlet*. 'Is she okay?'

'No,' he says shortly.

Jessa sits a little straighter and opens her books back up. 'Well, I can't ride yet. And Molly got sold.'

'I know. Laura said you weren't answering the phone and she needs the number for Glen Mitchell.'

'Who?'

'That orthopaedic farrier your mum used when Opal was a yearling.'

Jessa sighs and goes to shut her book, but Henry grabs her wrist. 'No. You're right in the middle. Finish what you're doing. I'll wait for five.'

Jessa nods. 'Thanks.'

Henry sits and drums his fingers for a minute, before his gaze settles on the dirty dishes in the sink. It is half an hour later by the time they leave the kitchen. Jessa has finished the last two paragraphs of her essay and all the dishes are washed, dried and packed away in a kitchen Henry knows as well as Laura's.

Upstairs, when Jessa bends over to rummage in a low drawer, Henry stares carefully out the window. She frowns into the drawer and eventually pulls out a scrap of paper.

She copies down the number and hands it to Henry. 'Here.'

He squints at it. 'I can't read your handwriting.'

'Laura can. She mastered cursive before she left primary school.'

'Good someone has,' he says, squinting at the dangling piece of paper.

Jessa glares at him.

Henry points at the flowers on her bedside table. Cameron gave them to her. I can tell because they are tied with a bow that has only one loop. Jessa calls them wings.

'You pick them?'

'Piss off.'

'I didn't know you liked flowers.'

'I *don't*.'

He cocks his head. He is pretending nonchalance, but I can see how carefully he is watching her, even as he grins lazily and shoves the piece of paper into his frayed pocket. 'Why they in your room, then?'

Jessa feigns a lunge towards him and he ducks, grinning. Then his grin fades and he sits down on the corner of her bed. 'I'm staying here.'

'What?'

'In Garras. I'm staying.'

'Oh. What about your mum?'

Henry shrugs. 'I just can't,' he says. 'I can't do it any more.'

Jessa reaches over, hesitates and then squeezes his shoulder. 'Sorry.'

He shrugs and Jessa clears her throat.

'My nan's coming,' says Jessa. 'For Christmas.'

'I like your nan.'

'She's bossy.'

'So are you. See ya,' he says, standing up and walking out the door.

She watches Henry through the window. She sticks her head out. 'Bush tracks?' she yells.

Henry gives her a thumbs-up without turning around.

That night, she sleeps in her own bed. She sleeps in her own bed through the night, without hissing or rising to join Bass in the bed that is now just his.

And when she wakes, and there's sun and she's under her horse competition ribbons and she can see Pebbles and Gus through the window, she smiles so hard it looks like she's on the verge of crying.

* * *

Rafferty is bent, swearing, over his business textbooks. He's hunched on the couch. I'd always made him move, when he studied there. And he's studying so much more, these days. He glances up as Jessa sits down next to him and switches on the television.

'I'm studying,' he says.

'It's your birthday! Dad says we're leaving in halfa. Screw study – watch something till it's time to go.'

'No.'

194

Jessa rolls her eyes and switches it off. 'Only coz it's your birthday. What's with all the studying, anyway?'

'Exams, idiot.'

'But, like, in general. You're studying more.'

Rafferty puts the book down. 'You know the feed store?'

Jessa nods.

'I don't want to work there for the rest of my life.' He sits back. 'Don't get me wrong, Reggie is brilliant and I've learnt heaps, but I don't think it's for me, you know?'

Jessa frowns, wraps her arms around herself.

'And I have no idea where I'll end up. And maybe all this study won't get me in anywhere, anyway. But it's worth a shot. I'm trying.'

Jessa stares at him.

'What?'

'Nothing. Just sometimes you remind me of Mum.'

* * *

Bass can't decide on a bull. He and Laura and sometimes Steve pore through the local papers, the studbooks online, the market sales.

The agricultural shows.

'I don't know,' says Bass. 'I just don't know. Does this mean this is all a bad idea?'

'No,' says Laura. 'It just means you haven't found what you're looking for. Look harder. He'll be there.'

* * *

The farm is yellow and wavering. My mother wears voluminous pants and strappy sandals and kisses Bass on both of his cheeks. Raff, Guy, Jake and Jessa are watching her from the shed.

'Your nan doesn't look old,' says Guy.

'You are such a *fucking* creep,' says Jake, shaking his head. 'How the hell am I related to you?'

Jessa smiles, leans in so that her arm is brushing Jake's.

'She looks so *clean*,' says Rafferty. He turns to the other three. 'Don't you think she looks *clean*?'

'She probably knows how to use bleach,' says Jessa.

'She looks clean,' says Guy. 'And *young*.'

Jake cuffs him over the ears. 'Would you knock it off?'

'Are you guys staying for dinner?' Jessa asks, looking up at Jake.

'Nah. Got something on. With Von and Davo. But thanks.' Jake smiles at her.

'Man, my shoulders are killing me,' says Rafferty.

'You're too weedy for manual labour,' says Guy, staring at him. 'You should work in a café. With pipes sticking out the walls. One of those disgustingly hipster places.'

'Uh huh,' says Raff, rotating his shoulder.

'They'll build up,' says Jake. 'You'll see.'

'How do you know?' asks Jessa.

Rafferty stares at her. 'He worked at the feed store, remember? All through high school. Your brain's like a sieve.'

'You're an arsehole.'

Guy slow claps. '*Brilliant* comeback, young Jessa. *Inspiring*.'

'Our brothers are dicks,' she says to Jake.

'You're fucking telling *me*.'

They wander inside where Bass absently makes everyone hot milk with cinnamon.

'Shit, I'm sorry,' he says when he realises.

'It's good. Delicious,' says Guy.

Raff sets his aside. 'Hot milk in summer. Yum.'

My mother stares around at them, grinning that smile of hers that always used to make me roll my eyes. *What?*

'Where's the Christmas tree?' she asks.

Bass glances wildly around and his foot starts tapping. Rafferty grins at her. 'We were waiting for *you*, of course! We're getting it today. Right, Dad?'

'Right. Yup. Right.'

'Dad's getting a special bull,' says Raff.

'A … special bull?'

'And Jessa says if I lock her in the chicken coop ever again she'll glue my dick to my leg.'

'I see.'

Bass rubs the bridge of his nose. 'Raff, go do the dishes.'

'There aren't any.'

'Go get the Christmas tree, then.'

'My car's nonexistent and I'm unlicensed.'

Jake laughs, claps Raff on the shoulder. 'No worries. We'll take mine.'

'I'm coming,' says Jessa.

'No, you're going to do something with your nan, while she's here,' says Bass.

'Sure.' Jessa's shoulders slump and she watches Jake and Rafferty disappear around the side of the house, talking loudly.

'I'm not that much of a boring old biddy, am I?'

'No! No, of course not.'

My mother winks at Jessa, nods towards the front of the house, where Jake has just disappeared. 'He's *quite* handsome, isn't he?'

'You're very clean,' says Guy.

* * *

Watching my mother in my house, I think that my parents were not always quiet. My father not always preoccupied with his work and newspaper.

I remember them sitting outside on the verandah, holding hands.

I remember my father flinging my mother around the living room, bellowing a Beatles song. The sound of her laughing.

Sometimes I confuse these memories with Bass and I.

Thinking of my parents as happy as us. It leaves a strange taste.

* * *

Tonight, Yvonne and Davo fight and Yvonne goes and stays with her sister. Guy and Jake settle in for the night. Bea comes over, and Henry and Laura. The tree is mostly brown and missing branches. My mother, who has her own fat little pine tree which she brings in each year from the porch, blinks at it.

'It's such a character,' she says. She has Rafferty's guitar in her lap. 'I've taken to putting sunglasses on my tree.'

'Thought a sophisticated city lady might appreciate a good drop,' Jake says, waving a couple of bottles of wine at my mother.

'Oh! Penfolds! Can't say I'm sophisticated, but I do love a good bottle of white. You know your wine.'

'I certainly do.' Jake grins. Nods at the guitar. 'You play?'

'Not even a little bit well.'

'Give it a go!' Rafferty calls.

My mum starts strumming it and I see Jake wince. 'Not bad,' he says.

They can't find the Christmas CD. I try to yell that it's in the sideboard cupboard, where it's been for the last twelve years. Rafferty pauses by the sideboard, rests a hand on top of it. He shakes his head and sits down, pulling Peggy Sue from where she's roosting on top of the wood heater and onto his lap.

Soon they start playing Paul Kelly and that seems enough. It seems just right.

Riesling. My mother's favourite. The smell of her perfume. She inhales it, sighs. And, for a moment, looks sad.

Bass can't find any fairy lights and only a handful of decorations, so they end up cutting stars out of tinfoil and Rafferty glues a face onto a toilet roll and sticks it up on top.

My mother can't stop laughing.

'What's funny?' Bea asks.

'The tree! Would you look at that tree? Cate would've *loved* that demented tree! Thank you so much for pretending you'd waited for me. I've had a blast.' My mother stretches and sets her wineglass aside.

'Is it wonky?' Laura tilts her head. 'It looks wonky.'

'It's wonky. Coz of the gum branches Guy stuck in.'

'It's Australian. It's *artistic*,' says Rafferty. 'I like it, Guy.'

'You're a true friend, Rafferty Carlton.' They nod at each other and Henry snorts. He's nursing a mug with a splash of Riesling my mother insisted he try.

Laura points at Jake. 'Say, you wouldn't happen to be the boy that Reggie said I *had* to hire for property maintenance, now, would you?'

Jake laughs. 'I worked for Reggie for years.'

'Thought so. You look familiar.'

'I find most people do, around here. Don't know all their names for shit, though.'

Jessa sits on the couch, staring out the window, her cheek propped up on her hand.

'You right, my love?' my mother asks.

Jessa nods, smiles. 'Just watching Opal,' she says.

* * *

Christmas morning is quieter than the night before. Jessa stays in her own bed, but is restless and gets up a little after five to sit on the verandah with her knees up under her T-shirt.

My mother sleeps gently, peacefully. She does not stir until the rooster starts crowing. She sighs, opens her eyes. She looks sad for a minute and closes them again.

'Just in case you're floating around somewhere, I love you. I think about you every day. Your children are beautiful. I miss you.' She opens her eyes again, gets out of bed and starts getting ready for the day.

I wonder how often she talks to me. I spend hardly any time with my mother. Fleeting moments. The way her brush slides over a canvas. Steam rising off a bowl of vegetables, for one. The music she plays in the car when she drives. The same three CDs. Over and over again.

I wonder if my mother is lonely. I wonder if she wishes my family lived closer. I wonder if she ever thinks of moving to Garras. I doubt she would. Being close to all the art galleries has always been important to my mother. She called it having her finger on the pulse.

They eat breakfast on the verandah. Rafferty has put reindeer antlers on Pebbles and brought him into the kitchen. My mother startles when she sees him.

'Can Guy and Jake come over?' says Raff, peering down at his phone. 'Their mum's still at her sister's.'

'The more the merrier,' says my mother, sitting down at the table, carefully avoiding Pebbles, who is trying to chew his way through a bag of bread on the table. 'Cheeky pony!'

They had said no presents, but Cameron presses flowers into Jessa's palm and Jessa has woven both boys a bracelet and oiled Bass's boots for him.

When Laura and Henry come by for brunch she runs out and stops Henry on the verandah.

'Merry Christmas,' he says.

'Merry Christmas.' She shoves a leather notebook at him, runs back inside.

Henry opens it slowly. My name is on the first page. The rest are blank. Henry grips it tightly and goes inside.

'For your recipes,' says Jessa. 'And your pen drawing things.'

He goes to hug her but she darts away. 'C'mon. Let's go do Opal before the boys get here.'

The book, Henry sets it carefully on the sideboard in the living room. I bought it just before I died.

A lurch.

It was going to be for my memories.

* * *

When my mother leaves the next day, Jessa hangs on to her for a long hug.

'Jessa?' my mother says.

'Hmm?'

'I think, if you're up for it, it would be very lovely for you to spend some more time with Bea.'

Jessa stiffens.

'It would mean a lot to her. She misses your mum. Just like the rest of us.' Jo kisses Jessa's head.

Afterwards, Jessa goes and sits in the shed and buries her head in a half-empty feedbag of oaten chaff.

'Jessa?'

She pulls her head out of the bag. 'What?'

'Here.' Bass has an awkwardly wrapped present in his hands.

She stares at it. 'No presents.'

Bass snorts.

'You're a day late,' she says, sitting up.

'I thought … I dunno. I just felt like I needed to wait.

Here.' He hands the present to her and sits down on a barrel by the door. Jessa unwraps it.

My tall laced riding boots. Jessa swallows hard.

'Reckon they'll just about fit you,' says Bass quietly.

'Yeah, I reckon,' she says, not looking up.

They sit there for a while, not speaking. Jessa running her hands along the leather of the boots.

'Well,' he says.

'Well what?'

'Do I get to see them on?'

Jessa struggles out of her old sagging boots and steps into my tall ones. Bass smiles, almost sadly but not quite. On the very edge of sad, but held there.

'They look great,' he says.

'Thanks, Dad.'

'C'mon. I'll make you a Milo. Then we can move the cows.'

Jessa groans and he tousles her hair. 'Just kidding,' he says as they walk out into the yard. 'Let's go eat crap and watch a movie. Think Raff has a Twisties stash in the sideboard.'

* * *

Jessa begins to teach Opal the difference between a working trot, a medium trot, a collected trot, an extended trot. She teaches her how to counter-canter. How to do a flying change in the middle of the arena. With Laura raising the jump poles higher and higher on the grids dragged into place, Jessa teaches Opal how to jump.

'I'll have to start putting her into the float when I have comps on,' says Laura. 'You'd be happy to do that, hey?'

Jessa shrugs, feigns nonchalance, but she can't stop grinning.

'How high was that one?'

'A metre, a metre ten, on the outside. You're doing great with her. Your mum would be so proud.'

Jessa smiles and presses a kiss to Opal's mane. 'Dad could still sell her,' she says.

'I think he's doing everything he can not to, Jess. C'mon, pick up the canter. Let's go through this grid one more time.'

Jessa learns that Opal can soothe her. That dipping her hands into dirt, that breathing in Opal's cheek, can be enough to alleviate whatever darkness is inside her.

Kissing that velvet place between cheek and nostril, Jessa learns to breathe.

* * *

Bass sits at the computer for fifteen minutes, toying with weather sites and playing solitaire. This man, who sits at the computer only under sufferance.

He glances behind him. Once. Twice.

Jessa is out with Michaela, slurping chocolate milkshake with a straw and marvelling at the even curls of Michaela's hair. Rafferty is slashing the grass around the house. Cameron is running through the back parts of Garras, listening to The Beatles through his earphones.

Bass types in *woman*. He types in *vagina*. He considers the two words, the blinking cursor. Then he types in *sexy*.

He clicks on the first site that comes up. The screen is filled with flashing fonts, sultry women with their legs spread for penises and dildos.

Bass hits escape. Presses the computer off. He sits there, staring at the blank screen. Glancing, once more, over his shoulder. The slasher is still roaring on the other side of the house.

Bass holds his breath for a moment then slams his fist down next to the keyboard. And his anger is so alien, so unfamiliar, that I find myself suddenly watching Rafferty, who is turning the slasher off. He takes off his gloves and is dusting his hands when he walks into the lounge room.

Bass startles and strides off into the kitchen, where he starts rattling things around, making a coffee.

'Dad?'

'What?'

'Bea called before. She's really excited about the Mulders'.'

'Good.'

'You invited her to the Mulders'? For New Year's?' Rafferty sits down backwards on one of the chairs and props his chin in his hand.

'Yeah, why?'

'She's … she's *Bea*. The Mulders have their party in a *barn*. There's one toilet and the floor has cow shit on it. She'll probably have a breakdown and start sweeping at five to midnight.'

'She didn't have any plans,' says Bass, sitting down with a glass of warm milk. There is no cinnamon so he has sprinkled ginger on it. 'She asked me what we were doing. What was I supposed to say?'

'You say, we're going to the Mulders'. There's lots of cow shit. You have a nice night elsewhere, now. Then you smile, pat her on the head and walk away.'

Bass rolls his eyes. 'When did you get so twerpy?'

'Think I've always been like this,' says Raff. 'Mum always said so anyway.'

Bass sips his milk, grimaces. 'Remind me to get more cinnamon, would you? Yeah, you've always been a twerp. You really think it's a bad idea? Her coming? I just … She's trying so hard and Cate was such a rock to her and I think she's feeling a bit … I dunno.'

'Adrift?'

Bass glances at Raff. 'Yeah. Exactly. Adrift. I'm worried she feels adrift.'

'It's not that bad an idea, really. She might even have fun. Just tell her not to wear stilettos.'

* * *

Jessa and Beatrice, wandering down the shiny well-lit corridors of Rosella Shopping Centre. Beatrice has her hair out and is already carrying an armful of glossy bags. She looks relaxed, happy almost.

'What are you doing tonight?' Jessa asks.

'Coming with you! Your dad invited me.'

Jessa stops walking. 'You're coming to the Mulders'?'

'Yeah.' Bea glances sideways. 'What?'

'Nothing! Nothing. Wear gumboots.'

'Are you joking?'

'Yeah. Yup. I'm joking. This is nice.' Jessa points out a conservative green dress with a high neck and low hem. 'For you, I mean.'

'I think I've well and truly got enough. Just remind me to get some nail polish on the way out. What sort of dress are you looking for? In particular?'

Jessa shrugs. 'I dunno. A dress.'

'Formal? Semiformal? Cocktail?'

'I dunno! Something for New Year's. Something for in the Mulders' barn.'

'Semiformal, then. Do you have shoes?'

'Yeah.'

'To wear with the dress?'

'Uh. No.'

'Okay. We'll get some shoes after we find the right dress. What colour are you thinking?'

'Blue. Dark blue.'

* * *

When we had been together for three years, Bass again gifted me an armful of sunflowers. They were pressed from his palm to my palm. My hands were sticky with avocado and cheeses. I was pregnant with the boys, feeling huge and always hungry.

'What do you think a sunflower means?' I asked.

He grinned that cheeky grin that lit up his eyes and softened his face. 'Well,' he said. 'That's easy. Pretty sure they mean the sun.'

* * *

New Year's Eve. Posters up in the main street of Garras as they drive through. Shops, closed early. The pub brimming with people making an early start on the festivities.

Jessa, climbing out of Michaela's mother's car at the start of our driveway.

'I can drive you up, hun,' says Michaela's mother. I can't remember her name.

'Nah. I'm okay. I like the walk. Thanks, though.' Jessa closes the door, grinning as Michaela pulls faces at her. Jessa watches as the car pulls away back down the road and then trudges up the driveway towards the house.

The house is quiet. Rafferty is at a friend's place in town, playing video games. Cameron is out running.

Jessa puts her bags down on the kitchen table. She's at the kitchen sink, pouring herself a glass of water, when she sees them.

Steve and her father.

Hugging near the chicken coop.

* * *

'Sorry,' Bass's voice is unsteady as he draws away from Steve's hug. 'It just hits me sometimes, you know? Even now.' He wipes his eyes.

'I think it's called being human,' says Steve.

They leave the side of the chicken coop. They start sorting through Bass's screwdriver set, packing them into the wooden case he has for them. Jessa is up in her room, throwing her dirty laundry into a basket and kicking her shoes across the floor.

'I need to sell her,' Bass says.

Steve shakes his head. 'You can't.'

'We need the money. Bank's getting shitty I've pulled everything out of the overdraft. Even selling the other horses hasn't helped as much as I'd hoped. And I'm still paying off the funeral.'

'Thought Cate's mum paid?'

'I'm paying her back.'

Steve breathes out and shakes his head. 'You'll come up with another way, mate. It's not worth it. Jessa'd be happier if you cut her arms off. You can't take Opal away from her. You just … can't.'

* * *

Henry ducks under Opal's neck. Dusty. He runs his hands through her mane and they come away grey and sticky with dirt and dried skin. Warm. Earthy. He is sweating in the sunlight, a glow to his forehead. The sky is cloudless.

Jessa, still on Opal's other side, is shaking her head, muttering.

'What is up with you?' Henry asks.

'Nothing!'

'You're so … What's wrong?'

'Nothing, I said!' Jessa flings her brush down onto the ground and drags the box closer so forcefully that Opal skitters sideways.

Henry pats Opal's neck. Soothes her. 'You're being so aggressive!'

'What the hell? Who even asked you?'

'I'm not attacking you,' Henry says. 'I just mean you're so …'

'Aggressive's the word you just used, arsehole.'

'It's not what I mean, though. Not really. Can you just listen? Like, tightly wound.'

Jessa rolls her eyes. 'Oh, much better.'

'Angry, Jessa. Okay? Angry.'

She stops brushing. 'Angry?'

'Yeah.'

She stares at him and he picks up a currycomb and starts cleaning the body brush he was using.

'Fucking arsehole.'

She scrubbed hard at Opal's coat, until the mare pinned her ears and stamped her foot on the hard-packed dirt.

'Are … are you going tonight?'

'Where?' she snaps.

'The party at the Mulders' place.'

'Maybe.' Her new blue dress, laid out on her bed. The colour of Henry's favourite saddle blanket.

'I'm going,' he says.

'Figured.'

'Do you …?'

She stops brushing. 'What?'

'Nothing.'

'I'm not angry,' she says.

Henry opens his mouth. Then closes it again.

* * *

The boys disappeared one afternoon. They were four and I'd left them in the living room to go to the toilet and start dinner.

When I came back the house was silent and the door was open.

I screamed. I'm not sure if it was out loud or in my head. But I remember the sound of my scream more than anything else. Its shrillness, how it encapsulated every shooting nerve, every pulse of suddenly unsettled blood.

I went running around the outside of the house. I checked the dam. I ran down the driveway to the road. I was running to the shed when I found them.

One on each of Bass's knees, making whips with bailing twine and gum branches.

'What?' he said.

They were so calm, while all I could hear was the pounding of my heart, my fingers slick with palm sweat.

And I had this strange sensation of looking in on my life. Of being absent.

* * *

Jessa has scrubbed her hands clean and put on some of the pearl-coloured nail polish that Bea bought her at the shops. She dabs perfume on her wrists, behind her ears and in the crooks of her elbows. She dabs it between her breasts.

Jessa needing a bra. It seems strange, still. Sometimes when I catch a glimpse of her shape, I have to remind myself that it is her. The new curves, the cleavage. Jessa, fitting into my boots. It's startling.

She plaited her hair tightly after her shower this morning and now gently unbraids it, pinning it away from her face the way she has seen Michaela do for parties and dinners.

A loud snapping noise. A cracker set off at the house next door.

Jessa pulls on the short blue dress that Beatrice bought for her and stands side on, breathing in her already concave stomach and pressing out her chest. She hears a sound. A jangle of metal and hoof on the driveway.

She is running before she has registered what it is. Before she has the words. Because she is Bass's daughter. She is a Carlton. And her breath is catching before she has reached the bottom of the landing, before she has seen Cameron unmoving in the middle of the yard. Before she has seen Rafferty, edging slowly to the shuddering dark shadow, pressed too tight against the barbed-wire fence line.

Jessa opens her mouth and screams. '*Opal!*'

Her voice sends a tremble through Cameron, who still doesn't take a step. Rafferty makes no sign that he has heard her.

'Opal!' Jessa says, quieter this time. Stopping a few steps shy of Rafferty.

'She's hurt, Jess,' Rafferty says. His voice is quiet and calm. *There's no milk in the fridge, Jess. Might have to have toast instead of cereal.*

Jessa's breath has been caught since she was on the stairs. She draws a heavy breath in and closes her eyes.

'I left the gate open.' Cameron has stumbled forward. Jessa shrugs him off, her eyes fixed on Opal. 'I'm so sorry,

Jessa. I left the gate of the yard open. I must've. I must've when I went to give them their hay. Her and Pebbles. And …'

'Shush,' Jessa says.

'She won't let me any closer,' Rafferty says.

Jessa holds a hand up to him. A slim finger, still not turning away from her horse.

The horse, lying on her side. Her back leg angled strangely behind her.

'Raff, I didn't mean to,' Cameron says. 'I just –'

'Cameron, don't,' says Raff, glancing over at him.

'But, I –'

'Cameron, just be quiet, all right? Just *don't*.'

'Someone get me a torch,' Jessa says. The fist illuminated by the house light is clenched. If she were not a metre away from the shuddering animal, she'd be swearing. Yelling.

Rafferty takes off at a run and by the time he has come back, Jessa is lying down by Opal's neck, crooning to her and scratching her wither. Her face buried in Opal's mane.

Rafferty lets his breath out. 'I told you it was bad.'

Jessa clears her throat. 'I need to see.'

'Jess …'

'Shine the torch.'

'Jessa, you don't need to. We need to call the vet and …'

She looks at him. Her expression is closed and sharp and he shakes his head, lifting the torch.

The wire has taken the skin and muscle off one leg. The bone gleams more pinkly than the moon. The leg, broken and strangely crooked.

'Fuck,' Cameron breathes, staggering back to the trunk of the tree. He retches loudly at the base of it.

'I'll go get Paul's number,' Rafferty says.

'No.'

'Laura's then …'

Jessa is breathing hard. Shaking her head. 'It's not fair.'

'Nothing's fucking fair. We can't just leave her. Let me get Dad back here. He'll know what to …'

Jessa ignores him. She leans her head into Opal's mane and breathes in. A deep breath, the smell of which she will always remember as the taste of her greatest sorrow.

The taste of her greatest joy.

'I love you,' she whispers into the flickering ear.

She stands up and is striding back to the house. Cameron, still by the tree. Rafferty, torch dropped. He runs.

'Jessa, don't you dare!'

She is faster than him and the gun, which Bass keeps for this very reason in a locked box, on a shelf in the study, is soon cocked in her hand.

She keeps it pointed to the ground as she goes back outside. If she had had it lifted, Rafferty, in his running, would have been within her range.

'Jessa, give it here.'

'No.'

'Jessa, I'll do it. Give me the fucking gun!' He makes a grab for it. She shakes him off.

'Fuck off! Are you crazy? Let go!' She is crying now.

He puts his hands up. 'Jessa, I'll do it. You love her. You can't. Just give me the fucking gun. You won't get over this.'

'I won't get over it anyway.' Jessa stops by Opal's neck and reaches down. She brings her dirty hands to her nose and breathes in. The smell of the dirt steadies her grip on the gun.

'Jessa …' Rafferty stops. 'Let me help you. Please.'

The gunshot is heard by most of the people in the area. Not a single person thinks it anything other than another early firecracker.

* * *

Bass hears the second early firecracker and the sound seems to slide down him like a droplet of water. Bass always came earlier, to the party. It happened every year. He would help the Mulders set up and we'd meet him there later.

Ken, with whom he once worked a dairy farm, nudges him. 'You right?'

'Yeah. Yeah, fine.'

The old shed has been strung with fairy lights and, judging by the clouds of smoke, reeks of citronella and dope. He finds himself blinking more and more slowly until all he wants to do is put his head down on the table and close his eyes.

This barn. Where he told me he had his first kiss, pressed up against the corrugated iron. This barn, where he had kissed fiercely and first pressed his fingers up and into that wet and warm place.

Rafferty has not changed his clothes. He is splattered with blood. Only two people notice. Bass spills his beer on the floor. He had been sitting with Laura in a quiet corner of the barn, with two bottles of beer. They'd been laughing, when Raff came in. Bass's hand had been on her leg.

Henry, in the middle of spiking the punch with Laura's vodka, comes running.

Bass grabs Rafferty around the back of the neck, as he used to do when Rafferty and Cameron were small. Were young. He steers Rafferty back out of the shed and into the paddock, which is hazy with gunpowder.

'What the hell happened?'

'Jessa shot Opal.'

Henry reaches them. 'Is Jessa okay?'

Bass closes his eyes. 'Why would she …?'

Laura comes out at a run. 'What's happened?'

'Jessa shot Opal,' Rafferty says. 'Cameron didn't shut the yard gate properly when he fed out tonight. Opal was out front and when she heard the crackers she tried to jump the fence. Pebbles is still out somewhere. But Opal. Broke a leg.'

'Did you get on to Paul?' Bass asks.

Rafferty shakes his head. 'She … she wouldn't let me. She wouldn't let me call anyone. She got your gun. I couldn't stop her.'

'Where is she now?'

'With Opal. I tried to get her away but she hit me.'

'Is Cameron with her?' Laura asks.

'He's at home, if that's what you mean.'

'Okay. I've had a bit to drink. I'll need someone to drive me.'

Rafferty holds out his hand. 'I'll drive. I can chuck the bike in the tray.'

'You've been drinking?'

Rafferty shakes his head. 'No. Not this year.'

Bass hesitates. Hands over the keys into his son's bloodied hands.

Laura looks at him. She looks tired. Suddenly exhausted. 'Where's the gun?'

'I took it off her. After. She let me, then. I took the ammo out of it.' He rattles his pocket.

I focus on Laura, realising.

There is so little to be done, so little she can do to help Jessa. To help any of them. She can't even help Henry, who disappears back to the city. Sylvia, who can't take care of him or of herself.

Laura sighs. Claps Rafferty on the shoulder. He flinches but reaches up to touch her hand.

'I'm sorry,' she says.

He doesn't say anything, but I see his fingers squeeze hers.

* * *

Laura, who has gone running to the city when Sylvia calls for far longer than Henry has been alive.

Once, we'd been sitting out on her verandah when the phone had rung. I'd stared Laura hard in the face, after. 'Why do you do it? She's not a little kid. She's a big girl. Same as me.'

'She's *not* you, though,' Laura said. 'She's stupid. Does stupid things, I mean. Gets into jams with dodgy people.'

'I know,' I said curtly. 'But … you can't save her forever.'

'I'm her big sister. Of course I fucking can.'

It was a tidal thing. The overexcited phone calls, the tense absence of her. Waiting for the next big plan, the next big thing. Then the tears, the yelling, the unanswered phone calls turning the absence into something sharp and slick. Something with edges.

Laura, exhausted. Out at competitions and teaching at riding clinics and riding her own horses. Sylvia had to go to rehab. Sylvia had a stalker. Sylvia got busted up pretty bad in a brawl.

'Is she mentally ill, do you think?' I asked one day.

'Of course she bloody is. I've tried to get her help but she never sticks at it. She's impossible.'

Sylvia had tried to keep in contact with me, after I came to the farm and settled down with Bass. It was sporadic, but for Sylvia it was a lot of effort. I went to the city regularly, just after I moved here. Spent weekends sleeping on her floor or in her bed if she'd picked up and gone to someone else's house.

'Here,' she'd said. Giving me a beautiful painting when I turned twenty-one. Of silver and blue and soaring shapes and shadows. It's up in the spare room. It's beautiful, but it always unsettled me. Made me uneasy. And I couldn't tease the painting from the painter. So I hung it out of sight. And twinged with guilt when I saw it.

I got back to her less and less. Particularly after the children were born. I was ashamed, I think. Of how much I had looked up to her. Of how much she had dazzled me. By how much I had been swept up by the glamour. Now all I could see was the murk and dark reflections. She was damaged, selfish. Watching Laura trying to help her – fix her – had made me hurt with sadness.

There was a court date. Something about possession. Henry stayed with Laura for a full six months while it was getting sorted out, and when he went back to the city again, Laura spent weeks crying. Never in front of me, never in front of anyone, I don't think. But her eyes were red and her face was puffy and blotchy from too much crying.

Laura, who introduced me to Bass at the Savannah Hotel in Garras that night. Whose bluntness had startled me, in the beginning. I had been a little scared, a little in awe of her.

Laura, right from the start, seemed as though she had it all figured out. She was methodical; she was honest. There was so little unexpected about her. No shocks. Just warmth, just routine.

I laughed more with Laura, in those early days in Garras, than I had ever laughed with anyone before. So different from Sylvia, who never stopped exhausting me, who never stopped being unpredictable.

Who never stopped terrifying me.

Laura, her back aching as she trimmed all our horses' feet. As she got up at five o'clock to hunt for Opal and then to help Jessa learn to ride her.

I wonder, who has gotten up at five o'clock for her? Who has bent, aching, over her horses' feet for nothing but a cup of cinnamon and warm milk?

* * *

Cameron is sitting on the verandah steps, head in hands. He doesn't look up when the car pulls in. Laura touches his shoulder.

'Is Jessa okay?' Bass asks.

'Where is she?' Laura shrugs past Bass without waiting for an answer.

'I don't know,' Cameron says. His voice is hoarse and thick.

Laura, heavy with drink, is nevertheless the quickest up the stairs. The shower is running. She slams the bathroom door open, making Jessa jump.

'What the hell are you doing?' Jessa snaps.

'I just … You're okay.'

'I'm getting the blood off me. Jesus, what did you think I was doing?'

After a moment of silence Jessa turns off the tap and Laura passes her a towel. Jessa wraps herself in it and steps out of the shower. Her face is pale and blotchy.

'I'll never forgive him,' she says. 'Ever.'

* * *

Dead livestock on a farm means a visit from the knackery truck. Our land is precious. Our land belongs, must belong, to the living. To us. To the animals still feeding off it. The crops.

There cannot be sentimentality on a farm, even one as small as ours.

But already I know that, on this one occasion, Bass will yield.

That he will dream of his daughter cocking the gun

towards her horse and pressing the trigger. Again and again. Over and over. Cold sweats. Waking in the night.

It will change him.

* * *

The boys sleep with Henry on the floor between them. Henry breathes softly, breathes evenly. He sleeps through the echo of the firecrackers at midnight; the sound of animals shying in their paddocks at the strange and unexpected sounds. He does not move from the tight ball he is in. Even when the other two stir, become restless.

The couch is more comfortable. It is longer and softer than the mattress he is on. But Rafferty dragged it into their bedroom and Henry curled up and went to sleep without a word.

Cameron cries into his pillow and Rafferty stares up at the ceiling and flexes his fists.

'Cameron, it's not your fault,' Rafferty says in the stillness of the house.

Cameron weeps, unbroken. Rafferty punches his pillow on the other side of the room. 'Jesus Christ,' he mutters. And takes his pillow into the lounge room.

He sits there, for a while, with his elbows on his knees and his chin in his hands. With his knees jigging and his teeth set hard.

Then he pulls on his boots and goes outside. He doesn't take a torch. The moon is out, but low. The sky starting to purple with dawn.

He walks around the back of the stables and checks the horses in the paddock. He stays there, for a while, staring out at them. Some gently grazing, others sleeping on the dry grass.

Then he walks towards the bush tracks and stops, listening. It is coming home, back towards the house, that he stops near the hay shed.

'You little bugger,' he says. Pebbles is curled up in a dozy ball in between two bails of hay. There is hay poking out of his mouth, even though he's fast asleep.

Rafferty stares at him for a while longer, his head tilted. He smiles, suddenly, even though Opal is dead over his shoulder, even though his twin brother is still weeping in the house. Even though I am dead and Jessa is wishing that she was too.

Rafferty glances back up at the house, then at Pebbles.

Pebbles doesn't startle or wake fully as Rafferty lies down and rests his head on the warm, satiny slope of Pebbles's shoulder. Pebbles turns his head around slightly, his eyes still closed, and snuffles Rafferty's head before sighing and falling back into a doze.

* * *

Jessa is lying in her room. She nods off, then wakes up hissing. And when she seeks out Bass, she finds Laura on the other side of the bed. Both asleep. Not touching.

And so she makes herself a drink. Cinnamon and warm milk. And she sits on the back verandah and pulls a feedbag over her. After a while, she cranes her neck towards the hay shed, where Rafferty is still sleeping next to Pebbles. Then she shivers and whispers under her breath.

I suppose she is whispering to Opal.

Then I hear her murmur 'Mum'.

* * *

Laura bred her first foal when she was in her mid-twenties and I was twenty-two.

It was a stillbirth and it was the only time I saw Laura cry.

She hacked its head off with an axe.

The skull still hangs in her shed. Tiny and coloured like a pearl.

I hated it at the time. Hated it, particularly, when I was pregnant. But there's something about it. Something sad and beautiful. Something that shifts things, just for a moment, back into perspective.

* * *

The next morning Henry wakes up on the floor between Cameron and Rafferty's beds. He is half off the thin mattress and yawns, winces, rubs his head and then sits up.

It is a windy morning. The jacaranda branches knock against the window and through it the clouds seem high and ruffled.

Henry folds up the blankets on the mattress and leaves the room without making a sound. He has slept in his clothes. His T-shirt is wrinkled.

Downstairs Rafferty's pillow is on the couch and his boots are missing from the basket by the front door.

Laura is pulling on her shoes. She has set up cereal on the table. Spreads for bread that has not yet been toasted.

'We're off,' she says.

'But ...'

'But what?'

He wants to see Jessa. It's painted across his face. But instead he swings his arms, glances up towards the stairs and follows his aunt out into the early morning sunlight.

'Will she be okay?'

'We're all okay until we're dead. Let's go.'

* * *

Laura dated a man called Johnny when Henry was young and first started coming to stay with her. Johnny was a good bloke, according to Bass. She met him at a party in the Mulders' barn. A New Year's Eve party, I think. I remember them kissing against the sound of fireworks.

He was broad with dark curly hair. Not conventionally handsome, but somehow beautiful. His smile lines, the belly laugh he was so generous with.

He helped Laura around the farm. He was a horse boy from a farm up north, near the border of New South Wales. He rode stock, but Laura didn't hold it against him the way she usually did when people didn't ride English.

There was talk about him moving in. About them starting up a serious breeding program at her place, turning the property into a stud.

And then it ground to a halt.

'He wants kids,' she said. Her foot jiggling. We were drinking smoothies at the café in town. Bea had taken the kids for me and I kept looking around for them, experiencing a jolt of panic when I failed to find them, then remembering that they were back at home with Bea on the verandah, butcher's paper and buckets of nontoxic paint. Henry was there too. I hoped Bea was keeping a close eye on Jessa, who still tended to attack him if she got the chance. She cried when he cried afterwards, though. I was never sure whether she cried at the shock of his tears or out of some sort of baby empathy.

'Now?'

'No. Not right away, but ... how can I? I've got my hands full with Henry. Sylvia ... and ... I can't ... I just ... I can't.'

They hung in there for a while longer, Laura and Johnny. On the day he left Garras, she came over and we watched *National Velvet* and drank champagne.

'It doesn't hurt, not like how I thought it would,' she said.

'That's good,' I said. Outside, the boys, Jessa and Henry were trying very hard to fly kites on the lawn. Cameron had gotten his up to about two metres before Rafferty jerked it back down. Cameron's lip was trembling. I was waiting for him to cry.

'I didn't love him, I don't think.'

I was quiet.

'Not enough to give him kids.' Her voice skidded. She had a long gulp of champagne. Stared hard at the television. 'Now,' she said, suddenly very brisk. 'Did you end up getting those kindergarten enrolment forms for me?'

* * *

There has not been such pain in the house since I died, I suppose. Watching them, I realise how much they had healed. How much this animal's death will, through Jessa, hurt them all.

I watch in pieces. And when I am not watching, I think.

I remember.

* * *

Sylvia fell in love with a man who had silver eyes. If Sylvia could ever love anyone, it was this man who sometimes opened a door for her, sometimes stopped speaking to her. This man, who painted huge, messy canvases and had handwriting that looked like it had been printed. He was tall with pale skin and dark hair and those unsettled grey eyes, caught somewhere between being blue and hazel.

He was handsome.

He smelt of oil paint and red wine and I sat carefully away from him on the few occasions we met up. I was with Bass by then. The man stared down at my engagement ring, my wedding ring.

He reached for my hand. His was warm, soft. 'Why the fuck did you say yes?'

He made everyone laugh, Sylvia loudest of all. He was clever, in this way. But his jokes had an edge; they were always at the expense of someone else.

It was not until years later that I learnt that Laura had loved him first. That he had left her, left Laura, for wild, unpredictable Sylvia.

'You lived in the city?' I asked Laura, eyes wide. I could not imagine him in the quiet of her bluestone house.

'For a while,' she said.

I could never properly gauge what it was she had with him. Not the magic, not the taste or touch or sound that is conveyed through stories and rolled eyes and too much wine on the couch after a girlie movie.

Bass said she met him doing a business course in the city. It was a short course, but she stayed there afterwards. 'Everyone here was stunned. You know? Can you imagine Laura being in the city by *choice*? Away from her horses?' He shook his head.

'It stretches the imagination. Did he ever come to Garras?'

'Nup. Not that I've ever heard of.'

'I can't picture Laura with him. I can't.'

We were sitting up in bed, eating pizza. I was pregnant with the boys, just. Hungry and nauseous at the same time.

Bass shrugged. 'Laura tells it like it is. She's ... strong and fierce. Clever. I dunno. I get why he was interested.'

'But why was she interested in him?'

Bass snorted. 'No bloody clue. He's an arsehole.'

'C'*mon* ... what do you think, though?'

'I guess he was her first proper relationship. If you can call it that. Like, she never really got involved in all the dumb relationship stuff in high school. I think he was so different from all of us blokes back here. I think he swept her off her feet and she let herself get swept. For a while.'

I cannot remember meeting him for the first time. Whether he had been a little distant. I cannot remember Sylvia glancing coyly away when I had no doubt asked how they met. Where he was from. I don't know when I worked it out, the moment when I knew.

Laura had loved him first.

Still loved him.

*　*　*

The flowers that Henry leaves against the kitchen door are bruised. His hair is slicked to his head and I wonder if there has been a rain shower. On his way off the verandah he snatches an old feedbag from the basket of shoes by the door.

He is a white blob as he stomps down the driveway.

And when Jessa finds them she stares out into the yard, where Bass is excavating the iron earth.

A grave.

Rafferty has put Pebbles back into the big paddock and covered Opal's body with a piece of blue tarp. He is dark under the eyes. I wonder if he has done it for Jessa or for Cameron.

There is so little speaking.

And I cannot think of many things more painful than the salt from Jessa's tears, a white mark upon Opal's neck.

Still gleaming.

*　*　*

I lose focus, then. I can't watch them. Not always. I suppose it's like sleeping, except I no longer sleep.

When I focus on them again, they are having dinner. Opal is buried. The tarp is folded in the shed.

Cameron has scratch marks on the backs of his hands and smells of dirty running shoes.

I watch Jessa through dinner. The focus of not getting lost in my own memories, where everything becomes a kaleidoscope and I am never sure who I am seeing or when I am seeing them. Sometimes it is a month that has passed. Sometimes a matter of minutes. Time trickles and gushes and I have no hands to stem the flow of it.

But I have noticed this: thoughts are painted on faces. I see them, splashed there like watercolour.

Jessa picks at the spaghetti Bass has made with red wine and garlic. The garlic is too strong and the meat not quite cooked, but Rafferty shovels it in like he does every meal, be it smoked salmon or a McDonald's burger. Cameron winces at the first bite, but Bass does not see and Jessa, across the table, sees but ignores him.

She is not listening to their conversation.

She stares out the window.

She is thinking about Henry.

About the flowers he has pressed against the front door.

Jessa holds her grief. She clears the table and dries the dishes and, as Cameron puts them away, she wipes down the table and wrings out the sponge.

It is only later, in the dark shed, with her head pressed into a quarter-filled bag of oaten chaff, that Jessa allows herself to cry.

* * *

Rafferty stares up at the ceiling. His fists are clenched, not under the covers. His arms are raised with goose bumps.

'It's not your fault.'

Cameron continues to cry.

'Can you fucking listen to me?' Rafferty sits up. 'I'm not doing this every night, Cameron. Cameron? Cameron!'

Cameron curls a little deeper in on himself. 'It is.'

'No. It's not. Shit happens. You know that. Fuck, we all know that. Look at Mum.'

'Opal's dead because of me.'

'Fucking hell. Can you see yourself? She's dead because I couldn't get the gun off Jessa. She's dead because Jessa shot her. She's dead because Henry found her. She's dead because Mum bought her. She's dead because she was born. Stop being so pathetic. You're better than this.'

'She'll hate me.'

'She's upset. Can you blame her? Fuck. But she'll get over it. She'll forgive you. You just need to fucking man up.'

Cameron catches his breath. 'Mum always said it was good to cry.'

Rafferty thinks of sleeping in the hay shed with his cheek against Pebbles's shoulder. How it was the deepest sleep he has had since I died. He settles back down on his bed. 'Mum didn't have to share a room with you.'

* * *

Beatrice took to reading up on horses when we were teenagers. Beatrice, who would enrol in a Masters of Arts, wanting to study myths and legends and then drop out after two months.

Her fascination with myths. Legends. The way she would draw butterflies and stars in the margins of her workbooks. She read things about them that I thought were useless. I wanted to learn about how to trim their hooves, the names of the different colours their coats came in, how to bridle them, saddle them. Ride them.

She told me horses stood for power, grace and beauty. For strength and freedom.

I think of this as I think of Jessa, her hands pressed into the dirt, her head hidden in the feedbag. I wonder what it is like for her to lose those things.

So soon after losing her mother.

* * *

Cameron sits in the counsellor's office. He is crying. There is an untouched piece of paper in front of him. A texta in his hand.

His eyes are closed.

'Take your time,' says the counsellor. 'Draw, talk, have a big long cry. Do what you need to do. This space is yours.'

'I killed her,' he says. 'I killed my sister's horse.'

'Your dad told me what happened. I'm so sorry, Cameron.'

'I killed her,' he says. And weeps.

He draws jagged lines and his hands are scratched and puffy. He cries some more.

I wish I could bring him tight against me in a hug. His pain makes him shake. His anguish. I wish I could hold him until his crying stops, until his breathing calms.

The counsellor squeezes his shoulder on the way out. 'If you need to talk, call. And you've still got those other numbers I gave you? The helplines, if you can't get through to me?'

He nods. Then he half smiles at her, as though he is embarrassed. He shrugs away.

Wishes.

* * *

I remember the nurses blinking when I told them Rafferty's name.

'Well, that's an unusual one!'

At first I explained how my grandma had always wanted a boy. How Rafferty was the name she had picked out. How my mother, too, had been waiting for a boy. How his name would have been Rafferty.

'Oh, how sweet!' the nurses said when I explained it.

The maternity wing of the hospital: full of little boys called John and Daniel and James and Matthew.

Sometime after they were born, I asked my grandmother where the name Rafferty came from. We were sitting on the verandah at the farm, my mother in the kitchen washing out bottles for me.

'Well, now,' she said. 'A story I read as a little girl. There was a boy called Rafferty who never stopped crying. He felt everything, you see. Sort of a sad story, now I think of it. But it's always been my favourite name.'

Cameron, weeping at school. His night terrors. How he grieved the deaths of the chickens when Bass wanted a roast for dinner.

Sometimes I felt I'd named them all wrong. That I'd mixed them up. Confused them.

Sometimes lately, though, I feel like I named them perfectly. That I named them just right.

* * *

Bass does a peculiar thing. He takes the wilting flowers that Jessa has thrown into the bin and takes them onto the verandah.

There, he sits. Under the arms of the jacaranda.

He unties the bailing twine and slits the side of a daisy's stem with his thumbnail. He pulls the stem of a second through the hole.

Slowly, methodically, he weaves his daughter's wilted bouquet into a daisy chain. He wanders out to the little herb garden that is going wild. The mint and chives are taking over.

I wish someone would cut them back.

Bass stands with the daisy chain gently in his fingers. He weaves some thyme in, around the flowers. Tucks in some sprigs of parsley and rosemary.

He then takes it back to the house and hangs it on one of the lower branches of the jacaranda.

He lets his breath out. He breathes in. Smells the herbs, his hand still touching the flowers.

* * *

Rafferty is sitting on the couch in Maggie March's garage. She is sitting cross-legged in front of him with a sheet over her shoulders. They are sharing a bottle of beer. Outside it is dusk, bruised and still.

'That's why I didn't meet you.'

'Jesus.'

Rafferty has a mouthful of beer. 'I get why she did it. I do. But fuck … I don't think I'll ever get her expression out of my head. When she came out with that gun.'

'But Opal couldn't have been saved?'

'No way. Her leg was fucked. She needed to be put down, but I could've done it, you know? It didn't have to be Jessa.'

Maggie is quiet for a moment. 'You said she's furious at Cam. For leaving the gate open.'

'She is.'

'How angry would she be at you, if you'd managed to get the gun off her? If you'd shot Opal?'

Rafferty is silent. Maggie climbs up onto the couch next to him. They don't speak.

Maggie reaches for his hand. I see her fingers squeeze tight against his.

* * *

Jessa is in the spare room, dragging Sylvia's big painting down off the wall. She lugs it quietly down the hallway, sets it against her bed while she pulls down all her horse ribbons. She hangs it there, above her bed. It makes the world tremble, that unsettled painting over my daughter's bed. She stares up at it, runs a hand over the signing. Then she sighs, braces herself and goes outside.

She stands where Opal is buried. It's near where she died. Bass did not have the equipment to move her somewhere else. Not gently. Not with dignity. Jake came over to help him and afterwards they stood quietly and Jake clasped Bass in a gentle, awkward hug.

Jessa doesn't move. Does not speak. She stands there, unblinking, staring at the pile of dirt.

She squats down and presses her hand into it. Starts to dig. She digs until her hand disappears and then she reaches into her pocket and puts an apple and a carrot in the hole.

Henry is just leaving the verandah, where he has quietly left another bouquet of flowers. He stops on the steps, slowly lowers himself until he is sitting. He watches Jessa. He watches as she pats the hole flat and sits with her legs crossed.

I had forgotten how silver his eyes are.

* * *

Cameron, alone. Standing by the jacaranda. He has one hand on the wilting daisy chain.

His hands are puffy and red. His face is blotchy. 'I'm okay,' he says quietly. So that the words don't carry any further than the reach of his hand.

He glances towards the quiet house, the empty windows. Then he unslips the daisy chain from the branch and takes it inside.

He puts it under his pillow. Those strange, strong smells.

* * *

Cameron and Rafferty, sitting at the kitchen table. Summer, still. They're drinking cordial and Rafferty has a plate of half-eaten toast by his elbow. There's a blowfly buzzing against the window above the sink.

Cameron's hand is scabbed up, but there is nothing weeping. There is nothing new. I hated seeing his hand, all scratched. It was a relief to see it scabbing, each time. Such a relief.

'Sam said she saw you and Maggie in the café across from the church.'

Rafferty finishes chewing and swallows. 'Who the hell is Sam?'

'Some girl I run with.'

Rafferty leans back in his chair. 'What?' he says.

'I just … are you …?'

Rafferty stares at him and Cameron just nods, swallows hard. 'You are. Okay. Right.'

'Cam …' Something softens in Rafferty's face. He is thinking back to the story of Cameron, crying against Maggie in her garage.

'It's okay.' Cameron gets up and goes outside. He watches Jessa standing by the grave and pulls live leaves off the jacaranda. He goes and pulls wild herbs from my overrun little herb garden. He stuffs them into his pockets, rubs them against his handkerchief.

He closes his eyes. Stills. He is thinking of the smell of green tea.

* * *

Jessa sits in Bass's car, her arms crossed tightly over her chest. Bass is holding the passenger door open.

Jessa stares through the windscreen. 'I'm not going.'

'I'm not asking.'

'Oh! You're telling?' Jessa glares up at him. 'What are you going to do? Drag me in there? Leave me in the carpark? I'm not two.'

'You shot your horse,' he says. 'You shot your horse in the head with a rifle. Now you're going to get up, get out of the car and go and see the counsellor.'

Jessa winces. She grips herself more tightly. 'I don't want to talk about it!'

He reaches down and grabs her arm. 'C'mon, Jess …'

'No!' She yanks free and slams the door closed. 'Fuck off!' she says.

* * *

All sorts of people told me that Jessa would be the soft one. That she would have everyone wrapped around her little finger and be spoilt silly.

Everyone said she would be girly. That the youngest with older brothers always are.

It was only after she had asserted herself that all sorts of people told me that little girls with older brothers were always like that. Hardened. Tough. Always trying to be another boy. To fit in.

The contradictions of raising Jessa drove me half insane. But watching her, watching her run away from her father in the carpark, all I am aware of is an incredible rush of love.

* * *

Henry doesn't kiss Jessa. Not how I always thought he would. With teenage awkwardness and uncertainty. With trembling hands and urgent lips, too wet. Too dry. Too much tongue. Teeth. Too pursed. Learning.

She is wearing the same clothes she was wearing in the carpark of the counselling centre. She and Henry are sweeping the stable, the dust of their brooms flecked with Opal's dark hairs. Jessa's catching breath. The strength it is taking not to cry.

Bass is still in the parking lot outside the counsellor's office. His hands are on the wheel and he is crying, his face slick with snot and tears.

'Cate. Cate. Cate. Cate!' A mantra, a prayer, a plea. It is pressed too hard from between his teeth.

At the farm, Henry is watching Jessa. His expression is thoughtful, sad.

'Jessa.' He takes the broom from her and she stands there, swallowing hard. Blinking away tears.

He sets both brooms aside and holds her face, a hand on each cheek. He rests his forehead against hers.

Jessa shakes him off. 'You smell like chaff,' she says.

He hesitates. Pauses. And then, so much more like a man than a growing teenager, he leans in and presses his lips to hers. The shock of it sucks away her breath. Empties her lungs.

All I can see, in the moments after, is Jessa. Curling a fistful of chaff to her nose and breathing in. The grit of it.

* * *

I don't think Laura ever told me that the silver-eyed man was Henry's father. I don't think she ever told me that she had loved him first. That, as much as one person can belong to another, she had thought that he belonged to her. That she belonged to him. I don't think she ever told me that she still loved him.

But things are painted across people's faces.

I wonder if I should have spoken to her, asked her, told her that I knew. That I had known since I looked into Henry's eyes that first time I met him, when he was two and Jessa clawed his face. How I had been made breathless not by their strange and familiar colour, but how deep they were.

How unlike his father's, even though they were the same silvery colour. How unlike his father's, even then.

* * *

Bass and Laura go out to my herb garden. They have seedlings and netting and piping and a trowel that I have never seen before. It's mild, the garden still caked from summer, but greening up. The claret ash is reddening. Autumn, again. So soon. Laura has her hair out.

'I'm not much use at this,' says Laura.

'Don't care.'

'Why now?' Laura, squatting down next to the bed, pulling out the clover and clumsily cutting back the mint. She puts a leaf in her mouth, chews.

'Cam's going through a rough patch.'

'That's an understatement.'

Bass leans in towards her. 'He's been sneaking herbs into his room. Ever since after Opal died.'

'Actual herbs? These herbs?'

'I thought it might … perk him up. Having it all fresh and redone. He's not up to doing it himself. He's getting his chores done and his running and that's about it, honestly.'

'Still going to see that counsellor?' Laura starts turning the soil.

'Yeah.'

'Jessa?'

'No. Can't even get her in the car to go. It's driving me mental – just when she needs it, you know? And I can't fucking even get her there.' He throws one of the pots across the bed.

'Sorry,' he says. He goes to get up but Laura grabs his sleeve.

'Stop being so bloody hard on yourself,' she says.

Her breath must smell of mint. I see Bass breathe in, slow and deep. Their faces are close. Then Bass turns away. 'These coriander are wilting. Let's get 'em in quick, hey?'

Laura starts digging, keeps turning. Too hard. The dirt goes flying.

* * *

Memories are watery, but more and more I see them, vivid. It makes me think that I might be here, long after Bass and Cameron and Rafferty and Jessa and Beatrice stop saying my name.

That I may be here for a long time. Or that I may be here for no more time at all. That the breath I am watching being drawn in, I will not see being exhaled. That I will simply cease.

And I am not sure whether this is a pleasing or upsetting thing.

Now, things simply are.

* * *

Cameron comes inside from feeding the cows. It's dry, restless. The leaves changing around the house. The kitchen door clatters open. Maggie, wearing a pretty green dress with her hair out. She puts her bag on the floor and smiles. 'Hi, Cam.'

'Raff's out fencing.'

'I'm here for dinner.'

'Oh.' Cameron does his best to hide his tattered shorts, scooting his legs under the table. His hands have healed. Are scarred, but nothing fresh. No scratching.

'Guess he didn't tell you.' She exhales. 'Do you need a hand? With anything?'

'No.'

'Well. Maybe I'll wait outside.'

'I'll … I'll bring you a drink.'

'Cameron?'

'What?'

'I'm sorry, you know. I am.'

Cameron nods, just once, and Maggie lets the door close behind her. Cameron runs upstairs and puts on a pair of shorts with no holes. Downstairs, he stares into the fridge, unblinking. He pours lemonade and goes outside to Maggie.

Jessa comes marching in, knocking into Cameron's shoulder as she passes.

Cameron looks at both of them. Looks from Jessa, making a racket inside getting her shoes off, to Maggie, who is staring out at the driveway.

'Thanks, Cam,' says Maggie.

'She hates me,' Cameron blurts out.

'She doesn't hate you,' Maggie says. 'Are you doing okay?'

Jessa comes back out barefoot on the verandah. 'He's in love with you. Did you know?'

Cameron flushes.

'She hates me,' he says, his shoulders curving. He goes inside and up to bed, puts his hand under his pillow where he grips the rosemary there. And his whole body trembles with the pain of it.

* * *

Rafferty and Maggie, sitting with Jessa at the kitchen table, nursing milk and cinnamon. Jessa is wearing one of Bass's hoodies and is picking at one of her toenails. She is thinking about kissing Henry. About how, for a moment, everything had felt okay. For a moment, she stopped missing me. She stopped throbbing over the loss of Opal. For that moment, with his lips pressed to hers, she was unburdened. She was lightened.

'You cracked yet?' Rafferty asks.

'Shut up.'

'Did Dad get you in there?' He leans forward. 'Roofie? Headlock?'

'Raff, leave her alone,' says Maggie, swatting at him.

'It should be you in there,' says Jessa. 'Not me. Everything always gets pegged on me.'

'Did you talk about Opal?'

'None of your damned business.' Jessa gets up, slams her mug on the table and stalks out.

Maggie swings around to face Rafferty. 'Why do you poke her like that?'

'Like what?'

'Like that! Don't poke her about the counselling. Don't poke her about Opal. It's not funny. It's mean.'

'It's not mean! It's just …'

'Just what.'

Rafferty blows out his breath. 'I dunno.'

'You do it with Cameron too. I've seen you.'

'Okay. I'm a fucking dickhead who picks on his siblings. Are we done?'

Maggie leans over and rests her head on his chest. He startles, but then drops his arms around her shoulders.

'You're better than that, Raff,' she says. 'That's all.'

* * *

Opal's grave has three visitors. Jessa goes out first thing in the morning and again at dusk. She often takes Opal's feedbag and lies there with it pressed over her head.

The grave is grassing over.

Sometimes she will take the tall boots that Bass gave her for Christmas out with her. She will sit and polish them, although they haven't been worn properly since I wore them. She will soap and polish and buff them.

Bass and Laura take turns buying apples and carrots and Jessa buries them in Opal's grave twice a day and it seems to soothe her. Loosen her. She breathes a little easier treading back to the house.

She doesn't talk to Opal. But sometimes she will sing. Murmured, half-forgotten nursery rhymes and lullabies. Songs from the radio she had learnt by accident, sitting quietly on the school bus.

Michaela comes over. She has baked a small carrot cake. They eat half, without speaking. And they press the rest into the grave. Jessa hugs her for a long time after that, and Michaela doesn't shy away from the acid, allergic sting of horse hair.

The other regular visitor is Cameron. He goes out at night, when Jessa is occupied indoors. He doesn't bury anything, doesn't sing. He sits out there with his strong-smelling handkerchief pressed hard against his nose. Sometimes he cries, but mostly he just smells the essential oils and sits with his head against his knees, his hands full of dirt.

'I'm sorry,' he'll sometimes mutter.

But otherwise he is quiet.

Henry comes by sporadically, without routine. Sometimes it is after school, when Jessa is off with Michaela. Other times it is early in the morning, or in the middle of a quiet Saturday.

He sits down, where Cameron sits. He sits with his knees brought up to his chin and he frowns.

He stares at the grave as if it is a puzzle that needs solving.

* * *

Laura and Bass kiss sometimes, sitting on the verandah. Soft, slow kissing that makes me feel hollow. After a few kisses, maybe cut short by footsteps on the stairs or in the kitchen, they will sit quietly, Bass with his arm looped around her shoulders.

Bass thinks of the night I died. He remembers returning home and seeing the silhouettes of Rafferty and Cameron and Jessa on the verandah. Waiting.

So quiet.

He remembers his panic. He remembers it white and grey. He remembers its colours and they make him feel old. Exhausted, like he needs to lie down and sleep for days.

He swallowed his panic, I think. At the time, he bit it down until it was a hard pellet in his stomach. Black and smoky.

Everything he felt was in shades.

And it was waking up that first morning with Jessa's hand linked with his that turned him back to colour.

Realising that he needed them as much as they needed him.

* * *

Cameron is eating his lunch in bed with a book open in his lap. Bass, who told Cameron and Jessa he was going to see Steve, is sitting on Laura's verandah with a beer.

Jessa is outside cleaning her father's Blundstone boots.

'I made it this afternoon.' Henry plonks a bottle of lemonade down next to her. He is sweating from the walk. 'Watcha doing?'

'Dad's shoes. I can't stand seeing them get all cracked and disgusting.'

'Need a hand?'

'No.' She sets the second boot aside and dusts her hands. 'Cameron thinks I hate him.'

Henry hesitates. 'Do you?'

Jessa shakes her head.

'You're a good person, Jess.'

'No, I'm not!' she snaps.

And there is nothing in this moment. Two teenagers, barely that, children in so many ways. Staring at each other. No horse between them. No patch of earth, neither squinting against the sun or swatting at flies or wiping a dribble of sweat from the eye.

Jessa looks away first, brushing her finger along the hair behind her ear. Leaving a trace of muddy oil.

'Jess?'

She ignores him. The feeling of butterflies, curdling in her stomach, painted across her face. 'Why do you keep leaving me flowers?'

'Why do you think?' He is looking the other way now. Both of them. Staring away from each other.

'Because you're sorry for me. Because I'm mean. And sad. Because you feel like you have to.' Her voice catches and I see her wince. Rub her fingers against her palms, like she does when her hands are full of dirt.

'I'm sad for you, not sorry for you.'

'Big difference.'

'It is, Jessa!' he snaps, glancing back towards her. 'If I was sorry for you I'd be all like, look how pitiful she is, isn't that a shame! But I'm not sorry for you. I'm sad for you. When I see you sad, I'm sad too.'

'I'm not sad. I'm angry.'

Henry pauses, glances away again. 'Well, I'll be angry too.'

And Jessa tenses, as though something inside her has shifted. Right through to her core.

* * *

Strange, that I cannot remember how I came to be in Garras. So often days blur together, decisions become distorted. I'm not sure what my trigger was; why I decided to pack my things into my car and drive out there.

When I was alive, this inability to remember distressed me, I think.

I remember the day I decided to stay in Garras. That decision carried weight. A future. So much more than the whim of driving out here with my car stuffed with clothes and my windows down and my radio blaring.

I think of how often I thought of moving somewhere. I had never travelled, not far, not for any longer than a week or two. Sometimes, I would feel so sad about it all I would just call in sick and if Sylvia answered I could hear her grin. 'I'll tell 'em you sounded like *shit*,' she'd say.

In Garras, I sometimes felt sad, but never about not having travelled. The world seemed bigger in Garras than it had in the city. Apart from when the children were very young, I never felt hemmed in, there. I never felt confined.

Itchy feet, my mother called it, when I was a teenager talking about wanting to go places. To explore. When she was younger, she'd had them. France, Italy, England, Germany, Ireland. She was saving up for Egypt when she met my father. And her itchy-feet money turned into a house deposit.

Sometimes I wonder if a little part of her was disappointed in us. In Beatrice and me. Neither of us had travelled very far. Neither of us had travelled for long. A few weeks in Europe just after we were married, a gift from my parents. Bass had wanted to ask them for money towards the mortgage, instead, but I'd shaken my head.

'We need to do this,' I'd said.

Sometimes I dream of Italy, the different smells. The room we had, tucked in a narrow street. The thinness of the pizzas.

Mum would call up and ask me to tell her about Italy for years after the trip. She would chime in with her own European stories and we would talk for hours. She never said anything about Beatrice and I both leaving the city for Garras. She never asked; she never commented.

Sometimes, when she visited, she'd sit on the hillside with the prettiest view and wrap her arms around her knees. 'I get it,' she'd say, and smile at me.

I felt it as a different rhythm to my blood. A quickening, a loss of rhythm.

That's how I think of my moving around. Of driving through the nights so I would be driving into the dawn.

I had been chasing my own rhythm.

Bass, leaning against the bar of the Savannah Hotel, smiling at me.

'This is Sebastian,' Laura said, grinning.

'Bass,' he said, holding out his hand, giving Laura a look.

With him, my rhythm changed.

I wonder now if that meant I was young. Too young.

I wonder if, when you grow older, your rhythm becomes fixed. Ingrained. I wonder, then, if you can be too old to be changed by someone else. Whether this is a good thing. Or sad.

The day I decided to stay in Garras was the day Bass asked Laura if he could move in with us for a bit. We had been seeing each other for three months, I think.

I was outside, but I saw Laura arch an eyebrow, glance over the top of her paper. 'Knock yourself out,' she said.

Bass and Laura together now. It is both a hollowness and a fullness, watching them. They are quiet, with each other. Gentle.

Their rhythms have already settled. Are whole.

* * *

Henry and Jessa are sitting by Opal's grave. It's cloudy and still and Henry has his knees up under his chin.

'What?' Jessa asks, without looking at him.

'What d'you mean, what?'

'What are you thinking about?' She asks it flatly, not looking. I wonder if she wants a distraction from Opal, from the pain of losing her.

'I was thinking about my mum.'

'Oh.'

'I miss her.'

'I thought you didn't want to see her any more.'

'Doesn't mean I don't miss her.'

'Oh.'

'And … sometimes this guy hurts her. He comes by and hurts her. They fight.'

'Well, that's stupid. Why does she let him come over?'

'Because she loves him, I guess.'

Jessa frowns into her knees. 'That's so fucked.'

Henry doesn't say anything. He is thinking of the silver-eyed man. He is thinking of his mother. He closes his eyes, hard, against tears.

And Jessa, remarkably, reaches for his hand. She squeezes his fingers in hers and rests her head against his shoulder.

* * *

The next thing I am aware of is Jessa and Henry sharing her narrow little bed. It is dark, the quiet of the deep night. Jessa has curled into herself, her back to Henry. She keeps tugging at the sleeves of her oversized T-shirt and I watch as she twitches and fidgets while Henry lies awake quietly beside her.

Above them, the picture swirls and disappears and looms and threads and almost seems to breathe to its own uneven rhythm.

Henry kneels up on the bed for a moment, touches his finger to his mother's signature. He doesn't say anything, just glances down at Jessa and lies back down next to her.

They are so young. Too young. Both hardened by their own yearning. Their own pain. Twinned. And in the stillness that follows, when they lie in the narrow bed and don't look at each other, I wonder if they have realised this.

Too late.

* * *

When my father died I drove to Melbourne to see my mother. I listened to songs that made me think of Bass. I cried, on and off. I drove with the windows down.

My tears were not all for my father. He was older than my mother. Older than Bass's parents had been when they died. My tears were from imagining my mother dying, Bass dying. Laura dying. Bea dying, all complications and confusion. I cried, thinking about how much my sister wanted to be my friend, how I couldn't bring myself to confide in her, to be joyful with her, when I knew – even then – that it was what she needed. That it was what would jolt her out of her strange limbo, which – I suspected – had started that night on the couch with the boy who didn't wait for a yes.

I cried, too, out of anger. Frustration. I mourned for myself, not that I had now lost a father, but that I had never had one who was what I needed. What Bea and I both needed. Who saw us. Who knew us. Not the way Bass knew our three, who were only young when their grandfather died.

When I arrived, it was to find the lounge room rug thrown over the verandah railing. Inside my mother was vacuuming. The kitchen floor was already mopped.

She was halfway through emptying the fridge and all of Dad's old clothes were in a pile by the front door.

'Mum.' My voice was a coin. Flat. Cold.

'Don't look at me like that,' she snapped.

'Don't you want to keep some of this stuff?' I tugged at the sleeve of one of Dad's shirts.

She glanced up and shook her head. 'No. No, I don't.'

'Do you want a cup of tea?'

'No.' She budged past me onto the verandah. 'Rug's nearly dry.'

'Mum?' My voice lost its hardness. She bustled back past me towards the vacuum. 'Mum …'

Mum looked at me for a long moment and put the vacuum down. 'Sit down, Cate.'

Mum made me a green tea and we sat on the verandah railing, on top of the drying carpet, and sipped at it.

'Did you hate him?' The question burst out of me and I winced at the words. At the sound of them.

'No. I didn't hate him.'

'Well, then. Why …'

'Because I want to remember him from earlier on. I want to remember when I first met him. I want to remember him like that. All this stuff does is remind me of how he was when we didn't really click with each other any more.'

'Click?'

'That's as good a word for it as any, don't you think?'

'I don't get it, though. I've never gotten it. Why'd you stay with him, Mum? Why'd you stay with him, when you stopped clicking?'

Mum sighed. 'Because it was comfortable, in its own weird way. I had my life and he had his. We never hated each other. We never really fought. It just is what it is. People change.' She shrugged. 'He had his research, I have my art, I have my own little community here. And we knew each other, knew how to live together, even when we grew apart. I don't expect it makes much sense to you.'

'Do you miss him?'

My mother glanced at me. 'Yes, I miss him.'

I'd closed my eyes. 'You're right. No sense at all.'

Sitting there, I remembered the feeling of my blood quickening. Its rhythm changing. I think of home, the pang of it. How I miss Bass, when he had kissed me goodbye only three hours before.

Clicking. Matching rhythms.

* * *

It's morning and everything is damp and still. Already the beehive in the gum tree behind the house is humming and the cows are calling for their breakfast. Henry's lemonade is on the verandah. Bass's boots still half oiled.

Rafferty has slept in the horses' paddock. On the nights he is not at Maggie's, he will put on a heavy jumper and go outside in the paddock. He will survey the horses, the ones dozing with a leg resting. The ones sleeping sprawled on their sides, the others dozing with their legs pressed up under them. There are so few of them, now. Only four. Some nights he will curl up next to Gus, who is like a sighing boulder and doesn't move until breakfast time. More often than not, though, he will sleep curled next to Pebbles. Pebbles sometimes wakes him up by chewing on his nose or nudging his shoulder. Pebbles, who is so much more subdued. Slower. Since Opal died.

'What the fuck are you doing?' Rafferty, standing in Jessa's bedroom doorway. He slams the door shut behind him and grass and mud fall off his jumper. 'Are you two fucking insane? Dad would *skin* you, Henry.'

'He's camping,' Jessa says. 'With *Steve*.'

Rafferty glances at her, a moment's curiosity and confusion playing across his face. Then he files it away for another time. '*Skin* you, Henry.'

'Calm down,' Jessa snaps. 'We just fell asleep.'

'I'm not stupid. Do I look stupid, Henry?'

Henry shakes his head. He's already standing up, dusting down his T-shirt.

'We didn't do anything!' Jessa snaps.

'More credible if you hadn't taken the one condom I had left in my wallet.'

Jessa wants to look at Henry. Wants to stare at him. Incredulous. Scornful. But instead she looks up at Rafferty, pulling a bored face.

'Why the hell would we take your condom?'

'Jess …'

'It was Cameron.'

'Cameron. Cameron?' Rafferty looks thoughtful. 'Our brother, Cameron? The boy who nearly got lucky but fucked it up by crying? The boy who's been a weepy mess since Opal? Yep. You're right. Definitely him.' He paused. 'Henry, grab your jumper. We're going for a walk.'

Henry glances at Jessa. 'Actually, I …'

'I'm not asking. Come on.'

Henry sighs and pulls on his jumper and shoes. Jessa is scrolling through her iPod. She only looks up once he's out of the room and only then to squeeze her eyes shut.

Outside Rafferty starts walking towards the bush tracks, lighting a cigarette.

'You're not going to, like, cut me into pieces and scatter me somewhere, are you?' Henry asks.

'You need to be careful.'

'I *am*. I mean … I'm sorry I took the condom, but …'

'No. I'm not talking about sex. I mean, you need to be careful with Jessa.'

Henry takes a deep breath.

'She's … she's fucked up right now, Henry. You probably know that just as much as I do. But she is. And the sort of person you are. I dunno. You're gentle, I guess. Even with all that mum shit you've got going on, you're gentle. And …' Rafferty breathes out a mouthful of smoke and glances sideways at Henry, shaking his head.

'I'm a big boy,' says Henry.

'She's not in a good place. I just … you both need to be careful.'

'I *know*.'

'Well.' Rafferty stares at him for a second and then butts his cigarette out against a tree stump. 'Let's head back.'

* * *

Rafferty thinks about when I died more than the others do. He thinks of it when he feels Maggie's hand, warm in his own. He thinks of it when he plays his games on the computer, when he tunes his guitar. He thinks of it when he's working at the feed store, where his back still hurts.

He thinks of it in the last dozing moments out in the paddock before he falls asleep in the early hours of the morning, when all he can see are stars and the clouds and the moon and all he can hear is the sound of sleeping horses.

He is thinking of a doctor's letter he found, outlining results for a test I had had. Of how the edge of it bit into his flesh and made him bleed. How he showed me. How we talked.

How we yelled.

How he went outside and punched a hole in the thin plasterboard of the shed we had tried to insulate.

He imagines me, often. He thinks of me, older than I was. He thinks of me staring at him like I don't know who I am looking at.

He thinks of it when he is trying to sleep. Again and again.

It is why he is awake when Cameron shudders and flails in the night.

* * *

Across the other side of the ranges, squatting outside Bass's tattered blue tent, is Laura.

Her beanie is pulled down low over her face and she's holding her hands over the steaming billy of black tea. Her breath comes out in white puffs.

'Bass!' She whacks the side of the tent. He grunts inside. 'Bass!'

There is rummaging, the sides of the tent being warped as he gets dressed.

And there he is, tousled, climbing awkwardly out of the low door.

'Shh,' Laura murmurs, pointing. A koala in a nook of a tree, nearly at their eye level. 'I didn't even notice. The whole time I was making tea. He was watching and I didn't notice.'

I am not sure whether it is a joyful thing, their togetherness. Joyful or agonising. For me, the two are coupled now. My family's joy without me brings such peace. *They're okay. They're okay. They're okay.* But it breaks me apart too. Breaks me open.

Bass sits down on the ground and does up his hiking boots.

'Laura?'

'What?'

'Do you think …?' Bass butts his heel against the ground, looks away.

'Spit it out.'

'Do you think she'd mind … this?'

'Cate?' Laura rummages in her canvas bag for the billy whackers. 'No.'

'You think?' His voice comes out sharp, desperate. He winces away from the sound but Laura keeps rummaging, does not look up. Gives him that.

* * *

Jessa is wearing the beanie that my grandmother knitted. She is sitting in class next to Michaela, but she is staring out the window. It's raining. And she is thinking about Opal. Her mouth is resting in the palm of her hand, her elbow on the table. Her chin quivers, just a bit.

She doesn't like to think of Opal in her grave. In the rain, the cold.

Michaela nudges her and Jessa glances to the front where Mrs Crowther is watching her. Mrs Crowther doesn't say anything, just keeps going with whatever it was she was saying and Jessa glances down, makes sure she's on the right page of the play they're reading as a class.

As Jessa heads out the door, Mrs Crowther glances up. 'Jessa, wait back a minute, please.'

Jessa crosses her arms. Mrs Crowther does something surprising, though. She wraps an arm around Jessa's shoulder.

'I could see how hard you were trying to stay focused, Jessa.'

Jessa just nods, doesn't look at her.

'It's hard, isn't it? When we're hurting. To pay attention for hours a day to things that seem pretty stupid.'

Jessa nods again, glances up.

'Just keep trying, Jessa. Like you're doing. Just keep trying.' She squeezes Jessa's shoulder. 'Okay?'

'Okay.' Jessa stays like that, for a moment, with Mrs Crowther's arm around her. 'Thank you.'

* * *

The trees down the main street are mostly bald. The few leaves still clinging are burnished and languid. Jessa sits in Beatrice's lounge room, her feet on the coffee table. She is eating Pringles, shoving in one after another, her eyes fixed on the television. Some American sitcom I used to rib her about. Did not really like her watching, but she is older now.

'Sure you told your dad you'd be here?' Beatrice calls. 'You know he'll worry if he gets home and you're gone.'

'I already said I told him.' Jessa's mouth pulls down a little as she talks, still staring hard at the television screen. Her forehead creases, just above her nose. 'I said I'd be staying with you for the next little while.'

She doesn't like seeing Opal's grave. The wet, muddy mass of it.

'Okay.' Beatrice pulls her phone out and sends Bass a quick text. I suppose he's now worked out how to use his mobile phone.

Then there is quiet. Beatrice, making soup in the kitchen. Jessa throwing the empty Pringles container onto the coffee table.

'How's your friend?' Jessa asks.

Beatrice stiffens. 'What friend?'

'The guy you have over to dinner. He comes after I go, sometimes.'

'He's fine.'

'Is he your boyfriend?'

'No.' Beatrice, her voice flat.

'So you just have sex?'

'Jessa!'

Jessa stares at her and she stares back. Then she turns towards the window.

'I forget how quick you're growing up. He's not my boyfriend,' Beatrice says. 'And you're right we just ... sleep together.'

'Does he stay over?'

'No.'

'What's his name?'

'Mark.'

Jessa is quiet and Beatrice sucks in her bottom lip. 'Jessa, did your mum ever sit you down and –'

'No. We have sex ed at school.'

'I just ...' Beatrice closes her eyes for a moment. 'God, this is awkward. But, if you have any questions or ...'

Jessa glances at Beatrice and there's a sort of panic. She does not want what Beatrice has. A man who is not her boyfriend, who does not sleep over, who just comes by for sex. She does not want that.

But she has nobody else to talk to.

Only the memory of me, when I said so little about anything to do with sex or relationships or boys. When I veered away from it, certain she was too young.

How, so quickly, she is growing up without me.

* * *

I remember being drunk in winter. Spiced wine for the solstice parties we threw before the boys were born. I remember the last person going home and Bass stoking the fire and then unbuttoning my blouse. His fingers always looked too big, too heavy. I remember watching him. Watching them unbuttoning. Marvelling at his delicacy, at the rhythm of them in motion.

'You know,' I said, lying on the floor. 'The saddest people are the ones who never cry.'

'How do you figure?' His lips against the pulse in my throat, his hands unclasping my bra.

'The sadness never goes anywhere if you don't cry.'

'What about people who do other things instead of crying?'

But I was not really listening. His words, when I think of them, are hazy. Maybe I only imagined him saying them.

My eyes closing. The heat of the fire on my bare skin.

It is the truth, though. That sadness is caught, is netted. That without tears – without something – sadness will seep into the deepest parts of you. Bass, who still buys my favourite tea when he shops. Who still has not changed the pillowcase I slept on.

Sadness is netted. And I don't know how to help him get it free.

* * *

I miss the smell of smoke. I miss slow cooked meals and a leg of roast lamb with garlic and rosemary pressed into the meat.

I miss my thick doona and how good it felt to be cold when I first got into bed and to have Bass's warmth, his solidness, to wrap around. To be near.

I miss reading by the warm light of the lamp in the living room. I miss the quilted blanket my mother made me.

I miss going out into the mist. The way my lungs hurt with the cold of it.

Winter. The stillness of the farm.

I miss being alive.

* * *

Sam is short and wiry and always wears her hair pulled back tightly from her face. There is no softness to her, nothing yielding, nothing that reminds Cameron of Maggie March.

She talks less, watches more. She is more serious, maybe. Mostly. But happier. She is not grieving, not mourning.

She gets things done.

She reminds me of Laura.

'I run because when I do, that's all I think about,' Sam says.

They are sitting on the verandah of her parents' house. The small yard, the gentle smell of lawn, then footpath. Everything is damp and tight. Winter. After rain.

Cameron nods. His breath steams in front of his face. Breathing ghosts. 'Me too.'

'I want to get a scholarship. Maybe at the Australian Institute of Sport. Only way ...'

'To get paid to run.'

Sam smiles. 'Over to the Mulders' and back?'

She doesn't wait for him to agree before her stocky little legs are taking her off down the road, her hoodie left behind on the verandah steps.

* * *

Beatrice folds Jessa's washing and leaves it at the foot of the little fold-up bed she has set up in her spare room. She touches Jessa's pillow, makes her bed so that there are no creases.

She leaves lunches out for Jessa, wrapped in paper bags. Jessa takes them and tries to eat what's inside at lunch. The sandwiches and dried fruit and crackers. But Jessa's not really very hungry any more and much of the food ends up in the bin.

Beatrice hums when she shops, now. For dried apple and Vegemite and Cheerios and tea.

I've never heard her hum before. The sound is strange. It's happy.

* * *

When it's warm, Rafferty sits in the hay shed and reads his notes. When he has to write essays, he sits at the computer that he mostly plays games on. Mostly, he switches the internet connection off and frowns at the screen.

It's winter, now. Too cold for the shed. He wears thick socks and drinks cocoa at the computer or on the couch.

Cameron studies in his bed, with his doona pulled up. He doesn't study as much as Rafferty does. He can't stay focused and ends up staring out the window or vacantly at his books, his fingers tracing the scarred backs of his hands.

He does not have Rafferty's intensity. When he moves, he does not have the dull ache of overstretched muscles that Rafferty has in his back.

When Jessa comes over, with Bea and not that often, she will stare at Rafferty long before he notices her watching him.

* * *

Bea has trimmed her hair a little. I don't know who else would notice. Our mother, probably. Certainly not Bass. He's sitting at the kitchen table with his arms crossed. The electric kettle switches itself off but he doesn't move.

'So?' says Bea. She has a pretty scarf on, wrapped tightly around her neck.

'Whatever you think.'

'Bass, it's not about what I think. You're her *dad*. What do *you* think? Is that new restaurant going to be too …'

'Too what?'

'Too un-Jessa?'

Bass raises an eyebrow. 'Un-Jessa?'

'You're right. Of course you're right. What about dinner here?'

'I suppose.'

'I'll call Mum. And Jake and Guy can come over too, right? And Michaela and Laura and Henry. It'll be fun.'

Bass wraps his arms more firmly around himself.

'We can all bring something.'

'Yup.'

'Bass?'

'Hmm?'

'Are you okay?'

Bass swallows. 'Yeah. Yup. I'm fine.'

* * *

The party is quiet. My mother is ill and doesn't make it to Garras. Beatrice makes a lasagne and a big salad and Laura brings soft drinks that explode across the table and kebabs, which Beatrice leaves in the fridge.

Cameron and Henry have spent the afternoon making a cake. It is a Saturday and the woodfire is burning. There is flour all over the bench.

'Like this,' Cameron says, showing him how to whisk the eggs.

'I *know*,' says Henry, rolling his eyes.

The cake is slightly uneven and the icing has dripped off, but Bass sticks a match on top and Jessa blows it out and in the momentary darkness that follows, I see her shoulders sag, her breath exhale.

Everything hurts and wavers. I find myself watching my mother sleep, her fist full of tissues, her nose red and full of cold.

Jessa has nothing to wish for.

* * *

A few weeks, maybe. Maybe longer, maybe less. I seek out Jessa. The trees on the main street are lush and green, the paddocks on the farm have dried and once again the yard is full of seed fluff from the silver birches. There are chooks broody on their nests. Jessa dumps her bag on the bathroom bench at the café in town and pulls out a makeup bag. She puts on mascara, some eye shadow and liner. She fixes up her foundation.

'I told my mum I'm sleeping at yours,' Michaela says, coming in after her. Jessa pulls off her school uniform, pulls on a T-shirt and a pair of jeans.

'Well, you are,' says Jessa.

'Yeah …'

'It's just Rosella! It's not like we're running to the city.' Jessa tugs her hair up higher, pulls on a jumper.

'Still …'

'Oh, c'mon!' Jessa zips her makeup bag back up. She links her arm with Michaela's. 'It'll be fun.'

Michaela grunts, rolls her eyes.

They catch the bus to Rosella from outside their school. They eat chips near the bus stop and then Michaela uses the GPS on her phone to guide them to a house with a hedge and roses and a pretty little apple tree in the front garden. The apple tree is blossoming. Spring, then.

Michaela glances at her. 'Ready?'

It is on dusk, just after. Jessa nods. 'Ready.'

* * *

I wonder what memories, what stories, my family carries about me. About how I died.

I wonder if they think about the last time they saw me. Cameron, I kissed on the head. I don't remember his face. The expression. But I watched him walking out across the garden. I marvelled at how tall he was getting. The long lines of his legs, his back.

His hair smelt of apples.

Bass, he was heading out too. I ran after him. 'Bass!'

'What?' He half turned, keys in hand. He was late. I forget where he was going.

'I … There's something I need to grab at the shops.'

'Sure. What?'

'I …' I frowned, stared back into the kitchen.

'I have to go, Cate. What do you want me to grab?'

I stared frantically towards the open cupboards, the closed fridge. Trying to piece together what I needed. Why I needed it.

'I gotta run. I love you. Call me when you remember?'

'Yeah …' I frowned into the kitchen. I didn't watch him leave.

* * *

Jessa and Michaela at a party. There is music and drinks and some people who were in the years above them at school. I recognise some from Cameron's race days. Pale curtains, blowing in and out of an open window, even though the night outside looks cold. There are snacks and boys who look eighteen and older. Older than my boys. Older than Jessa.

Jessa and Michaela drink canned vodka snuck from a bath filled with ice cubes. Jessa flicking the bottom of her jumper. There is music and giggling and silly dancing and a goon bag going around the room.

Maggie March is there with a group of her friends, sitting near the fireplace with a bottle of champagne. She sees them and frowns. She gets up.

'Jessa, what are you doing?'

'Nothing.'

Maggie sits down next to her, brushes a piece of hair off her cheek, and Jessa shrugs violently away. 'Your dad would have a fit.'

'He wouldn't care.'

'Bull,' says Maggie. She smiles at Michaela. 'Michaela, right? I'm Maggie.'

'Yeah, I know. Raff's girlfriend, right?'

Maggie half shrugs, smiles. 'Yeah.' She tousles Jessa's hair. 'What are you even doing here? I still hear stories about you bitch-slapping Jason when he offered you a UDL.'

Michaela chokes on her cruiser. 'You what?'

Jessa rolls her eyes. 'I didn't bitch-slap him and he was keeping me awake. Idiots.'

Maggie sat down next to her. 'Look around, kid. Same idiots here.'

'What are *you* doing here, then?'

'Me? My friends like the idiots. I like my friends.' Maggie shrugs. 'Besides, I hate those band gigs Raff likes. Places too small for live bands.' She shudders. 'So when there's a band or something on that I don't want to see, I hang out with my friends. Or when I want to hang out with my friends, he goes to the gigs.'

'Huh,' says Jessa.

'You girls having fun?'

'Well …' Michaela glances at Jessa. 'It's kinda boring. Honestly. All the cruiser's done is make me sleepy.'

Maggie smiles. 'Well, we can run you home. We're going back to the Savannah in a while. How were you gunna get back?'

Jessa shrugs.

'Shit, Jessa. You can't nick out to another town at night without an escape plan. What happens if you don't get a ride back?'

'Taxi.'

'Bullshit – they don't run out here. You know that. Bus stops at eleven. Raff and Cam don't have their licences yet. Way too far to walk. You gunna call up Bass?'

'No.'

'Guy? Steve? Bea?'

'*No.*'

'*Oh.*' Maggie glances at her, has a swig of champagne. 'You were gunna call up Jake.'

Jessa doesn't say anything. She finishes the rest of her cruiser, stares hard at Maggie. 'I'm getting another.'

Maggie watches her go, shakes her head a bit. 'This was her idea, hey?'

Michaela yawns. 'Yup.'

* * *

The jacaranda is flowering. It flowers in late spring. Last year it flowered late. There were still flowers on it after Christmas. There were still flowers on it after I'd died.

The whole shape of the house, of the land, changes. With those flowers, the colour of them. The mass. They don't smell, not the way the jasmine and the roses smell. How the freesias smell, when they bloom just after winter.

But the jacaranda. There's something about it.

* * *

'Not Bea's,' Jessa groans from the back seat.

Maggie's curly-haired friend glances back at her, continues to drive down the main street. They're in a little green hatchback with P plates in the windows.

'If she hurls, I'm going to kill you, Mags.'

'She won't hurl,' says Maggie. 'Will you, Jess?'

'Don't you dare hurl,' Mic hisses. 'I'm a sympathetic vomiter.'

'Stop talking about vomit,' Jessa groans. She coughs. 'Take me home. Take me to the farm. Please. Not Bea's.'

Maggie sighs and rolls her eyes at her friend. 'Just drop me off there too, hey? Not sure who'll be home and I think the little one might need some help.'

'*Not* little.'

'This driveway?' the girl asks.

'Yeah. Thanks, Lucy. Thanks heaps.'

At the house Michaela and Maggie get Jessa out of the car. Bass's ute isn't there. He's at Laura's. I can see Rafferty, home from his gig, playing a game on the computer.

'Wow,' he says when they drag Jessa into the hallway. She glowers at him, staggers up against the wall.

'Someone thought they were ready for a big-kid party,' says Maggie.

'Not my idea,' says Michaela.

'Let's just dump her on the couch,' says Raff.

'Don't *dump* me,' says Jessa, sliding down the wall to the floor.

Raff sighs and reaches down for Jessa. She smacks him. 'No! Staying *here*.'

'Seriously,' he mutters, picking Jessa up like a feedbag and carrying her over his shoulder. She squeals and kicks

270

her legs. One kick lands very close to his crotch and he grunts and drops her onto the couch.

'Seriously?' he says.

'She was at Anton's.'

'Why the fuck were you at Anton's? You don't even know the guy! Do you know him?' he asks Michaela.

'Nup. Jessa wanted to go to a party. So I went with her.'

'You can hardly talk, Raff,' says Maggie. 'Mic – can you run upstairs and get her pillow and blanket? I'll go get her some water and toast.'

Michaela disappears and Maggie hums as she goes into the kitchen.

Rafferty looks down at Jessa and notices the tears. Running a tiny track down her cheekbones and onto the couch. Rafferty strokes the hair off her forehead. 'Well, the bright side is you won't be going near cruisers again any time soon.'

She breathes in a ragged breath, buries her head into the couch cushion.

'I miss Mum,' she says. She starts crying. 'I want my mum!'

Rafferty doesn't say anything. He strokes her forehead. 'You're an idiot, Jessa.'

Maggie comes back in and Raff stands up. 'Gunna go and dig out a bucket from the shed. I can spot a hurler a mile off. Be back in a sec.'

Maggie sets down the toast and water and sits by Jessa's feet. 'How you feeling?'

Jessa groans. Mic comes back down with the pillow and blanket. 'Where do I put 'em?'

'Jessa? Put your head up, honey. There we go. That's it. Just chuck the blanket over her feet. She can pull it up if she gets cold.'

Jessa sniffs. 'Not cold.'

Rafferty brings the bucket in and Jessa throws up spectacularly a moment later and then begins to cry. She curls on her side and sobs.

'You guys go to bed,' says Raff. 'Mic, crash in Jessa's. Maggie, you can crash in mine. Cam won't care.'

Maggie raises an eyebrow, does not look entirely convinced.

'Think he's at Jason's tonight anyway. Seriously. Go. I've got this.'

Maggie kisses his cheek. 'You're awesome.'

Rafferty grunts, but turns and watches as she climbs the stairs, two at a time.

Jessa continues to cry. Rafferty doesn't say anything. He just empties the bucket and brings it back and drags the armchair closer to the couch.

'Raff?'

'Hmm?'

'I can't stop thinking about it. All the time.' Her eyes are squeezed shut.

'What?'

'Mum. When I … It's all my fault.'

'It's not your fault, Jess.'

Tears. I never understood when people said tears were coursing. That they coursed. But right now, down Jessa's cheek, they're coursing. They're like a river, a creek after rain. Swollen and flowing and full of everything unknown.

* * *

The last time I saw Laura, we were out for a coffee on the way back from looking at a horse she liked. I was meeting Bea in town afterwards. So I watched as Laura slapped money on the table and stood up, needing to get home to do the afternoon feed.

'I'll pay,' I said, staring at the money. I straightened the note so it was in line with the edge of the table.

'I got it, Cate. It's fine.' She was frowning at me.

'What?' I asked, staring at her properly for the first time that day.

'You … You right? You seem weird.'

'I'm just tired.'

Laura snorted. 'Tired my arse. There's something bugging you. I can tell.' She squeezed my shoulder. 'Come over for a cuppa, hey? Or I'll come over to yours. When you're ready to talk. About whatever it is.'

* * *

Rafferty and Jessa are quiet in the living room. Rafferty leans in and tells her something important. I can tell by the expression on his face. She drunkenly lurches for his hand and then she cries and he cries.

'See? It wasn't your fault.'

And I know that it's about me.

She clings to him. She sobs.

* * *

Cameron walks down the driveway with his hands in his pockets. It's sunny, bright. The trees are still. It's cold in the mornings, sometimes frosty. Even in spring, when the world unfurls.

He goes into the kitchen and runs up the stairs. Maggie March is curled on Rafferty's bed. She is still in her clothes from last night, the jeans and silky purple top. Her hair is loose across his pillow and her hands are tangled in the sheet. She's not under the doona. Cameron can see the goose bumps on her arm. He swallows hard. His breath catches and he quickly dumps his bag and goes back downstairs.

He pauses in the living room, staring in at Jessa who is holding her head and groaning.

'What's up with you?' he asks.

'Hungover,' says Rafferty, popping up behind him with a cup of coffee. 'She's completely the-sun-is-burning-my-eyes-stop-the-room-moving hungover. It's like watching a lamb learn to walk.'

They move into the kitchen. 'Huh. Should we ... do something?'

'Oh, she'll be right. I just made her drink some fizzy lemon. She'll perk up.' Rafferty hands Cameron a coffee.

'Thanks. How was your ... gig ... thing?'

'Pretty cool. I don't think I want to do more, though. I don't really like performing.' Raff sips his coffee, puts his feet up on the kitchen table, wiggles his toes. 'I like playing in the garden best. I like doing parts of songs.'

Maggie comes in. 'Raff, how's – Oh, hey. Cam. How was Jason's?'

Cameron shrugs, has a big mouthful of coffee. It burns him and he winces, sets the mug back down. 'Fine. Good. Yeah.'

'It's been a while since I slept in a chair,' says Rafferty, cracking his neck.

'You slept in a chair?' Cameron's voice suddenly brightens.

'Yeah. Someone had to make sure Jessa didn't do a drunk runner or vomit anywhere inappropriate.'

'Mic's still asleep,' says Maggie.

'Oh,' says Cameron. He smiles a bit. 'Cool. Reckon I should make pancakes?'

'*No*,' says Jessa. A groan. '*No* cooking. *Please.*'

Bass comes in, fresh faced and clean shaven after his shower at Laura's. 'Full house,' he says. 'How was last night?'

'Yeah, awesome,' says Rafferty.

Bass peers into the living room and frowns. 'What's up with your sister?'

'Food poisoning. Haven't seen her chuck like that since she was five.'

'*Food* poisoning, hey?' Bass claps Rafferty's back. 'Good on you for watching her back, but I can smell the shitty lolly water you guys drink from here.'

'Sorry, Dad,' says Jessa, head still in her hands.

* * *

I drift from them, after. The image of Jessa weeping on the couch too painful, too fiery and hot to go near or touch. I think about the sound of hooves on hard-packed earth. The smell of lemon-scented gum and the slick feel of reins in sweaty, trembling fingers.

Cameron and Rafferty, lying in their childhood beds. The window is open. They're both on their backs. Rafferty is flicking through messages on his phone, frowning slightly. Cameron is staring at the ceiling.

'Cam?'

'Hmm?'

'Happy birthday.' Rafferty sits up. 'We're *adults*. Crazy, hey?'

'Crazy.'

Eighteen. My twin boys are eighteen.

They eat pancakes for breakfast, side by side. Cameron brews a pot of herbal tea and sits it beside them. Bass comes in, dirty from his morning chores. He takes his hat off and sits down. 'Happy birthday!' he says. He tousles both their heads.

'Thanks.' Rafferty stretches. 'Doesn't feel like much of a birthday. Fucking exams.'

'You've got one today?'

'I've got *two* today. Cam's got one tomorrow. Maths?'

'General maths.' Cameron stuffs more pancake into his mouth. He reaches for his workbook with his other hand and Rafferty smacks it. 'Not during breakfast pancakes!'

'I need to study.'

'*After* breakfast pancakes,' Rafferty says.

'I'll give you your presents tonight,' says Bass. He stands up. Claps their shoulders. 'Let me know what time you need to be driven in, Raff.'

'Nah. I'll be right. Jake's running me in. Guy and I are going for drinks at the Savannah when we're done.'

Bass smiles. He shakes his head, leans against the doorway. 'Eighteen. I have adult children. How the hell did that happen?'

* * *

Summer. I watch the house, the bleaching of the world around it. The grass and leaves and heavy pastures.

I am thinking of memories.

Of how I cannot remember the last time I saw Jessa. The last time I saw Rafferty. Sometimes, there is a whisper of it. A hand, a voice fishing for a sentence. The smell of rain and wind.

And then I am watching Bass standing outside the house in the rain, staring in at our family, without me. The shadows, the short, thick grass, the naked arms of the jacaranda.

Only this time, I notice something different.

Rafferty, sitting by the window, watching Bass. Watching for his father. Waiting for him to come inside. To come home.

* * *

Jessa is in her room, stuffing clothes into her schoolbag. It is evening and outside Beatrice is talking to Rafferty.

'You coming home soon?' Bass, in the doorway.

'Maybe.' Jessa zips her bag up and grabs a schoolbook from her bedside table. Her wardrobe is already mostly empty.

'Jessa.'

'Bye, Dad.'

'Jessa! Will you just hold up a minute?'

'Bea's waiting!'

'Jessa, you need to ...'

Jessa glances at him, shrugs past. 'I saw you with Steve next to the run,' she says coldly.

Bass frowns the way he does when he's confused, trying to piece something together. All those months ago, when the world was in autumn, turning cold and red and naked.

'Jessa ...'

She shrugs away from him and slams her bedroom door on her way out.

* * *

The front paddock made strange with a tattered marquee. The jacaranda dropping purple flowers. The boys' birthday, I suppose. Belated.

Bass and Steve are settling hay bales underneath the marquee. Tarp and fairy lights and old wine barrels to rest drinks on.

'Jessa not around?' Steve asks.

'Nah. Been at Beatrice's since I got back from the camping trip.'

'Right.'

'I used to kid myself a bit, think she liked being here because of me and the boys. But I guess it was just about the horses. She hasn't been around in two weeks.'

'Right.'

They stand, shoulders nearly touching, staring at the paddock. Rafferty and Guy digging a fire pit big enough to bury half the town, and Cameron patting one of the Hereford calves through the fence.

Sam is nearby. She is in a pretty dress and has her hair loose around her face. She is watching Cameron. Waiting, I think, for him to notice her. But when he does look around he reddens and turns back to the calf, pretends to be checking something on one of its straight, healthy little legs.

'Hey,' she says.

'Hey,' he mumbles.

Out of her running gear, smelling of icy perfume that reminds him of Beatrice, she is unknown.

She touches his arm and he has to brace to stop himself shrugging it off.

'Umm … want a drink?' he says, walking off without waiting for an answer.

Her footsteps behind him are slow, confused. He gets her a beer and across the tent Maggie nudges Rafferty. 'Cameron's *girlfriend*,' she whispers.

'Cameron!' Rafferty yells, but Cameron makes no sign that he has heard him. Instead, he takes Sam's arm and they go and sit by the fire pit. Cameron sits next to her, shoulder to shoulder.

I can tell by his breathing that he is convincing himself that he's at an athletics day. That he's just finished running.

It's the only way he can loosen his shoulders, the only way he can stop from clenching his hands into unhappy fists.

* * *

Soft cheeses. Sunflowers. Photos of me with the boys and Jessa. With Beatrice and my schoolfriends. Someone had scanned them, printed them, stuck them up on pinboards around the marquee.

'Looks good,' Henry says.

'Thanks.' Cameron is securing the last one with fishing wire.

'Do you know if …'

'I don't know if Jessa'll come.'

Henry nods. 'Right, well.'

And they stand in silence. Rafferty arguing with Bass over fire restrictions by the fire pit. Steve setting up a table for drinks.

And of course that's when it hits me. This time of year. The marquee.

They are celebrating what would have been my fortieth birthday.

* * *

Sometimes I would stare at Bass and he would stare at me. 'Having a mushy moment?' he'd ask, setting aside his paper and leaning in until our noses were almost touching.

'No,' I said one time, kissing his nose. 'Just thinking about which bits of you are in the boys.'

I traced my finger along the line of his nose, his cheekbones, his strong jaw. 'Even your lips.' I brushed them with mine. 'It's the strangest thing. Nobody really tells you about it, do they? How you spend years just staring at them, looking at all the bits and pieces of them

that come from you and me and your parents and Bea …
But they're so much themselves, too. You know?'

Bass kissed my forehead. 'I know. But thank *God* they
didn't get that sulky little mouth,' he said, twiddling my
lips.

I batted him away. 'Do you really want to play that
game?'

'No,' he said, straightaway. Grinning. 'I really, really
don't.'

His hand. It was roughened, tanned. There was always
dirt around the nails and in his knuckle creases, no matter
how hard he scrubbed.

It was warm against mine. 'Stupid big hands,' I said.

Bass smiled. And kissed all my fingers.

* * *

Jessa is wearing the blue dress Beatrice bought her for
New Year's.

The dress she was wearing when she shot Opal.

She spends fifteen minutes putting her hair up in such
a way that it looks casual, as though she has just woken
up and rolled out the front door without a mirror in
between.

She puts Beatrice's mascara on. Dabs on a little lip
balm that Michaela gave her.

'Nearly ready, Jess?' Beatrice calls.

'Yes. Is … do you know if Steve's going?'

Beatrice sticks her head into the room. 'Steve? Your
dad's friend, Steve?'

'Yeah.'

'No idea.'

Jessa runs her hands over the dress. Down the front of it. I don't know whether it was splattered with Opal's blood or whether it somehow stayed clean. I am surprised, seeing her in it. Surprised she has not thrown it out. Burnt it.

They pick Michaela up on the way. She is wearing a pretty satin dress that makes her eyes look very blue. They pull up at the farm just as the fairy lights are turned on.

'Your mum would've loved this,' Beatrice says.

I look at the yard. At the tattered marquee and the cows at the fence, watching. I look at the sunflowers and the barbecue and how, already, there is laughter and chatting. Friends from Garras and old friends from the city. Friends from my job at the music store and university and where I used to agist Gus. Friends of Bass's who I don't know very well, friends from the boys' and Jessa's schools. Horse friends and competition friends.

Friends.

My grevillea and roses are decked in glow sticks and solar lights. Pebbles is tethered by the marquee with a piece of cardboard: *Pony Rides*. There is a box with *Memories – put one in!* written on the side.

Cameron has had some soft drink and is laughing with Sam now, one hand on her knee. The feel of her dress makes his ears go red, but he keeps his hand there, drinks another can of cola.

Monique Masters, whose little boy I had tried to get Jessa to befriend in kindergarten, stands with her back to the marquee. She wipes her eyes and her girlfriend puts an arm around her. 'Her children are so beautiful.' Her crying doesn't stop.

Rafferty is with Maggie, one arm loosely around her waist. He is introducing her to my mother's sister, Aunty Mim, who has flown down from Townsville. I have only met her a dozen times in my whole life. She is wearing a skivvy and jeans and five strands of coloured beads. Maggie reaches for them, runs them through her fingers. Aunty Mim smiles and takes them off for Maggie to look at.

And Bass is laughing with Taylor Mulder and then the food is brought out. Bea heads into the kitchen, setting everything up. Getting the food heated and cooked and out to everyone. Yvonne and Marg Mulder help her.

Her cheeks are red.

Mum comes in and presses a kiss to her shoulder. 'You're doing a brilliant job.'

Bea flushes further, smiles.

Yes. I would've loved this.

* * *

Jessa catches sight of Jake, shirt sleeves rolled up to his elbows, drinking wine, not beer. She likes that. It makes him different. She stops moving. Just watches him. His slow and measured movements. His broad shoulders, beautiful face.

'Jake's working for Loz now,' Henry says. He is thinking how best to slot his arm around Jessa's waist. He is wondering whether she will feel cool and dry or warm and damp. I can tell. The shift of his body, the way he is breathing carefully.

'Jake,' she says, still watching him. She glances away, back at Henry. 'You brought drink?'

'Yeah.'

She tugs at his sleeve. 'Let's go have some.'

The two of them disappear from the back of the marquee. Only Rafferty notices. He is standing with Maggie by the food table. His expression is closed. Maybe a little sad.

Maggie turns, sees Henry and Jessa disappear into the darkness.

'Do you want me to go after them?' she asks.

Rafferty shakes his head.

* * *

When Jessa rode Opal; when she breathed in the smell of leather and hay; when she dipped her hands into the dirt by the jacaranda. She is thinking of a night in winter when she was outside in a parka, making sure the ponies had thick enough rugs on. She turned back to the house and saw Rafferty and I talking. Yelling. She saw Rafferty storm out of the house and punch a hole in the side of the shed.

Later, she stood there. She stood in the rain and traced her hand around the hole that Rafferty's fist had made.

'Mum ...' The door clicked shut loudly behind her.

Inside I was nursing a wine, staring out the dark window.

'Mum. What's up with Raff?' She remembered shrugging off her parka. Leaving it in a sodden pile by the kitchen door.

My voice is sweeter, I think. Remembered by Jessa. Like I am singing. 'He's upset.'

'Why?'

'It's not a big deal. How's Pebbles?'

'Sulking.'

'Opal still dry?'

'Yeah.'

'Thanks for checking them, Jess.'

She nodded. She watched me sip my wine, stare out the window. She was overcome, in that moment, with a desire to slip into my lap as she had when she was smaller. She didn't, though. There was something about me, something in how I was sitting, that dissuaded her.

'Well … night,' she said. She paused, one hand resting on the door frame of the hallway. 'Goodnight, Mum,' she said, louder this time.

I stayed quiet.

* * *

The party on the lawn. The Beatles are playing and people are laughing. Bass, his hand on Laura's leg under the table where he's eating roast lamb, one-handed.

If anyone approaches he draws it back up, onto the table. It's done casually, lazily. Nobody seems to notice. Except my mother, who is on the other side of the marquee. Who is deep in conversation with an old schoolfriend. My mother, who sees everything.

Across the lawn, with her hair out, Bea is watching them too. Her expression is unreadable, but her centre seems to give way a little bit. Seems to collapse. I think of that day when she brought the groceries over. I yearn to see someone draw her in, draw her close. Draw her into a hug and tell her that she's been seen.

Nobody even seems to notice that she's there.

Laura is wearing mascara. A tiny bit, just on her top lashes. It makes her look younger. Look sparklier.

She is wearing the green dress she wore when she was my bridesmaid.

'It's okay, isn't it?' she asks Bass. 'I wasn't sure. I wanted to wear something nice. Something ... proper, you know? It's the only dress I've got and I don't get dresses. I don't get the etiquette.'

He squeezes her leg under the table. 'You look beautiful.'

I wonder if maybe it's not the mascara at all. Not the dress, which I don't remember sitting quite as perfectly as it is sitting now. I don't remember it catching the light in quite the same way. I wonder if it's Bass who has made her look younger. Made her glisten.

* * *

Henry and Jessa sit on the verandah. In front of them the marquee is huge and alive. Bright and noisy and beating.

Henry retrieves his bag from inside and pulls out a drink bottle.

He hands it to Jessa and she drinks. A long draught that makes her pucker.

'Ugh,' she says, wiping the back of her hand across her mouth. 'So, how long's Jake working at Loz's?'

'No idea. He's good. Good with the horses. She's

happy. Reckons she's not as young as she used to be.'
Henry grins. 'I reckon she must have a fella.'

Jessa passes the bottle back to Henry and he has a sip,
barely enough to wet his lips, and slips it away into his
bag.

He is thinking of whether he should kiss her. Whether
he is reading too much into the slight turning away of
her body. The crossed arms.

'Do you miss her?'

'Who?' Jessa startles, uncrosses her arms.

'Your mum.'

She snorts. 'Of course I miss her. That's the dumbest
question anyone's ever asked me. *Ever.*'

'Sorry.'

They sit quietly. Henry berating himself in silence.
Jessa thinking about Jake.

'I miss my mum,' he says.

'I know. Where is she?'

'I don't know.' He is thinking, in that moment, of the
silver-eyed man.

'That's not the same as my mum. It's not the same as
her being dead.'

Henry winces. He swallows hard. Briefly, before he
snaps it away, he thinks that it would be easier if she was
dead. 'No. I know.'

More quiet. Jessa picks at a loose splinter of wood
coming up from the verandah floor.

'I'm sorry about your mum,' Jessa says.

'I know.'

* * *

Cameron thinks of the night after I died. He is thinking of how he dug into the backs of his hands so deep they had felt like they was burning. Smouldering. He had woken from dreams of being on fire. Had rolled over to wake Rafferty. But Rafferty was already up, sitting on the window ledge. Not sideways, not like he normally sat. But with his legs out, leaning forward. Like he was going to jump into the branches of the jacaranda.

Cameron switched the light on, checking the backs of his hands. Groggy, still dreamy, making sure they weren't smoking, melting.

When Cameron looked over again, Rafferty was sitting back sideways. Sitting like he always did.

Cameron rolled to face the wall.

And neither of them slept.

* * *

Guy comes over and gets Rafferty in a headlock. 'Where's the slug bucket?'

'Geddoff! I'm trying to stay clean.'

'Jake's handing out crackers,' says Guy. 'He's very helpful.'

'My nana's here. She said to say hi to you.'

'Oh! Your nana! She's so *clean*!'

There is no lengthy speech. There is no minute of silence. There is no discussion of how I died. There are just stories. Endless snippets of stories. It's strange to think that it is me binding all of these people together. Even though I am gone.

Even though I am not really here any more.

'Remember that beautiful dress she wore to your eighteenth?'

'Strange how she was such a quick walker and so young when she was potty trained, but she didn't speak till she was four!'

'We used to go riding, when we were teenagers … She'd borrow a horse off me … Then she got Gus …'

It's strange. These people. This marquee of people. They have not forgotten me. I am remembered as more than the reason for my family's grief. This fills me up. Makes me think of warmth. I think of sinking into a steaming bath after a day out with the cows or horses. After a day competing or training or working. How my muscles loosened. My tension with it. Everything soft and joyful.

* * *

The fairy lights from the marquee are still glowing through the window when Bass stumbles back into the room. His footsteps are heavy, ungainly. That's how I used to be able to tell if Bass was drunk.

Bass pauses in the doorway and breathes in. His breath catches and he lurches over to the dresser where he still keeps a lot of my things. He fumbles with the drawer where I kept my favourite perfume, but pauses, his attention caught by a sudden thud outside. 'All good!' someone calls and Bass reaches into the drawer and brings out not the perfume but a card. Thick, cream coloured, with Bass's sprawling writing.

I would have no other companion in this life but you.

Bass finds this in the card he gave me after Jessa was born. He stares at it, stumbles backwards onto the bed and cries.

I try, then. I try to yell at him. I try to yell his name over and over again.

His breath evens out.

He sleeps with the card pressed between his fingers.

* * *

At the same time that Steve is unhooking the fairy lights and Bass is curled on the bed with the card in his fingers, Rafferty is at Maggie March's. Everything is bleached of colour. They are in her bed, which is pressed hard up against a wall with a window. Through that window is the brick wall of the neighbour's house. Rafferty closes the blinds when he is over there. Hesitant, I think, so close to other houses. Other people. Growing up on a farm where the closest person was still a couple of minutes' drive away. He is not relaxed in town, although he would never say so.

The curtains closed against the moon, he traces her face, her breasts, her legs in the moonlight and kisses her between the eyes.

He is thinking that their hearts are beating at the same time. He is thinking that there is nothing as good as this feeling of her skin against his. Of how, when he lies on top of her, she matches his breathing. So that when he is breathing out, she is breathing in. How, when she does that, he feels so close to her.

'I love you,' he says.

'I love you too,' she says. She does not make him wait. Does not hold it over him, leave him vulnerable, for longer than it takes her to breathe air into her lungs.

I think of Cameron, waking in the night with panic attacks.

Cameron should have been with this girl who says 'I love you' straight back. Cameron, who needs gentleness. Who needs gentleness so badly.

* * *

Henry and Jessa walk out into the paddock. Gus groans in his sleep as they pass. They stop on the far side, where the ground begins to curve down and the breeze is stronger.

They lie down, head to head, staring out towards the valley where there are lights and shadows and everything moving.

'I don't want to go back to school,' says Jessa. 'My stupid brothers have finished. Can you believe that? They never have to do another test or sit in another stupid classroom.'

'What if they go on to uni?'

'They're not. Not yet anyway. They're taking a gap year.' Jessa turns to Henry. 'I shouldn't have said that. About your mum. I shouldn't have.'

'No.'

'I'm a shit.'

'Sometimes.' Henry stretches. 'But mostly not. I'm so sleepy. I reckon I could fall asleep out here.'

Jessa yawns widely. 'I'm not sleepy.' She turns onto her stomach, stares out towards the valley. 'It's so hazy tonight. After it's rained, you can almost see the city. It's just this tiny, tiny light.' She points.

'Smokey, you mean. There must be a fire somewhere,' Henry says. He pauses, sends Laura a quick text on his mobile, asking if she's noticed the smoke. 'Bloody early for fires,' he says.

'Hmm.'

'I wonder why they built the house back where they did. Imagine the views you'd have if you'd built it here.'

'Mum said the same thing to Dad. He said it would've been more expensive. She wanted to build a little granny flat here for the two of them when they got old.'

'What about the house?'

'She said that'd be for Cameron. That he's the firstborn so he has to stay and look after them and let them out for walks and change their nappies.'

Henry snorts.

'Yeah, well for ages Cameron thought she was serious.'

Henry puts his hand near Jessa's, but she doesn't move hers closer. She stares hard towards the city, then up towards the stars.

'Jake's so nice,' she says. 'I'm glad Loz hired him.'

Henry yawns. 'Yeah. Me too.'

* * *

It is still dark, still quiet. Henry and Jessa are still lying in the curve of the hill. Henry is watching Jessa. Watching the minute gleam of her eyes, the way her hands are crossed over her body as she stares out into the night.

He pulls himself up. He moves gently, rolling closer towards her. He takes a deep breath and kisses Jessa's temple. His heart is pounding, thumping. So strong he feels like he is breathing to the beat of it.

Her eyes are open, but she doesn't move, doesn't shuffle closer or pull away. He kisses her cheek and she finds his hand. She squeezes it. And Henry flops down next to her. His heart stays fast.

His heart stays hopeful.

* * *

Dappled shadows, the sun beating down and the smell of burning. I can't smell it, not any more. But I can see the thickness of the air. I know that smell.

I remember it.

Laura is on her verandah, hands on hips. She is feeling the wind, her radio blaring on the scuffed table by the door. Cameron is sitting there, thinking about Sam.

Jake comes up onto the verandah and sits down. 'Just re-arranged your hay. Should be able to fit the tractor in next to it, now.'

'Thanks, mate.' Laura sits down on the step and stares out at the smoke.

'Fire still out of control?'

She nods. Inside Henry is cooking something with zucchini and pumpkin. 'I've been trying to get on to his mum. If that wind change they're predicting comes in, I want him away from here. It's only fucking November. This is unbelievable.'

'I can take him to my aunt's place. She's just outside the city.'

'That'd be a three hour drive.'

Jake shrugs. 'I don't mind. Just let me know.'

'Thank you.' Laura stares at him for a long moment and then back out over the verandah railing. 'You look like shit.'

'Hmm. Davo's been round. He and Mum get pretty rowdy.'

'Fighting?'

'Nah, mostly not. They just get drunk and loud and stay up too late.' He yawns. 'But it's all good. They're moving to his soon. Guy's going to TAFE in Melbourne. I just need to find a place.'

'Henry!' Cameron calls. 'Have you diced it really small?'

'I'm doing it myself! You're just moral support! Moral support is *quiet*!' Henry calls back.

Laura smiles a bit and turns back to Jake. 'You can stay, you know. Hen and I, we're pretty quiet.'

'Really?'

'I've got the bedroom in the loft. Gets a bit hot, but it's okay at night.'

'That'd be great. Thank you. Heaps.'

Laura smiles.

He nods and gets back up. 'Better get back into it.'

'Sit for a minute. It's thirty-five degrees. Henry! Can you get Jake a cold drink, please?'

Jake sits down and Henry brings him out a ginger beer.

'It's still fifty kilometres away,' Henry tells him, gesturing to the smoke.

'That's nothing out here,' Laura snaps. 'You need to learn some respect for fires.'

Henry shrugs. 'I do respect them.'

Laura snorts and goes back to making some sort of list.

'Loz?' It's Henry, leaning close to her.

'What?'

'You looked really pretty the other night. With the black stuff on your eyes.'

* * *

The air is hazy, the wind slow. It is like being submerged. It is like drowning, but with the dryness of it all.

The sirens at the CFA keep stopping and starting.

Cameron goes to Sam's, once Henry has finished cooking. They are looking at maps of hiking trails in the area, trying to work out if there are any places they haven't tried. She is wearing a baggy T-shirt and a tiny pair of shorts. She has a little bit of makeup on, but it has made her face look shiny. She has cut watermelon up for them, but she is the only one who has been eating it.

She stares down at the map, sucking on a slice of melon. Looking. Hunting.

Places they have not yet run through.

Cameron has a battery-operated radio that he keeps tuned to the local emergency news.

'Are you okay to do this now?' Sam asks, watching as he twiddles the tuner, stares out the window at the smoke haze.

'Yeah. I'm fine.'

'It's a long way away.'

'Yeah, I know. I just …' He runs his hands through his hair. I see Sam looking at his scarred hands. The rawness of them, even healed.

She pulls one of his hands down. Pulls it down into hers and he stares at it, stares at her. There is a standing fan rotating around the room. It reaches them and Sam's hair flies around her face.

'Those sirens. They just mean that the rig's going out. It doesn't mean anything else. It's not the community siren. That goes for ages. Then you know something's up. Nothing's up. It's all okay.'

'Yeah,' says Cameron. He pulls his hand away from Sam's. He presses his fingers to the back of his hand until the skin fades white around the contact. 'Yeah, I know.'

* * *

'To Cate,' my mother had said, holding up her glass.

'To Cate.'

My twenty-first birthday. Already engaged and beaming. Coconut on my birthday cake. Orange juice tangy with lemon and vodka.

I was wearing a black dress I hung on to for years afterwards. That I hoped, one day, to give to Jessa.

There is a photo from this moment. My mother giving the toast. My father sitting behind her with his arms crossed, but smiling. Bass with his arm around me, his champagne glass to his lips.

Beatrice. Watching him. Watching us. Something about her expression sad. Yearning, maybe.

Beatrice, on the couch. A 'no' choked up in her throat.

Strange, how a composed and older sister can break your heart as easily as a young and frail one. Back then, of course, I didn't think that way. I was glowing with happiness and hugging it to myself. It's only now, looking back, that I see it. That my heart breaks.

* * *

Rafferty and Guy are in the city. It's sunny, still. A tram rattles past and Guy grins. There is gum on the footpath, seagulls perched nearby on a low bluestone wall. 'Man, I love those things.'

'Trams?'

'Trains, trams. Used to want to be a conductor when I was little.'

Rafferty shoves his hands in his pockets. 'You're such a wank.'

'You should come down, you know. Rent a place. We could study together.'

'I don't wanna do horticulture.'

Guy rolls his eyes. 'Another course. Whatever you want. You got a pretty good mark, yeah?'

'Yeah.'

Guy offers him a cigarette and Rafferty shakes his head. 'Nah, not smoking any more. Bloody expensive and I don't particularly want to up my chances of deadly diseases. And if I studied down here I'd live with my nan. Rent free and all that.'

'Suit yourself, Pandora. What'd your dad say?'

'Huh?'

'About your *marks*.'

'Didn't ask what we got. Me or Cameron.'

'That sucks.' Guy stares up at the buildings above them. They're in Russell Street. I recognise the theatre. 'What's Maggie doing?'

'Maggie's going up to Sydney. Doing some osteo course.'

'Shit. You going up with her?'

'No.' It is too far, too far from Garras. She said they'd work it out somehow. They'd make it work, being in different states. He hasn't seen much of her since then. He is reeling. It has hit him in the stomach like a flying hoof.

'So?' Guy says.

'So *what*?' Rafferty snaps.

'What'd Cameron get?'

'He did well. Bit lower than me, but not much.'

'Funny. Everyone always had him pegged as the smarter one. Guess he's just less of a drunken arsehole.'

'Delightful.'

'So.' Guy stares at him.

'So fucking what?'

'Are you going to come and study?'

'Maybe! Just fucking drop it. I'm deferring this year.'

'Deferring?' Guy's eyebrows arch up. 'You applied?'

'Of course I fucking applied. They *make* you. We were in those classes together.'

'Yeah, but I thought we just put law and science and medicine and stupid things down at Melbourne Uni that we'd never get into.'

Rafferty is quiet.

Guy stops walking. 'Are you fucking kidding me? What course?'

'Science. But I'm going to do music, I think. Maybe. I dunno.'

'You got into fucking science at Melbourne Uni? Jesus. Congrats, man.'

'I might not end up going. I dunno yet.'

'Still.' Guy stares at him. 'Hey, let's go get a beer. My shout. Then we can get the train out to whatsit TAFE.'

They start walking down the road again. There are shadowy patterns beneath the trees. People walking slowly, staring up at the sky.

* * *

'I didn't want to visit Nan today,' Jessa says for the sixth time in as many minutes. She is hunched up against the passenger door of a rattling, rusted old car that I think Cameron has borrowed from Rafferty. They're on the freeway, somewhere past Rosella. 'It's too hot.'

'Shush. I'm *driving*,' says Cameron.

'If you can't talk and drive at the same time, you shouldn't have your licence.'

'You're sweet.'

'Shut up. Dad doesn't even *want* those shelves. He doesn't like that kind of stuff.'

'He asked us to grab it.'

Jessa snorts. 'He asked *you* to grab it. He didn't ask me.'

'Jessa, can you stop whinging? Please?'

Jessa makes a huffing noise and turns the radio off.

'How's Bea's?'

'Shit. She won't leave me alone. I've been staying at Mic's a lot. Her mum's cool. Doesn't care.'

'Well, Bea's lived by herself for how many years now? It's probably really weird having someone in her house.'

'Well, she shouldn't have *asked* me, then.'

Cameron changes gears. 'You could come home.'

'No.'

'Why?'

'Because you killed my horse.' Cameron winces and doesn't say anything for a while. Jessa's nose puckers like it always does when she's caught in a lie.

I wonder, though. Why now. It's to do with Opal, with that open gate and the feeling of the gun in her hand. But, it's more than that. It is Laura, pressed against Bass's side, untouching. It is watching Steve hug her father outside the chicken coop. It is Henry, that night they went too far.

She needs to be held.

And Beatrice, for all her fussing, does not know how to hold her. Draw her in. She plaits her hair instead. She buys her clothes or offers to buy her little china figurines or overly sparkly jewellery.

Jessa mumbles something into the door.

'What?' snaps Cameron.

'I said I'm sorry.'

* * *

When Laura turned thirty, the boys were toddling and I was pregnant with Jessa.

'She doesn't want a party,' Bass kept saying as I rattled off plans for balloons and streamers and a big cake. I was wearing my elastic waisted jeans. My greasy hair was up in a knot on top of my head.

'She *says* she doesn't want a party,' I said.

'I've known her since we were kids. She's not a party person, Cate. Blood'll shoot out her ears at the sound of the first party cracker.'

'Charming.'

'Seriously. You just need to chill, you know? Put your feet up, have a rest.'

'I'm *fine*,' I snapped, shoving past him to get to my phone.

'Cate,' said Bass, using his slow voice. 'Cate, I think you're looking for projects to do, seeing as you can't ride.'

'Thanks, Captain Obvious.'

'Cate?'

'Hmm?'

'Why the fuck do you have Sylvia's number up on your phone?'

'What?' I shoved the phone out of sight.

'I just saw Sylvia's name. On your phone. You said you'd lost touch.'

'We have. Sort of.'

'Cate …'

'What? It's no big deal.'

'How would you feel? If you'd asked me something and I'd lied?'

'Fine.'

'Bullshit. You'd feel like absolute shit.' He ran his hand around the back of his neck. 'I *hate* secrets.'

'That shirt is ugly on you.'

'Can you be serious? Please? You say I don't talk enough – well this is me trying to talk!'

'Shush, you'll wake the boys.'

'All I'm asking is that you don't keep stuff from me. Even stuff like that.'

I rolled my eyes. 'Fine. Alright. Jeez.'

Secrets. I'd given so little thought to them. I'd never had a big one, neither mine or someone else's. Not really. No secrets.

But I know now. How they crawl into you. Into the deep places you can't reach. They take a hold. Are insidious.

I know.

There are so many things I would have done differently.

* * *

'Can I stay with you for a while?' Jessa, not looking at Laura. Not daring to. They are unwinding a pressure bandage off Gus's leg. There's still smoke. I can see it through the stable door.

'Yes. Why?' Laura asks.

'Because I'm not okay to come back here. Not yet. And Beatrice is driving me crazy. I've been staying at Mic's heaps, but I'm starting to feel bad.'

Laura grins at that. 'Bea trying to girlify you?'

'No. She's been okay with that. She just hovers. I don't like it.'

Laura is quiet for a moment. 'Why aren't you ready?'

'I'm just not.'

Laura puts aside the bandage and starts pulling away the cotton padding. She stares hard at Jessa. 'Jessa Carlton,

I've known you since you were a bump in your mum's belly.'

'I know.'

'I've never let you get away with things.'

'I *know*.'

'Why aren't you ready? Why now?'

Jessa swallows. 'I just … Opal and …'

Laura eyes her for a long moment and then nods. 'Okay. Well, you can stay. Sleep on the couch. Henry has dibs on the spare room.'

'Henry could stay here,' Jessa says. 'He loves hanging out with Cam and Raff. And Dad's been teaching him about the different cow breeds.'

Laura considers this. 'I'll ask him. He might like it.'

'He would.'

Laura stares out into the smoky day. 'It's controlled now.'

'What is?'

'That fire. It was bloody close to Garras. Shit, you haven't been following it?'

'No. Dad does the fire stuff.'

'That's all well and good, but you still live here, Jessa. You're not a little kid any more. You've got to step up with these sorts of things.'

Jessa starts rewrapping Gus's leg bandage.

Laura cocks an eyebrow. 'And you should think about it.'

'What?'

'Going home.'

'I'll be next door. I can go there all the time.'

'But you don't go there. Not enough. You're not the only one who's still hurting, Jess. If you stay with me, you're going to be spending a lot of time at home. Got it?'

Jessa's expression has clamped down.

'Okay,' she says.

* * *

Afterwards, I blamed pregnancy hormones. I told Laura they'd made me go crazy and Bass backed me up, rolling his eyes to the ceiling.

'She's lost it,' he said. 'She's seriously, completely lost it.'

'I put the ice creams I bought in the dryer,' I said. 'By *accident*.'

Laura snorted. I only got one-word responses from her for a week afterwards. The longest, I think, that she was ever angry with me.

The party had started off nicely enough. We'd had it at the Mulders' barn. Streamers, balloons, cupcakes with thirty on them. Laura had baulked at first. At the number of people, at the noise and the booze and the music.

But I'd made it for *her*. The booze was her favourite. The songs were all ones she knew the words to.

She'd relaxed, started laughing and chatting and I'd wrapped some streamers around her head and she'd let me.

'Beautiful,' I'd said and she'd rolled her eyes.

'Who said this was a bad idea?' I'd asked, sidling up to Bass. Except, as pregnant as I was, I couldn't sidle very well. It was a backwards waddle.

Sylvia arrived after midnight. The lanterns were burning low and someone had set the fairy lights to flicker. I didn't recognise her at first. She had dyed her hair dark, had a huge wrapped present in her arms. A canvas.

Then she got closer to Laura and I choked on my drink.

She was pregnant. And she was with the silver-eyed man. His arm was around her waist.

* * *

Jessa watches Jake. It's a hungry watching. Damp and consuming. She is disappointed by how little time she is able to spend with him. It shows on her face. He works hard, stays focused, even when Laura is off the property or in the living room making lists or going over accounts.

'Wish that brother of his was as hardworking,' Bass grumbles to her. He tried hiring Guy to help him do some fencing.

Jake weeds her garden beds and goes up and fixes the damaged bits of the roof. Laura gives him free rein. He gives her receipts from the hardware and feed stores and she reimburses him in his next pay.

He insulates the ceiling of the loft. 'Figured Henry'd probably be moving on. He's getting pretty grown-up and I won't be here forever,' he says when Laura stares, dumbstruck, at the insulated walls.

'Shit. That's amazing. Thank you,' she says.

He grins, goes back to waterproofing her winter rugs.

Henry stands in the living room. He is slowly packing up his clothes into a bag. He leaves the big suitcase he has brought where it is. He hopes he won't be gone long.

He is watching her. Does not see how she is watching Jake.

* * *

I can't remember what my hands looked like. I wonder about this as I watch Laura and Bass, leaning into each other in the kitchen. They are eating pancakes off the same plate. I can't tell who has fried them up. The dishes are piled high in the sink. There is washing detergent, a full rack of drying dishes. There is sun streaming in through windows that look clean. There is jacaranda on the table in a vase. Laura brushes a finger against it and wipes her mouth with the back of her hand.

'Strange,' Laura murmurs. 'How I never even looked twice at you. All those years. You may as well have been a sack of dirt.'

'You're sweet.'

She knocks him in the ribs and he coughs. 'When did you ...?' she trails off.

'When did I what?'

'I dunno.' She touches the flowers again. The water in the glass vase ripples. 'I dunno. When did you ... like me?'

Bass snorts and a piece of pancake goes flying. 'Like you? Are we in grade three?'

Laura doesn't look up from the flowers and Bass feeds a piece of pancake to Mac. 'After Cate ... everything was in pieces. I can't even remember most of it. But you were here. Every morning, you looked for Opal. You ... you did their feet, with your bad back. I don't know what we ... what I would've done.'

'You would've been fine.'

'No. We wouldn't have.'

Laura is smiling, still staring at the flowers. She is thinking of the silver-eyed man. Of how different Bass is.

How different she is with him.

* * *

Henry sleeps on the couch at our place. At night he stares out the window towards Laura's place and sometimes he breathes out a deep sigh.

'Sleep in Jessa's room,' Bass said. 'She won't mind.'

But Henry baulked, shook his head. He goes up there sometimes. When the others are out. He stands in the doorway of her bedroom. Sometimes he'll sit on the bed, run a hand over the pillow, across the doona. Sometimes he'll lie down, stare at the ceiling. Heave a huge sigh and get back up again.

He stares up at his mother's strange painting. Traces the signature.

Once he fell asleep on the bed, staring up at it.

Cameron came home, stuck his head in the room. 'Thought you were Jessa.'

Henry blinked, sat up. 'Sorry.'

'It's a weird painting, hey? It was a present for Mum but she said it gave her the willies.'

'My mum painted it.'

'What? Really?' Cameron comes in and sits down next to Henry. The springs creak.

'Yep, really. That's her signature.'

'You're sure?'

Henry snorts. 'D'you know how many times I've had to forge it on school forms and stuff? I'm one hundred percent sure. Besides, I recognise her paintings. They're all the same.'

Cameron stares up at it. He frowns.

'It's ... eerie.'

'It's her insides.'

'What do you mean?'

'My mum's paintings are all of her insides. It's all chaos and battling and things banging into each other. It's weird to look at because it's so real.'

'I know what that's like. That painting.'

Henry picks at a stray thread on Jessa's doona. 'Me too.'

The painting. I watch it, long after the boys disappear into the next room. I watch the arching shapes, the sharp-edged ones. The brushstrokes. So vivid. They look like they are still moving across the canvas.

The motion of it.

I remember. It always made me feel sick.

Like I was looking in on myself.

Like Sylvia had painted me.

* * *

On this night Henry is sitting on the couch with his legs crossed, staring across the room at the heavily stacked bookshelves. His head is tilted slightly, reading the spines. He glances up but does not startle as the back door snaps open.

'Henry?' Raff flicks the light switch on and Henry blinks. 'What are you doing here?'

'I'm staying here for a while. Been here for two days already.'

'Oh … right.' Rafferty has been at Guy's place. Drinking, playing his guitar, sometimes half letting himself believe they'll be in the city together next year. He's been out to dinner with Maggie tonight, but they were quiet, mostly.

'Yes, really. Jessa's staying over there and somehow convinced Laura that I'd like to stay here. Laura actually said the word *treat*.'

'Wow.'

'I know.'

They are silent for a moment. Rafferty walks across the room and sits on the end of the couch. 'Heard anything from your mum?'

'No,' Henry says, flat and fast.

'Do you ever? Hear from her?'

'No.' Henry starts picking at a stray thread on the couch.

'Are you going back?'

'No. I'm staying in Garras.' He doesn't look up and Rafferty doesn't say anything else. He claps Henry on the shoulder when he stands up and glances back at him from the doorway.

'You want the light off?'

'No … it's okay. Leave it on. Please.'

* * *

I remember, in a sudden rush, how it was that I came to be in Garras. It is a simple memory, short and sharp. Of Sylvia eating a quiche with her sunglasses on top of her head.

She had decided that she wanted to be a florist. We were scouting places along Bridge Road for her to work while she looked for a course.

'You wanna go bush? Go to Garras. My sister still lives there.'

'Where the hell is Garras?' I asked.

'Two hours away.'

'Cheap land?'

'No night life. Getting out of there was the best thing I ever did,' she said, staring hard across the road.

'Huh,' I said, watching her. Watching her closely.

'I'm going to specialise in wedding flowers. That's where the money is. And I love weddings. Who the hell doesn't love weddings?'

'What's it like?'

'What's what like?'

'Garras.'

Sylvia had shrugged. 'Pretty, I guess. Lots of horses.'

'Are there many comps there? Horse comps?'

'Fuck, I dunno. There's this massive ag show every year. Lots of people compete in that.' She considers for a moment. 'Actually, there's lots of competitions. Laura says. Anyway – flowers, right? Wedding flowers.'

I stopped listening. I'd heard of Garras Ag. The grounds always looked beautiful in the photos I'd seen in magazines.

Garras, I thought.

* * *

Jessa leans into Scrap and, for a moment, stops brushing. He glances back at her, large ears pricked. He is eighteen hands tall. A pinto-Clydesdale cross with feathers on his legs.

Jess brings a bucket over and stands on it. She starts humming. Starts brushing his mane out.

Across the aisle Jake has the radio on and is seated on the brick floor with his legs crossed. In his lap is a jumble of Laura's bridles and martingales. Her girths and spare reins. Some of them I vaguely recognise as mine. A seventy-five centimetre girth when she had a breaker who didn't fit into the dozen she already had. A sweet-iron bit for a mare who kept her jaw rigid against rein pressure.

'I should be done by next month,' Jake says.

'If you're lucky.'

'Was that a Jessa offer to give me a hand?'

'No. I'm busy.'

'Yeah, I can see. There's a lot of Scrap to brush.'

Jess doesn't reply and Jake goes back to his sorting.

All of her insides are smiling.

* * *

It was the only time I saw Laura cry, that night I invited Sylvia to her thirtieth birthday party at the Mulders' barn.

Laura just stared at the two of them. Sylvia, one hand under her bulging belly, his arm around the small of her back. Laura strode outside. 'I need the loo.'

311

I waddled after her. It was a beautiful night. New moon, all the stars out. The whole pinpricked mess of them that you missed in the city or when the moon was full.

'Loz?' She was next to the portaloo, bent over, bracing herself above her knee

'Loz …' I went to put an arm around her but she shrugged me off.

I expected her to go off at me, which was part of the reason why I had followed her away from the party. Loz wasn't known for her discretion when she lost her temper. But she just kept crying. The wrenching, wounded sobs when something was broken and there was no way to fix it.

'I'm really, really, really sorry. I don't know what the fuck I was thinking.'

She nodded, but didn't speak. After a while she slid down until she was sitting on the ground and she let me put my arm around her after I'd managed to hunker down next to her.

We didn't speak. She went quiet and I thought she had stopped crying, but when I looked at her, the tears were still coming. Silently.

She was staring up at the pinpricked sky.

* * *

Laura rolls onto her back. She is on Bass's side of the bed. When you lie on your back your right arm is on the edge. Bass sleeps on my side now. As he did when Jessa would come creeping in, having woken herself up with a hiss and a start.

I wonder if he misses her coming in every night. I wonder if he dreams of it.

My pillowcase has been changed. They're all white pillowslips, now. New ones.

Laura is flicking the headboard with her finger. Bass has an arm over her stomach. 'I know it's not about Scrap. She's never even looked twice at him! But it's so good to see her riding again.'

'Why's she doing it, then?'

'To be close to Jake.'

'Guy's brother?' Bass is quiet for a moment.

'Would he do anything?' Bass's voice is tight in the gloom. I see his arm tighten over her midriff.

'No.' She pauses, reaches for his hand. 'No. He wouldn't. No way.'

* * *

Newborn Jessa, hissing and angry, caught in the crook of my arm. I was at Laura's. The boys were in a playpen in the next room. I had dragged the chair so I could see them clearly. I'd already learnt, only weeks after they'd started toddling around on their feet, the value of supervising them constantly. I was still recovering from the scratch marks they'd managed to key into my favourite dressage saddle with one of those benign toddler sporks.

Propped on Laura's cluttered desk was the canvas Sylvia had painted for her. It was large, cumbersome. At odds with the faintly 1920s feel of the rest of the bluestone cottage. Laura had once told me that her mother and grandmother were both like her, that they had never really seen the point of redecorating. Life was short. You did things that mattered.

'Well?' I asked. Jessa hissed more loudly and I unhooked my maternity bra.

'I don't know.'

It was all swirling colours, bright and organic, rather than the geometric, darker shapes that Sylvia had used in her other works. This one was ripe, thrilling. It had a vitality about it, as though just by looking at it you might become less tired, less worn. Brought back to sharpness and clarity.

'You could sell it,' I said, but the words stuck in my throat as I breathed them. Selling it was not an option. I knew that, but I was hoping to avoid what I suspected was coming. My mother loved art. She was an artist. For her, a gallery was like a church. From a young age Beatrice and I had been taken to gallery openings. One of our first life lessons was to never *ever* touch a painting or a wall at a gallery.

I held my breath. I waited.

Laura looked at me. 'You reckon?'

I realised, in that moment, how little Laura ever actually looked me in the eye. She was looking me in the eye now. Something almost pleading about her expression.

I took a deep breath. 'You do what you have to do,' I said.

I closed my eyes as she started slashing, but afterwards, when the canvas was in tatters and she'd stomped on the wooden frame, the sight of the strips on the floor, the splintered wood, was almost enough to move me to tears.

I made myself look. I made myself set Jessa down in her pram and help Laura pick up the remains and shove them into a garbage bag.

My penance.

* * *

Cameron decides that Sam smells like flour and cinnamon. Like a bakery, when things are still unmixed. Uncooked.

Sam has her P plates and they spend their weekends driving out to race days.

'Did you bring it?' she asks him as they head out along the highway, the back seat of her hatchback piled high with bags.

'Yeah,' he said. He rummages around and pushes a CD into the player.

Nick Cave fills the car and Sam grins. 'Nice.'

'It's sort of weird, isn't it?' he says.

'What?'

'I dunno … racing, but not for school. It's weird.'

'Driving ourselves out.' Sam shifts gears. 'Very grown-up.'

'What time are you running?' he asks.

'I'm not.'

'Huh?'

'I didn't qualify.'

'Oh.' Cameron can feel her watching him out of the corner of her eye. Then a truck cuts her off and she slams her palm against the horn.

Later that day, Cameron kisses her. It's an overcast, still afternoon. He's untying his running shoes and she's holding a can of Coke he bought her on the way. It must be warm by now. He stuffs his handkerchief into his back pocket.

Cameron won his race and his heart was still pounding. It would seem spontaneous to Sam. Natural. Fluid. But I see Cameron tensing through the shoulders. The way he settles his breathing deep down into his belly before he leans in.

It is quiet. Small. With Maggie March he had expected something large and luscious. Something that would shift him.

When they pull away, pull apart, his eyes are pressed closed.

'Cam?'

He startles a little bit, the image of Maggie March, smiling at him, disappearing from his mind. 'Yeah,' he says. 'I'm great.'

* * *

Laura is fiddling with the dishes in the cupboard. The good dishes she inherited from her mother.

Once, putting those dishes away, I asked her why Sylvia was the way she was. It was after Henry was born. After he had stayed with Laura that first time.

'Our family wasn't a happy one,' Laura said.

'But you turned out brilliantly! I don't get how you could both ...'

'People deal with things in different ways, Cate,' she said sharply. 'I got sort of rigid, I think. I like things how I like them. I plan my days carefully. I like my space. I bottle things, I think.'

'And Sylvia?'

'Sylvia just went wild. Chaotic. I dunno.'

'I shouldn't have brought it up. Sorry, Loz.'

Laura shrugged. 'Don't be sorry.' She pauses, sets a plate down. 'You know what's funny, though? I always thought my way of coping was better. That my way was … superior to hers.'

'Loz …'

'But now. Now, I dunno. We're all just doing the best we can. I don't think there's better or worse. There just *is*.'

* * *

Bass is staring at the cheque for Opal's insurance. He is staring and staring. It is more than he thought she was worth. He is thinking of his bull. He has a picture of it from a magazine, a set of details, highlighted in front of him.

'So?' says Steve.

Bass glances at him. 'Gimme a minute.'

But he doesn't call the number he has underlined. He stares at the cheque. He stares and stares and finally folds it up, puts it in his shirt pocket.

'I can't buy the stupid bull,' he says.

'What are you going to do with the money?'

'Pay Jo back. Get back up to speed with the mortgage. Put some aside for … for Jessa. For the boys. I can't do it. I can't spend this money on a bloody bull.'

'Weren't you getting a loan anyway?'

'Yeah ... a loan's ... A loan felt different.' He flushes. 'God, I sound like an idiot.' He rests his head on the table. 'I'm going soft in my old age.'

Steve pats his head.

'You'll work it out.'

Bass groans.

* * *

In the quiet and secret world I had imagined after my death, it was always Beatrice who moved in with Bass. Beatrice who would mother my children and sleep in my bed. Beatrice, who had loved Bass, I think, from the moment she first saw him sitting on Mum's couch.

Beatrice who, in this other world, fitted as easily into the crook of Bass's arms as a load of hay or a bobby calf.

But it is not Beatrice.

It is beautiful, fierce, intelligent Laura. Laura told me time and time again that she is damaged as Sylvia is damaged. But differently, too.

It seems strange now, to imagine such a thing. Beatrice all angles and order and uncertainty. Bass all golden and flowing. Beautiful Bass, so chaotic and full of life.

I am not sure how many of my memories have seeped away. How many are slowly seeping. I wonder if eventually I will have none left. That I will be watching my family, or the children of my children, perhaps even their children, and suddenly it will be as if I am looking down at strangers. Staring at them. Bewildered.

* * *

Coming back from Laura's house with a box of cocoa, Henry sees Jessa watching Jake. Sees the expression on her face.

She is in the yard, curled in the shadow of one of the gum trees with a mess of dirty bridle parts in her lap. Henry opens his mouth, half steps forward, then stops himself.

Straightens.

He goes back to our farm and sets the cocoa on the table. He stares at it.

'Jessa still at Loz's?' Rafferty asks, coming in and opening the fridge.

'Yup.'

Rafferty frowns and leans against the fridge door.

Henry stares back at him. 'What?'

Rafferty tilts his head. 'Nothing. Just weird, is all. Her taking off there.'

'It's Jake,' Henry says, shortly, busying himself with mixing bowls and cocoa.

'Huh? *Jake* Jake?'

'Yes *Jake* Jake. Jessa likes him. Can you pass me the milk?'

Rafferty passes it to him. 'I …'

'Don't tell me I told you so. Don't you fucking dare,' Henry says, flatly.

'I was going to say I'm sorry. That's fucked.'

'It's Jessa. I should've … I didn't even …'

'You can't see that sort of stuff coming.' Rafferty sits down. 'Not till it's too late.'

'I know how Cam feels now. With you and Maggie. I know how he feels.'

Rafferty winces at that. 'She's just got a crush. That's all.'

Henry smiles a small smile. 'Maggie?'

'Ha ha. Jessa.'

'It doesn't look like that. It doesn't look like a crush.'

'Well, it is. She doesn't even *know* Jake. And anyway, he's a good guy. He wouldn't … *do* … anything. She's a kid.'

Henry's mouth tightens and they're quiet.

Rafferty starts swinging his shoulder around and Henry stares at him. 'What the hell are you doing?'

'Bloody shoulder's killing me. Don't know how people work at the feed store for years and years. Or do anything like that, to be honest. It totally fucks you up. Only four shifts left. Thank Christ.'

'I mean this in a completely non-creepy way. But. Would you like a massage? I'm good.'

Rafferty raises his eyebrows, considers for a moment. 'Yeah, all right.'

He is already sitting backwards on one of the kitchen chairs. He leans his upper body over it and Henry grabs his shoulders.

'Holy shit,' says Rafferty. 'Holy shit, you're good.'

'I know.'

'You could do this. As a job. People would pay … whatever … you … asked … Oh … that's … fucking … *good*.'

'Yeah, knock it down a notch or I'll feel creepy and have to stop.'

'Right.' Rafferty clears his throat. 'Beer and footy, eh?'

'Beer and fucking footy.'

Bass comes into the kitchen. He blinks at them. 'Right,' he says. He opens the fridge and gets out some milk.

'Beer and footy, Dad!' says Rafferty.

Henry nods. 'Beer and fucking footy, eh?'

* * *

Bea is shopping with an old friend from school. She looks like she is in Melbourne. Certainly, she is further from Garras than Rosella.

There aren't piles of clothing and sparkly jewellery in the bags she's carrying. There are some shirts for Bass. A new pair of boots. A book on guitars through the ages.

'That everything?' her friend asks. 'I still need to go to Myer.'

'Yeah. Just need to pick something up from that fancy new printing place,' she says, heaving up the bag with the boots a little higher on her arm.

'I paid online,' she tells the person at the service desk. He looks up her order.

Her friend raises an eyebrow. 'What did you get? Is it for your mum?'

'No,' says Bea. The man passes her the box. 'It's for Jessa.'

It is a delicate pendant with a picture of Opal and Jessa. In the picture they're galloping. In the picture it's winter.

'Extraordinary,' says her friend. She puts her glasses on and peers closer.

* * *

Sylvia begins to call Laura. The calls are long, weeping, angry, stilted. Wanting him back. Wanting him home.

She starts calling our house. The phone rings at all hours and Bass disconnects the line at night.

On this day, when she calls, Henry answers. His stomach is stilled and cold. The kitchen smells of brownies and his hands are sticky with oil. Rafferty has fallen asleep on the couch after his massage. Henry stares out the window, towards the nook where Laura's farm begins.

Sylvia is talking about a herb garden and new pots and going shopping and new bed linen. She is talking about baking a turkey for Christmas. Henry grits his teeth.

He thinks of Jessa, watching Jake.

School is about to finish. The long stretch of holidays before the next year starts. I see him swallow. Close his eyes.

'Okay,' he says. 'Fine. I'll come back. Just stop bloody calling.'

* * *

This one still dusk, a few nights after the day he kissed Sam, Cameron gets up off the computer and pulls on his running shoes.

Sam texted Cameron periodically for the couple of days after their kiss, but Cameron couldn't bring himself to text her back. He had weeded my rose beds, run the bush tracks. He had stuck his head in a feedbag, to see what it was like. It made him sneeze, made his eyes go watery. He wondered at Jessa.

Now, Cameron presses his nails against the backs of his hand, but doesn't scratch himself raw. He picks some roses from my garden and wraps their stems in foil.

He runs to Sam's house. She answers the door in gingham pyjama shorts and a singlet top. She crosses her arms over her chest.

'What?' she asks.

He hands her the flowers and she takes them. She brushes her hands over the petals, most wilted and bruised from his run.

'They're beautiful,' she says.

He doesn't say anything. His breath is catching. He cups her hand, draws her in.

They kiss on her parents' porch.

She doesn't feel his trembling.

* * *

Jessa is lying on Laura's couch with a laptop on her stomach when Henry comes over to collect the last of his things. Sunlight. A still day. Perfect riding weather. It is strange to see Jessa inside.

'Where are you going?' she asks, setting the laptop aside and sitting up.

He fishes some socks out from behind the television. 'Home.'

'But … I thought you were staying here now.'

'Well, I'm not.'

'Oh. Shit.' Jessa stares up at him for a moment.

'Don't bother,' says Henry.

'What do you mean? *Don't bother,*' she mimics.

He stops moving. 'Do you even *see* me?' he asks.

'Why the hell are you so pissy?'

He stares at her for a long moment. 'I don't love you any more.' At the door, he glances back at her. 'I don't.'

The door snaps shut and he strides out of sight.

Then Henry stops. He exhales, closing his eyes. I realise, watching, that part of him has been hoping not to go. Part of him has been hoping that Jessa would fight for him. Fight for him to stay.

Back at the house Jessa is sitting on the couch with her head in her hands. Her breathing is heavy. Hard in her lungs. She swallows, stares up at the ceiling. I can see her trying to do the breathing exercises the school counsellor taught Cameron. I can hear her trying to lengthen each breath.

Swallowing hard against tears.

The sound of her hiss.

* * *

Early onset dementia. Not Alzheimer's. Something different. Something rare and fast moving. Something that made all the saliva leach from my mouth. Turn dry.

One of our paddocks in summer. Cracked and endless. The pain of it.

It's how fear tastes.

I swallowed hard. I didn't like the specialist's office. I preferred the wood and cream walls of the Garras GP. 'So ... that's why I've been having the mood swings?'

'Yes. And the trouble with fine motor control.' The cards I had written in for the twins' birthday. It had taken me half an hour, my handwriting erratic. Dizzying.

'We'll keep going with the tests. We'll do more CT scans, MRI and quite a few cognitive and memory tests that we'll do at close intervals to mark decline.'

'How long do I …'

'We don't know until the results come in, Cate.' He stared at me in the eye. 'It's degenerative. It's virulent. But let's wait until we know more, until we get the next round of tests done, before we get into all of that, okay?'

I'd nodded, unable to speak.

The doctor took off his glasses, rubbed the bridge of his nose. 'It's … exceptionally rare. At this age. Your age. Very, very rare.'

I nodded. Swallowed.

He put his glasses back on. 'And trouble swallowing. And you mentioned you were not as steady riding as you used to be?'

'I could sit anything.' I paused, watched the doctor typing things into his computer. 'I'm thirty-eight,' I said. The words came out like a question.

I stayed with my mother in the city while I got the tests done. I just told her I was having pain in my leg after coming off Thai the week before. I curled up in my childhood bed, which she had left intact as she turned the rest of the room into her studio. I looked at my mother's paintings. They were green and red and fluid and moving.

They were dizzying. They were alive.

I wanted to cry, but the tears wouldn't come.

Sometimes fear stills them. I'd never been so afraid.

* * *

Laura and Bass, settled side by side on the lounge, sharing a beer with a lemon wedge pressed into the neck of it. They are watching the late night news. The lights are off. The windows open, moths thumping against the flyscreen, drawn to the faint glow of the television.

The world outside is so dark.

Upstairs Cameron is trying to throw out his old school things and Rafferty is asleep, still feeling hungover from the night before.

'I always wondered,' Laura says, not looking at Bass. 'You and Beatrice ... did you ever?'

'Of *course* not.'

'But do you think she wanted to?'

Next to her, Bass is suddenly feigning sleep. The beer still clenched damp and upright in his hand.

* * *

I rehearsed telling them. I remember it, how I rehearsed telling Bass. I imagined the way his face would fall. How he would not look at me. Not properly. Not again. He would look at me the way people look at something that is going to cause them more pain than they have ever experienced before.

He would withdraw from me. In ways he could not help. His speaking, his tone, the way he touched me. Like I would break.

And in that way we would drift apart, become separate, while we were still married. Breathing. Parenting.

And my death, when it came, would hurt him. But his tears would be tangy with relief.

Rafferty, punching a hole in the wall. How he yelled at me, ripped at his hair. He had found the letter, confirming the results, giving me a breakdown of all the tests I'd had. I'd requested the letter. As though I needed to see it, not just hear it. Read the words. Feel them under my fingers.

Rafferty awake at night, thinking of me forgetting him. Over and over again.

Raff. The only one who knew.

* * *

The same afternoon, I think. Bass stands in the doorway of our room. His room. He rubs the back of his neck. His hazel eyes. They flick from the wardrobe to the drawers. To the boxes sticking out from under the bed.

He touches the card he gave me, still on the dresser. Still there.

He closes his eyes and goes and hunts around for the cordless phone. He fiddles with it before he dials. He wipes his nose and clears his throat.

'It's me,' he says. 'It's Bass. I need your help.'

Bea doesn't knock when she comes. She is wearing jeans, her hair in a bun. She has brought big striped bags and some plastic boxes. She has worn her sensible shoes.

Bass is still sitting on the bed, staring. Staring up at the wardrobe.

'You right?' Bea asks, sitting down next to him.

He nods. 'Let's do this.'

* * *

Fourth term is trundling towards an end. Jessa sometimes sneaks out of school early and will walk the seven kilometres from town. She will vault onto Scrap, dozing in the paddock, and ride him out and along the road.

'This is not working!' Laura, idling the car next to them at three o'clock in the afternoon. Her voice makes Jessa jump. 'Turn him around and get your bum home. Now.'

Jessa watches as Laura wheels away down the road. She sighs as she turns Scrap around. They trot a little of the way back, but mostly Jessa walks home, staring up at the sky. The trees.

She leaves Scrap in the paddock and wanders up to the house with her arms crossed. Laura is on the verandah, threading a double bridle together.

'You're going home,' she says.

'What?' Jessa frowns.

'You heard me. This isn't working. You're not spending any time at home, you're wagging school and riding bareback along an eighty kilometre an hour road without a helmet. You're going home. Being here isn't helping you.'

'But you said –'

'I said you could stay if you spent some time at home. When's the last time you were over there?'

'Not that long ago.'

'It was to pick up the last of your things. I'm not wearing this, Jessa. That's it.'

'But Scrap –'

'He can go home with you if you like. You can ride him along the bush tracks.'

Jessa stares at Laura, her expression closed. 'I thought–'

'I want what's best for you. Being here isn't. So that's it. You can stay tonight and pack up your stuff, but tomorrow – tomorrow I'm taking your things next door while you're at school. Got it?'

Jessa ignores her. She's staring out towards the stables.

* * *

Bass and Bea have stopped for a break. They're sitting in the bedroom with some lemonade, Bea cross-legged on the floor. The wardrobe is all open, the boxes pulled free.

Out in the hallway, there are more cupboards open, more drawers hanging crooked. There are boxes and bags, piles of letters and photos and albums and old riding gloves and bras and half-eaten boxes of chocolates all white and shrunken.

'What about this?' Bea holds up a black dress. The one I wore to my twenty-first.

'Keep. Put it in the Jessa pile. Cate always wanted her to have it.'

Bea runs a hand down it and then puts it on a pile next to the wardrobe.

'Your life together,' says Bea, fiddling with her empty glass. 'It's … I didn't realise how full it was.'

'Full?'

She flushes, sets the glass down. 'I'm so sorry, Bass,' she says. 'I'm so sorry you lost her.'

* * *

The phone rings at Laura's. It's dark, the trees still and cold through the windows nobody ever bothers to pull curtains over.

Jessa wakes, a hiss in her throat. As she looks around for the phone, Laura comes into the living room and unearths it from her worktable.

'Hello? Yes.' She stiffens. 'Where?' She scribbles something down on a piece of paper. 'Okay. I'm leaving now.' She hangs up.

'Who is it?' Jessa tugs the blankets up higher so that they cover her shoulders. Laura sits down at the end of the couch to pull her boots on. 'What time is it?'

'Henry's mum. It's only eight-thirty. You just dozed off.'

'Is Henry okay?'

'I fucking hope so.' Laura grabs her keys from the table.

'Can I come with you?' Jessa's voice is small, childish.

Almost before Jessa has finished speaking Laura is shaking her head. 'It's not right, Jess. I'm sorry.'

'Okay.'

'I can run you home on my way.'

'No. You're in a rush. I'm okay here. I'm all tucked up.'

'Well, all right.'

'Loz?'

'What?'

'Take care, okay?'

Laura grunts and slams the door as she leaves.

* * *

I remember pulling up outside Laura's house, that first day I came to Garras. The beautiful bluestone cottage. The unkempt garden.

She came out in her old boots and stared at me. She was beautiful, like Sylvia. But differently. Sylvia, all new clothes and makeup and hair carefully styled and curled.

Laura had the same long legs, the same thick hair. Everything about her was darker than Sylvia, though. Her hair didn't have highlights; her face and arms were tanned against the white singlet she was wearing; her brown eyes had creases in the corners.

She crossed her arms. Bare feet, her jeans rolled up.

'You need a map?' she asked.

'I'm Cate,' I said. 'Sylvia said she called you.'

Laura sat down on the verandah step. Yawned. 'Sylvia lied.'

I remember my palms suddenly feeling damp. The feeling of having unexpectedly missed a step down a flight of stairs. 'Oh. Well, I'll keep going. She just thought you could point me around, I guess.'

Laura snorted and piled her hair into a bun on her head. 'What did you say your name was?'

'Cate.'

'And you're planning on staying here? For a while?'

'Yeah. I mean, if I can find a place and it's not too expensive.'

'Well, you're well shot of her.' Laura stood up. 'I'll get you the number for the hotel in town. You can make a booking and I'll write down the directions. Come in.'

'Thank you. I'm sorry to just land on your doorstep like this.' I shut my car door and followed her up onto the verandah. 'That's a nice saddle,' I said, pointing at the brand-new Kieffer sitting on a rack by an old wicker chair.

'Thanks,' she said. 'Just cleaning it.'

'Have you tried their new jumping one?'

'Whose new jumping one?'

'Kieffer's.'

'Ah, a horse girl.' Laura held the door open for me. 'You have any?'

'My gelding Gus is at a friend's place. I'm hoping to stay here for a while. Maybe a long while. I'm going to float him up once I'm settled. I really want to breed and train them. That's why I'm out here.'

I still remember that feeling of warmth, talking about moving. It was the horse side of things, but more than that. I could breathe better in the country. I didn't feel so unsettled.

'What do you want to breed?' Laura poured me lemonade in a mug and pushed it across a table thick with horse magazines.

I sat down. 'Well, performance horses. Eventing, specifically. Warmbloods, if I can get the broodmares. And I'd like to retrain off the tracks.'

'If you could pick any warmblood sire,' Laura poured herself a lemonade, 'who would it be?'

'Value. No question. So many of the modern stallions are too heavy. He's so light and athletic. You could put him over thoroughbreds or heavier warmbloods and still win.'

Laura was looking at me with narrowed eyes. 'You working at the moment?'

'No.'

'Well, the hotel's a tourist trap. You can stay in my spare room while you look for a place.'

'Really? That would be amazing. I could pay ...'

Laura waved a hand. 'Cook me a meal and we'll call it square. Go grab your stuff and I'll see if I've got any clean sheets.'

As I watched her go I realised I was trembling. She and Sylvia were complete opposites. The only thing they had in common was this strong presence, this sense that they saw every part of you.

* * *

Jessa is curled on the threadbare couch, a doona wrapped around her shoulders. She is trying hard not to think of Laura driving in the rain. Of Henry, waiting for her in the city.

Rain in summer scares Jessa. She is scared of oil slicks, of spinning out of control.

'You don't like storms?' Jake's voice is friendly, airy. He doesn't look at her as he pulls milk out of the fridge and starts rummaging in one of the cupboards. 'Laura asked me to pop in, make sure you're all good.'

'I don't mind them,' she says.

Jake finds some cereal and pours it into a bowl with some milk. He shakes the milk carton, peers inside and takes two long gulps from it. 'It's not bad manners to drink from the carton if it's the last bit,' he says. 'That was the house rules when I was little.'

'My brothers always drink from the carton.'

She, quite suddenly, is behind him. Leaning against the fridge with the doona still over her shoulders. 'Well, Raff does,' she says. 'Cameron's too tight.'

'Tight?'

'Square.'

'Ah.' Jake rinses out the milk carton and sets it next to the drying rack. 'You know, I still don't get how people can't tell them apart.'

'I know,' she says, inching closer. 'Cameron's the nervous one. Raff's the annoying one.'

Jake laughs. 'Bloody oath. He and Guy used to drive me mental when we were younger. Still do, but it's not as bad.' He turns around and nearly bumps into her. 'Oops!' He pats her absently on the head as he takes his cereal back into the living room.

'It's weird, Guy in the city. Too bloody quiet.' Jake grins. 'You follow the football?' he asks, reaching for the remote.

'No.'

'Oh.' He sounds disappointed. 'There's a good game on tonight.'

'You can watch,' she says. 'I don't mind.'

'Sure?'

'Yeah.'

'Awesome.'

On the couch she stretches her feet out until they're edging into his lap. In the same airy way that he patted her head in the kitchen, Jake scoots down onto the floor and crosses his legs, cereal in hand, not looking away from the television.

'Who's that?'

'Edwards. Bloody brilliant.'

'How come?'

'See how coordinated he is? He could kick a ball here and have it hit a mark all the way up in the gulf.'

'Oh.'

She, too, slips down onto the floor. 'You cold?'

'Nah. Thanks, though.'

She is studying him. 'You could be a football player, I reckon. You've got the arms for it.'

Jake bursts out laughing, a pleasant laugh right from deep down in his stomach. And as he throws his head back, Jessa seizes her chance, quickly straddling him and pressing her small, unhappy face to his.

His laughing stops. For a moment he seems to waver. Or maybe it is just his brain catching up, adjusting to this sudden change. 'Jessa.' His voice is sad. As easily as lifting a doll, he lifts Jessa up and off him. She stays sitting there, absolutely still. Her heart pounding. Her face filling with blood and heat.

'Jessa …' he says again.

'I've got to go.'

He raises an eyebrow at her. 'Go?' Outside a huge clap of thunder makes her wince.

She wraps her arms around her legs and says nothing.

'Jessa,' says Jake. 'You're beautiful.'

She makes no sign that she has heard him. Does not move or speak. Her eyes, fixed on the door, do not move.

'I'm twenty-four. You're – what? Fourteen?'

'Fifteen.'

'Same diff.' She scowls at him and he holds his hands up and grins. 'It wouldn't be right. Nothing like that would. I'm too old for you.'

She is silent.

'Jessa?'

'What?'

'Do you get it?'

'I'm not stupid.'

'You're beautiful and smart and special. But I'm nine years older than you. Later on that's no big deal. But right now? Right now it is.'

She nods. Just once.

* * *

On the verandah, Bass rolls a cigarette he will not smoke. He can hear their voices through the window. He has driven over to see Laura. He received a barely decipherable text about her going to get Henry. He was hoping to catch her before she left.

'You're beautiful and smart and special. But I'm nine years older than you. Later on that's no big deal. But right now? Right now it is,' he hears Jake saying. There is a pause, Jessa's muffled voice. 'No!' Jake's voice, incredulous. 'I'm not watching the horseracing replays! It's my bloody day off!'

Bass stands and breathes out, loosens a crick in his neck.

The world beyond the verandah is dark and windswept,

thunder clapping and lightning, over the ranges, luminous against the swell of clouds.

He stares out at it for a while. Realising, in the calm and in the dark, it is no longer just me that he misses.

* * *

Sitting in the doctor's office, twisting up tissues in my fingers. Staring up at the certificates that hung, framed and behind glass, all down one wall.

'So, trouble sleeping?' He typed as he spoke, not looking at me. 'How are you moving?'

'Not great.'

'Well. I'll prescribe you the benzos. Just go easy on them. Take them exactly as directed.'

I nodded. 'Just so I can sleep,' I said.

Those long nights, so scared that my stomach clenched into cramping. I couldn't stand Bass touching me. As though I would wake up changed; wake up worse. Wake up and recognise less of my world. As though I wouldn't wake up at all.

* * *

This is what I did. I asked Rafferty not to tell anyone. Not to tell Bass. It seems such a selfish thing, now. To have given him that much to hold. So young. But I suppose I was grieving. Grieving for myself. And grief does strange things. Twists and distorts.

If I could change one thing, it would have been asking Rafferty to keep it secret.

I think of the way Laura sometimes looks at Henry, at the silver in his eyes.

Her pain. She hides it, mostly. She squashes it down and away.

It is a different pain, a harder pain, to have someone leave you by choice. To take that step away from you, knowing it is away.

Knowing that there is no way back.

'I can't believe you haven't told Dad yet! What the fuck!'

I picked up my cold tea, looked away from him. He had found me in the barn, where things were quieter. Where the smells of leather and dirt and horse sweat and things old and well used always calmed me. Soothed me.

'When are you going to tell him? Huh?'

'Soon.'

'*Soon?* Mum, what the *fuck*. Just tell him.'

'I will.'

'For fucksake!' He punched the wall. He cried out, held his fist. 'It's cowardly,' he said. 'It's fucking cowardly. Not telling anyone. Not telling us. You tell him, Mum. You tell him or I will.'

If I had one wish, it would be to untell Rafferty. It would be to hide the letter that he found before he saw it. It would be to look at him, stare at his eyes, and notice all the ways he is different from Cameron. Notice each fleck of his irises, the different fall of his hair. The way he walks with such grace. It would be to hold him so that I could feel his heart beating against me. To tell him how much I loved him. To tell him about all the little things I remembered from his life.

The way he used to smell books. The first time he climbed onto Gus.

To hold him.

* * *

Maggie and Rafferty are sitting by the open window. The curtains billowing in and out, as though the world outside is breathing.

Maggie is quiet, staring at him.

Rafferty's breathing is ragged. She has brochures for Sydney Uni in her lap. She has started packing her bags. The pinboard above her desk is bare.

Rafferty's voice trembles. His arms are wrapped tightly around his body. 'I shouldn't have told you. I'm sorry.'

'Does your dad know? About your mum?'

He clears his throat. 'No.'

'Why didn't you tell him? It's a big deal. It's huge. He needs to know. Jesus, Raff. How can you not have …?'

Rafferty leans forward, like he's telling a secret. 'I hid the letter. Went through all her things before Dad had a chance to. Made sure there was nothing in there. I burnt them. And he didn't want any details from the report. He said he knew what killed her and knowing the details wouldn't change anything. I was kind of relieved, kind of sad about that, I think. Then I kept waiting for the right time. I kept waiting and waiting. And then he got his shit together and how can I tell him now? How can I drag him back there? Back to all that pain?' Rafferty blinks hard a few times. His eyes are watering. 'I told Jessa.'

'What? Recently?'

'I told her. That night she got pissed. She was crying, saying it was all her fault. Dunno if she remembers or not, but I had to tell her.'

'You need to tell your dad.'

'I can't.' Rafferty's voice cracks and he leans forward against his knees, like a little boy. Like a little child. He cries and cries.

The washing machine, somewhere else in the house. The sound of a budgie tickling its beak against the bell in its cage.

Maggie tries to bring him closer, tight against her. Tries to kiss him and hold him, but he stays rigid. He stays away.

'Raff,' she murmurs.

Rafferty shudders. Doesn't move. I can see him wiping his eyes.

* * *

I want for Jessa to love Henry as I love Bass. I want everything about her to quicken when she sees him. Later, as the relationship steadies and becomes solid, I want her to look up and miss him when he disappears through a doorway. I want her to listen, as I have listened, for the sound of Henry's tyres crunching down the driveway towards the house.

When she closes her eyes against sadness, I want her to relive a moment of time she has spent with him. I want her to think of his hands, touching her. His eyes, the way they stare at her as though she is the most beautiful thing he has ever seen in his life. I want her to relive all the little fragments that make up the kaleidoscope of long years shared. I want her to smile to herself as she thinks of galloping together through the bush tracks, as she thinks of that day they had sex when they were far too young. How nervous he had been. How, in hindsight, it makes her heart ache. Tender.

I think these things as I watch her sleeping. The gentle rise and fall of her chest. Sprawled on Laura's spare bed.

She is dreaming of him coming home.

* * *

I always told everyone I wanted to be buried at the base of the jacaranda. It had looked so beautiful that day we came to look at the farm. Amazing, how a single tree can bring a place into motion. Into sound and colour. How that tree brought the asbestos in the roof, the lurching fences, the dusty floors, into something that we would one day love.

Bass has the urn with my ashes hidden in the bottom of my wardrobe. He made sure it stayed there, pressed into the deepest corner, while he and Beatrice cleaned and sorted around it.

Around me.

I don't think anybody has ever asked him where he would scatter them. When he would do it. It has been something that is just his. This last thing that he and I would share.

It is the same night that he rushed around to Laura's and overheard Jake talking to Jessa. It is the same night that he stood on Laura's verandah and did not smoke the cigarette in his fingers.

It is still raining. There is still thunder. I know how the farm smells. Wild. Thick. Like things being born and loved and dying.

Bass takes my box of ashes out onto the verandah and starts digging. The ground is soft, dark. It yields in a way that is like something sleeping.

He digs down into the tangle of the jacaranda's roots. And when the spade can no longer wedge in between them, Bass kneels down and digs with his hands.

He digs down deeply, angling the hole towards the base of the tree. It takes him a long time, I think. He is drenched and stiff and panting when he finally pulls himself up onto the edge of the verandah, bracing himself above the knees as Cameron does after a race has been run.

'Cate,' is all he says. He tips the ashes loose into the hole and watches, for a moment, as the rain dampens them into the dirt. Then he begins filling the hole. The dirt all blurred.

And I feel a strange calm. The deepness of it, like the pull of sleep.

* * *

Rafferty sleeps in the curve of Maggie's body. His arms are flung out, his mouth open a little. He breathes evenly, breathes long. She is cupped around his back, her head propped up on one elbow. She is restless, staring out the window. It is raining. The world outside is dark with the static of it. She touches Rafferty's face and his eyelids flicker but do not open.

She traces a finger along the stubble on his cheeks, the bridge of his nose and down his jaw. She runs her hands along his arms and down his sides.

She stares down at his eyelashes, at the fanning of them. The way they falter when she touches him.

Rafferty sleeps how he slept when he was a small boy.

So different from how he has slept since I have gone.

Softly. He sleeps wholly.

* * *

I remember. I remember the warmth of the day. How it was muggy, windy. Like a storm was coming, except it didn't. It didn't come.

I had been sitting in the bedroom. Thinking, slowly. Slow thinking. Of what I could do.

There was nothing. Nothing I could do. The pills I had, they had helped me sleep, but the sleep was heavy. It was like waking up from drunkenness. I felt unwieldy, hungover and heavy. Now, the bottle was cool in my hands, but I couldn't. Couldn't do that. I wouldn't.

To any of them.

I couldn't do it to myself.

I screamed, I think. Made some noise. In my memory, it is a scream. The same sound, I suppose, that I think of when I remember the day the two boys went missing from the living room.

I was going. Too quickly. Too quick.

And then that noise. That noise I remembered as a scream.

* * *

Bass, pressing the dirt down with the flat of the shovel. He is crying, now. That soft, embarrassed crying that men do when they are alone and frightened.

He pulls himself up onto the verandah and curls up, curls in on himself. He sleeps like that. Wet on the wood. The shovel still in his hand. Gripped there.

So tightly.

* * *

I had left my bedroom, my throat still ragged with the noise. Throbbing like something raw. It was still that same, muggy day. I tripped over Rafferty's guitar and swore.

'You ready?' Jessa asked, stepping in front of me as I entered the kitchen. She was in her jodhpurs, a T-shirt. She was smiling.

'What?'

'Are you ready? Our ride, remember? You said you'd ride with me.' That closing in of her expression. The hardening of it.

'Jessa … I can't … Not right now. I'm sorry.'

Jessa stomped her foot. 'You don't do anything with me! Not lately! Nothing!'

'Jessa …'

'You ignore me! All the time! You don't even look at me! Look at me!' Jessa wrenched my face until I was staring her square in the eyes. 'It's like you're not even really here. And you were yelling at Raff.'

'What?'

'The other night. You were yelling at him. I saw you. And he was so sad that he punched the wall.'

'Okay – we'll go. We'll go for a ride. Just let me …'

'No! I'm going by myself! I'm too mad at you!' Jessa stomped out onto the verandah and disappeared towards the barn.

In my memory, my cheeks tingled. In my memory, they kept tingling for the rest of my life. The last place my little girl touched me. Wrenching my face so we were looking at each other. So we were staring each other in the eye.

I watched Jessa saddle Pebbles. I watched as she disappeared into the bush tracks at a canter. I waited for a bit. I did Cameron's breathing exercises. I looked down at my fingers. I splayed them, brought them together into a fist. Splayed. Fist.

It was Opal I brought into the barn. Opal I groomed and saddled. It took me ages to bridle her. Just a quick ride, along the tracks. Just a quick ride, until Rafferty got home. Just a quick ride, before I pulled him aside and told him that I was sorry for being a coward. That I was sorry for not telling them.

Just a quick ride, before I caught Jessa in a hug and kissed her hair and told her that I loved her. That I was sorry.

Just a quick ride.

I would tell the others that night. Bass, Cameron, Jessa, Laura, Beatrice. My mother, who would cry on the phone. This would not be Raff's weight to bear alone. The horror of it. Of knowing he was losing his mother, when nobody else knew.

Grieving.

The decision made my breath come just a bit easier. My hands still shook, though. My stomach still hurt. My balance was off. My balance wasn't like it used to be. It was like my feet were in water. Trapped in a tide.

Opal was unsettled under me. Skirting sideways and shooting forwards with her rear pressed down. She felt, I think, everything I felt. In those last minutes before I fell, she was trembling as I was trembling.

* * *

Cameron is bent over the herb garden in his running shoes and shorts. He keeps having to brush flies away from his face. Cameron has kept herbs under his pillow since Opal died, pressed there. He clings to them in the night. I can never tell if he's sleeping or not, when he reaches for them. Their shape, their smell soothes him.

I wonder if his dreams are different.

I wait for him to stuff handfuls into his pocket and secret them up to his room, like he usually does. But instead he keeps adding to the bunch in his hands. Basil and sage and thyme and dill. Mint and chives. He ties them with a ribbon and, when Sam appears, red-faced and sweating from the run over, he presses them into her hand.

She smiles and inhales and I know they must smell strange, too strong. The smell of Cameron's dreams; his hurting. She reaches for his hand, which is scarred but not raw. I wonder if it will always be scarred.

* * *

In my final hour, when I went galloping off on Opal into the gum trees, I was so full of my own trembling, my fear, my anger. So consumed by it.

I did not look to see which way Jessa had gone along the bush tracks. I did not look for the gritty, fresh tracks of Pebbles's hooves in a gallop. I did not listen for the sweet sound of Pebbles's feet striking the hard ground as Jessa started to head back.

I do not remember what happened when she found me.

I do not remember the sound or the colour.

But looking at Jessa now, I can imagine her pain. I can imagine her panic.

Jessa. All this time. She thought I had died riding after her, searching her out in the bush.

Jessa, hissing in the night. Weeping on the couch while Raff stroked her head.

She thought I had died because of her.

* * *

Red-faced and panting, Jessa sets her bags down on the verandah and sinks into the old lounge chair set up there. She has walked all the way from Laura's. She bends down to pick up Peggy Sue, who is wandering busily down the verandah.

The jacaranda is flowering. Pale and purple. Like the first colouring of a bruise.

Jessa strokes Peggy Sue's black feathers. They look green and blue in the shifting sunlight. She murmurs to her, stares at the jacaranda. At the shovel, still cast and muddy on the verandah. She murmurs things to Peggy Sue that I cannot catch. And Peggy Sue makes sympathetic clucking noises and puffs out her feathers when Jessa sets her down.

Jessa drags her bags back up the stairs. She is still panting, red in the face. It's sunny, still. The curtains inside are all flung open.

'You're back,' Rafferty says, stopping on the stairs. He is rotating his sore shoulder, around and around.

'You gunna give me a hand?'

'After your long journey?'

'Where's Dad?'

'Out back. Why?'

'I said something shit to him. That's all.'

Rafferty bends down and picks up Jessa's bags. 'About what?'

Jessa ignores him, pushing past into her room.

Rafferty puts her bags down next to her bed. 'Jess. You know … how I told you … about Mum? How she was sick?'

Something in his tone makes Jessa turn around, sit down on the edge of the bed. 'What about it?'

'I was thinking about telling Dad. He's so good, you know? With Laura and everything …'

'Laura?' Jessa frowns.

'Yeah … Laura,' Rafferty says, slowly. He tilts his head. 'You can't be *that* thick. You didn't realise? They're not hiding it very well.'

Jessa squares her shoulders. 'Of *course* I knew.'

Rafferty snorts and then sighs.

Jessa peers at him. 'You seem … different.'

'Different how?'

'Just calmer or something. I dunno.'

Raff shrugs. 'But what do you reckon?'

Jessa shakes her head. 'No,' she says after a while. 'Don't tell him.'

Then they are quiet, still. She nods out the window. 'Look. Did you see? He's just buried her ashes.'

* * *

Beatrice, sitting down on the couch. Her phone is pressed up against her ear. Her hair is out. How much I always loved it. I'm not sure if I ever told her how pretty she looked with it out. How it softened her somehow.

She has crackers on the table. Dip she has been munching on. We are alike in this way. We eat when we are nervous. When we are sad or frightened or lonely.

'Mark. It's me,' she says. 'Look. I want to say something and I don't want you to interrupt me. I've been meaning to do it in person, but every time I try to, I just clam up. And I can't clam up. It's important. I need to say it. I don't want this. I don't want you coming over like you do. It's cold, what we do. It's cold and it's empty and I want more. And if you want more, too, well, we can have more. With each other. But if you don't, that's it. Because I don't want to do it any more. I don't want to do it like this.'

* * *

The road home. I can tell from the dapple of the leaves. The scars on the tree trunks, disappearing through the car windows.

'I need to stop in at Bass's,' Laura says.

'Oh,' says Henry. He slumps a little in his seat. His face is painted with Jessa, that flickering expression on her face that last time he saw her, lying on the couch with her laptop on her stomach. How much he wants to apologise. 'Okay.'

When they pull up, Laura glances at him. 'You coming?'

Henry rubs the bandage on his head. 'Give me a minute.'

Laura sits with him.

'They weren't just talking,' he says.

Laura exhales. 'I know.'

'He was choking her and then he hit me when I tried to stop him.'

'I could see.'

'I don't know why she always makes out like he's a good guy. He's a …'

'I know.'

Henry drums his good hand on the window. 'She loves him.'

Laura sighs. 'She does.'

'Mum told me about you and him. Mum told me how you used to go out with him.'

'She did, did she?'

Henry rubs his eyes. 'It's why I keep going back to her. It's why I let her get away with so much. Because you worked things out. You got away. And if you did, maybe she will too.'

Laura is quiet.

'She's not stupid. I just think if she tells him to fuck off then she'll be okay, you know? He's why she's so ... I dunno ... chaotic? Is that the word?'

Laura opens her mouth. The words on the edge of her tongue are tremulous. How she had not worked out anything. How she would have followed him anywhere, anyway, anyhow. How it was only that he left and she knew she could never outrun Sylvia. Could never outdo her.

Strange, she thinks. That this has suddenly become her greatest strength.

Henry closes his eyes and Laura leans over and rests her forehead against his for a moment. Then she shuts the door and pauses at the jacaranda, at the empty urn. She nudges the patted-down earth with the toe of her boot and glances up at Bass, sitting on the verandah with Peggy Sue on his knee and Mac by his feet.

He is stroking Peggy Sue's soft feathers. He is dark under the eyes, but seems calm. He smiles a bit sadly at Laura and she half smiles back.

'You buried her.'

He nods.

She reaches out a slow hand and touches the lowest branch of the tree, still looking at Bass. Her whole face is soft. Softer than I think I've ever seen it before. Her lip trembles and she braces it, hard. 'You're covered in mud.'

'I know.' He holds his arms out away from his body and Peggy Sue clucks and flutters to the floor.

Laura points at his muddy, cracked boots. 'Shameful.'

He nods. That half-smile.

Laura, her hand still on the lowest branch. 'Have you had dinner?'

'Cameron's cooking something,' Bass says, standing up. He waits for her, for a moment, but when Laura doesn't move, he touches her cheek and goes inside. He gives her that.

Laura doesn't say anything. I didn't think she would. But she stands there, her hand on the branch. Closes her eyes.

She squeezes the branch until her fingers hurt.

* * *

Jessa is flipping through photos of Opal. Thinking how Opal's coat is so dark in the photos, she almost looks blue. How she always has an ear pointed towards Jessa, whether she is standing next to Opal. Whether she is in the saddle or behind the camera. Jessa has never noticed this before.

She hears the kitchen door snap shut. She hears Laura's voice and drops the photos on her bed. She pauses for a moment, catching her breath. The sudden racing thud of it.

She walks to the kitchen, her nails marking little crescents in her palms. 'Is he okay?'

Laura shrugs. 'Ask him yourself. He's in the car.'

Jessa goes outside with her feet bare. She flings open the passenger door so that Henry startles and winces, touching his head.

'I thought you were at Laura's,' he says.

'No. I'm back home.' She swallows hard. 'You … you're hurt.'

'Not badly.'

'What happened?'

He glances down. 'Mum and … him. Got into a fight. I tried to stop them and ended up with stitches.'

'Are you okay?' She reaches out to touch him but stops herself.

'It doesn't matter.' He tries to sit up a little taller in the seat, but presses on his sore wrist and winces.

'I'm really sorry,' she says. 'I was awful that last time I saw you. Really, really awful. And … everything else. I'm sorry.'

Henry stares at her. 'You know, I don't think you've ever said sorry to me before. Ever.'

She takes a deep breath. 'Well. I'm sorry.'

Henry bursts out laughing.

'You're such an arsehole, Henry Thompson.'

She catches his hand then. Feels it, warm and full of life, against her own. Jessa breathes in, a deep breath that makes the small bones in her neck and back crack. That stretches the skin over her chest, her stomach, her shoulders.

And then my little girl lets it out. This breath that she has been holding.

Everything fades. Gentle. Like how a breath would look.

Let go.

* * *

Things are quieter now. More darkness. I see in images, in flashes. I see things in still moments that I explore, in whatever constitutes my memory, in the long darkness between.

I see Rafferty, curled on my childhood bed in a room filled with my mother's paintings. He writes some things down into a journal with a university crest on it. He sets it aside and pulls out a book.

It has *This belongs to Maggie March* scrawled on the inside cover.

* * *

I see Jessa, forehead to forehead with a chestnut colt. I can see her breathing in the smell of him. As she once breathed in dirt. There is sunshine and a breeze that makes the leaves dance. That makes the colt shy, arch his neck. He snorts. Laura, in the shade. Her laughter.

* * *

Cameron is sprawled in the sun with a beer in his hand. He is in his running shoes, his running shorts. His chest is heaving, his cheeks are flushed. He is somewhere with tall trees. Somewhere I don't recognise. He has creases around his eyes. Smile lines. He is breathing. His hands are smooth and calm.

* * *

Beatrice, standing in front of the empty white wall of her living room. Her furniture is covered in white sheets and piled into the middle of the room. She has a paintbrush in her hand. A peachy colour. Somewhere between yellow and pink and orange. Her hair is shorter. It frames her face. She has tied it up in a scarf.

* * *

Bass. My beautiful Bass, standing on the verandah of our old house. Standing there, with greying hair and strangely hairy knuckles. A Scotch in one hand. His other linked in with the lowest branch of the jacaranda. It's in flower, gentle and purple. The colour of it matches the colour of the sky as the sun sets. As it smudges everything.

Up and away.

Acknowledgements

Thank you to all my beautiful family and friends – I'm incredibly lucky to be spending my life in such good company. I could fill this book twice over with all the wonderful ways I've been supported, nurtured and loved by the people in my life.

Firstly, to all the people in the publishing world who have encouraged and had faith in this story. Thank you.

In particular, I would like to thank and acknowledge the inspirational Katharine Susannah Prichard Writers' Centre for the residency that gave me the space to dream this story up.

Thank you to Sally Bird, who started off as my agent and became a friend, mentor, counsellor and everything in between. Thank you to Catherine Milne, who has had her hands full wrangling an over-enthusiastic twenty-something along her first publishing journey. Thank you also to Jane Finemore, Shona Martyn, Denise O'Dea, Julia Stiles, James Kellow and everyone else at HarperCollins Australia for making this story into a book. Thank you to

Chandani Lokuge, for the most inspiring classes I've ever taken, and Ross Berry for much love and many stories. Thank you to Meg Mundell for championing my work and boosting me when I most needed it.

Thank you to Madeleine Ulbrick for daily support, Sharon Flitman for reading early drafts, Andrew Pitts for being my talented IT guru and Kathryn Stephens for once reading an entire novel I had written in 8-point font. Thank you Anne Parkes and Anne Tidyman for ruining all future managers/colleagues for me. You've both taught me so much in so many ways and I'm so lucky to have spent so many amazing years working with you. Thank you Geraldine Pitts (my other mother and pony soulmate). Thank you to Jessie Cole for being so warm, insightful and generous – I'm lucky to have found you! Thank you to my dad, who's loved me fiercely and proudly since I was born. Thank you, too, to Bern and George.

Thank you to all the writers, editors and publishers out there who have personally encouraged me and given me incredible opportunities. Also thank you to the writers whose work has shown me, again and again, how beautifully stories can be told. Without you, I wouldn't be writing. And a big part of me would be missing.

Thank you to my amazing husband, Ben, who reads everything I write (including this story about fifteen times) and still says he loves me. Lastly, thank you to my mum, who has encouraged me in every single way a mother can encourage her child. Your love of writing, horses and books has become mine.